Catherine Armsden

Dream

a novel

House

bonhomie press

Copyright © 2015 by Catherine Armsden.

All rights reserved. No part of this book may be reproduced in any form without written permission from the publisher.

Library of Congress Cataloging-in-Publication Data available upon request.

ISBN 978-0-9905370-4-5

Manufactured in the United States of America.

Interior design by Rose Wright.

Jacket design by Andy Carpenter and Rose Wright.

This book has been set in Berkeley Oldstyle Book.

Published by Bonhomie Press, an imprint of Yellow Pear Press, LLC.

www.yellowpearpress.com

10 9 8 7 6 5 4 3 2 1

For my sisters, Gay and Beverley
and for Lewis, Elena and Tobias Butler

Maybe it is a good thing for us to keep a few dreams of a house that we shall live in later, always later, so much later, in fact, that we shall not have time to achieve it. For a house that was final, one that stood in symmetrical relation to the house we were born in, would lead to thoughts—serious, sad thoughts—and not to dreams.

Gaston Bachelard, The Poetics of Space

Dream House

On a mean Maine day in April, the house could only stand and wait. Sleet shushed against its walls; bare branches scoured its windows. Only two hours earlier, the day had been mild, bathed in a harsh white light unabated by leaves that would come in May. The promise of spring had seduced crocuses out of the earth and gardeners pushing wheelbarrows from their sheds. After lunch, a vicious storm barreled in, whipping the village of Whit's Point as if in punishment.

In the cellar of the house, the furnace groaned to keep up with the dropping temperature. Rooms were warm despite the inhospitable weather and still breathing with the evidence of their inhabitants, who'd left the house in some haste, expecting to be back within the hour. The bathroom light had been left on, a wet towel forgotten on the bed. The smoky aroma of bacon filled the kitchen where a slice of bread and a stick of butter sat out on the table. Tea bags slumped in two cups of cold water. The sink faucet, which lately required extra attention, dripped water into the bowl beneath it.

The only sign that leaving had been intentional was the blaring TV—a precaution taken to keep unheard-of burglars at bay. To a robber, the house might have seemed an unworthy target: small and stylistically unremarkable, a typical early nineteenth-century box with a steep, gabled roof and clapboards badly in need of paint. Four rooms were downstairs, four rooms up, a single bathroom, and a pieced-together kitchen. In the comfortable, slightly crowded rooms, unfussy antiques mingled with simple, modern furniture. Several small oil paintings of landscapes and people doing quiet, ordinary things adorned the walls. Wool rugs and linen slipcovers in soft shades of green, tan, and amber showed the weariness common in houses of country retirees; certain stains persisted until they finally went unnoticed. Despite its humble first impression, to those not in a robber's rush the house might have revealed an undeniable elegance, a hint of something more. If one were to open the antique mahogany box on the living room table, one could behold unexpected treasures—bits of history that auction houses might have taken an interest in. And there were the very old and crazed oil portraits, their size and their subjects' patrician noses too imposing for any room except the tall, narrow stair hall.

Two hours had passed. Still, the inhabitants had not returned. The ship's clock in the living room chimed on the hour; a second later, the lighthouse clock in the kitchen tooted in imitation of one famous lighthouse or another. TV soaps came on, their depiction of humanity mirroring the weather's rage. With no one home to switch them off, accusations and proclamations disturbed the house's coziness—though this was nothing new to these rooms.

Another hour, then another. On the table, the bread hardened; the butter softened and turned a deeper shade of yellow. The bowl beneath the leaky faucet was nearly full. Dampness from the wet bathroom towel penetrated the blanket and then the bedsheets. By five-thirty, a layer of ice made the front steps dangerous. Rooms darkened. The automatic timer under the living room table turned another notch and a lamp snapped on. Without the usual evening thermostat adjustment, the furnace lost its battle with the plunging temperature, and the air inside dipped to sixty-five degrees.

On TV, it was time to assess the day. Later there would be broad-casts from the Middle East and the White House, but first, local news and weather: school closings and an approval for an expansion of the outlet mall, an award for a courageous firefighter.

Another gust—the house shuddered; storm windows rattled. The news moved on, as did the storm. Robbed of its inhabitants, the house could only stand and wait.

Two days passed before a friend trusted with a house key came in and turned off the TV. She emptied the garbage, washed the dishes, and threw out the butter. She cranked tight the kitchen faucet and clicked off the bathroom light. After some hesitation, she watered the geraniums wintering in the kitchen window, and the potted cyclamen and chrysan-themums. She looked around to be sure everything was in order. On her way out, she turned the thermostat down to fifty-four. She locked the door and checked it twice.

A few evenings later, she drove by and peered up the driveway. She thought she saw a faint light coming from the house. "Only your imagi-nation, Annie," she told herself. In fact, every day at five thirty, the timer beneath the table would set the lamp ablaze. As if the house were remind-ing the world: I am still here. As if it had a life of its own.

Now I don't yet know why houses have so much grief concealed in them
if they try to be anything at all and try to live as themselves. But they do.
Like people in this I suppose.

Frank Lloyd Wright, Frank Lloyd Wright: An Autobiography

Chapter 1

On a rainy Sunday night one week after her parents' car skated off the road into the woods, Gina Gilbert pounded and kicked the old front door that had swelled against the jamb until it suddenly gave way, pitching her, soggy and luggage-laden, into the tiny entry hall of her childhood home.

Her sister, Cassie, stepped inside behind her. The chime of the ship's clock greeted them, followed by the sad moan of the lighthouse clock.

"Cape Ann," Cassie said. "Ten o'clock."

"It smells horrible in here," Gina said.

The fat, blue ceramic lamp on the living room table was already on, its wide shade standing sentry over a collection of framed family photographs. Gina squinted to shut out the room. The cold, early darkness and crowded, closed-up rooms were the lesser reasons she'd come back here only in the summers since moving to California thirteen years ago. Tonight, the sepia-toned lamplight was not just forlorn but tinged with death. Gina's legs threatened to fold under her. "Cass," she said, "I think I'm going to bed."

Cassie touched her arm. "It's still early. We'll be okay. We're here together. Besides, I made us some applesauce cake."

Gina draped her wet coat on top of Cassie's on the newel post and followed her sister through the living room to the kitchen.

"It smells even worse in here," Cassie said. "Skunky and like something is rotting." She pulled the string that switched on the ceiling light. The hodge-podge kitchen, which doubled as the laundry room, filled with a harsh glow.

"Oh, God. *Look.*" Gina pointed to mice droppings on the floor. "They've moved in already."

Finding the garbage can empty, they checked the cupboards for spoiled food without uncovering the source of the odor. Cassie sliced up the applesauce cake and handed a piece to Gina on a napkin. She ate dutifully. "Yum," she said.

"I actually made the applesauce for it—from Macintosh apples," Cassie said. "Comfort food."

Cassie's momentary perkiness faltered in recognition of this current absurdity; she looked as pale and defeated as Gina felt. The sisters shared a crooked smile, small features, and delicate skin that tanned easily. At five-foot-two, Cassie was four inches shorter than Gina, but her broad-shouldered athleticism buttressed her role as older sister, which, at fifty, she still took very seriously.

When the teakettle whistled, Cassie pulled two herbal teabags from her purse and Gina understood they'd be sitting down together at the old pine table in the foul air. There they ping-ponged practicalities: bills, insurance, pensions, auction, flowers, canceling this, ordering that, boxes, trucks. Gina had traveled all day from San Francisco and as soon as Cassie had her in the car at Logan Airport she'd hit her with the news that Mr. Hickle, their parents' landlord of fifty years, had called to tell them they had to be out of the house by the end of the month. The prospect of moving out on top of getting through the funeral nearly suffocated Gina.

Now, the stench in the room began to work on the food in her stomach. "Something died," she said.

Cassie looked at her blankly. Gina stood, opened the door to the small shed built off the kitchen, and gasped. A dead skunk lay just past the threshold, feet splayed out, a clear plastic cranberry juice bottle stuck on its head.

Behind her, Cassie barked, "Shut the door!"

"It's dead."

For the first time all day, Gina felt alive. She insisted on taking care of the skunk herself, finding some rubber gloves under the sink and a pair of tin snips to cut the bottle off the skunk. She wrapped the animal in two old swimming towels from the shed and then walked through the rain to the garage, where she laid it on the floor. Should she bury it? she wondered. Did the town dump even take dead animals?

Ocean Spray Cranberry Juice was her mother's favorite. Gina imagined the skunk rummaging in her parents' recycling box that only got emptied every couple of weeks and then blundering around the shed terrified, possibly for days. Feeling a fresh surge of anger about human carelessness, she trudged back to the house.

Upstairs, Cassie was sitting on her childhood bed, her face glowing in the light from her computer. "Jake's Wi-Fi password still works," she said, referring to the next-door neighbor.

Gina took her laptop into the bathroom, where she knew the connection was better, closed the toilet lid, and sat down to check her email. She was relieved to see that most of her architecture clients still seemed to be respecting her absences of the past week; there were a few easy questions from contractors and employees, and one message from her ever-eager client, Jeff Stone: *Know you're tied up. When you get a chance, give a call. Thanks much.*

She answered a note from her husband, Paul, who wrote before leaving for his book group that all was fine at home with their children, ten-year-old Esther and six-year-old Ben. Gina had called Paul at work three times from Logan Airport, getting his voicemail every time. It had been wrenching to leave her family, and she was especially worried about Esther, who'd missed two days of school after her parents' accident, crying almost continuously. Paul, Esther, and Ben would fly out on Friday for the funeral on Saturday. Six days! It would be the longest she'd ever been away from them. She looked at her watch; the babysitter would be helping the kids get ready for bed now. She wrote Paul a quick report on her trip, closed her laptop, and went back to Cassie's room.

"The sheets for Dad's bed are in the bottom drawer in your room," Cassie told her.

Your room, Gina thought with dread, crossing the hall. Since she'd left home, she'd always stayed in Cassie's room when visiting. Her own was connected by a door to her parents' room—a war zone. Her father had moved into it fifteen years ago when he was exiled from the marital bed. His twin bed was, as usual, meticulously made, not a wrinkle in the cotton bedspread. His hearing aid lay on the bedside table. Three pairs of shoes were lined up at the foot of his bureau, all of them leaning to the outside.

She took the sheets from the drawer and pressed them to her face, seeking reassurance in the fresh crispness of cotton dried outdoors.

Cassie appeared in the doorway wearing a too-small Andrews Academy T-shirt that Gina knew had been sitting in Cassie's bureau for at least thirty years. "G'night," she said, embracing Gina in a strong, protective hug.

"G'night," Gina murmured into her sister's neck.

Cassie went back to her room, and Gina slid between the cold sheets, turned out the light, and lay listening. Somewhere near her head, a loose cable outside slapped the clapboards. Now and then a gust whooshed the rain against the house, and the window rattled. Then, for a few moments when the rain seemed to cease, she thought she could hear the house breathing; she listened reluctantly, the way one listens to the dying.

She folded the pillow over her head, and after a long time, dozed off for what seemed like only seconds before a bumping noise woke her. She got up, went into the hall, and pushed up the window. Heavy drops of rain splatted her when she stuck out her head, though the frigid air smelled more like snow. Looking down, she followed the dark legs of a ladder, rising from the driveway up the wall.

"Cassie!" she yelled at her sister, hunched at the top of the ladder in their father's big yellow slicker. "What're you doing?"

"The goddamn shutter's banging! One of the hooks is busted!"

"It's four a.m.!"

"*Someone's* gotta fix it!"

Gina pushed the window down, remembering how exhausting Cassie could be. She brought big energy and superlatives to every situation: fabulous! devastating! mind-blowing! Cassie didn't just work, she *busted her butt*. She owned a catering business in Rhode Island and was known for her three-alarm chili-mint-kumquat and tequila salad that was *awesome!* In addition, for years, she'd put her energy to work helping her parents with the house and then, with the same good-humored vigor, complaining about it to Gina.

Gina went back to bed feeling guilty about Cassie's hard work, and guilty about her own infrequent visits here. Guilt had always created tension between the sisters; still, Gina wondered not for the first time, if there could be anyone closer to a woman than her sister, with their shared nature *and* nurture. The shock of the accident seemed to have melted through layers of time and the small things that had come between them, exposing their sisterhood at its most potent. She and

Cassie had spoken every day since the accident: planning the funeral, working on acceptance, or else giving in to their unacceptance. If it weren't for their talks, Gina wouldn't have been able to face the daily routines in San Francisco that had seemed painfully distant from the tragedy.

Since stepping inside the front door, though, nothing felt real. Instead of the deep tête-a-têtes they'd had on the phone, she and Cassie had been speaking in clipped code, as if in these rooms, there wasn't enough air even for complete sentences, let alone their pain.

The power of this house! Her parents' death had not rendered its rooms impotent; being here still made Gina feel diminished and flighty—birdlike. "The house should be the church of childhood," she'd once read somewhere, and she'd thought, *ha*!

The rain had stopped. In the bright morning light, the house vibrated with a mocking cheerfulness. Gina carried her toiletries to the only bathroom, where Cassie had started to clean out the medicine cabinet and drawers; into a box she'd dumped dozens of Howard Johnson's and Quality Inn soap bars, boxes of Band-Aids, nail clippers, and a cupful of unused dental floss. Gina plucked her parents' toothbrushes from the holder and threw them into the wastebasket along with her father's dental bridge, several long-expired medications, lipsticks, and ancient bottles of foundation.

She picked up a ceramic ashtray painted with the Italian words *casa senza donna, barca senza timone* that had sat on the chest of drawers forever. While brushing her teeth as a little girl, she'd said the words in her head having no idea what they meant, but enjoying their musical sound. When she finally learned their meaning—"a house without a woman, a boat without a rudder"—she realized the ashtray's longevity was due not to its usefulness, since no one had smoked in the house for years, but to its message. At different times, the proverb had mystified and infuriated Gina; her mother had indeed been at the helm of their household, but she'd steered like a mad captain!

Gina dropped the ashtray into the wastebasket and turned on the shower. Because there was no functioning outlet in the bathroom, Cassie had plugged her hair dryer into an extension cord that ran from a bedroom; now, the fact that the cord didn't allow Gina to fully close the door made her crabby.

She was drying off from her shower when the bathroom door popped open.

"Oh!" Cassie said. "Sorry!" The extension cord squeaked as she tried to pull the door shut.

Gina clutched the towel to her, feeling as she had as an adolescent, making futile attempts at privacy in the house's one bathroom.

She dressed in Cassie's room and headed downstairs past the large eighteenth-century portraits of Mr. And Mrs. Eugene Banton, who seemed to ask her with a thin-lipped grimness whether the aristocratic likes of them could expect a more dignified future beyond this humble home. The portraits, of Gina's maternal great-great aunt and uncle, were among the heirlooms passed down by the Banton family— "Pronounced the French way," her mother always instructed, "not to rhyme with *Scranton*." One of several dignitaries who adorned Gina's family tree, Sidney Banton, had been George Washington's private secretary. In 1785 he'd built a home in Whit's Point, "Lily House."

A mile down Pickering Road from Lily House, Gina and Cassie had grown up in this rental with only a sampling of the family valuables: Chippendale chairs, swords, and Sidney Banton's writing desk. The elegant antiques lent an unsettling incongruity to the shabby-around-the-edges house but didn't alter her family's unfussy country lifestyle a bit; their free-range pet rabbit, Honey Bun, had chewed the bindings off more than a few eighteenth-century volumes as well as the fringes of two Oriental rugs.

"We're going to auction you off," Gina told the Banton portraits. "I don't care who you're related to. You're ugly."

When she reached the bottom of the stairs, she kept walking out the front door into the cold morning. She stood on the lawn and raised her arms to the heavens, grateful for the sunlight and other things, like the ground, that were true and important everywhere and to everyone, no matter what.

The skunk! she remembered. She ran to the back of the house and into the garage, a balloon-frame structure that for at least ten years had looked like it might collapse any moment. She grabbed a shovel. The skunk's grave would be where they'd always buried their pets—in the back field, still visible from the kitchen window.

Carrying the bundled skunk to the field, she worried about the risk of her shovel turning up a bone or two from Missy or Painter, their springer spaniels, or Honey Bun.

She set down the skunk and picked up the shovel, bringing the blade down. As it hit the earth with a loud thump, she staggered backwards a little.

"The ground's still frozen!" Cassie shouted.

Gina looked up to see Cassie, standing in the shed doorway. "It's *April*," Gina yelled back, as if the seasonal thaw had irresponsibly missed its deadline. She trudged to the garage with the skunk.

Back in the house, she went straight to her laptop and discovered that York County Solid Waste Disposal had a website with a paragraph on the disposal of dead animals.

Line a garbage can with two heavy-duty trash bags. Wearing gloves and using a shovel, place the carcass in the bags. Tie off each bag and dispose *only at dead animal composting area. $200 fine for disposal of carcass in any other recycling area. Dead animals may be dropped off on Tuesdays and Saturdays only.*

Gina went back to the garage, stood over the bundled skunk and said, "Tomorrow," as if the skunk should know she had a plan.

"So here's the list," Cassie said when Gina walked back into the kitchen.

Pencils behind both ears, she was standing in front of the open closet jammed with tableware spanning their mother's entire socioeconomic history—Rose Medallion, Limoges, Dansk, Corning Ware. The dishes were packed so tightly and with such strict order that moving anything had always felt like a test.

"First, we should throw out as much crap as we can," Cassie said. "Second, figure out what should go to the auction guy. Third, call in the consignment lady and then Goodwill. Oh!" Cassie was suddenly a fountain of tears.

"Cassie?"

"I'm so sorry!"

"About what?"

"That I'm making us sell everything."

"It's fine; we've been through this. I'm okay with it."

Cassie was broke. Her husband, Wes, had lost his software engineering job out on route 128 two years ago, and they had three teenagers and two maxed-out credit cards. Gina and Cassie had agreed to assign a value to each of the house's furnishings so that if there was something Gina wanted, she would buy it from the estate. Everything else they'd try to sell.

"I just wouldn't be able to stand it if you got mad at me," Cassie said. "All that fighting that Mom and Aunt Fran did when they were dividing up the Banton *things*!"

"We're not going to fight," Gina said. "We aren't fighters."

The memory of her mother and aunt poked Gina with two cold, witchy fingers. She shivered and pulled her phone from her pocket, hoping she might be able to catch Paul between his patients. Again, she got his voicemail.

"Jeez, Gina," Cassie said when Gina hung up without leaving a message. "That's the third time you've tried Paul today. Are you that worried about Esther? Her dad's there."

Gina bristled. She missed her kids painfully and perhaps unreasonably, too. Secretly, sometimes she was seized by the fear that if she turned her attention from them, they could be swept off the earth. "It's not the same with Paul," she told Cassie. "You know a mother empathizes with her kids in a way no one else can."

Cassie rolled her eyes. "Well, not *all* mothers," she said. They exchanged a grim look, a kind of emotional osmosis that came with their history—our *sistory* they called it.

They got to work on *#1 Throw out all the crap*, beginning in the kitchen with corks, jars, and twist ties, mounds of hoarded plastic cutlery and stacks of plastic cups from Barnacle Bob's—her parents' favorite fish 'n' chips place. Then, with an unspoken understanding, they separated and began eviscerating the house room by room, stuffing thirty-gallon garbage bags to be taken to Goodwill or the dump.

Upstairs, Gina pulled from a blanket chest a sack of hems that their tiny mother had cut from her skirts. She was about to shove it into a garbage bag when she felt something hard; she fished around and pulled out a slender cardboard box, secured with a rubber band.

Inside was a scrap of burgundy-colored velvet labeled, "A piece of Gen. Washington's cloak" and a tightly folded piece of paper with a large tag attached that said, "Lady Martha Washington's hair." Carefully, she peeled back the delicate ancient paper to have a look. The tiny nest of dark strands gripped her with a fascination that years of her mother's reciting the family history had failed to inspire.

"Cassie! Come here!"

Cassie bounded up the stairs, and when Gina held out her findings, she drew a deep breath. For a few moments, they beheld their treasure with silent reverence.

"God!" Cassie finally burst out. "Was Mom *hoarding* these? Why didn't she sell them! She thought it was so important that we got to spoon our sugar from Sidney Banton's silver bowl every morning, and meanwhile, she and Dad could hardly pay the coal bill."

Cassie's tirade so soon after the accident made Gina squirm; though as usual, she completely agreed. Cassie stood and gestured to the leather bound books—several bearing presidential signatures—that they'd cleared from the bookshelf. "And the things here aren't even the half of it. Do you remember all the beautiful stuff at Lily House?"

"Only vaguely," Gina said. She hadn't been in Lily House since Fran had lived there. When Fran died in the 1970s, the house was sold with all its furnishings to the New England Historical Society. Her parents' best friends, Annie and Lester Bridges, had been Lily House's caretakers for years.

"Annie and Lester really want us to come by," Cassie said. "I'd like to see them, but . . . you realize that everything in that house should be *ours,* and going there . . . It's like salt in the wounds. I know I shouldn't be thinking this way, but it's just . . . " Cassie gazed, glassy-eyed, out the window. "Wes didn't get that job he was so hopeful about last month."

Gina stroked her sister's muscular back. She knew Cassie hated to talk about money; they'd been taught not to. "I know," she said. "Something will change."

Make a place in the house...which is kept locked and secure; a place which is
virtually impossible to discover...a place where the archives of the house or
other more potent secrets might be kept.

Christopher Alexander, A Pattern Language

Chapter 2

By the end of Tuesday, Gina's parents' fifteen-year-old VW station wagon was fully packed for the dump. Gina loaded the skunk between the centerboard from a long-gone family boat and several faded bolts of paisley cloth, vintage 1970. She had just put the key in the ignition when Cassie popped out of the house and said, "Damn, the skunk!"

"Tuesday's dead animal day," Gina said.

"Yeah, but I just remembered the dump closes at three-thirty on Tuesdays."

Gina dropped her forehead to the steering wheel. She'd slept only five hours last night and was vibrating with fatigue and frustration. After a few moments, she climbed out of the car and gazed up at the promising blue sky. The weather had no rules, she thought; there could be a sudden thaw, and she would be able to bury the skunk.

Back in the house, Gina stood above the two-foot-by-two-foot opening in the attic and lowered down boxes covered with dust and bits of tar from a sloppy roofing job to Cassie. At least thirty of the boxes were filled with photographs and negatives from their father's commercial photography business that he'd operated from home; others held the artifacts of their childhood. Cassie and Gina carried them down to the living room, leaving a trail of black behind them.

"Check this out," Cassie said, pulling something framed from a box. She turned it for Gina to see. "My junior year French award. And..." She reached her other hand into the box. "Ta-da! The Miss Andrews Academy Award."

"Pretty hot stuff," Gina said.

Cassie laid the documents back in the box. "Yeah, well, I remember Mom told me back then not to have them out for people to see because it was too braggy."

"I'm sure. But she bragged about us to other people."

"Only when we weren't around to enjoy it. Remember how she'd say, 'Don't let it go to your head'? Have you ever, even once, said that to one of your kids? She called it 'being modest', but I think she was just jealous."

Cassie's insight was knife-sharp. Their mother was impossible—not just volatile, but childish and manipulative. Gina had always been reluctant to share achievements with her. Now she wondered: how could a mother feel competitive with her children? She'd always hoped that Esther and Ben would surpass her in feeling fulfilled in life.

"Not to mention," Cassie said with a snicker, "she hated that boys liked us."

A foghorn blew. "Nubble Light, five o'clock," Cassie said. "Time to drink."

She went into the kitchen and called, "Damn! I wanted to pick up some wine." Gina heard the jangle of bottle openers that hung on the door of the tiny liquor cabinet in the bottom of what had once been the water heater closet. "Vodka, gin, scotch, and vermouth. How about a martini?"

"Sounds good," Gina answered, though she didn't like martinis. She was beginning to feel as if her older sister was the host and keynote speaker of a days-long event at which Gina was a guest.

Gina stood and shifted to the living room window that framed the cove and harbor. The window! She'd forgotten, during these brooding, interior days, the escape it offered. Their mother had dreamed of replacing the one double-hung sash with glass doors. But Gina had always thought the narrow window made the experience of viewing the waterscape more intimate and poignant because, when standing at it, there was only room for one. The tide was high, and in the late afternoon light, the cove was a gloomy gray. Trees on the shoreline hadn't yet leafed out, but already someone was sailing a small boat from the harbor. Gina wished she were that sailor, but she was lost on a sea of boxes in a house that seemed far from home.

With Cassie still distracted in the kitchen, she decided to take her phone into the piano room to sneak in a call to Paul.

"I have a call to make before my next appointment, so I can't really talk," Paul said, when she reached him. "We're all fine. Esther's quiet but seems engaged with school again. Check in later if you want to talk to her. You okay?"

Gina reported that she was and said goodbye, missing her kids even more than before the call.

In the kitchen, Cassie gave Gina's arm a playful pinch. "You're such a helicopter mom! You have to stop this before your kids are teenagers. All the attention you give them might backfire."

Cassie had hit a nerve—Paul, too, often accused her of hovering over the kids. "Do you eavesdrop on your kids, too?" she said, regretting that she'd taken Cassie's bait. She opened the refrigerator and looked at the date on a bottle of green olives. "The olives expired a year and a half ago."

"Olives never go bad," Cassie said.

Gina chose to believe her about the olives. But while Cassie finished making the martinis, she plucked old jars of mayonnaise, mustard, jelly, pickles, ketchup, marmalade, salad dressing, chutney, and capers out of the refrigerator door and set them in the sink. "Do we have to recycle all these, or are we exempt, under the circumstances?"

"Save the skunks," Cassie said, pointing to the garbage can.

She handed Gina the martini and they returned to the living room where Cassie took stock. "Well? There are the portraits and the Civil War weapons, books, and some good silver here that would be more valuable melted down. Not all that much."

Silently, they continued sorting through boxes; for Gina, the martini created a pleasant haze between her and their situation.

When the landline rang, it startled them both. Cassie jumped up to get it.

"Annie!" she said into the phone, "Yes, we're buried. Okay, sure, thank you—we'd love to. See you soon."

"I thought you didn't want to go to Lily House," Gina said, thinking, I certainly don't.

Cassie slugged the last of her drink. "I've had a martini. Things look different."

Gina and Cassie drove past the stone wall built by the Historical Society to buffer Lily House from the road. At the end of it, a modest sign hung from a post.

Lily House
Home of Sidney Banton
Built 1785
Open to the Public
(By appointment only)

In her mind, Gina saw her mother shake her head at the sign with disapproval.

Cassie sighed as she pulled into Lily House's driveway. Though it was more than a hundred years older than the rental, it was evident that the generous-sized Georgian colonial, with its bright yellow clapboards, black shutters, and welcoming wide porch, had been much better cared for.

As the sisters climbed the porch steps, Cassie asked, "When *was* the last time you were here?"

Gina tried to answer but her breath caught in her throat.

"Cassie! Gina!" Annie beamed when she opened the door. "Lester? They've come!"

Annie wrapped an arm around Cassie and then Gina, reeling each of them in for a hug. Gina felt small and limp next to her. At five-foot-nine, Annie was eleven inches taller than Gina's mother, and Gina always imagined those inches balanced the power in their friendship. When Annie pulled back from them, she wiped tears from her eyes. "Oh, you girls," she said.

Lester appeared at the end of the hall with a broad smile. "Well, well! Cassie and Ginny! How wonderful!" He made his way toward them on one metal crutch, his companion since childhood polio.

"*Gina*," Annie corrected Lester. "She hasn't been *Ginny* in years."

Cassie grabbed Gina's wrist and squeezed. "Wow, it's exactly as I remember it!" she exclaimed, stepping into the living room ahead of Annie and Lester.

The darkness that had enveloped Gina all week suddenly deepened. The last time she'd been in Lily House was thirty-five years ago, the day her Aunt Fran committed suicide here. That the arrangement of furnishings had been frozen in time by the Historical Society seemed macabre. She tried to maintain the slight blur from the martini to keep her mind skittering along the surface of things.

But Cassie's big eyes widened. "Wow!" she exclaimed. "I think I remember every single thing in here. The Shaker chairs . . . the gorgeous tea set? It was Martha Washington's." She ran a finger along the belly of the teapot. "And the lolling chair that George Washington sat in when he came here," she said, her hand brushing the velvet seat. "We never got to sit in it because it was always 'Fran's chair.'"

"Welcome to your family museum!" Lester said. "We'd love to entertain you here in the living room but it's off-limits, of course—no sitting allowed."

They followed him into what Gina remembered her mother calling the "piano room," though now it was clear to her that it had been built as a library. "This is Annie's and my living room."

"So which rooms can you and Lester actually use?" Gina asked.

Lester explained they used the piano room, the large kitchen, and as their dining room, the sunroom. They slept in the "summer ell," an addition off the kitchen that originally had been built for summer guests but had since been winterized.

"How about a glass of wine?" Annie offered. Gina was about to say, no, thank you, but Cassie said, "We'd *kill* for a glass of wine!"

Cassie winked at Gina, and Gina resigned herself to whatever Cassie had in mind. At least she'd always liked Annie and Lester. When she was young, she'd recognized them as unusual: a mother with a profession playing violin in the Maine Symphony, a father who worked as a high school guidance counselor. Both tall, they filled a room, and in their frequent visits to her family's house, Gina felt their physical presence like old, comfortable furniture as much as family friends. She'd memorized Annie's big, arty necklaces and her perfume, Lester's tweedy sweaters and his penny loafers—exotic, because her father had never owned a pair—and their party drinks: Annie—gin and tonic, Lester—Michelob beer. They'd loved her father's puns and her mother's cheese soufflé. Their two sons, now in Alaska and Boston, were quite a bit older than Gina and hadn't been around much when she was growing up.

"Dearies, how's everything going over there?" Annie asked when she returned with the wine. "You poor things. Is everything set for the funeral? What can we do to help?"

"It's an unholy mess!" Cassie said. She described the house cleaning in detail, including the adventures with the dead skunk, but not, Gina noted, the discovery of Martha Washington's hair or George's cloak piece. While Cassie chattered, uneasiness rolled through Gina as she imagined memories, nested wasp-like in these walls, ready to swarm.

"Gina?"

Annie stood over her with a wine bottle. Gina looked at her wine goblet and seeing it was empty said, "No, thank you." Annie refilled Cassie's glass.

"There's something different about this room," Gina said.

"Wow, the architect speaks!" Lester laughed. "You don't miss a trick. We moved the piano some. In the summer, the sun coming in that window was murder on the instrument."

Below the bookshelves, under the piano, were panels that Gina knew were actually secret cabinets where toys had always been kept. She thought about those toys now: wooden animals, small sailboat models, an old doll with one arm missing; her fingers itched to touch them. She stood, realizing the alcohol had gone to her head. "Would it be okay if I ..." she laughed. "I just can't resist." She ducked under the piano and slid on her knees to the wall where the panels were. She knew just how to press them to make them slide open.

"What the heck, Gina?" Cassie said. "Oh, are you looking for the toys?"

Gina opened each of the three doors and peeked inside: empty. "They're not there," she said, feeling ridiculous.

"Your ancestor Banton was a secretive guy," Lester said. "That's not the only hiding place he had."

Cassie gasped and jumped from her chair. "Did you find the Washington letters?" she shouted.

Mortified, Gina crawled out from under the piano, bumping her head as she tried to stand. Did Annie and Lester know about the Washington letters? she wondered. Their mother had always told them they were a secret. As George Washington's private secretary, Sidney Banton had supposedly hidden some important letters of the first president's in Lily House.

"No, no," Annie said. "Good heavens! You'll be the first to know if we find the Washington letters."

Cassie's flushed face sagged with disappointment. As if possessed, she walked the perimeter of the room, pressing on the panels of the wainscoting.

"Over here," Lester said, squeezing behind the piano bench. "Take a look." Placing both palms on one of the wall panels, he easily slid it to the side, revealing a cavity about eighteen inches wide.

Cassie and Gina peered into the compartment. "This must've been where Sidney Banton hid all the important stuff he had of George Washington's," Cassie said when Lester had closed the panel. "How come Mom never told us about it?"

"She said she didn't know it was there," Lester explained. "I think it must've been because the piano was up against it all those years. The Historical Society people knew about it, though."

"And Sid dropped in maybe six months ago, and he knew about it," Annie added.

"*Sid Banton?*" Cassie said. "What was he doing here?"

Sid, Fran's son, was Gina and Cassie's only cousin, eight years Gina's senior.

"He's thinking of moving back to Whit's Point. I would imagine he was interested in checking in on the house where he grew up."

Gina detected sarcasm in Lester's remark, and no wonder. She and Cassie must have seemed more than a little drunk—off the wall. In the awkward silence that followed, the angry voices of Gina's mother, Sid, and Fran pushed into Gina's head; she nearly turned to see if they'd come into the room.

"Fran and Sid must've taken everything in that hiding place," Cassie said, as if she, too, had heard ghosts. "Including the Washington letters."

Lester smiled. "Well, now that's funny, because Sid thinks you two must have those letters," he said.

"*What?*" Cassie's face looked ready to pop. "He's so full of it! The Bantons were all liars and loose cannons!"

Gina touched Cassie's arm to stop her from unleashing more. She felt the constriction of memories, of night pressing in, of wishing and wanting for things that couldn't be had.

"Will you stay and have some leftover chicken?" Annie asked.

Gina raced Cassie to answer. "Thank you, Annie, but we've got a lot to do at the house before the funeral and should get going."

As the four of them walked to the front door, Cassie's eyes swept over the room and she sighed. "Mom always wanted to live here," she said.

"Oh no," Annie said. "I don't think that's true. Not *always*."

Lester opened the door, and Cassie and Gina stepped out. "Listen, you two," Annie said, "I want you to come back, anytime. Don't be strangers."

In the driveway, Gina took the car keys from Cassie and had the thought that this was another *last*: the last time she'd be at Lily House. Like all the other *lasts* this week, she put it in a box that would sit until she dared to open it.

When they got back to the house, Gina put some water on to boil for pasta, and they went back to work, numbly sorting through the things from the attic.

"Did you see Sid's stuff?" Cassie pointed at a box, and Gina reached over and pulled out a model airplane labeled "WW2 P 51." Underneath it were more boy toys—a book about military uniforms, a filthy baseball, and a photograph of their mother beaming at a young Sid, holding the tiller of their O Boat. In his smiling boyish face, she saw the flash of hurt she remembered about him, the long dark eyebrows so arched they could suspend a bridge. She held up the picture for Cassie to see.

"Mom was *obsessed* with him," Cassie sneered.

Gina knew that after a couple of drinks, Cassie wouldn't be able to let the subject of Sid drop; she couldn't stand him. Their mother had adored Sid as a little boy. He was two when she became pregnant with Cassie, and she was so sure she was carrying a boy that she'd never picked out a girl's name. She let this bit of information slip in front of Cassie when she was thirteen, establishing a life-long resentment.

"Sid lived with us for a while, you know," Cassie said. "But Mom never told us why. She taught him to sail, not me, because he was a *boy*."

"Cass, he looks like he was about nine. She taught him and not you because you were, like, *six*."

"Right. Do you suppose he'll show up at the funeral?"

Gina shrugged. "Probably. They *were* his only aunt and uncle."

Cassie groaned, and Gina filled with dread too; she had her own awful memory of Sid. She was ten when she last saw him at Fran's funeral, where he was cloaked in black and Banton enmity. "You must speak to Sid," her mother had coached her, squeezing her hand. But after everything that had happened, Gina couldn't bear to even look at him.

"I can't believe he had the gall to tell Annie and Lester he thinks *we* have the Washington letters," Cassie said. "It can't be a coincidence that he got into the antiques business in New York—he probably funded it by selling family stuff from Lily House."

The thought that family fighting over *things* like the Washington letters could go on for another generation made Gina's stomach hurt. "You never know," she said. "Maybe Mom's the one who was lying about who had what."

"Well we know she wasn't above lying," Cassie said.

Gina felt suddenly that her time with Cassie at the house, taxed enough by grim circumstances, was churning into a downward spiral. She resolved not to entertain any more negative commentary about their mother or any other family member.

Reaching into a bag full of Christmas tree ornaments, she pulled out a box containing an angel made of glass with a delicate halo and lacy wire wings. Every year, the girls had taken turns climbing up to place her at the top of the tree. Gina was about to remark on its loveliness when Cassie crowed, "Look! It's the angel with nine lives!

Veteran of Christmas wars! God! Mom found a way to ruin every Christmas! She just had to have a fight with somebody. Fran. Or Dad. Or me. *Whoever.*" She began to laugh. A soft, gurgling laugh that slowly swelled to a whoop.

Her laughter seemed impetuous and was so forceful, Gina felt an almost physical sensation of being pushed away. "Cassie, you're drunk!"

Cassie slapped Gina's knee. "Imagine just *canceling* Christmas on your kids! It's so awful it's hilarious!" She laughed harder, rocking back and forth on the rug, tears streaking her cheeks. "Was *that* the last time you were at Lily House? The year of the Christmas-that-never-was? Or did you forget—remember your *wall-of-forgetting*?"

Gina felt the strength drain out of her. Cassie was right—that was the last time Gina had been at Lily House. But it was Cassie who seemed to have forgotten—maybe because she'd been away, happily skiing with a friend—that the canceled Christmas had come on the heels of Fran's suicide.

Cassie was still tittering. "Stop!" Gina yelled. "Please stop!" She flushed with heat as if she were wrapped in plastic. "We need some fresh air in here!" She lurched to the window and flung up the sash. "Shit!"

"The storm windows are still on," Cassie said. She slumped onto the couch. "I'm sorry. It's because of all the work fixing the shed roof. I was up here fifteen weekends this year, and we only got the ones upstairs off. I'm *sorry*."

"Stop apologizing!" Gina snapped. "It doesn't matter—it's not our house!"

"Oh," Cassie said, "It's just that . . . you're hardly ever here and now there'll be no reason for you to come east." To Gina, Cassie looked a lot like their mother right now, her body sunken into the couch cushions, tears that turned her big eyes into glittery martyr jewels.

"Don't be silly! I'll come to see you in Providence."

"It's just not the same. Here . . . now . . . without the house."

"Cass, stop! What're you saying? You've always griped about coming to Maine. And anyway, we were miserable here. Admit it. You're as finished with the house as I am." Her eyes stung with the uncertainty of this stern pronouncement.

The ship's clock chimed, followed by the groan of a lighthouse and for the first time, Cassie didn't announce which one. She stood and slinked into the kitchen.

With a shaking hand, Gina carefully laid the glass angel in its wooden box. When she heard Cassie draining the pasta, she joined her, and they sat down and plowed through their dinner, topping it off with Fig Newtons. After they'd washed the dishes, Cassie fell asleep on the living room couch. At nine thirty, Gina, hardly able to keep her eyes open, dragged herself upstairs to bed.

As on previous nights, she felt utterly alone in her father's bed. She pictured Esther and Ben, reassuring herself that somewhere, she still belonged to someone, and reached for her phone on the nightstand. She had to tell Esther that she'd never again leave her in her time of need, if she could possibly help it.

"Aw, I forgot she was going to have dinner at Julia's," Paul said, when Gina asked to speak to Esther. "How'd the rest of the day go?"

Gina described their visit with Annie and Lester, but her conversations with Cassie felt too convoluted to talk about. "I wanted to prepare Esther for the funeral," she said. "I'm afraid she'll feel . . . I just . . . I hate not being there with her now."

"You can't be in two places at the same time," Paul said. "Esther knows that. And I'm here." He took a breath. "Gina . . . "

In his protracted pause, Gina heard everything he wanted to say:

you worry too much . . . you don't have to be the perfect mom . . . it's okay for them to grapple. Things he'd told her over and over again, but she didn't buy.

"You need to worry about yourself," he said now. "Right? If you're very anxious, how about taking the Xanax I gave you?"

She was too exhausted to call him on his paternal tone. "No," she said. "Whatever. Just tell Esther she can get ahold of me anytime if she wants."

After they'd hung up, Gina thought about how attending to her children always made her feel strong. Now, feeling small and vulnerable in her childhood room, she realized that comforting her children soothed the confused and inconsolable child within herself. Was there something wrong with that? With *her*? Maybe Paul was right: she needed to find a different way to ease her anxiety

She lay awake for an hour, listening as Cassie locked the front door and thumped upstairs to bed. When the house was silent, she tossed in her father's exile bed for a few more minutes until she could stand it no more. There was no way self-comforting was going to happen in *this* bed, in *this* room, in *this* house!

She jumped out of bed, shivering with a violence a blanket wouldn't fix, and crept into Cassie's room. "Can I sleep with you?" she asked.

Cassie slid over in the double bed, and Gina climbed in beside her as she had so many times before.

"You're shaking," Cassie said. "Why didn't you tell me you didn't want to sleep in there?" She caressed Gina's shoulder, and they were both quiet for a while. Finally, Cassie said, "I'm sorry about earlier. You know, it's different for me, being in this house. I couldn't have spent so much time here if I hadn't had a couple of blowouts with Mom. It's why I can laugh about it all and you can't."

Gina rolled onto her side, her back to Cassie. Since they were very young, the sisters had bonded over struggles with their mother; now, the distinction Cassie had made caused Gina to feel even more isolated. The defenses she'd been keeping up for days were weakening. But she wouldn't let them; there was still too much to get through. When Cassie hugged Gina close and cried, her warm, minty breath puffing into Gina's back, Gina sensed that although her sister claimed to have "let it go," her shuddering was not just about the sudden death of their parents—though that would be enough—but also a mourning for what had come before, here in the house.

In the sagging bed, Gina was alone on an island in the dark, dreary night with the one person who understood.

Cassie stopped crying and rolled over. Soon, her icy cold feet found their way to Gina's calves, as they always had when they slept together as girls.

Gina folded the pillow over her head. When Cassie said something, she peeled it away. "What?"

"You haven't cried the whole time we've been here."

Gina had felt the tears, swelling inside her. What Cassie didn't know—because Gina hadn't yet found the words for it—was that even before their abrupt and monumental loss, something else had been stealing from her, something more insidious and stealthy. "I can't," she said. "Not yet."

"You still always sleep with a pillow wrapped around your head?"

"Yup."

"I'm sorry you ended up with the bedroom next to Mom's."

"It's not your fault."

A house: a shelter against heat, cold, rain, thieves and the inquisitive. A recep-
tacle for light and sun. A certain number of cells appropriated to cooking,
work, and personal life.

A room: a surface over which one can walk at ease, a bed on which to stretch
yourself, a chair in which to rest or work, a work-table, receptacles in which
each thing can be put at once in its right place.

The number of rooms: one for cooking and one for eating. One for work, one
to wash yourself in and one for sleep. Such are the standards of the dwelling.
Then why do we have the enormous and useless roofs on pretty suburban
villas? Why the scanty windows with their little panes; why large houses with
so many rooms locked up? Why the mirrored wardrobes . . . the elaborate
bookcases . . . the consoles, the china cabinets . . . ?

Le Corbusier, *Towards A New Architecture*

Chapter 3

The morning after the funeral, Paul, Esther, and Ben piled into Cassie's car so that she could drop them at the airport on her way back
to Providence, where she had an evening event to cater. Watching
her family drive out the driveway, Gina felt a frantic urge to run after
them and jump in the car. But there was still much to do, and she
owed it to Cassie to stay a couple more days.

The auction man arrived at ten-thirty to pick up the house's more
valuable furnishings. "There're some real treasures here," he said. "You
might be surprised by what they fetch." Sliding open the drawer of
a Banton family desk, he asked, "Have you gotten everything out of
these drawers? Oh, wow! Look at these!" He plucked out several small,

worn frames. "Sixth plate daguerreotypes. Signed 'New York, 1841.' Wonderful!"

Yesterday, Gina had seen the daguerreotypes but hadn't even taken them out to look at them. They'd been tucked in that drawer for as long as she could remember and had become fixtures over time, like faucets and hairbrushes. What excited *her* were the piece of George Washington's cloak and the lock of Martha's hair, now tucked in her carry-on bag. She and Cassie had decided not to even mention this fresh discovery to the auctioneer until they'd researched the best thing to do with them. Since Cassie's house had been broken into recently, she insisted that Gina take them with her to San Francisco.

Neighbors and friends had picked up most of the rest of the furniture and now that the auction items were cleared out, the house was nearly empty. Even the ship's and lighthouse clocks had been packed away, their voices silenced. Without Cassie's big personality to fill up the rooms, Gina experienced the echo of death even more acutely.

She went upstairs and sat on the toilet lid, looking for solace in her email. She opened the last of five from her clients, Mitzi and Jeff Stone, whose two voicemails she'd neglected to answer. She'd brought their drawings with her, expecting they'd want to talk and finally made a date with them for a Skype conference the next morning. She spent most of the afternoon answering the string of emails from clients and contractors that felt like a lifeline.

At five o'clock, she loaded up her parents' car with more boxes and bags and headed out Halsey Road to Goodwill. She made her drop, trying not to think about her mother's tiny cardigans and tiny shoes and the hardly-worn wool trousers of her father's that were stuffed beneath the knot of the black plastic bags. It seemed indecorous that owing to size and convenience, trash bags had become the default carry-all—for life, for death, and everything in between, like garbage.

When the car was empty, Gina turned around and drove back into the center of Whit's Point to pick up some groceries at Tobey's Market, the only commercial establishment in town and whose sign boasted "The Oldest Family-Owned Store in America." She pulled into the parking lot, filling with apprehension. She could run into *anyone*!

She dashed into the store, wishing she had her sunglasses to hide behind. It was dinnertime, and the place was nearly empty. In summer, tanned yachters from boats moored in the harbor perused the sparsely stocked shelves, sporting Patagonia miracle fabrics, traditional red shorts and Topsiders. But April was slow for Maine merchants. A couple of older local men in khakis and wool L.L. Bean jackets lingered at the register, complaining about the shrinking of Wheat Thins over the years and the "useless and ugly" crosswalk that had just been painted between Tobey's and the post office. "If you can't cross the street in Whit's Point without a bunch of damn lines to tell you how to do it, you should stay at home," one of them said, and the other said, "Ayuh." Gina was relieved that she recognized only the cashier in the store, who was one Tobey or another.

Everything inside the store had changed except the most complete inventory of Campbell's soups in America, the anemic iceberg lettuce that dominated a paltry selection of California produce, and the creaky wood floor. Rubbery-looking croissants and a self-service coffee bar—complete with soymilk—had replaced the display of Devil Dogs, Yodels, and Ring Dings; there were handmade wreaths, straw baskets, and homemade preserves for sale. What was once the quintessential country mom-and-pop grocery had become a caricature of a quintessential country mom-and-pop grocery.

She carried her omelet ingredients to the register and handed her money to . . . *Robbie* Tobey, she remembered now, who had been a year ahead of her in school and had smashed up his father's truck out on

Halsey Road when he was sixteen. "Thanks," he said, without looking at her.

Walking back to the car, a man approaching her stopped abruptly.
"Gina?"

"Kit!" She leaned forward with the impulse to hug her childhood
friend but caught herself and drew back, offering him her hand. Kit
shook his head with a smile.

"Grease," he laughed, holding up his hands. "I've been workin'."

Kit's aged face and baldness were a surprise, but it was his familiar, piercing gaze that put Gina momentarily at a loss, taking her back
twenty-eight years, when she had last seen him.

Kit's brow creased. "Well, wow. I was really shocked about the
accident. I didn't even know. I was out of town for two weeks and just
got back yesterday."

"Yeah," Gina said. Emotion welled up in her, and she looked at
her feet. Kit lifted his hand as if he might reach out to comfort her, a
possibility that only flustered her more.

"Well, anyways, you're lookin' good, despite everything."

When she still couldn't respond, he asked, "So, do you have the
house now?"

Again, he'd caught her off guard. "Oh, no, Mom and Dad didn't
own the house. They rented it; remember? For fifty years, actually.
Cassie and I've been packing it up. The landlord's putting it on the
market soon."

"You kiddin' me? They *rented* all those years? I guess I forgot
that. What an amazin' piece of property! That *view*! You lookin' into
it? What's he wanna get for it?"

"$998,000. And the place is falling apart."

"Sheesh! Crazy!" Kit shook his head. "Hey—have you got a few
minutes? I wanna show you somethin' I know would interest you,
down at the dock."

Gina's heart raced the way it had at the funeral yesterday. It had been overwhelming, catching up with so many people on decades of life, meted out in little morsels. With Kit . . . she didn't have the wherewithal to be anything but superficial, but he was her oldest friend.

She glanced at her car, calculating how quickly she'd be able to get to it. "Oh, I wish . . . I can't though. I've got a dinner thing." She was sure Kit could see the lie; she felt awful. But her body was telling her, *bolt*.

"No problem. Well, I gotta get some grub here before they close up. Come find me at the dock sometime if you're around."

Gina said she would, and Kit turned and walked away, a hint of hurt in his posture that she remembered well.

When she walked into the kitchen with her groceries, Gina startled a mouse who scampered into an impossibly small slot between the stove and the wall. She imagined her mother, reaching for a pot from the pot rack that was no longer there. She grabbed her phone, put in her earbuds, and played the last chapter of an audiobook while she cooked. When the novel ended, she moved on to an episode of *This American Life* that she'd downloaded. She maneuvered the few utensils and dishes they hadn't given away, her hands robotically moving in front of her while her mind was basted with clever talk. She listened as she ate her omelet, and while washing the dishes, she switched to her playlist, singing along with Judy Collins's "Who Knows Where the Time Goes" and Bob Dylan's "Not Dark Yet." She sang out loud and hard—"behind every beautiful thing there's been some kind of pain"—someone else's poetry, true, but the words spoke for her. No more muted feelings—tonight, if she couldn't cry, she would at least sing down the house.

She dried her hands and walked through the living room, where she imagined her mother again, this time on the couch that had been taken away, holding a G and T, her legs curled under her. She was everywhere, the breath and heartbeat of the house. "Let me in," she seemed to say now.

In the bathroom, Gina answered more emails as Blind Faith's tender "Can't Find My Way Home" poured into her head, nearly swallowing her up. She went into Cassie's room at eleven, took out her headphones, undressed, and reached in her suitcase for her sleep shirt. As she pulled it out, the folded paper that held Martha Washington's hair came with it and fluttered to the floor. Her heart pumped—the first president's wife's hair! In her carelessness, it could have disappeared, like those restaurant receipts and used bus tickets left in her purse until they turned to pulp.

She searched her belongings for something to put the hair in for the journey home and came up with a container of spare contact lenses. She shook out the lenses, slipped the wrapped hair inside the box, and shoved it into her toiletry kit.

When she finally crawled into bed and turned out the lights, she was still uneasy. Her head was so noisy that she reached to take out the earbuds that were no longer there. All at once, words spoken during the past few days rushed in: dangling conversations with old family friends at the funeral, Kit's questions, Annie's invitation to stay at Lily House. To everyone's request wanting to help, to cook, to comfort, she'd smiled gratefully and said she was, "All set thank you." Having kept herself unknown to people in Whit's Point for so long, she felt undeserving of their kindness.

Death was everywhere in the dark tonight. It filled the place next to her where Cassie had slept and when it pressed its cold feet against her shins, Gina turned on the light and bolted out of bed. Grabbing the box of Martha Washington's hair, she ran downstairs to the shed. Martha's remains would have to spend the night on the shelf, next to the bag of birdseed. She locked the kitchen door tight.

Back in bed, she lay awake, wired and vigilant, not a drowsy bone in her body. She wasn't Gina Gilbert—mother, wife and architect; she was Ginny Gilbert—colt-limbs curled, lonely, scared.

By ten o'clock the next morning, Gina had labeled all the boxes of her father's photographs for Cassie to move to her garage, given the stove and refrigerator to Jake, the neighbor—tokens of appreciation for three years of mooching off his WiFi connection—and fastidiously scrubbed the bathroom in preparation for her Skype meeting with Jeff and Mitzi Stone. She left notes for Cassie, locked the windows, emptied the garbage, and turned off the furnace. She returned Martha's hair to her toiletry kit. Finally, she took a screwdriver, removed the old brass Banton doorknocker from the front door and put it in her suitcase. She'd always liked how the claw clutching a ball had nested in her palm.

Her suitcase was packed and stood by the front door. There was no way she'd spend another sleepless night in the house; after her Skype meeting with the Stones, she'd drive Paul's rental car to Logan Airport and stay at a hotel before catching her noon flight tomorrow.

She carried a box of books to the bathroom and spread the Stones' drawings on top of it. At ten o'clock, she sat on the toilet lid and tilted her laptop screen so that Jeff and Mitzi hopefully wouldn't see the tank.

When they were connected, Jeff's face appeared against their kitchen cabinets; next to him, Mitzi had her cell phone pressed to her ear.

"How are you holding up?" Jeff asked, gesturing to Mitzi to get off the phone.

"Ma, I'll call you back," Mitzi said. "I'm just starting a meeting with my architect. Okay. I will, I will. I love you, too."

Mitzi hung up and leaned into the screen, the symmetrical curves of her hair rocking against her cheeks.

"I'm okay, I think," Gina said. "It's been a rough week."

"You poor thing," Mitzi said. "Thanks *so* much for agreeing to talk today." Thin and high-strung, she was dressed in an orange workout top and a Giants baseball cap. Her phone chimed with a text and when she picked it up to look at it, Jeff said, "Mitzi, put it away! That's rude."

Mitzi stuck out her tongue at Jeff and winked at Gina. "Is it true what they say—that remodeling destroys marriages?" She laughed as if such a thing could never happen to her.

Gina cringed, wondering if she'd be able to rise to the occasion this morning of being the Stones' architect, a position she'd been navigating for over a year. The Stones had moved from St. Louis and bought a fifteen-thousand-square-foot Tudor Revival mansion in San Francisco that sat on a hill of solid rock, one-hundred-twenty feet back from the street. When Gina first toured the house, she'd been awed by its audacious expenditure of space, the colossal volumes that seemed to presume inhabitants who themselves were larger-than-life and had a royal-sized entitlement to earth and air. The walls of the main rooms were lined with low wainscots and pierced with mean little windows—like the eyes of a behemoth. Worn from neglect, the house was clunky and visually busy, with a tortuous floor plan.

A tear-down, Gina had thought to herself. She'd wished away the thick, stucco walls and in their place, imagined planes of light—perhaps a double-height living room—that celebrated the large and luxuriant yard, filled with sun and tall trees. She wasted no time in making her proposal to Mitzi and Jeff. Without missing a beat, Jeff had said, "I want that." Mitzi had been harder to convince, explaining that she associated the house's imitative European style with classiness. Gina's solution—to retain the façade while completely recreating the house behind—would satisfy both Mitzi's vision and San Francisco's codes enforcing the preservation of potentially historic buildings.

And now Mitzi clapped her hands, rattling her gold and jade bracelet every time Gina pointed out a detail that defied tradition; she cooed about the "architectural statement" they were going to make to the world—or at least, to Pacific Heights. Besides the façade, she remained committed only to the size of the original house. "We want a home where everyone can visit. Plus, we want to have four bedrooms for our kids," she'd explained.

So far, there were no children; Mitzi had confided to Gina last month that they'd been trying to get pregnant for three years.

"Gina," Mitzi said, reaching for something. She held a page of a magazine up to the screen. "I thought this was a great idea—a gift-wrapping room. When you think about it, we women spend half our time wrapping presents, you know? Could we make something like that?"

"Why not?" Gina said. "You have the space."

"Fabulous!" Mitzi beamed. "I am just *so* excited about this house! I was wondering, do people with nice homes in San Francisco ever name them? We've been to Jeff's client's place in the Hamptons—one of those big, shingled houses with a huge porch and a widow's walk? On the east coast, a lot of homes have names. His is called 'Firefly House.' Isn't that romantic?"

"Mitzi," Jeff patted her hand. "Gina knows all about houses with names; she's an Ivy League-educated east-coaster." Jeff, a Harvard Business School alumnus, grinned at Gina with an air of fraternity.

"Oh, yeah!" Mitzi said. "Maine. Did the house you grew up in have a name?"

Gina glanced at the original claw-foot tub with its jerry-rigged shower, the peeling ceiling paint, and the cracked black-and-white linoleum. "No," she said. "No name."

Mitzi's phone rang. "*Ma,*" she said into the phone, "I'm still in my meeting. No, September's no good. Okay, thanks—you're too adorable. Love you." She hung up. "My mother!" she complained. "But she's like my *best friend.*" She caught herself, and her hand flew to her mouth. "Oh, Gina, I'm so sorry. I wasn't thinking . . . "

"No worries," Gina said, feeling a vacancy inside more cavernous than Mitzi could possibly imagine: the missing of her mother that she'd experienced long before her mother had died.

An awkward silence followed. "Can we talk about bathrooms?" Jeff finally asked. "I really think a house with this many bedrooms deserves five baths."

Gina counted to ten in her head and recited her mantra: "needs expand to meet the budget available." Aloud she said, "No problem. Let's see." She shifted her laptop so she could stretch the roll of tracing paper over the drawing, and with her pen quickly reconfigured the second-floor laundry room and closets to accommodate another bathroom. She wondered: How would Mitzi and Jeff feel, shuffling around those rooms, if having children didn't work out? Five bathrooms, two dishwashers, and an au pair apartment didn't have fertility powers. She held up the drawing for them to see.

"Gina, where are you, anyway?" Mitzi said, leaning toward the screen. "Are you, like, in a *bathroom*?"

Gina stood and quickly rearranged her laptop. "Oh, yeah. It's the only place in the house that gets a good connection."

Jeff smiled, baring his over-bleached teeth. "It looks quaint," he said. Gina was relieved that they seemed reluctant to ask where, exactly, she was staying.

"Okay. Great," Jeff said, looking at his watch. "We've got the baths. Thank you for indulging us." He flashed his smile again. "What I love about architects," he said, his voice suddenly silky, "is that you ask, 'What *can* we do—what is the dream?' instead of, 'What *needs* to be done?'"

After more than an hour of talking with the Stones, Gina closed her laptop and sat for a moment, soaking in the sunlight pouring through the bathroom's high, east-facing windows. No amount of space, of marble or fancy plumbing fixtures, she thought, could match the luxury of beginning the day in a sun-drenched room.

She stepped down the stairs, put on her fleece jacket, and walked out of the house with her suitcase. She locked the front door, her hand unsteady as the bolt thunked into place. Turning over the key with its twenty-year-old paper tag in her hand, she had the thought that she should do something ceremonious with it. She set her suitcase on the porch, ran down the hill to the cove, and with a dramatic sweep of her arm, hurled the key; when the water swallowed it, she immediately regretted her impulsiveness.

She climbed back up the steep hill to the narrow band of level lawn that had been their patio. "The view!" she remembered Kit exclaiming yesterday. Indeed, it was a celebrity view, having appeared on the covers of magazines and calendars as captured by her father's camera. Unlike the breathtakingly wide, uninterrupted ocean of the West Coast, this panorama offered places for the eye to rest on its way to the horizon: the shimmering, horseshoe-shaped cove rimmed by tall, straight spruces, two tiny islands, a changing cast of picturesque boats, the lighthouse marking the harbor's outer edge. Many a painter had set up her easel in the yard, but Gina and her family had always agreed that simply sitting and watching as the landscape changed from moment to moment was a creative activity in itself.

All of her adult life, every year on arrival here, Gina had dashed from the car to stand in this spot, embracing the smells and scenery of her childhood, her parents' ecstatic welcome and summery moods. But after a few days, a kind of winter would move into her; the optimism she'd arrived with would fade and she'd begin looking forward to leaving—sometimes, in the final few hours, nearly holding her breath. There would be the tearing away from her parents at the door on departure day, their tearful eyes and resigned waves from the driveway. As Paul drove toward the airport across the Piscataqua River into New Hampshire, he would put his hand on Gina's knee to ease her melancholy. Her relief to be leaving had made her feel at once unyielding and impotent, like a bad daughter; her wish that things could be different had swelled like a balloon in her chest.

Halfway to the airport, she'd always felt a shift as she turned her gaze ahead to the fresh, wide-openness of the opposite shore. Compression, release: the cycle would begin again as winter turned to spring; she would plan their next trip to Maine, both hopeful and dread-filled. A struggle, but a predictable one and, in its own way, life-affirming. How would life be now, without that cycle?

It was unfair that on this day, cerulean sky, glistening water, and brilliant light would conspire to create a visual feast—a last supper. She put down her suitcase, set up a chaise facing the view and collapsed into it.

Once she was down, she was transfixed, her senses drugged. She felt her purposefulness drop away, leaving her helpless to rise from the chair.

When she was a teenager, her mother had sat in this spot, perhaps even in this very chaise, and often said, "Sitting here, who could have a care in the world?" To Gina, the declaration had sounded hollow, even cruel, given that, in this house, her mother had created all the cares in the world.

For more than two hours, Gina gazed out across the landscape, her back warmed by heat reflecting off the house's white clapboards.

Finally closing her eyes, she was visited by another memory: when she was three or four, on summer afternoons, her mother would sometimes let her take a nap curled up next to her on a chaise. Now, she could hear her mother's heart beat beneath the breathing pillow of her breast, feel the tickle of wind on her bare arms, the sun that would leave her upturned cheek pink. Gradually, her limbs lightened and seemed to float away; she succumbed to a peacefulness so profound, she thought she might be sleeping.

A neighbor's lawnmower startled her awake at five o'clock. She stood and picked up her suitcase. The cove was richly colored and velvety. A tranquil sea, fading light, goodbye. Her suitcase held a few treasures, it was true. But of everything the house possessed, this view was what she wished she could take with her.

As she crossed the front yard toward the driveway, the house seemed to stir. She looked up just as something crashed to the ground, hitting the brick walkway with a clatter. A window shutter, she discovered, the one Cassie had climbed up to fix. Its fasteners were worn through. She glanced again at the house's façade, feeling unsettled by the asymmetry caused by the missing shutter. "You'll be okay," she heard herself say.

It was time to go! She fetched the garbage can from behind the house, tossed the splintered shutter into it, replaced the can, and got into the car.

She couldn't turn to look back up the driveway as she drove out, didn't feel her usual relief as she crossed the bridge out of Whit's Point. This time, she experienced a release too big, like a fish being spewed into open water. A sickening turbulence and its disorientation, a freedom thrusting her forward, the kind of rushing freedom one could drown in.

We are searching for some kind of harmony between two intangibles:
a form which we have not yet designed and a context which we cannot
properly describe.

Christopher Alexander

Chapter 4

Insomnia! From the bedside table, the numbers on the clock taunted Gina—two, three, four o'clock. San Francisco's windy, clear days of April and May had blown by, and June found her six pounds lighter—proof that lying awake was a grueling workout. In those wee hours, she plunged into a black chasm teeming with shapeless sorrows. She longed to cry out loud. "They expect you to be sad," Paul had told her. "You have feelings, too."

But she would never let her grief drift like a miasma into the rooms of her sleeping children, making them choose vigilance over sleep.

The numbers in the clock flashed seven, and Ben's rosy-cheeked face appeared in the doorway. He waited, as always, for Gina's smile to invite him in and then climbed into bed beside her. She strained to follow his whispered stream of chatter that began with a Byzantine description of a computer game and ended with, "But you have to have special software for that."

"That sounds really neat," Gina absentmindedly cooed, pushing her nose into his soft blonde curls. She mourned: tomorrow was Ben's last day of kindergarten; how much longer would he come in for a snuggle? "I'm such a lucky Mom."

"What? Mom, are you listening? We don't have the right software!"

"You're right! I'm sorry. Well, maybe we'll see if we can get it. Hey, kiddo, time for us to get up and get ready."

Ben wrestled himself out of bed, waking Paul, and went to his room.

"How'd you sleep?" Paul asked, as he did every morning; it had become rhetorical.

He stood, yawned, and put up the window shades. From the bed, Gina saw blue sky out one window, and out another, fog cascading over the white Victorian cornice of the neighbors' house. They were several miles from the Bay, but she could hear the moan of a ship's horn, confirming that the fog hovered at the Golden Gate.

Paul looked at her, his face full of concern. "I can get them breakfast if you want to try to go back to sleep."

"No, no," Gina said. "I'm okay." Her morning ritual with the kids, their steady expectations of her, were what lately had given her the will to get out of bed each morning.

She stood and went to find Ben, who was squatting over his *Illustrated Encyclopedia of Machines* dressed only in his underwear. "Look," he said. "Elevators are just like big pulleys."

Gina knelt next to him and said, "Cool," more about his boundless curiosity than the impressive diagram of the elevator. She put some clothes out for him. "Here you go. Get dressed now, okay?"

"Can we work on the rocket when you get home tonight?" he asked. A quarter of his floor was covered with plastic K'NEX pieces

and the beginnings of a complicated rocket model they'd been building together. It was apparent to Gina that he had better innate spatial
skills than she and probably could have constructed the rocket alone.
But he liked having her help.

"Sure," she said. "We could finish the fins."

Ben turned his big eyes up at her and studied her face. "Your
voice sounds different," he said.

Gina cleared her throat. "Really? How is it different?"

"Older."

Wilted inside, she smiled and hugged him. "Hmm. Well, I *am*
older than I was yesterday, right? And so are you."

She surveyed his floor—origami paper and Legos, an open package of flower seeds and a small dirty sock—and even surrounded by
the kid mess and primary-colored plastic, she felt the inevitability of
his growing up, looming like a kidnapper in the shadows.

And Esther! In her stuffy, quiet room, filled with the nature she
was deprived of growing up in the city: shells and rocks and bird
nests, bits of obsidian, sea glass, cow bones and feathers, several cacti
and a Venus Flytrap, Gina could almost hear her daughter growing,
exhaling her innocence into the room. Everywhere, there were clues
that she was ready to be older. Last week, Gina had been rummaging
to find an overdue library book and came across a stash of tam-
pons behind Esther's cherished collection of *Redwall* rat adventures.
Esther hadn't started her period yet, but the fourth grade curriculum
included a detailed unit on puberty, and it was so like Esther to be
thoroughly prepared—even, possibly, years in advance. Later, she'd
come home from school with the news that she'd decided she wanted
to go to sleep-away camp this summer. She'd never wanted to before,
and that night, in private, Gina and Paul had differed about whether
she was ready to be away for two weeks. "She's been so ambivalent,"

Gina had reasoned. But Paul didn't worry about the kids when they were out of his sight; he imagined only the best: their pleasure at being with other children and under the enlightening influence of other adults. "Maybe it's Esther's mom who's the most ambivalent?" he'd said to Gina.

He was right, and it wasn't just about camp—she was relieved when the next day, Esther reversed her decision; she was already dreading the days when Esther and Ben would leave for college. Surely this was not normal!

Esther was still asleep, curled facing the doorway. Every day she looked more like Paul, with her sharply contoured face and dark hair, but her long, flat eyebrows were from Gina's mother. Gina opened the window curtains to reveal six scraggly petunias still wearing a few anemic blossoms. She'd planted them in the window box to mitigate Esther's view of the neighbor's brown siding, four feet away, but lately she'd neglected to water them.

She kissed Esther's cheek. "Time to get up, Estie."

Esther's eyes fluttered open. "Did you look for a photograph for my project?" she asked.

"Not yet. But I will now."

Gina left her and went down the hall to the study. The room was lined with books—volumes of architectural theory and mono-graphs on the lower shelves, and above, novels—upright, piled, lying, leaning—but also photographs of family: the inheritance of a photographer's daughter. She'd returned from Maine with a box of childhood photos and in the middle of the night when she couldn't sleep, she'd been looking through them obsessively, the way one looks for something lost. Like the novels, the photos were stories that had already taken place. She wondered when she would she begin to select which stories to keep and which to throw away. Did people ever lose their fear of forgetting?

Now, in more than three decades' worth of photographs, she was determined to find a recent picture of her parents alone for Esther's project. But so far, Eleanor and Ron had shown up only in groups, usually with one of Gina's children: Esther with grandmother Eleanor sailing the Cape Dory in Maine, Ben and grandfather Ron rowing the dinghy, Esther—a year older—with Ron and Eleanor, standing on their dock. Their stage for all these activities was the luminous cove that had always made everyone their photogenic best. In the pictures, her parents sparkled with jubilance; they *had* been jubilant, as though with their grandchildren they were experiencing the joys of parenting for the first time.

Finally, the perfect photograph appeared, taken on her parents' fiftieth wedding anniversary—the diminutive Eleanor looking cheerfully up at Ron, who held her hands in both of his. A picture is worth a thousand words, she thought, and can hide a thousand more.

On the desk, the phone rang; Gina picked it up. "Dearie, it's Annie Bridges. I couldn't reach Cassie, and I bet you're running around trying to get out of the house at this hour. But I wanted to tell you that the 'for sale' sign at your house is gone."

"Wow—thank you, Annie, for letting me know. We all knew it was going to happen, but it still feels kind of strange."

"It sure does! Well, I'll let you go. We'll chat at a better time."

When Gina hung up, she was buzzing; Annie's news had triggered the memory of Cassie's call about her parents' accident two months ago. After that call, too, she'd been standing here in the study, trying to fathom the loss, feeling as if there were something she should be doing but rendered helpless by geographical distance.

She turned to leave the study and glanced at the framed sixteen-by-twenty, black–and–white photograph of the cove that sat on the desk, waiting to be hung. As soon as she'd returned from Maine, she'd gone to look for it in the storage closet and had taken it to be framed. She resolved to put it up today, when she got home from work.

In the bathroom, Paul shaved; Gina put in her contacts. Ben came in and pulled out the stool to brush his teeth.

"I got a cancellation today, so I have a couple free hours beginning at eleven," Paul said, rinsing his razor. "What's your day like? Think you might be able to get away? We could go up to the property—it'll be nice and warm there."

A year and a half ago, they'd bought a place north of the city, in Marin, that they were planning to remodel and move into. Gina hadn't yet been able to come up with a design she was happy with, and she knew Paul was getting impatient. She had the time to go to the property today. But she balked at the pressure it would put on her to get going on the plans.

Paul smiled at her in the mirror. "Aw, come on. The weather will be like summer there. It'll be a good break for you," he said.

Gina managed a smile. "Okay." But she thought: what I really need is a break from myself. And a good night's sleep.

Ben left and Esther came in and handed Gina a hairbrush. "French braids, please," she said.

"Won't it be nice to have a second bathroom?" Paul said.

"I like this," Gina told him, wanting to counter his insinuation for Esther's sake. She pulled the photograph of her parents out of her bathrobe pocket for Esther and braided, occasionally glancing up at her family in the mirror, absorbing the tender scene as deeply as she could. This was an unexpected side effect of sleep deprivation; she'd discovered it created a slower internal pace that made her more present in these ordinary moments with her kids.

Esther looked back and forth from the photo to herself in the mirror, her long eyebrows shifting up and down. "This is a perfect picture," she finally said. "They look so happy."

"See you in a few," Paul said, kissing Gina goodbye after breakfast. Gina loaded Esther, Ben, and their springer spaniel, Stella, into the station wagon and drove to school.

At eleven, after a difficult meeting about expensive change orders with the Stones and their contractor, Gina left her office to pick up Paul. When she opened the car door, she was horrified to discover Stella panting and pacing in the back.

"Stella! Oh, no!" She'd brought Stella so she could come with them to the country, but had forgotten to take her into the office with her. She assessed the temperature inside the car: because of the fog, it was still cool. She poured bottled water into Stella's travel bowl, and Stella lapped it up.

Rattled, she drove toward Paul's medical office. Usually as she crossed town cresting the succession of hills, views of the pastel city and bridges would lift her spirits. Not today. The wind and gray muted everything: color, shape, expectations, the time of day, her mood. She was dropping stitches, getting flustered, feeling the glass half-empty more and more each day, and she couldn't blame it only on lack of sleep, though that wasn't helping.

She pulled into a loading zone near Paul's building and watched him cross the street. Tall and athletically built with a cropped beard, he appeared younger than his forty-eight years. She noticed he was wearing his new Italian high-top shoes that he was so proud of.

"Boy, this car needs a good clean out," he said when he got in. He gathered a binder, paper cups, and an old roll of drawings from the floor and threw them into the backseat. "Feeling okay?"

Gina rolled her eyes at him. "I think I only slept three hours last night. Also, my clients don't need an architect; they need a shrink!"

Paul laughed. "I take it you just had a difficult meeting?"

"Not difficult, exactly. More like crazy. You know how the Stones' house is set at the back of the lot? They've decided they want

the garage to be right under the kitchen, so they have an idea about
tunneling through the hill from the street all the way to the house.
But the thing is, once they drive in, they won't have room to turn
around. They want a turntable installed so they won't have to back
out. It'll mean *months* of grueling neighborhood meetings."

"Is it legal to do that kind of massive excavation?"

"Sure. The question is, is it *moral* to blast away almost a thousand
cubic yards of the planet just because you can?" Gina sighed. "All my
clients just want more and more of everything."

Paul smiled the all-knowing smile she'd come to dread. "Ah," he
said. "Is this the architect's indictment of those who don't understand
that 'less is more,' or are you perhaps a little envious that your clients
have no qualms about saying exactly what they want?"

She groaned; it was all of the above. She'd felt lucky after she'd
first opened her office twelve years ago and jobs had flowed steadily
her way, but recently she'd been wondering if, in building a thriving
business, she'd compromised her architectural vision. While some
residential clients, like the Stones, had given her ample freedom to
assert her ideas, most just wanted her to put a barely artful spin on
their own versions of beauty and function. Le Corbusier and Palla-
dio hadn't looked over Gina's shoulder in a long time. Their cries of
"Light! Space! Proportion! Harmony!" were too often drowned out by
"Payroll! Budget! Schedule!"

On the Golden Gate Bridge, the wind gusted with fog so wet that
Gina had to turn on her windshield wipers. But within minutes, they
emerged from the envelope into blinding sunshine. She was groping in
her purse for her sunglasses when her phone rang. She didn't answer,
but listened to the voicemail from a contractor trying to get a final
inspection on a project.

"Bob here. We got that bitchy electrical inspector. First she
wanted to know why we'd use ugly steel windows on an old house,

and then she told me the architect was stupid for using a plug strip instead of putting the outlets in the backsplash—blah, blah, blah. She left without even checking out the electrical panel. She's holding us way up, Gina. If we don't get these inspections . . . "

Gina ended the message, and they drove on in silence. Her head began to throb.

Soon they were on the small road that wound through oaks and scrub brush, mailboxes, and garages of weathered redwood that signaled "neighborhood," though not a soul could be seen. Eucalyptus trees drooped along the road, not from perpetual thirst, as Gina had thought the first time she'd seen them, but because that was what eucalyptus trees did.

Gina parked in a stand of trees on the north side of their two-acre property that stretched south toward a shallow valley bounded by low hills. Since their first frigid summer in San Francisco thirteen years ago, she and Paul had dreamed they would move somewhere warmer and closer to nature, with an easy commute to the city.

Paul took off his new shoes and put on his sneakers. Gina got out and opened the tailgate; Stella shot out, her short tail wagging. Under the blazing sun, Gina felt enervated as she and Paul walked toward the derelict '60s ranch house, with its flat roof, splintered redwood siding, and cheap aluminum sliders. She tried to conjure the excitement and confidence she'd felt a year and a half ago when she'd tentatively begun a modest plan for it. Usually, when she worked on the schematics for a house, a feeling about the site, both sensory and emotional, would take over and inform her design decisions, right down to the window trim. Here, she could imagine the sun on her shoulders as she bent over a garden they would plant. The crunch of brown August grass under her sneakers as she climbed the hill to the south and the smell of ripe fruit from the lone peach tree . . . searching for toads and lizards with Esther and Ben and, after they'd gone to bed, sitting out under the stars with

Paul, the air still warm and fragrant.

Yet as soon as she put hand to paper, her creative impulse froze. She couldn't see the house. While her projects for clients zipped along, her own unimagined, undrawn house weighed on her. She hated that Esther and Ben would be missing another summer here, where they could be outdoors all day.

Standing in the heat now, the image that did come to Gina was of Ben and Esther in Maine, running down the hill to pick blackberries, barn swallows circling overhead.

Here, hawks, or some other birds of prey—Gina had not yet learned to identify them—surveyed the field below. Paul strode away from Gina, leaning to pick up some tiny piece of litter. When he reached the lilacs they'd planted near a stand of eucalyptus, he gave them the once over, turning a leaf in his hands. "Oh, no," he said, "looks like we're losing them."

Gina ran to inspect the bruised leaves. "I can't believe it! We killed them! It's way too hot and dry here."

When they'd gone to the nursery in early spring, the grass a lush green, the earth rich and fragrant, she'd spotted the lilacs and couldn't help imagining the purple flowering bushes that had grown to tree size around the house in Maine. It was wrong to plant them in this parched place; early June and already the grass was straw-colored, and the dusty earth rose in clouds behind their shoes.

Paul stretched out his arms and smiled. "Maybe someday we could put in a pool. It would be great here."

"Yes," Gina said, trying to picture a turquoise oval sparkling in the sun. Instead, she saw the cove in Maine, breaching the dock at high tide.

Paul fetched the cooler from the car, and they sat down on the scratchy grass in front of the house and looked out over their property, as they had so many times before. The insistent banging of a lone hammer could be heard, coming from the "good side of the hill" (as the real estate agent had put it) where a thirty-thousand-square-foot Mediterranean Revival villa was under construction.

"I'm so ready to be doing this house!" Paul said. "Aren't you?"

"Uh-huh," Gina said.

"We just need a little something on paper that we can discuss."

"I know."

"Gina . . . "

She looked up at him. Goose bumps broke out on her arms.

"Are you cold?" Paul said. He stroked her arm. "The lilacs will come back. If they can make it through those brutal New England winters, they can make it here."

She wouldn't correct him, but he had it backward. Months of cold earth around their roots were exactly what lilacs needed to produce abundant blossoms later; this was part of their magic. The lilacs were *dead*.

Paul opened their cooler and handed a sandwich to Gina; they ate silently until several wasps, hungry for ham, drove them to the car.

They decided to take the coastal road home. Feeling out of sorts, Gina asked Paul to drive. In half an hour, they were back under the blanket of fog; just as the ocean came into view, the sun burned through, restoring the blue to the water. Gina squinted into the light, so white and penetrating it nearly shrieked, lending super-realist clarity to the textures of the landscape.

"It's gorgeous, isn't it?" Paul said.

Reflexively, Gina agreed because she and Paul had always agreed about what was beautiful in life. Now, she realized how foreign the Pacific still was to her. In fourteen years, she'd never navigated its windswept waters—she, who'd bailed and rigged and tacked since she was nine. Only occasionally did she swim in it; it was an exquisite temptress, too cold to touch. She knew that Paul, too, missed the time they'd spent when they were first together back east, bodysurfing at the beach and swimming in Walden Pond. The night they met, they ditched a sweltering party in Cambridge to drive to the pond for a swim. Gina had pulled her swimsuit from her glove compartment saying, "You never know when you might need one," and Paul had laughed, delighted. They'd treaded water and talked for nearly an hour; at one point, she remembered discussing the physics of levers and jaws, subject matter where their two professions—architecture and medicine—intersected. Walden Pond had been a black, still clearing in the forest with no sign of life except the racket of peeping. The immediate connection she and Paul had felt with each other had been breathtaking.

Those years, that intimacy, felt too distant to her now. Recently, she suspected that Paul probably barely recognized the confident, spirited Gina he'd married. Challenges had always made her energy rise, her eyes shine brighter. "I'm movin' to crazy California!" she crowed from Paul's '64 Mustang as they crossed into Kansas, heading away from the East Coast for good. Her entrepreneurial zeal had saved her from continuing to draw elevator cores for a corporate firm, and within a year she'd hung out her "Gina Gilbert, Architect" shingle. Moments after delivering Esther, she'd cried, "Let's have another one right away!" Paul was cautious and made moves slowly; her vigor had always been enough for both of them. Now, she feared her malaise was threatening the balance they'd come to rely on.

The car hugged a sharp curve, and she felt the cliff's plunge in her stomach. This famous winding road had never before made her uncomfortable, but now she saw how close to the cliff's precipice the passenger was, how blind the curves were. Anything could happen: a bicyclist, a deer, a car from the opposite direction swinging too wide.

The road might not be swept away today in a mudslide because it wasn't the rainy season, but at any moment an earthquake could send it tumbling into the sea.

Paul swerved around a bicyclist, and Gina felt her lunch rise in her throat. "Paul, pull over!" she rasped.

He stopped the car in a turnout. Gina got out and stood shivering in the bracing wind.

She stared up at the restless, gray expanse of sky where gulls drew invisible lines, then down at the restless, empty gray expanse of ocean; sky and water together were like an impossible jigsaw puzzle in which every piece looked the same.

The nausea receded, Gina returned to the car, and they began the descent into the valley of dripping redwoods and eucalyptus. When they left the trees and turned onto the straight lane of freeway, she was relieved.

"Sweetie, I'm excited about the house," Paul said after a while. "But I don't want you to feel pressured about the plans for it. Give yourself a break; you've been through a lot."

Gina was silent for a few moments. Finally, she said, "Nothing feels right."

They'd reached the Golden Gate Bridge where people on the walkway clowned for cameras; others clutched their jackets closed against the wind. Tourists, everywhere. She felt like one, too.

"You're not yourself now. It takes time," Paul said.

Gina let her head fall back on the seat. Why did people say that, she wondered, as if it were the flu? Since her parents' accident, everything had changed somehow. And yet, certainly not the day-to-day. She'd only seen her parents one or two weeks a year during the past decade. Still, the *idea* of her parents at the house in Maine, drinking Lipton tea at the kitchen table or touching up the paint on the porch, animated by the occasional phone call with her and the kids, had admittedly provided more comfort than the *reality* of being with them. This is the way it is, she'd always told herself about their family dynamic, which even Paul conceded was dysfunctional. But buried in that resignation was a kernel of hope: as long as her parents were there, there was the possibility her relationship with them could change. Now, it was frozen stuck; *the way it was* felt like a kind of failure, a colossal waste of human potential for growth and acceptance.

Paul was right; it took time to mourn. But it wasn't only loss she felt. Her parents' death was a period at the end of a long, difficult sentence whose words had conveyed more urgency and pain to Gina the more she'd aged. In the past few months, it seemed to have shaken the very foundation of her courage and contentment. She felt unmoored—like a tent with one of its stakes pulled out of the ground, flapping and folding in the wind.

They rode in a humming silence punctuated by the thumping of the bridge's expansion joints and Stella's panting. When they arrived at his office, Paul pulled over, kissed Gina on the cheek, and got out of the car.

Gina climbed into the driver's seat and just as she pulled away from the curb, her phone rang. It was Cassie.

"Cass," she said when she answered, "I'm driving, can I . . . "

"I'm sorry!" Cassie interrupted "But you've gotta hear this. Sid just called and left a message that he bought the house. *Our* house. He wants to discuss his plans for it."

"*Our* house?" Gina ran a yellow light and noticed a cop parked at the intersection.

"Cassie, it's illegal to talk on my cell while driving. Wait—hold on." She laid her phone on the seat next to her and pressed "speaker."

"It's so awful! Just spiteful!" Cassie's agitation filled the car, making it hard for Gina to breathe.

"You know, Sid's bought and sold, like, three houses in Whit's Point in the last ten years. He's just buying ours to flip it, too," Gina said, thinking this might somehow reassure Cassie.

"Oh, how horrible! What will he *do* to it? I just *can't* talk to him."

"Then I guess I'll have to."

"No!" Cassie practically shouted. "You can't. He wants something from us—besides the house, I mean. He thinks we have something, and he'd probably do anything to get it."

Gina's mind was not on her driving; she needed to say good-bye. "Let me think about it, okay? Email me his number. You and I will talk."

They hung up. Gina's head felt foamy with confusion. As usual, she'd been so intent on calming down Cassie that she couldn't register how *she* felt about Sid's buying the house. Cassie's distrust of their cousin was over-the-top, she knew, but Gina wasn't eager to talk to him, either. She'd associated him with inexorable family hostility for so long that she imagined any contact with him could suck her into a vortex of pain. She was sure he felt the same way about her and Cassie—he'd long ago distanced himself from them. He hadn't even shown up at her parents' funeral.

But what could she really know about Sid? She'd been Esther's age when she last saw him. Why was he coming back into their lives now?

A book is a home for a story
A rose is a house for a smell
My head is a house for a secret
A secret I never shall tell!

Mary Ann Hoberman, *A House Is a House For Me*

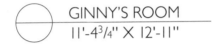

GINNY'S ROOM
11'-4³/₄" X 12'-11"

Just when it seemed her mother's birthday was doomed, Ginny's father was struck with the idea of a family trip to the Museum of Fine Arts. Eleanor had frowned at his other ideas of how to spend the day: lunch at Howard Johnson's or a drive to the mountains.

"Okay, the museum—that's good," she had said, and Ginny, her father, and maybe even the timbers of the house, having been in suspense all morning, sighed with relief.

The Gilberts wound out Pickering Road, mounded on both sides with colorful leaves.

As they approached Lily House, Eleanor said, "Slow down, Ron. *Look!* They finished the roof job. The color of those new roof shingles is all wrong."

Ginny turned to look. Everyone in the car expected Eleanor to remark about something or other every time she drove by Lily House. Wasn't the field behind it getting high or the barn needing some paint? From her mother's vigilance Ginny gleaned that Lily House was her mother's *real* house, the one she would move into if Fran weren't living there. Because her mother and Fran didn't get along, Ginny had only been inside Lily House a handful of times.

"Stop!" Eleanor now commanded. "It's *Sid*—in the driveway. Let's see if he wants to go to the museum."

"Oh, honey, you don't really want—"

"Certainly I do! Pull in."

Ginny slumped in her seat. Cassie had left for her first year of boarding school six weeks ago, and Ginny missed her almost unbearably; it didn't seem fair to have your sister leave home when you were only nine. They were going to pick her up at school to go with them to the museum, and Ginny had been looking forward to having her to herself in the backseat. Plus, for some reason, Cassie hated Sid, and she'd be mad he was coming.

Ron pulled into Lily House's driveway, and Eleanor got out. Ginny couldn't remember the last time she'd seen Sid. She took in his bell-bottom corduroys and jean jacket, the dark hair that reached jaggedly for his shoulders, and the cigarette clamped in his mouth and decided he looked like a musician on the cover of a record album, lanky and loose. He appeared to be fiddling with the windshield wiper on Fran's car.

Sid looked up at them, plucked the cigarette from his mouth and ground it into the dirt with his boot. He didn't move toward them when Eleanor got out of the car.

"Oh, boy," Ron said.

Sid and her mother exchanged a few words, and Sid disappeared into the house. Eleanor marched back to the car. "Fran will come up with some reason he can't go with us, of course. Even on my birthday."

Ginny hoped she was right. Ron started the engine, and Eleanor said, "Turn it off. We'll just wait. I haven't seen him in three years, for God's sake. She's just jealous! She's been jealous since the day I was born!"

Lily House's door opened. Sid stood on the porch with his knapsack for a few moments, as if still deciding.

Eleanor said, "Oh!" and her face lit up the way it did when she'd see a Jack-in-the-Pulpit in the woods. She got out of the car and climbed into the backseat with Ginny.

"Why does he get the front?" Ginny asked.

"Because he has long legs."

Sid's knapsack landed on the floor in the front seat. "Thanks for the rescue, gang," he said when he got in. "Nice Pontiac, Ron." The car filled with a smoky smell.

"Sid's coming to the museum with us!" Eleanor announced gaily. "Then we're going to drop him at the bus station to go back to Chapin. Ginny, say hello."

"Hello," Ginny said.

"So how's school, dear?" Eleanor asked Sid. "Are you still painting?"

"Still painting. Senior year. A lot of work. Not much sleep. On top of it, I was up half the night with Fran, so if you don't mind, I'm going to take a little snooze."

Sid slumped against the car door. Eleanor looked out the window. Ginny stewed; her mother would never have allowed Cassie to get away with such rudeness.

No one said a word. Halfway between home and Boston, they stopped to pick up Cassie at Andrews Academy, the all-girls boarding school that Eleanor's "summer person" friends had recommended when Eleanor complained that her older daughter had gone boy crazy and her teachers didn't challenge her. Andrews had given Cassie a scholarship, and her wealthy godmother had provided the balance of the tuition. To Ginny's astonishment, Cassie had been fine with going away to school and didn't even tear up when they dropped her off in September. Ginny had cried hard that night, in bed.

When the station wagon pulled up in front of the dormitory, two girls wearing carpenter's overalls walked by, and Ron chuckled, "Would you look at the outfits?" Cassie bounced down the steps smiling, her long blonde hair shimmering against her navy loden coat. She hadn't gone for the "hippie" look yet, Ginny noted with some relief.

When Cassie spotted the sleeping Sid, her mouth dropped open.

"Oof," she said, sliding onto the seat next to Ginny. "What's Sid doing here?"

"He's coming to the museum with us!" Eleanor said. She put her finger to her lips to keep Cassie from saying more.

Cassie pinched Ginny's arm lightly, signaling her annoyance. "Happy birthday, Mom," she said. "Pretty jacket, Gin."

Ginny looked down at the red-and-purple plaid that had caught her mother's eye in the bin at Filene's Basement on their semiannual shopping trip. Now, she floated in Cassie's sweet smell—Prell, she knew; their mother had taught them to wash their hair with soap, but Cassie had graduated to shampoo.

Eleanor opened the cooler and passed the girls the cucumber sandwiches she'd made.

"Our chorus sang at chapel this morning," Cassie said.

"Oh, how nice, dear. Something classical? Hymns?"

"We sang 'Blowin' in the Wind.' It's a Peter, Paul, and Mary song."

Eleanor clucked her tongue and shook her head, dispersing her disapproval over the backseat.

Cassie said, "It smells like pot in here."

Sid woke up as they were parking the car in the museum lot. "Whoa, where'd we get Cassie from?" he said, twisting to peer at them.

"I'm their firstborn, remember?" Cassie said. Eleanor shot Cassie a frown.

"So," Sid said, grinning at Cassie. "You going to that Woodstock concert next weekend? Going to be good."

Eleanor's head cranked hard to look at Cassie. "I'm only kidding, Ellie," Sid said. "She's way too young for that."

Cassie got out of the car and motored toward the museum entrance. Ginny trailed behind, wondering why Sid rankled her older sister so and feeling fairly certain that one of them was going to ruin the birthday.

But something came over her mother, Ginny noticed, whenever she stepped inside a museum or concert hall; here, at the Museum of Fine Arts, her mood and even her height seemed to elevate in proportion to the majestic domed lobby.

And now, Sid cocked his head and said to Eleanor, "Your coat, Madame?"

"Well, certainly sir," Eleanor beamed as Sid lifted her coat from her shoulders.

Cassie looked at Ginny and frowned. As the family followed the crowd toward the grand staircase, an older woman with a large emerald dragonfly pinned to her blazer lapel bent down to say to Eleanor, "Your daughters are just lovely!"

"Well, aren't you nice to say so," her mother said. She looked her girls over proudly, and Ginny stood up straighter. "And this is my nephew," she said, turning with a sweep of her arm, only to realize Sid had drifted away.

Experienced museumgoers, the Gilberts spent a respectable amount of time on each painting, careful not to block the views of others. Today, Ginny had a hard time concentrating on the art because she was busy monitoring Cassie and Sid, who seemed to be steering clear of each other and the rest of them. At least Ginny's father—balding but handsome, she thought, in his tweed sport coat—had placed his hand protectively at the center of her mother's back and for once, Eleanor didn't pull away.

Now, her father lowered his head to catch her mother's murmured remarks to Ginny.

"Isn't it interesting how quiet his colors are compared to the others? Just exquisite!" Ginny and her father leaned their faces closer to Eleanor's; the rapture emanating from her felt almost like love. "You can see the way he made the shadow with different shades of blue and purple."

Her mother touched Ginny's arm, and the three shifted to the next painting. "And look at the simple, soft shapes in this one," she said. "Don't they remind you of your paintings?"

They did, Ginny thought, but only because they seemed inaccurate, like hers.

"Psst!"

Ginny swiveled to see Sid, her mother's coat hooked on his thumb over his shoulder, peeking at her from around the door frame of an adjacent gallery. Behind him hung an intriguing and enormous black-and-white image. Keeping an eye on her family, she moved toward Sid into the room where a sign announced, "The Pleasure of Ruins."

Sid poked her in the back. "Hey, don't look so sad."

"I'm not sad," she said.

Sid laughed. "Look over there at your sis."

Ginny turned; Cassie looked like she always did: pretty, serious.

"She'd rather be anywhere but here. But it's your mum's birthday. Your mum and mine, they're sensitive and get their feelings hurt easily. So we have to try to be extra nice to them."

Now, Ginny *did* feel sad. "I know," she said.

"Cheer up, kid! We're in the presence of greatness." Sid gestured to the artwork. "This is the really *great* stuff," he said. He was standing so close to her that she could *feel* his excitement, as if bugs were jumping from him to her. She circled the room, trancelike, astonished by the photographs covering the walls: columns rising from rubble and huge blocks of stone standing upright in a field, heavy crumbling walls and windows with only sky behind. Their labels read: "Stonehenge," "The Parthenon," "The Forum," "The Baths of Caracalla." The images filled her with a wonder she felt in her bones.

She'd nearly forgotten Sid was there until he said, "These places are more alive in death than most places are at birth. They're cool, huh?" Ginny almost understood what he meant; mostly, she jittered with the idea that he'd speak to her in this grown-up way. "What do you think?" he asked.

Ginny looked at him, wondering what in the world he expected her, his nine-year-old cousin, to say. His dark eyes danced. "I like that they're mysterious," she said.

"Ginny?" She almost didn't hear her father, who'd come up behind them. "Great shots, aren't they?" he said. But it wasn't the ruins that captivated her now. Still under Sid's spell, she slid her hand inside her father's, and they left the gallery to once more traipse through the halls of Degas and Van Gogh and Bonnard and the three M's: Monet, Matisse, and Morandi.

At dinnertime, the Vietnam War silently flickered on the TV as it did every night.

The kitchen was cramped and brightly lit, with uncurtained black windows that steamed up from a single boiling pot. A birdcage hung in one corner, but their liberally supervised finch, Pepe, was not inside, having found a warmer place to perch somewhere in the house. While her father peeled potatoes and opened cans of corned beef hash—a favorite quick dinner of their mother's—Ginny put candles on a small cake in her father's darkroom. The birthday had gone smoothly enough; all the way to the bus station to drop off Sid, Eleanor had plied him with questions about which colleges he was interested in ("No idea"), whether he had a girlfriend (he didn't), and if he'd be in Whit's Point for the summer ("I hope not."). When he got out of the car, Eleanor said, "He's so handsome. I can't believe he doesn't have a girlfriend." Cassie had said, "Maybe because he smokes pot. Or, maybe he likes boys." Ginny had braced for her mother's reaction, but all she'd said was, "Poor thing. He's awfully good to his mother." Then she'd said to Cassie, "Too bad school's so important you couldn't come home for my birthday weekend." Gina had squirmed while Cassie explained in a tight voice that she'd had a long play rehearsal on Saturday.

Now, Ginny was already missing Cassie, but she excitedly eyed the wrapped presents on the worktable. The biggest one, she knew, was a white Singer sewing machine that would replace her mother's ancient black one.

After dinner, her father lit the candles on the cake, and Ginny carried it into the kitchen singing "Happy Birthday." Her father set the presents on the floor next to her mother's chair.

"Well," Eleanor said, looking down at the sewing machine box, wrapped in Christmas paper. "What a surprise—poinsettias in October!"

"Oops," Ron said, shifting his weight awkwardly. "Guess I was just reaching for the biggest piece in the box."

Ron helped Eleanor pull the paper off the sewing machine and stepped back, as if it might explode.

"Wowie!" she exclaimed. "A sewing machine! Now let's see . . . are you going to learn how to sew, Ron?"

Her father's nervous laugh. "Oh . . . well, sure, why not?" They'd been warming the kitchen with the open oven, and it had grown too hot; perspiration beaded on his forehead.

Eleanor unwrapped Cassie's present—a knit hat—and said, "Ooooh."

Ginny waited, excited about her present—a pair of pajamas. They were her idea, even though she knew her parents usually slept without anything on, which she surmised was because pajamas were a luxury. Her father had taken her to Riversport to buy them. She picked out a cotton pair with green and white stripes; her mother was practical and wouldn't like frilly, silky ones.

As Eleanor unwrapped the pajamas, Ginny stood at her elbow and held her breath. Her mother picked up the starched, long-sleeved shirt-style top, inspected it, then looked up at Ron. She carefully laid it back in the box.

"Why, Ginny!" she exclaimed, pulling Ginny toward her. "Thank you, sweetie." Ginny looked into her mother's face. Her lips were smiling, but her eyes were not.

Late at night Ginny was awakened by her mother's shout, "This goddamn pigsty!" Silence. Her father, mumbling. She looked at the door that connected her room to her parents'. In the past few years, it had become dangerous, like the door she'd been told never to open if she smelled smoke and the wood felt hot to the touch.

"You don't know anything! She'll turn that boy against me . . . Oh, how I loved him. He could have been mine . . . " Her mother wept, steadily and quietly enough that it nearly lulled Ginny back to sleep. But then a mournful tune filled the darkness: "Happy birthday to me, happy birthday to me . . . " Her mother's singing was so creepy Ginny wished she'd go back to crying. Her father mumbled. Her mother: "You really have no idea; do you!" Then, a tearing sound: zripp—zripp—zripp!

"Oh, honey, don't . . . " Her father's plaintive voice.

"Don't touch me! You think I'm just going to be the servant in this pigsty for the rest of my life? Well, don't count on it! This isn't life…this is some kind of death! Oh . . . oh . . . oh . . . I wish I could just die."

The door was burning; her mother's cries leapt through its old wood like flames. Ginny wrapped the pillow around her head and scratched it with her fingernails, scratch-scratch-scratching away the world. Tonight, she would begin to practice forgetting; she would build a *wall-of-forgetting*. The less you heard, the less there was to be forgotten.

She must have dozed off. She awoke to the squeal of her parents' window sash going up and slamming down.

It seemed like hours before she could fall back to sleep.

In the morning, she raised her shade slowly, so the noise wouldn't wake her parents. It was so early that it was still dark, and across the cove the silhouette of pine trees was just barely distinguishable against the sky.

After switching on the light, she stretched up her arms and looked around her room. Was it a "pigsty"? It was messy but in a good way, in her opinion, because the mess was what she herself had created. Everything else in the room—desk and bookshelves, bed and bureau, pale pink walls and most of her clothing—had been passed down to her. She'd divided the room into zones: one for sleeping, one for homework, one near the window for thinking and reading, one for dressing, one for art making. She'd nearly covered the pink walls with her artwork; everywhere, there were so many animals and books and knick-knacks to look at, that the looking nearly silenced the world outside the room. Perhaps, she thought for the first time, she should sleep with her light on.

She began picking up the clothing layered on her desk chair, separating dirty from clean. The dirty things went into a pile near the door; the clean things she hung up in her closet or folded neatly in drawers.

She went to her easel and flipped through sheets of newsprint. None of the paintings she'd made of flowers and bowls of fruit looked real. When she took her sketchpad outside, on the boat or in the yard, lines and brushstrokes seemed to have wings. But here in her room, she couldn't get the shapes right. She thought of the ruins at the museum that seemed more like creations of nature than of human hands. She thought of the mysterious Sid and wondered when they'd meet again.

After sorting through every one of her drawings, she selected a few to clip back onto the easel. The rest she stacked on the floor next to her dirty clothes.

Now, she carefully placed the tubes of paint in their box in order by color. Pinched the dry, hard spots off her modeling clay, then rewrapped each color. Switched her Cray-pas around in their box, matching each one with its named slot. She eyed her art supplies; organized in little rainbows, they were as tantalizing as the cookies in a bakery case. She liked arranging and deranging them almost more than drawing with them.

Through the door, she heard her father snore, like a warm-up for the blub-blub-blub of a lobster boat starting up now, on the other side of the cove. She hastily assessed her cleaning effort. With everything in its proper place, the room looked bigger, sleeker, its horizontals and verticals clearer. Surely, she thought, this would make her mother happy. If she was still alive, that is. On mornings after a night like last night, she could never feel sure she would see her mother again.

It was seven o'clock, time to get back in bed. She turned off the light and went to the window. The sun was up, and it set the edge of the red sumacs ablaze. The rocks of Miller's and Poison Ivy Island were black against the midnight blue sea; the trees were losing their leaves, and she could see all the way to New Hampshire. When she turned ten next year, she'd be allowed to sail their boat across the harbor and river mouth, to New Hampshire. To another state, *by herself!*

She raised her window, unlocked the storm window and propped it open at the bottom to get a feel for the new day. Her eyes dropped to something on the porch below her parents' window. She squinted. Lying next to the empty planter boxes were the green-and-white striped pajamas she'd given her mother, shredded and in a wad, their tags still attached.

Quickly, she put down the window, threw up her *wall-of-forgetting*, and climbed back into bed.

The hall floor creaked, and soon she heard her father moving toward her bed. This morning, she would pretend to be asleep; she needed to feel the caress of his fingers on her cheek.

"Get up now, okay sleepyhead?" he whispered.

She waited, relishing the tender stroke of his hand that assured that her mother was still alive and that she hadn't yet made her father leave. Finally, she opened her eyes. Her father looked like autumn in his brown khakis and red-and-black checked shirt. It didn't seem like too much to hope he might offer a sympathetic acknowledgement of what had gone on during the night. But he never did.

Glancing around the room, he said, "Wow! Pretty spiff."

In the kitchen, Ginny sat at the table with a bowl of Rice Krispies and opened her notebook. "I need Mom's help with homework questions," she told her father.

"Something I can help you with?"

"No, it's about ancestors."

Her father looked very hard at something on the floor. "I guess I better wake her up," he said and headed upstairs.

Ginny looked out the kitchen window and saw that the pajamas were gone from the porch. Something thumped the ceiling above her; the bathroom door slammed. Her father's slow footsteps on the stair. Back in the kitchen, he dropped two slices of toast into the toaster and put the teakettle on to boil.

Finally, Eleanor came in, her blue bathrobe tied loosely around the waist, her eyes puffy. Ginny felt almost sick with relief to see her mother alive. But a moment later, she hated her for last night's declaration that she wished she were dead. "Brrr," Eleanor said. "Winter's coming. Rigor mortis is setting in."

"Can I ask you my homework questions now?" Ginny asked.

"Fire away," her mother said, sitting down at the table.

"Okay. Number one, where did my ancestors come from?"

"England and France, mostly. We're descended from kings! Haven't I shown you the genealogy book your grandpa made?"

Her mother glowed, as if a light inside her had switched on. She left the room and came back carrying a large, black notebook.

"Here—look. You remember your ancestor Cassandra Westwick, the Salem witch, don't you?" she said. "The one Cassie's named after? She was an honest-to-goodness witch from Salem, burned at the stake and everything! And you see . . . here's your grandpa, Sidney Banton, and here's his father, Sidney Banton, and so on, till you get to the Sidney Banton who owned Lily House. He was the one who was George Washington's private secretary; and did you know that the president came to visit him at Lily House once? He did, and he sat in the Hepplewhite lolling chair. You know the one I mean?" Ginny was pretty sure she knew the chair, but her mother didn't wait for an answer. "And the president—George Washington—left some important letters— letters from Thomas Jefferson!—at Lily House. The letters disappeared after the president died, and some people think Sidney Banton burned them up, but your grandpa was positive that he hid them in the house somewhere." Her mother tilted her long, dark eyebrows at Ginny. "Now *that's* not something you can tell anyone about, though, okay?" Ginny thought her mother looked a little puffed out, like Pepe when she was cold.

Sidney Banton: Ginny had heard the name all her life, and it occurred to her for the first time that fame was why his name had been passed down through generations, to her grandfather. Now she wondered how Sid ended up with the name, since it was his mother, not his father, who was a Banton. When she asked her mother, she frowned.

"Oh. Well, since Sid's father ran off before he was born, Fran didn't see why Sid should have his last name, so she gave him her last name, and it worked out, because Sid's the only grandson, and it would be a shame for Sidney Banton's name not to be passed down."

Her mother fell silent and looked far away, out the window. "God only knows . . . Fran has probably done something with those Washington letters. Oh, well, doop-de doo," she said, shutting the book. She shook her head. "All those precious *things* at Lily House."

Her father must have thought she was talking to him. "Well, there'll be a war about them someday," he said. "I think it would've been better if your father or grandfather had just given it all away to a museum or library or something." He buttered the toast and put it on a plate in front of her mother, apparently unaware that she was glaring at him. When he slipped a teabag into her cup and began to pour steaming water from the kettle into it, Ginny felt suddenly panicked that someone was going to get burned.

"Give it away? *Give it away*? It's all we've got, goddamn you! Give it away and *then* what? We can go live in a tent for the rest of our lives?"

Ginny peered into her bowl of beige Rice Krispie mush.

"Oh, okay," her father said. "I'm really not the one to . . . "

"You've got that right—you're an *idiot*!"

"Okay, I'm an idiot then," her father said, looking like he'd just eaten something sour.

Ginny felt the cereal rise in her throat and swallowed hard. She looked at the clock, then at the last question on her paper, "What makes you proud of your ancestors?" She didn't ask it out loud, though; it seemed like a personal question.

She and her mother pressed their lips together in their ritual goodbye kiss.

Her father walked her to the front door, and she turned to give him a worried look. He gave her shoulders a squeeze. "Better get a wiggle on. See you later, alligator."

She was halfway down the walk when she turned abruptly.

"Daddy—" she called, turning to see him still standing at the door. "Were there any real ancestors on your side?"

"No one important that I know of, honey," her father said, putting his hands in his pockets. "Your grandfather brought us to America from England when I was a baby. He came to find a better job here as a toolmaker."

Ginny rarely saw her paternal grandfather from Michigan, but she loved the way he said "garage" to rhyme with "carriage." She remembered him playing his marimba and singing in a rich baritone voice. He knew a lot about things, it seemed, like juggling and electricity.

When she got to her desk at school, she opened her notebook and answered the question, "What makes you proud of your ancestors?" She wrote: "They were smart and interesting, and some of them can sing."

On the way home from school, Ginny zipped her jacket and put up her hood. The air's cold edge reminded her that Halloween was only six days away.

She stepped into the house and felt immediately that the storm her mother had whipped up last night hadn't passed. No one was in the kitchen, and the darkroom door stood wide open. She put one foot on the stairs to go up, but when she caught her mother's crying from the bedroom, she went back outside.

She ran down the hill to the fort she'd built on the rocks at the edge of the cove with salvaged, waterlogged plywood. It was her refuge when the house didn't feel safe, when she'd been marooned by things she didn't understand. The three-sided structure was open on the cove side and equipped with a few old kitchen utensils. It was just big enough for two: Ginny and her best friend, Sandy.

Ginny wished for Sandy now, wished it were summer, when the days outdoors never ended. Instead of Sandy, she got Kit, her next-door neighbor who now stood peering in at her. He was two years older and a boy, but he was better than no one. She moved over so he could sit down. It was nearly high tide, and the water nipped the rocks. They listened to the *shush-shush-shush* of their neighbor scrubbing the weeds off the bottom of his boat, already hauled out for winter. In a few months, storms would push the water over the rocks; the fort—at least most of it—would wash away. In May, Ginny would build another.

"Wanna go rowin'?" Kit asked.

They climbed over the rocks to the dock and pulled in the dinghy on the outhaul.

While Ginny set the oarlocks, Kit bailed out water with a cut-off Clorox bottle. Pointing the bow to the center of the cove, Ginny rowed with long strokes, watching the funnel swirls made by the oars. She loved the freedom of propelling the boat through the water; when she pulled back the oars, it felt like spreading her wings.

In the boat, Kit was silent, as usual. He was shy and spent a lot of time alone, building complicated rafts that he steered around the cove with a long pole and fixing lobster traps for people. Since he had no brothers or sisters at home and his parents were divorced, he was often available. She'd known him since she was two, and there was something comforting about his gentle smile and curly hair and the old green army jacket he wore every day.

She and Kit didn't speak until they were nearly to the other side of the cove, and Ginny said, "Mom told me this morning that I'm related to kings, but I don't believe her."

"Probably everyone is if you go back far enough."

Ginny thought about this. It seemed likely; first there was Jesus, and then kings and queens, then George Washington and witches, and then everyone else.

"Do you think that means my family was rich once?"

"Maybe. But lots of people, like my dad's parents, lost all their money because of the Depression."

Ginny considered Kit's explanation. She'd heard about depression; Cassie often talked about "Mom's depression," and that Mom did such-and-such because she was depressed. Of course, Ginny thought, her mother's depression was probably why they never had enough money. Things were starting to make sense.

She rowed a big loop around the cove while Kit looked for minnows over the side. When he spotted a school, she scooped them up with the bailer and in the same movement released them in a small waterfall. After a while, they hauled the boat up on the far side of the cove, rolled up their pants, and scavenged along the high tide line, collecting mussel shells and good fort-building wood. Ginny's legs itched from the tall grass that grew along the spongy mud bank. It had turned straw-colored.

When it was close to dinnertime, Ginny took the oars, and they headed back. Halyards of the few remaining boats moored in the harbor slapped against their masts, sounding like a percussion section that had lost its orchestra. Had it been that long since summer? She could still see her mother's smile and ocean eyes sparkling against the sail of their dinghy. Now the October light flagged, staining the sky pink.

The tide was turning, and a fresh breeze came up, strong enough to edge the dinghy shoreward, but not enough to keep her mother's wail from reaching them. "Goddamn you to hell!" Slam! The back door. Ginny pretended not to hear and laughed nervously, the giggling like ginger ale settling her insides. She gazed up the hill at her plain white house—small and vulnerable, as if it could blow down the hill in one big storm. Her bedroom window was a black eye; but soon, her mother's window blazed and sobbed, a sound as familiar to Ginny as the cries of seagulls settling at night.

Ginny was certain all the ears on the cove must have been trained on her house. Kit wouldn't look at her.

Finally he said, "Are they gonna get divorced?"

Ginny felt she might fold in half, but she sat up. Anger clenched her hands tight as she dug the oars deep into the inky water. "I wish they would," she said.

You've got to bumble forward, into the unknown.
Frank Gehry

Chapter 5

Two weeks later—another inhospitable June morning, desolate with fog. Gina sat in her storefront office reviewing a set of drawings in anticipation of her eight-thirty meeting. As was her inclination, she lingered on things that dissatisfied her, starting with the virginal twenty-pound bond paper on which the floor plans had been plotted, untouched by an architect's hand, and the prints—no longer the iconic blue, fragrant with ammonia, but an odorless white, printed offsite and delivered in a roll. There were the drawings themselves, corrupted by the computer's distinctly unhuman mistakes: a wall missing its inside line, an incomplete dimension string, and worst of all, the ghost of a demolished room floating in the middle of the Stones' living room. Before computer-aided design, lines were drawn with deliberateness! Qualities! Each had been assigned a special line-weight, then pulled across the vellum by a loving hand, leadholder twisting between fingers, traveling just beyond the intersection with another line to make a crisp corner. CAD lines were all the same, and all were sprinters, finding the quickest path between two points. Her clients' drawings were as artless as a wiring diagram. Looking at them, Gina felt her artistry faltering, too. Wasn't something important in the design process lost when the brain and the hand didn't make their connection on paper? Besides, she loved the feel of the rough vellum, the graphite on her fingers, the whir of her electric eraser.

CAD was a form of sensory deprivation, she thought now, not unlike the fog-wind that swirled outside the windows, stirring up eddies of soot and sushi bar flyers, shutting out spring.

At eight forty-five, Jeff Stone called to say something had come up, and they wouldn't make it to the meeting. Gina pushed their drawings aside and cleared everything off her desk so she could use her Mayline parallel rule, the only one in the office. She pulled her year-old schematic drawing for the Marin house out of the flat file, laid it on her desk, and had just rolled some tracing paper over it when her cell phone rang in her purse. She fished it out, and when she saw her friend Joni's name on the screen, she gasped, "Oh, no!"

In the open, loftlike office, her seven employees craned around their partitions to look at her. "Joni!" She said quietly into the phone, "I completely forgot about book group last night! I'm so sorry! I know. No, I'm okay, I think, except I'm still not sleeping well, and I was so out of it that I didn't even check my messages last night. And—aghh! I was supposed to bring the entrée. What did you *eat*?"

After more apologizing, she hung up and went into the conference room for some privacy and rested her head on the table. She felt terrible. It was not like her to forget her plans; she always looked forward to seeing her friends. Though now that she thought about it, she'd been fending off their caring efforts all spring. She tried to reconstruct her evening the night before and realized she'd been preoccupied with their trip to Marin all through dinner. Only later, when she and Ben had been working on the rocket, had she felt present.

She gathered herself and returned to her desk. For an hour, she pushed her pen around the tracing paper, considering sun angles and wind direction, views and the slope of the lot, while trying to resolve the lines that would contain the house's rooms. While she drew, her mind's eye drifted through the rooms of the Maine house, up the steep stair to the window with its view of the cove. She found herself wishing they weren't restricted to a one-story house by a ridgetop ordinance in Marin. She tried an "H" scheme, a courtyard scheme, a bar scheme, and a wall scheme. Her trash can filled with the crumpled evidence of her failure. She felt a strange, bracelike tightening around her chest and shifted in her chair, unsuccessfully trying to relieve the sensation.

Determined to take the plans to the next level, she put the tracing paper aside and taped down a sheet of vellum, hoping the commitment to a more serious paper would somehow force progress. She drew her squeaky Mayline down its cables, placed her triangle against it, and began to draw, the black lines of her leadholder emerging reluctantly, vibrating against the bright white paper. Occasionally, her young employees stopped by her desk and briefly watched, as if she were demonstrating a lost art. Another half hour, and her eyes burned and blurred with fatigue. She looked down at what she'd accomplished: nothing.

Gina and Esther had a tradition of going out for milkshakes on the last day of school. This would be Ben's first year to join them. Gina left work early so she could change her clothes before picking them up. Walking in the front door of the house, she nearly tripped over the recycling box she'd forgotten to put out, and Stella danced around her, letting her know she wanted a walk.

She was making tea in a travel cup when the doorbell rang, sending Stella racing to the front of the house in a spasm of barking. Gina followed, opening the door to two blue-blazered, beaming young men, one of whom was saying, ". . . and it looks like this one's built to the maximum allowable envelope."

"Hi, Mrs. Goodson?" The other man said, one hand caressing

the portico column. "We're from the Town Real Estate Company? Perhaps you heard that the home here on your block—2323—sold for $2.2 million last week? Mrs. Goodson, we're wondering if you were thinking about selling your home."

Gina froze, trying to make sense of what he was saying. "*Excuse me?*" she said. "No, no . . . Mrs. Goodson is my husband's mother. This was her house but hasn't been for seven years."

The agent cocked his head and furrowed his face as if she were an unintelligible old woman. "Mrs. Paul Goodson, right?"

Gina felt the brace again and now her heart banged against it. "Right, but no, I'm not . . . I'm Gina Gilbert. Paul Goodson is my husband, but we're not selling his . . . " She shook her head and waved her hands. "It's not for sale!" She shut the door hard and stepped back on Stella's foot, eliciting a sharp yelp. "I'm sorry, Stella!"

The walls of the narrow hallway pressed in; she was tight and hot, toast in a toaster.

Hoping Paul would be between patients, she pulled her cell phone from her purse and called him. When he answered, she said, "I feel really weird. Sick, maybe; I don't know."

"Do you think you're just exhausted? I could pick up the kids if— "

"No!" she said, too firmly. "It's their last day." She'd never missed a last-day-of-school milkshake celebration and was determined not to.

"They'll understand if you're not feeling well, you know. I could take them for milkshakes a little later."

"No. I'm okay," she lied. What did she want from Paul? Certainly not his usual advice to not worry about the kids. "Cassie really wants me to call Sid to talk about the house," she blurted, to change the subject.

"I thought you'd decided not to. Is this what's upsetting you?"

"No. I don't know. It's just . . . A couple of real estate agents just rang our doorbell and wanted to know if we were selling our house!"

Paul laughed. "It's just the real estate business. They do that all the time."

"It's not nice."

Paul was quiet. Then he said, "Gina, what's this about?"

What's this about? she parroted in her head. She and Paul rarely quarreled, but lately arguments seemed to sprout like weeds in some dark room inside her. "I can't design our house, Paul. I've filled a trashcan ten times with shitty plans. It's like I'm so polluted with other peoples' houses I can't see my own. But how can we even know what a new house will mean to us? We're living in your parents' house now, *your* house, and the only house that has ever felt like mine is three thousand miles away and wasn't even mine."

"Gina . . . " Paul started.

Why didn't he just say the first thing that came to mind? Gina thought. What she'd always loved about him was how he never turned away from emotion. He didn't just mist up over sad movies; he *cried*.

In his silence, she imagined he was fuming. She was the one who'd jumped on the chance to move into his childhood home when his mother decided seven years ago that she could no longer maintain it. He and Gina had been renting a two-bedroom, third story walk-up, and Gina was pregnant with Ben. When she'd asked Paul if it would be strange for him to live in his family's house, he'd said not at all, even though she knew he had some sad associations with it, growing up as an only child with a father suffering from multiple sclerosis. The decision to move in was one of those made when one spouse provides the forward thrust. Now, she knew that Paul felt an insistent desire to create a home whose history would begin with her, Esther, and Ben.

"Do you think . . . " Paul spoke slowly, deliberately, "that maybe you're romanticizing the Maine house? It was a beautiful place to grow up, but you've been trying to leave that house for as long as

I've known you."

Emotion surged through Gina. "Yes, but the house has always been there, if I wanted it. Now it's leaving *me*. *Here*. What am I doing *here*?" She felt the constriction in her chest that she'd felt earlier. "I don't even know where I belong anymore."

Paul was silent. Then he said quietly, "Do you think you're depressed?"

Her cheeks burned. She didn't want a diagnosis; she wanted him to grope around in the dark with her instead of looking for the light switch.

Paul's patient had arrived, and they hung up. Gina raced downstairs to the garage and backed out of the driveway too fast, nearly overlooking a young woman on the sidewalk who frowned at her when she mouthed, "I'm sorry." She drove toward Esther and Ben's school, her head swimming, alternating waves of heat and cold moving up and down her body. She was seized by a desperate urgency to tend to this familiar task, something routine that would reset her internal machinery: Esther and Ben. Milkshakes!

Robotically, she moved back through the intersections, timed lights—traffic moving smoothly. Doing okay. At a stoplight, she felt her body almost catch up with her, and she took a deep breath. Almost there; just have to get to the carpool line . . . Picturing Esther and Ben, her heart calmed. Then she was in line, and Esther spotted her from the sidewalk.

"Hi, Mom," Esther climbed into the backseat without looking at her. "Last day of school! Milkshakes, right?" She pinned Gina with a look that left no room for "maybes."

"You bet!" The musical confidence of Gina's words was a promise to herself that no matter what, the day would end with happy ceremony. "Where's Ben?"

"He's somewhere. I think the little kids all had parties cuz it was the last day. So maybe he's still getting his stuff."

Gina needed this routine to be the same as it was every day. She needed Ben to be here, *right now*. The car behind her honked. "Shit!"

"Mom!" Esther scolded. "They just want you to keep moving up."

Gina inched forward, her eyes raking the sidewalk. Kindergartners she recognized were getting into cars in front and now behind her. Ms. Symington, Ben's teacher, strode toward the car and leaned her elbows on the open passenger window, revealing a lacy turquoise bra.

"Hi! Are you missing Ben?" she said. She was pretty, charismatic, and exuded the kind of confidence that could only be attributed to a happy and secure childhood. "Yes, I see you are," she said. "Hmm. Keep moving up, and I'll go see where he is." She trotted back to the building in her denim pencil skirt and red ballet flats.

Every part of Gina seemed to float away, as if being repelled by the heavy pounding in her chest. Something I ate, she told herself. Ben's probably in the bathroom or trying to find his sweatshirt. Keep moving. She kept her eyes glued to the sidewalk while Esther launched into a description of her day. Gina didn't hear a word.

Moments later, Ms. Symington returned without Ben, still not appearing worried. "So, Alex Bender thinks he went home with Luke Stern for a playdate?" she said, looking uncertain. "But you know they're only six, so you can't really . . . "

Gina reminded herself: intelligence was a must, but remaining rational was next to godliness. A low, growling "No!" erupted from her.

In the mirror, Esther looked aghast.

"Well, hang on. Let me investigate some more," Ms. Symington said, and she left.

"Nothing to worry about, Estie," Gina lied.

"I *know* that. Why is your face sweating? You know Ben. He probably just . . . forgot his lunchbox and went back to get it. He's so out of it."

Esther's reasonableness did not reach Gina. Her body was in

a state of emergency, her heart drumming out the long minutes as she watched ecstatic kids run out to greet their parents. Finally, she couldn't sit in the car any longer. She pulled to the curb, got out, and went around to open Esther's door.

"Come with me, Estie, please."

"No, Mom, you go look."

"*Now*, Esther!" Gina barked, and when Esther didn't get out, she took her hand and pulled her.

"Mom!" Esther yanked her hand away, gaping at Gina. "What's wrong? Calm down!" She straggled behind her mother and Ms. Symington into the school.

Inside the building, Ms. Symington went one way and Gina and Esther went the other. Against the chatter of children in the hallway Gina concentrated on the amplified tap of her own shoes on the linoleum floor. She and Esther ducked in and out of every classroom on the first floor, the gym, the art room, the music room. With each empty classroom they passed, Gina felt the chest girdle squeezing. My son is missing!

She jogged up the stairs to the second floor. Esther skipped steps to keep up with her, every now and then pleading, "Mom!" The hallways blurred, colors of student artwork flashed strobe-like, faces they passed smeared into the noisy atmosphere. They reached a dead end, and Gina whirled around to see Ms. Symington coming toward them. She shrugged, so casually, thought Gina; how naive she is! Kids disappeared into thin air every day.

"He's here somewhere," Ms. Symington said. "Please don't worry."

"I *am* worried!" Gina snapped. "He's gone!"

Esther's mouth dropped open in a mortified O.

"Please, Mrs. Goodson, we have very good security, and there's really no place he could . . . "

"We'd better call the police!" Gina concentrated on her breathing because, should her attention slip for a second, she felt it might just stop. She was coming apart—a concrete structure in compression, no rebar. She stumbled to the wall to lean into it so she could rummage through her purse for her phone.

"Are you okay? Please don't . . . " Ms. Symington began. "Mrs. Goodson," she said too firmly, her good-with-six-year-olds face too close to Gina's. "Please calm down—we . . . "

Ms. Symington, all confident five feet eight of her, blurred; from the human smudge emerged a hand, snaking toward Gina.

"It's *Gilbert*, not Goodson!" Gina drew what felt like her last breath and thrust out her own hand, searching for an anchor. She felt the heat of Ms. Symington's thin wrist, the hard, cold metal of her bracelet. Recognized Esther's gasp. She turned to see her daughter's face, pinched with horror, and withdrew her offending hand. Ms. Symington's ballet flats clicked away down the hall. Beyond her, Gina made out first the tiny frame, the posture, the orange sweatshirt, and then the face, smiling now: Ben.

"I *told* you!" Esther yelled at her mother, and at last, the few gaping children in the hallway scurried away.

Gina wanted to make a fast retreat home, but now the milkshake outing seemed even more important; adhering to tradition might be her only shot at redemption as far as Esther was concerned. At the drive-in, she and Esther were silent while Ben prattled on about the distance of certain planets from the sun. Gina *oohed* and *wowed* while monitoring the sinking foamy chocolate in Esther and Ben's glasses. When the last strawful had been slurped, she stood and said, "Ready to go?"

Once home, she went straight upstairs to curl up in a ball on the bed. She heard Esther tell Paul loudly on the phone, "Mom grabbed

Ms. Symington and had a heart attack or something!" Minutes later, Paul came into the house and up the stairs. He poked his head into the bedroom; when she didn't stir, he quietly said her name. She breathed heavily to let him know she was sleeping, alive.

As he was about to shut the bedroom door, his cell phone rang. "Yes, Felicia," he said. Gina's eyes popped open. Felicia was head of Ben and Esther's lower school. She strained to listen, but Paul's voice trailed off as he went downstairs.

She lay stunned and staring at the dusty ceiling medallion, wanting only to run away from herself, from her vibrating body. She'd done what she'd promised herself she'd never do: lose it in front of her child. Was she becoming her mother?

Her eyes fixed on the photograph she'd brought home from Maine, which she'd finally hung between the two windows. From the bed, it provided a third "window"—the view of the summer cove, its sinuous shoreline rimmed with pines and opening to the boat-studded harbor. She visualized Whit's Point in a kaleidoscope of other seasons, too: in fall, a sky dashed with geese; elms heavy with snow in winter; in spring, lush with lilacs and blossoming apple trees. She would not let herself dwell on any one of these landscapes, instead conjuring a slender ribbon of images to tow her away from her troubled thoughts. She felt herself slipping, gently sliding into the images, into the house in Maine, into sleep. Then, she was awake again, her heartbeat insistent.

The last good slumber she'd had, she realized, was on the chaise in the yard in Maine.

She needed to feel that peaceful prelude to sleep again. What had brought it on? Not just the soothing, familiar landscape. Something inside her had opened during those last hours alone. It was as if for the first time, without her mother's dominion over the house, without the noise of Cassie's extravagant emotions and snappish commentary, she could hear the house speak—just to *her.* After years of keeping her hatches battened while there, she'd let the house in.

Her mother had slipped inside her, too. Even the falling shutter had seemed to convey what she always thought her mother felt, but wouldn't say: "What will become of us now that you are leaving?"

This time, imagining her mother's question had touched Gina with a pang, not of guilt pushing her away, but of protectiveness, pulling her back. Her parents had died long before she'd finished with them; as long as their presence still flickered in the house, she couldn't let them go, couldn't let the house go.

"For as long as I've known you," Paul had said today, "you've been trying to leave that house." Gina knew he was right. She was still trying to leave, to put the house and all that happened there behind her. But the only way to leave was to go back.

She slid off the bed and gathered the courage to face Paul, Esther, and Ben. Deciding a prop would be helpful, she retrieved the basket of clean laundry and carried it to the family room. Paul put down the paper and peered at her. From the couch, Esther and Ben looked up, wide-eyed.

Gina set down the basket, sat on the floor, and began folding. "I think I'll go . . . I'm *going* to Whit's Point for a few days," she said without looking up.

"Are you going to stay at Gran and Granddad's house?" Ben asked.

"No!" Esther barked. "Gran and Granddad are *dead*."

Ben ran out of the room and up the stairs. Esther put her hand over her mouth as if to say, "I don't know why, it just popped out." Sobs sputtered from her. "I'm sorry! I'm sorry!"

"Shhh, it's okay." Paul stroked her back.

"No, it's not!" Esther cried, raising her blotchy face. "*Nothing's* okay!" She glared at Gina with searing accusation, stood abruptly, and ran upstairs.

"Gina," Paul said, "what happened?"

Gina heard emotion in Paul's voice, but she continued to fold with retail-like precision. The neat piles of clothes mocked her; within a few days, the same items would sit at the bottom of the laundry chute, and the cycle would start again. Finally she said, "I need to go to the house. I don't know if I can talk to Sid, with everything that's gone on between our families. But I'm not ready to just . . . I need to be there again."

"Is this the right thing for you now? When would you go?"

"In two weeks, during the time we set aside to go camping. I know it screws up our vacation, but since I'd already planned to be away from the office then . . .. It would only be for a few days."

Paul sighed. He was petting Stella, gathering handfuls of her hair, and in his slack posture, Gina read his disappointment and concern. She felt awful changing their family trip.

"Why don't we come with you?" he said.

"No," Gina said firmly. "I need to be there alone."

"Are you sure? I'm worried about you, Gina. What happened at school? Esther's really upset."

Gina stopped folding and looked at Paul through flooded eyes. "The teacher was . . . I thought I was going to . . . I lost my balance."

Paul's expression implored her to elaborate, but she looked away. He stood and walked to the window, then back again. "I would just feel so much better about your leaving if I knew what happened today. You've been really out of sorts and going to Maine has always been tough for you."

Gina calmly tried in vain to smooth the wrinkles in the shirt she was folding. "Paul, I'm asking you to trust that I know what I need."

Standing over her, Paul sighed. "Okay," he said. "You should go. But don't tell me not to worry, because I'm going to."

He leaned over and kissed her cheek. Gina smiled, picked up the laundry basket, and left the room, relieved that at least the awful day was over.

That is why people look to the past. Their nostalgia is not the result of an interest in archaeology . . . nor of a sympathy for a particular period . . . Nor is it a rejection of technology. People appreciate the benefits of central heating and electric lighting, but the rooms of a Colonial country home or of a Georgian mansion—which had neither—continue to attract them, for they provide a measure of something that is absent from the modern interior. People turn to the past because they are looking for something that they do not find in the present—comfort and well-being.

Witold Rybczynski, Home

Chapter 6

After two weeks of uncomfortable business-as-usual—the kids at day camp, conversations with Paul focused on logistics—Gina was at the airport saying goodbye to her family. Esther and Ben were somber, unaccustomed to Gina's being away. She kissed them both, and Esther blinked back tears. Gina knew the scene she'd made at school would hang over Paul and Esther until she could offer an explanation, but she had none.

Paul hugged Gina. "I'm still sad you'll be having your birthday out there," he said.

She flapped her hands against his back. Esther was watching them, her mouth pinched in concentration. "Me, too. But it's okay. I'll call you from Annie and Lester's tonight," Gina said. She pulled away from Paul, her shirt damp with perspiration though the airport was cold.

As she walked away, she turned and called, "Love you, guys!"

Love you, guys: her cheerfulness sounded so phony! Feeling as she did, she wondered how in the world she would survive being without her family for four days.

At Logan Airport, she caught the bus that would take her an hour and a half north to Riversport, New Hampshire, one town south of Whit's Point, Maine. She'd been outside for only a few minutes, but already she was sticky from heat and relished the bus's chill as she slid onto the plush seat.

From the window she took in the disparate sights of Route 1 north: a Greek Revival house with a "DiAngelo's Funeral Parlor" sign plastered against its fluted columns; beside it, a picket fence encircling a display of turquoise pools; a Mr. Tux shop whose plywood bride and groom were dressed in soot. Across an enormous empty parking lot stood a colonial barn, its ancient weathervane peeking out over a giant green-and-red dragon promising authentic Chinese Cuisine. All were rooted in a sea of black on this June day, hot-enough-to-fry-an-egg black, appearing liquid in places, as though asphalt had flowed from some nearby volcano.

This stretch of Route 1 was an authentic sample of America, though not an uplifting one. Soon, Gina began to notice that not everything had succumbed to the highway. A white clapboard house clung to a patch of green just big enough for a laundry line and a chained-up German shepherd. An occasional majestic, century-old tree sprang from the center of a parking lot, its canopy providing an oasis of shade for the cars huddled below it. And Queen Anne's lace sprouted from cracks in the asphalt, reaching up to hug the highway guardrail. Despite the continuous assault of noise and poisons, of greed, ugliness, and extreme weather, in the New England tradition, these survivors held their ground.

She turned from the window and let her head fall back on the headrest. Thirty-one years in New England hadn't made *her* resilient. She hadn't had another episode like the one at school that day, but still she felt fear waiting in her recesses, as if all this time she'd been flourishing from the ground up, while under her, fragile roots struggled to keep hold. When she was younger, she wanted to explore, to be productive, to be excited by life. Now, more than anything she wanted to be *strong*.

She thought of Esther and Ben and felt her hand slip into her carry-on for her phone. But she stopped herself. She was determined this time to focus on being only here, undivided and self-reliant.

Her shoulder pressed the window as the bus swerved off the highway into the parking lot of King's Clam House, its last stop in Massachusetts before reaching New Hampshire. A group of shirtless boys waited in line at the takeout window, brushing sweat from their foreheads with their T-shirts. Gina could almost smell the fishy grease mingling with the flat odor of scorching asphalt. It made her queasy, but it was summer, *real* summer, not like bundling up to hover over the barbeque in San Francisco.

Along the highway, the asphalt let up, giving way to lush grass and woods of maple, ash, and birch trees, already at their deepest summer green. In California, Gina missed this abundant green and the undisciplined, untended growth that graced the New England landscape. In California it was housing that grew this way: forests of pitched-roof variations on an affordable dream house sprouting from hillsides, flanked by identical trees, each with its own IV of water to fool it into believing it was not growing in a desert. Unfair, perhaps, but making these comparisons was irresistible; every year, no matter how hard she tried to play the detached tourist, she found herself drinking in the lushness of eastern summer.

The bus exited the wide, pristine highway at the "Entering Riversport" sign and, as it squeezed through the twisty city streets, seemed to pass from one century into a previous one. Colonial houses stood shoulder-to-shoulder along both sides of the street, some brick, most wood, and nearly all with window shutters, a later Victorian embellishment. Riversport bore the signs of prosperity brought by Yuppie refugees from Boston: concrete sidewalks widened and replaced with brick, uniform rows of trees, Starbucks.

Warm air, thick with ocean saltiness, embraced her as she stepped off the bus. She found herself surrounded by the moist flesh of evening strollers so took off her thin sweater and tied it around her waist. She loved the intimacy of exposed limbs on a warm summer day. People greeted each other, hands touching skin, bare heels pulled up out of sandals by a hug.

She searched the street for a taxi to take her the remaining five miles to Whit's Point. She'd be staying with Annie and Lester, and they'd offered to pick her up at the bus station, but she'd told them "No, thank you;" her need to be alone was so pressing that she hadn't even told Cassie she was coming east.

In the taxi, she opened both backseat windows to let in the sea breeze. In a few minutes they were crossing the Piscataqua River, which separated New Hampshire from Maine. Lobster buoys were pulled flat against the water's surface by the river's powerful current. A frantic crowd of seagulls dove at the wake of a fishing boat roaring downriver with its catch.

Entering Whit's Point, she felt the drop in temperature that never failed to surprise her. The road wound through an unkempt townscape that had barely changed since she was a child. Unpruned trees threatened phone lines, a jungle gym she could remember climbing on now rusted in a yard, mailboxes bore the same names they had for decades. Farther along were the formidable entrances to the Naval shipyard and the brick schoolhouse where Gina had attended junior high. Then there were only the tired but stalwart houses lining the road with their unapologetic boxiness, white, gray, or yellow clapboards, and tall chimneys. She liked to look at them every year, to see how they might've changed. "You still designing houses?" an architecture school classmate had asked her last year, as if she were stuck in some evolutionary stage. But she'd always been a respectful admirer of houses. Not houses presented in magazines as lifestyle showcases, but houses as objects in the landscape, like trees, and as containers of life. Tall bare-boned houses that sprouted from the middle of vast, flat farmlands, the tiny stone cottages of Ireland, Native American dwellings in the recesses of cliffs. Even the monotonous rows of tiny, expressionless facades in San Francisco's Sunset District were intriguing—to think of the multiplicity of stories behind those ubiquitous picture windows!

But *these* were the kinds of houses her clients often yearned for, she thought; not just their old windows or gable roofs or the patina of something old, but something sensory about them, like the way sunlight slanted through a window. Not the staccato of balusters below a porch railing, but the memory of friends gathered on the porch to eat popcorn and play Monopoly in a thunderstorm.

As the taxi swerved around two bike riders, Gina sucked in her breath. The driver caught her eye in the mirror. "The bridge into Whit's Point was up for an hour today," he said. "Some clown in a yacht got his signals crossed, and there musta been four boats under the span trying to sort it all out. What a mess."

Gina laughed, but her heart galloped. In a moment after they'd passed the high school, she could see the bridge. It was up. Not even all the way yet, and there was a line of cars waiting. She hadn't counted on this little delay; she'd made every arrangement she could think of to avoid surprises on the trip.

Leaning out the window, she spotted the culprit, a tall-masted sloop motoring up-river. To distract herself from her thudding heart and the tingling in her shoulders, she imagined herself in the boat, lightly sunburned and relaxed after a long afternoon sail. But she was immediately back, trapped in the taxi. The bridge was up, no way out. She closed her eyes and wiped her moist palms on her thighs.

Once, waiting in this spot with her parents, she'd been the villain. She was twenty-two, had been up for the weekend, and they were taking her to the bus station to go home to Boston.

Just before they reached the bridge, her mother had said, "Why don't you give us a key to your apartment? It would be so convenient for Daddy and me to stop in there when we're in Boston shopping."

In the backseat, Gina had seethed. She had had a powerful sense her mother was wrong, on principle, to ask for the key, but it was confused, as always, with her own guilt about being secretive and unwelcoming. Giving them a key would have meant her apartment could be subject to her parents' scrutiny without notice. She had pictured the incriminating evidence they might encounter—like her boyfriend's T-shirt hanging on the bathroom hook—and had imagined Eleanor descending into a self-pitying harangue about how her daughter had failed her. But *not* giving them a key would have been felt as a brutal rejection, like all of Cassie's and Gina's assertions of independence.

The gravitational pull of their mother's suffering had kept Gina and Cassie in a tight orbit around her. Gina had never said a flat-out "no" to her mother before. Beyond wanting to avoid conflict, there had been pragmatic reasons for this, like Eleanor's threat to cut off her college tuition. But Gina was financially independent now and would soon start paying off her school loans. In the front seat, her mother's silence screamed. Gina prepared her speech, short and devoid of words that might Velcro themselves to Eleanor's memory.

She had cleared her throat. "Mom," she had said, her eyes focused on the back of her mother's seat. "I don't—"

"Say no more!" Eleanor had shot back.

The car had crested the hill, and Gina had seen it: the line of cars at the foot of the bridge and the subtle movement of the span rising in the air. There had been a race that afternoon, and there was a parade of masts lined up to go under the bridge. Gina's stomach had lurched as her mother let out one of her been-stabbed-in-the-heart wails. "Oh-oh-oh! After everything I've done for my children, and this is what I get! Am I really that rotten?"

Eleanor had spoken these words so many times that they were incapable of eliciting empathy. She had bawled. Her feet had been up on the glove compartment as she slathered rose-scented Jergen's lotion onto her short, sturdy legs. Ron had tapped his finger on the steering wheel and stared out to sea. Gina, her stomach clenched, had watched a peaceful green settle over the water as, one by one, boats had made their way to their moorings. She had learned to navigate the schisms between the ugliness inside and the beauty outside and had found that over time the contrasts, like complementary colors, sharpened her experience of each part.

Remembering the scene now, Gina suspected those fifteen minutes waiting for the bridge had defined the relationship she would have with her mother for the rest of her life—the final, deferred act of her childhood, sitting in the backseat, her jaw set, resolutely holding her silence. Language, time, or circumstances had defused other conflicts sparked by her defiance, but this act, this simple utterance of "I don't," words too close to "no" for her mother to bear, was crystalline.

What had made Gina's independence such a heartache for her

mother? Gina had wondered, again and again. She'd believed with time, her mother would come to understand the nature of her own deep discontent and its effect on her family. Instead, Gina had watched Eleanor's woundedness age in her eyes. Now she was gone.

The bridge was on its way back down, but it was too late: her body had been hijacked by heat and then cold and her chest tightened, like that day at Ben's school. The car crossed the bridge and passed the Congregational church and the rose-covered pergola where she and Paul had been married. Then the scenery blurred. She held the door handle and closed her eyes.

"So what's the address on Pickering Road again?" the driver asked.

She opened her eyes to see Lily House's stone wall. "Right . . . here . . . this is good," she said.

The driver pulled over, and she scrambled out of the car. Paul was right; she shouldn't have come. She paid the driver, and he tugged her suitcase from the trunk. When he'd driven away, she again reached for her phone to call home but then stopped.

She leaned against the stone wall, focusing on the things that usually brought her comfort: the warm, fading glow of a summer evening, the rich smell of the sea, and the humidity that put a gentle wave in her hair. But she felt like a stranger—as if she were observing herself from a distance: a slender woman, dressed in pale summery clothes, her light brown hair twisted into an unfastened braid. She might have been painted into a landscape like this one, appearing serene, her trembling imperceptible.

She gathered herself and stepped up Lily House's porch stairs.

Lester answered the door with a big grin. "Ginny, you great girl, how are you?" He held a handful of paper. "Wow, haven't seen one of these things in a long time!" He nodded at the T square poking from Gina's bag.

"She's *Gina* now, Lester." Annie stepped into the hall wearing Bermuda shorts and a sleeveless white blouse. She took Gina's suitcase and gave her a quick hug.

Lester planted his hand on Gina's shoulder and stepped back to inspect her. His weathered face creased with a grin. "You must be starved. Come sit down—dinner's ready."

Gina put down her bag and followed Annie and Lester, glancing into the living room as she passed. The six sash windows were thrown open and an enormous bouquet of what must have been ten different kinds of flowers sat on a table. The house was redolent of the hearty dinners the older generation cooked, too heavy for a hot night. She hoped she'd be able to muster an appetite.

As if sensing she wasn't feeling her best, Lester pulled out a chair for her at the table in the sunroom. "For you," he chuckled, sliding the paper he was holding in front of her. "Your clients have found you already."

He disappeared with Annie into the kitchen.

The sunroom door was open, giving Gina a view of the blue hydrangea bushes through the screen. She sat down on the creaky antique chair and picked up the paper. A couple of her clients had nearly panicked when they heard Gina would have Internet access only on her phone, so Annie and Lester had borrowed a fax machine for her visit, which now sat on one end of the sunroom table. While an eggbeater whirred in the kitchen, she read:

To: Gina Gilbert

From: Allison Brink

Gina: Here's a description of everything I'd like accommodated in the remodel. The kitchen should open to the family/dining area. This "great room" should not be so large that it's not cozy, and should have a place for intimate family meals as well as formal dining for larger groups. The room should include a seating area and a couch and chairs for watching TV and playing video games, a desk for the computer, printer and fax, and an area for the children's homework and art projects. I can't stand clutter, so there should be ample storage for all supplies, as well as cabinetry that will hide the TV from view. Also, my grandmother's upright piano will need to be in this room. Because the kids and my friends like to help cook, I'd like a Wolfe professional twelve-burner range; state-of-the-art lighting, and a gigantic window overlooking the garden. There should be an oversized kitchen island and a place to put away small appliances to maximize counter space. Do you think you might have something to show me by tomorrow?

"Just put it right here like this," Gina overheard Annie instruct Lester. "Don't forget the lemon pepper."

How would it be, staying at Lily House? Gina wondered, trying not to think about her unease in April when she'd been here with Cassie. The nearest hotel was twenty minutes away, and she'd wanted to make the trip efficient and inexpensive. No rental car, no hotel. Annie and Lester knew Sid had bought the house, and Gina had told them vaguely that she wanted to revisit it; they'd been thrilled she was coming and hadn't asked questions.

"So what's the job?" Lester asked, when he and Annie had brought out plates of roast beef, mashed potatoes and corn-on-the-cob. "I mean the fax—I didn't read it, but it looks . . . complicated."

"You did *too* read it, you fibber!" Annie scolded. If she'd embarrassed Lester, it didn't show.

"It's a potential new project, yes," Gina said. "Allison's a surgeon, a recent divorcée and mother of two who relies so completely on her Guatemalan housekeeper that her three-year-old son speaks no

English. She hopes opening up the main rooms will give her more togetherness with the kids during the two hours a day that they're all at home."

"Huh." Lester shook his head at his roast beef. "Think a remodel will solve her problems?"

"I don't know," Gina said. "This is the fourth project I've done for her. She's a serial remodeler. It's a kind of addiction, I think."

"Well," Lester said, leaning back in his chair. "You probably know the story about Thomas Jefferson, how when his wife died ten years after they married, he became consumed with remodeling Monticello. He added two half-octagons and several years later, a dome. His house was a construction site until three years before his death."

Gina laughed. "At least he was his own architect. Fewer meetings." She thought of her clients who'd remodeled for years to keep up with the changes in their family lives and sometimes missed the deadlines. Like one couple who was still perfecting an elaborate teen rec room even though their son had had his first child and moved to France.

"You hear about people in California," Lester said, " . . . how they . . . I don't know . . . "

"Lester, please pass Gina the butter," Annie interrupted, shooting Lester a look that Gina, not Lester, noticed.

"Hold on, Annie." Lester planted his knife and fork on the table like ski poles. "I just mean, it seems to me people are trying too hard to have it all. Is having a family nowadays just running a small business in a house that has a fancy kitchen and jets in the tub?"

Lester took a bite of roast beef and peered at Gina. All at once, she felt his criticism might be aimed at her.

"Gina's had a long day," Annie said quickly. "She doesn't want to hear your cynical views on modern parenting."

Lester wiped his forehead with his napkin. "Okay, you're right. Boy!" he said. "How about this weather—hot 'nuff foah ya?" Again, he turned his gaze on Gina. "What about your property up north . . . Marin, is it? Paul was telling us about it after the funeral. Any progress? It's a *vacation* house, right?"

"Oh, no!" Gina said, her body tightening as if she'd been accused of something. "It's a remodel—it would . . . *will* be our full-time . . . our *only* house. We have the permits. Now I've just got to get busy and draw the plans."

"Well, then," Lester said. "Easier said than done, I'm sure."

Gina nodded and Lester seemed to know she didn't want to say more. When she asked them how their sons and families were, Annie said, "Mike and Karen are visiting Randy and Susan in Alaska this week. But Mike usually comes up every third weekend with one or both kids. Karen sometimes stays home. I don't blame her—they're a rowdy bunch! It must be dreamy to have the house to herself."

Gina wondered, would she find it "dreamy" when her kids were gone? It was hard to imagine; her own mother had made her empty nest seem like solitary confinement.

"Is that a hint, Annie? Should I take a trip?" Lester teased good-naturedly.

"Take a trip, Lester, *please.*"

"I think she likes her violin more than she likes me sometimes," Lester said. He reached over and squeezed Annie's shoulder and she laughed.

Despite her unease, Gina soaked up their mutual esteem and affection and felt intuitively that they respected her privacy, too. They didn't mention her half-eaten dinner while they were washing dishes together or question why she wanted to turn in early.

Gina couldn't remember ever having been in Lily House's one-story "summer ell," which was off the kitchen and housed two small bedrooms and a tiny bathroom. She was enormously relieved that she wouldn't be sleeping upstairs where Banton ghosts surely would be lurking. The guest room was predictably New England: blue pin-stripe wallpaper, a braided oval rug, a cotton quilt. Annie and Lester had taken out a chair to fit in a worktable for Gina that overlooked the yard and placed a vase of zinnias—Annie couldn't have known they were Gina's favorite—on the bureau. The one window was propped open with a wooden ruler but offered not a breath of air. She stretched out on the high, four-posted bed and aimed the fan on the nightstand at her face.

Crickets peeped; a motorcycle roared by on the road. Some-where, but not close, a dog barked. The floorboards squeaked outside her room, a door bumped shut. When she thought Annie and Lester were settled in for the night, she crept to the bathroom she would share with them. Out of the hot silence of the house came Lester's voice. "That's what money . . . " he said. The thump of shoes against the floor. Then, "It's just real estate to them."

It was curious how clear his voice was, and Gina stooped to dis-cover a rectangular hole in the wall near the baseboard under the sink, perhaps cut for a heating vent. She kneeled to look through it. A similar hole was cut in the plaster of Annie and Lester's room, and she could see their floor.

Gina brushed her teeth and padded back to her room, alert and prickly. It would be hours before she fell asleep—jetlag, the smothering heat, the smart of criticism. Now, she sensed the ghosts of Lily House, loitering like a gang outside the bedroom door, waiting to pounce.

Rooms which are too closed prevent the natural flow of social occurrence and the natural process of transition from one social moment to another. And rooms which are too open will not support the differentiation of events which social life requires.

Christopher Alexander, *A Pattern Language*

PIANO ROOM
12'-5½" X 12'-11½"

"Isn't it just lovely?" Ginny's mother said in her movie star voice. "There isn't a breath of wind, and the snow is sticking on every little branch."

Mother and daughter stood looking out the piano room window at the huge elm tree that had been transformed by the night's surprise snowstorm into a lacy veil of white, delicately outlined by black branches. Against the gray sky, it looked more like a pencil drawing than a real tree. Ginny stared, entranced. At ten, she'd come to rely on such beauty, on the harmony it inspired; as she stood in silence with her mother, a fleeting but immutable understanding passed between them.

"Good morning!" her father said when Ginny and her mother came into the kitchen. He was squeezing the last drops of juice from an orange and despite his kid-like grin of disorganized teeth, he looked distinguished in his dark gray sweater.

"Ron, I think you'd better get the camera out and shoot that tree after breakfast," her mother said. She was scrambling some eggs, and they sizzled when she poured them into a pan.

Ginny's father set four glasses of orange juice on the table and put his hands in his pockets. "I don't think I'll have time today. Bruce Ruby's coming in so I can shoot his bread."

Her mother reeled around, spoon midair. "What? You're kidding! *Today*?" The spell of the elm tree had broken.

"I thought I told you that last week, sweet pea. He needs to get his catalogue out the first of the year."

"I'm sure he does."

Ginny could have predicted this conversation, her mother's sarcasm that heralded a fresh conflict. She turned and looked out the window, where the snow was so deep that bushes spread out like dunes on a wide white beach. Icebergs that had been forming in the cove all week made it impossible to tell if the tide was in or out. Six geese scuttled up the hill, looking for handouts from Ginny's mother, who often tossed them breakfast scraps. The outdoor world was so smooth and without lines their house could be set in a cloud; the kitchen, in comparison, appeared cluttered and worn. Ginny wolfed down her eggs, determined to get outside.

"After you practice," her mother said. "And somebody's going to have to get that laundry in."

On the back porch, Ginny's breath made a cloud around her head, and the cold bit her cheeks. Clothespins marched down the line like white bunny ears; beneath them hung the laundry, frozen stiff. She yanked the line in and after pulling off the pins, laid the crunchy clothes in the bottom of the basket. Upstairs, she draped them over the long hall railing and spread the socks on the radiator.

In the piano room, she practiced her violin, letting the notes float directly from the page to her fingers so she could keep her mind free to think about other things. Her squeaking was accompanied by the

crunch and shoosh of her father's shovel, thrusting coal from the
cellar bin into the furnace. Soon, he was with Ginny in the piano
room, setting up floodlights, preparing for Mr. Ruby. Ginny finished
practicing, put her music away in the bench, and pushed it as far
as it would go under the piano, an old out-of-tune upright that was
not nearly glamorous enough to have a room named for it. "Every
house should have a piano," Ginny had heard her mother say, even
though she didn't know how to play. Connected to the darkroom by
a door, the piano room was also her father's office and studio. And,
on special occasions and after a lot of furniture shuffling, it became
the dining room.

Ginny liked the room best in its studio mode, full of lights, cameras, and her father's customers—all of which made him seem more
important—and she felt a twinge of excitement, anticipating Mr. Ruby.

Stuffed into her snow clothes, Ginny plunged into the white
silence beyond the front porch where only the tracks of their dog,
Painter, disturbed the powdery surface. She leaned to grab a fistful of
snow; it tasted deliciously fresh.

The "Ronald Gilbert—Commercial Photographer" sign that
hung on the garage was whited-out. Ginny grabbed the toboggan and
towed it around back to the best sliding hill in the neighborhood. A
gang of kids had already packed a good track and were standing in
line at the top of the hill, waiting their turns to go down. She was
disappointed not to find Kit because the plow had pushed up giant
piles of snow in the driveway, and she wanted him to help her build a
fort later. Since he was twelve now and in junior high, she didn't dare
to go knock on his door.

After an hour and a half, Ginny's snow pants were soaked, and
her toes felt dead, so she headed back to the house. In the front hall,

she peeled off everything with her numb fingers and sat down on the stairs to thaw. Soon the ache set in—her toes first, then her fingers. When she was younger this sometimes made her cry, but now she got a certain pleasure from the pain of play.

Her mother was on the phone in the living room. "I know, Annie, but things don't just disappear," she was saying, " . . . at Lily House. Fran? Who told you that? I haven't any idea; we're not speaking. But I s'pose I'll invite her to dinner; it's Christmas. *Sid?* This weekend?"

"Honey?" Ginny's father yelled from the piano room. "Bruce Ruby's headed up the driveway!"

Eleanor put down the phone and streaked past Ginny up the stairs. "Quick! Help me get this laundry out of here!"

Ginny and her mother grabbed the laundry she'd hung over the hall railing. A pair of underpants floated down the stairwell; she scooped it up and sat on it just as Mr. Ruby let the brass fist knocker hit the door. Her father went to the door, put his hand on the doorknob, and waited for the all-clear signal from her mother.

"Okay, Ron!" Her mother kicked shut the bathroom door and disappeared into her room.

A few minutes later, she emerged dressed. She brushed past Ginny, who was still sitting in the middle of the stairs watching her father and Mr. Ruby bring boxes and boxes of baked goods into the piano room.

"Hello, Bruce!" Her mother smiled and held the door as Mr. Ruby, looking dwarfish in his big brown overcoat, brought in the last box. "And how is everything with you?" She showed no hint of her earlier resentment.

Mr. Ruby set the box down on the piano room floor as Ron began opening each one and pulling out bread, cakes, cookies, and éclairs and placing them on the white linen tablecloth he'd spread over a platform on the floor. The house filled with an intoxicating sweetness. The two men crawled on their hands and knees to arrange flowers and plates and bread, sitting back on their heels to consider the composition, then rearranging. They joked and laughed, and Ginny thought: everyone likes Daddy.

Now and then, her father stood behind his camera to look through the viewfinder and directed Mr. Ruby with his hands. "No, we can't do that; it'll slide out of the frame," he'd say, or "a few too many éclairs on the platter." Mr. Ruby would shuffle around the bakery goods. "How about this?"

"Better. Hold on a minute. Nope, I think there's too much bread here for one shot."

"You're the boss, Ron."

You're the boss. Ginny loved to watch her father at work in this room where he could be the boss. When he pulled the family station wagon over to the side of the road to photograph something scenic, Ginny's mother would be there, directing where to put his tripod. But when the piano room became his studio, he was in charge. He seemed to stand taller, to speak more loudly and move more decisively. Only he knew the secrets of the camera, with all its crazy tricks.

Mr. Ruby and his confections created a holiday sensation in the house: convivial chatter in the piano room, the scent of sugar and vanilla, treats that showed up on the kitchen table. The next day, Wednesday, he brought apple muffins, scones, and donuts. On Thursday, éclairs and butter cookies. Ginny was hopeful that all the sweetness might keep out the sad spirits that sometimes haunted the house at Christmas time.

But, with the piano room tied up with the photo shoot, Ginny and her mother had to cram their activities into the living room and kitchen, behind closed doors. Drop-in friends were out of the question.

Mr. Ruby stayed late, so Ginny and her mother ate dinner most nights in front of the TV.

By Friday, Mr. Ruby's fourth day, Ginny noticed her mother didn't even greet him when he arrived, and she was barely speaking to her father. Cassie, who was on a ski trip with a friend's family, called at lunchtime. Eleanor held the telephone while she stirred soup on the stove. "Well, honey, the snow does sound perfect, but I'd still like you to come home Sunday as planned. Everyone's coming for dinner Monday, and we need to decorate the tree before then, and we can't do that without you . . . I know it's only one more day . . . what? Because I'm your mother; that's why."

On the kitchen table, Ginny was signing Christmas cards. She and Cassie smiled up from this year's Christmas picture bundled in stocking hats and wool coats, bearing hastily wrapped empty boxes. As usual, they were standing in front of Lily House's front door. When Ginny had asked her mother this time why they didn't take the Christmas photographs in front of their own house, her mother had said, "Well, because it's not really *our* house," which had made her sad.

Eleanor moved away from the stove, stretching the phone cord into the living room. "Cassie? Oh, hi, Judy. Yes. I know, the snow sounds . . . Right, I know she was, but . . . Uh-huh. Well . . . "

Ginny knew her mother was backing down; as tough as she was with Cassie, she wouldn't dare press Cassie's friend's mother. Ginny's spirits sank. She wanted—*needed*—Cassie home for the tree decorating, a reliably festive family tradition in an otherwise unpredictable season.

"Okay, well, she can do what she wants, then. You bet, Judy. Bye."

Eleanor put down the phone and stood over it with a defeated hunch. It rang again, and she picked it up. "Hello? Why should I be mad? Obviously, your friends are more important than I am. *You* feel bad? What do *you* feel bad about? Sure, I know. Well, have a good time."

"Have a good time" was one of those things her mother some-times said in a way that made having a good time impossible.

Mr. Ruby and Ron worked through the weekend. Late on Sunday afternoon, restless and lonely, Ginny went outside to her snow fort to escape her mother's bad mood. Under the biggest pile left by the plow she had dug a room wide enough to spread out her arms, with a skylight and a window that looked out on the driveway. It was clean and quiet inside. She lay on her back with her knees up, watching clouds slipping across her rectangular piece of sky. The black fringe of the elm tree, stirred by an occasional gust of wind, floated in and out of the frame.

"You in there?"

Kit peered at her through the fort's window, all braces and red cheeks. He found the fort's opening, crawled through, and stretched out beside her in his camouflage jacket. "Nice fort . . . for a girl," he teased. Ginny swatted him, and he caught her hand in midair. "What're you gettin' for Christmas?"

"I dunno. Mom's been in such a bad mood I doubt she's even gone shopping yet. What're you getting?"

"My dad's gettin' me a guitar. I'm gonna learn all the songs on *Abbey Road*."

"What's *Abbey Road*?"

"You know, the Beatles."

Ginny knew the Beatles. Kit had taught Ginny how to play some Beatles songs on the harmonica. "Then will you teach me to play?" she said. "During vacation?"

"We're drivin' to Pennsylvania for Christmas. Tomorrow. We don't get back 'til the day before school."

Ginny took this news like a kick to the head; she felt lonelier by the minute. "Why didn't my mom tell me?"

"She wouldn't know. She doesn't exactly talk to my mom."

It was true. In fact her parents didn't socialize with any of Ginny's school or neighborhood friends' parents. "Why is that?"

"My mom says your mom is snobby."

The front door slammed. Ginny sat up and spied her mother through the fort's window, trudging down the front steps.

"Ginny, you in there?"

For a fleeting moment, she thought not to answer. She wished she could stay in the fort with Kit for the rest of the day, staring up at the clouds. But she stuck her hand through the window and waved.

"I should go," Kit said. "See you." He left, his boots crunching sadly away on the packed snow. Ginny crawled out of the fort and joined her mother in the driveway.

"What're you two up to in there?"

"Just talking."

Her mother looked her over with disapproval in her eyes. It seemed like she didn't like Kit as much as she used to.

"C'mon. Let's drop in on Fran!" she said.

Ginny was stunned. As far as she knew, her mother hadn't seen Aunt Fran in almost a year, since Grandpa's funeral. Since then, her mother's phone conversations with Fran had sounded like an angry chained-up dog. *She's just plain avaricious!* her mother always said when she hung up; Ginny had never seen or heard the word *avaricious* used anywhere, except to describe Fran. But every year, her mother insisted that Christmas was for family, avaricious or not.

Ginny crawled out of the fort and shuffled behind her mother to the car.

"I brought your game bag so you'll have something to do," Eleanor said, handing her the cloth shoulder bag Ginny had made at Brownies.

When they were on Pickering Road, her mother said, "Fran's in really bad shape. Her neighbor doesn't think she's left the house all week. Family is family," she added as they were passing Tobey's Market. When they passed the church she said, "You don't just ignore your family during Christmas, though your father and Cassie are doing their best to."

Ginny slumped in her seat. Her mother's pinched voice betrayed that she was dreading the visit as much as Ginny.

But her mother's eyes swept over the big yellow house as they pulled slowly into the lane. In the snow, Lily House did appear especially elegant and inviting, Ginny observed; its windows, with all their little panes, already glowed with a warm light. For the first time, it seemed obvious to her why Lily House had a name and their house didn't.

"Sid's car. He's up from New York," her mother said, pulling in next to a Chevy Malibu. The news cheered Ginny; Sid's presence could take the edge off the sisters' feud, and perhaps he'd have something interesting to talk to Ginny about, like the ruins at the museum last year.

Eleanor shifted into park and stared out the windshield for a few moments. Then she said, "Sid's eighteen." She opened her door. "C'mon," she said, almost smiling. "It'll be fine."

Ginny followed her up Lily House's front steps. At the top, her mother grazed the porch railing with her fingertips. "Look at this porch," she said, her face brightening like the moms' in TV commercials. "It's hard to imagine in the snow, but in the summer . . . when I was working in Boston, I came up here every weekend. Fran was already living in the house, and she and Bill Holloway and I played bridge out here every Saturday afternoon . . . I hated bridge, but it was the only thing Fran liked to do . . . Bill and I would always want to go sailing, but Fran was so jealous . . . " Her mother turned to her suddenly, as if she'd forgotten she was there. "Well anyway, we had a big hammock," she went on, "and after Sid was born . . . Oh, what a sweet child he was. Cassie was all prickers, but Sid was the cuddliest little boy. He just *adored* me!"

Though it was about Cassie, Ginny noticed her own feelings were hurt. Her mother once again threw her gaze over the porch and said, "Isn't it beautiful, Gin?"

"I like our house better," Ginny said. She waited for her mother to agree.

"Well, there are houses, and then there are *houses,*" she said.

Her mother gently pushed Ginny's hair out of her eyes and knocked on the door. When no one answered, she knocked again.

After another long minute, the door opened, and Sid, his face swollen and unshaven, stepped toward them holding a glass of something. He was not the stylish and enigmatic young man Ginny remembered from the museum, just a sloppy teenager, his cowboy-style shirt spilling over the wide leather belt that seemed to be barely holding up his hip-huggers.

"Oh, gracious me," he said. "Mother, look who's here."

Fran appeared in the hallway, dressed in a maroon cardigan that was buttoned wrong. She was taller than Ginny's mother and more delicate. And though she was only two years her senior, she looked older; her face was lined and puffy. "Well hello, Ginny," she said. She attempted a smile that teetered and then fell, as if it had lost its balance.

"Hi," Ginny said. Something was wrong; there were not enough lights on in the house, and the air felt heavy.

Her mother said, "Merry Christmas," took a big step forward, and embraced Sid—with one arm, because she was holding a bag with two presents for Fran and Sid in the other. "How are you, dear?"

Confusion flickered in Sid's face—a startled smile, then a furtive frown. Fran's big dark eyebrows seemed locked at the top of her face. Sid backed away from Ginny's mother. "Just groovy, Ellie . . . Eleanor," he said. "After all, it's Chrizmiz. Want a drink?"

Her mother said, "Oh, no. We just wanted to say hi."

"Well, I know I want one," Sid said.

Ginny's mother didn't take her eyes off Sid until he'd left the hall. As Fran led them past the living room into the piano room, Ginny noted there was no Christmas tree. Her mother's hand flitted across the furniture as she walked by.

Fran sat in the George Washington chair. Eleanor set the bag with the presents on the piano and sat down opposite her sister, her eyes caressing the portraits on the wall. Ginny settled at the card table in the corner where she could track the conversation but wouldn't have to participate. She slung her bag over the back of the chair. On the table next to her was a carved wooden frame with a photograph of two little curly-haired girls dressed in sacklike dresses and what looked like neckties, and black booties. She was surprised she could tell from their features that they were her mother and Fran; they were turned to each other, giggling.

Her eyes wandered around the piano room—a *real* piano room, with a grand piano that her great-grandfather had played, one of the things that must have made her mother think Lily House was a *house* and not just a house. At Lily House, the piano room was larger and taller and never had to change into something else; here, instead of the kind of bookshelves her father threw together in a cellar, there were built-in shelves that reached almost to the ceiling.

But there was no scent of holiday baking and no dog with a jingle bell on its collar.

Sid returned with his drink but didn't sit down. "Mother and I've been having quite the afternoon; haven't we Mother?" His smile was wrong for the sharp edge of his voice.

"Oh, well," Ginny's mother said breezily. "So tell me what you've been up to in the big city!" Her smile, too, looked forced.

Sid took a big slug of his drink. "Well, Fran? Are you going to tell her, or am I?" Fran looked at her lap, and Sid turned to Eleanor. "It seems you and Mother have been squirreling away more than just the family *things*. A little history, too. *Secrets*."

Ginny watched her mother's face go blank and understood that something terrible was coming.

"So, no one wants to talk about where babies come from?" Sid asked. "Okay, then why don't we talk about your favorite topic: the *things*. Mother's a little paranoid that you've been accusing her of stealing," he said.

Ginny's mother drew her chin back indignantly. "Sid, *really* dear!" she said, glancing at Fran. "This is not the time . . . your mother is . . . "

Sid's face twitched. "A liar? You've got that right."

As Fran flew out of the tall-backed Washington chair, it rocked like a stiff old man. "You're worthless! Get out!" she yelled.

Ginny's mother jumped up and wedged herself between Fran and Sid. She looked ridiculous, Ginny thought, holding her chin high, as if to make herself taller. Sid and Fran still glared at each other.

"You've gone too far!" Eleanor barked at Fran. "Don't you dare hurt him!"

Ginny watched, incredulous, heart tapping. Saliva collected in her mouth the way it did before she was going to throw up. Sid bent slightly at the waist as though he'd been slugged, turned, and left the room. Ginny heard his loafers scraping up the stairs.

"Go ahead and walk out on me!" Fran shouted after him. "Everyone else does! But you're never getting any of it, if I can help it!"

Ginny closed her eyes and thought: this is what hate sounds like.

The low cabinets behind the piano were filled with toys that she was too old for, but at least in the corner on the floor, she wouldn't have to watch the fight. After coaxing open the sticky cabinet doors, she pulled out the musty but comfortingly familiar toys: wooden zoo animals and matchstick cars, tiny stuffed bears and pinwheels, fake money and yellowed dice. She turned them over in her hands, her back hunched against the anger that flew around the room.

"How could you!" her mother snarled at Fran. She flopped down on the chair.

"This is none of your goddamn business!" Fran snapped. "I suppose your idea would have been to lie to him about his father for the rest of his life. That's what *you'd* want. Because you just can't stand the idea that I had Bill Holloway and you didn't."

Ginny closed her eyes, wishing she could squeeze her ears shut to escape her mother's and Fran's dangerous-sounding words. "My-old-friend-Bill Holloway–who-was-shot-down-in-the-war," her mother often said.

"That's just asinine!" her mother shouted. "You didn't deserve Bill, and you don't deserve his son—you're not fit to be Sid's mother! Who stayed up at night when he was a baby and took care of him when you were . . . were licking your wounds! I did! He should've been *my* son!"

Ginny turned away from them and closed her fist around the pair of elephants, folding deeper into her thick wool coat.

"*Your* son? Because you're such a good mother, you think? Ha! That's a laugh! Your timid girls. You probably make them as miserable as you make me."

At this, Ginny felt a stabbing urgency to jump up and run out of the house. But she didn't move.

"How dare you!" her mother cried. "You have no idea what it means to work hard . . . You've had your whole life handed to you on a platter—you got the house and the Holloway's . . . *keep-quiet* handouts! You got two years of goddamn college that you *wasted* when you dropped out. That education could have been *mine*, but I didn't get the chance! Because of *you!* You wasted it, just like you're wasting your life now. And don't you think I don't know you've stolen things from this house!"

Fran huffed and began to weep. Ginny heard her get up and stomp out of the room. Her mother's footsteps followed.

The shelves of books closed in around Ginny; a blade of orange light sliced through the window, illuminating the cobwebs that clung to the piano's underside. She hunched over the little animals, dividing them into pairs and lining them up, smallest to largest—a miniature Noah's Ark—but her mind was on Sid, whose boots squeaked across the floor toward her. She held her breath.

"Life's just secrets and lies, cousin Ginny," he said, standing over her. "My own mother's been lying to me all my life. Turns out my father wasn't some asshole who ran off to South America after all. Nope. But the Holloways thought they were too good for us. So they all lied."

"*Your* mother . . . " Sid went on. Ginny braced herself. "She always told me she loved me, you know. I was her 'little boy.' But neither of them knows how to love someone; they just know how to lie." He kicked a giraffe across the room. "Secrets and lies! Well, I have a secret of my own, but it's not going to be a secret for long."

Heart pounding, Ginny rocketed to her feet and turned to Sid. Fumes from his drink enveloped her. "You're the liar!" she yelled. "You're a messed-up drunk!" Her knees nearly folded under her. Sid's lips quivered, and his eyes were glassy. Ginny backed away from him, nearly falling over the toys.

Her mother stormed into the piano room, expression resolute, body stiff. "Put the toys away, Ginny. We're going."

Jangling with fear that her mother had heard the nasty words she'd shouted at Sid, Ginny stuffed the toys into the cabinet. She followed her mother out to the entry hall where Fran stood looking lifeless as a statue, holding a Christmas present.

"We're family, you know!" her mother snapped.

Stone faced, Fran held the present out to Ginny, and Ginny reached for it.

"Certainly *not!*" Eleanor snarled, snatched the gift and dropped it on the hall table.

When Eleanor had turned her back, though, Fran took the present and quickly stuffed it into Ginny's game bag. Ginny looked back at Sid.

"Congratulations," he said. "You're all experts at being cruel. I can't wait to get the hell out of here. This is one sick family. You all deserve each other." He looked at his mother, then at Eleanor, then straight at Ginny.

Shaking, Ginny slinked out the door behind her mother, one hand pressing the present deeper into her bag.

In the car, Eleanor announced, "I guess I won't be asking them to dinner after all. She's just lost her mind."

Ginny started to cry.

Her mother said, "Oh, it's not worth getting upset about."

But it was; Ginny could see the tears in her mother's eyes, and she herself had never in her life felt so sick when she wasn't actually sick.

"If she thinks she can stay in Lily House till her dying day, she's got another think coming," her mother snapped. "She just grabbed that house, like she grabs everything."

"My stomach hurts," Ginny said.

They passed Tobey's Market. "We'll get you some ginger ale when we get home."

Back at the house, Ginny ran upstairs to her room and pulled the present from her bag. Fran had given her little things every Christmas and in the car Ginny had schemed that she'd open the gift immediately, throw away the wrapping, and never mention it to her mother. But the tag on the package said "For Eleanor." She panicked. She couldn't throw away someone else's gift, but her mother would be furious if she knew Ginny had accepted it. She'd have to hide it until Christmas day when, surely, her mother would no longer be angry.

The Christmas tree stood waiting in the living room. Her father had brought it inside the night before, and its fragrance had begun to overpower the aroma of Mr. Ruby's sweets. The box of ornaments sat on the floor near the front door, next to a mound of green light strands. Every time Ginny walked by them, she thought of Cassie and wondered if she would be home in time to decorate the tree with them. She hadn't heard Cassie's name since the phone call with her mother.

On Sunday, Mr. Ruby started packing things up. Ginny felt a little sad that he wouldn't be coming anymore, but at least maybe her mother would cheer up. She sat on the steps and watched Mr. Ruby and her father carefully packing up the baked goods and folding the white tablecloths. As they unclamped the floodlights from their stands and coiled extension cords, they shared stories about their customers. Her father had to work all weekend, but it seemed to Ginny that he and Mr. Ruby had been enjoying themselves. And, she hadn't had to practice for days.

It was nearly nine o'clock when Mr. Ruby finally loaded the last box into his van. He came back to the house carrying a large, flat, red box and called out for Ginny and her mother. When the family had congregated at the front door, he handed the box to Eleanor.

Smiling and tipping his hat, he said, "Thank you, Eleanor, for your patience and most generous hospitality. Merry Christmas!" Then he was gone.

The night was still and cold enough that icicles had formed at the corner of the porch roof. When Mr. Ruby's taillights had disappeared from the driveway, Ron lifted the top of the box. The three of them peered into it at a dazzling heap of Christmas cookies—stars frosted in green and red and white, blinking like little neon signs. Ginny's mouth watered at the thought of their creamy sweetness.

"Well," Ginny's father chuckled, "I'm almost sorry to see him go. He's kind of a fun fellow." Smiling, he turned to her mother. "Why don't we decorate the tree now? Where's Cassie? Wasn't she supposed to come home tonight?"

Her mother looked up at him with eyes flat and gray like beach stones. Stepping out onto the porch, she raised the box of cookies over her head, leaned forward and heaved them into the night. Then she snatched the ornament box from the floor and flung its contents out with the cookies. Green and red balls, miniature sleighs, and Santa mice rained down, hit the crusty surface of the snow and slid a little before coming to rest. Glowing white under the porch light, the yard became celestial, constellations of cookie stars scattered below a black starless sky. Ginny's world turned upside down.

Her father stood at the bottom of the stairs staring at his feet. A minute later, he trudged upstairs where her mother had fled.

"Don't 'honey' me!" Ginny heard her mother yell. "If you and Cassie don't care about Christmas, maybe we just won't *have* Christmas this year!" The bedroom door slammed.

Ginny sat in the living room with the blank Christmas tree. She and the tree seemed to belong together at that moment, robbed of all Christmas spirit, sentenced to wait and wonder: was it possible to just *not have* Christmas?

A storm raged in her head. She couldn't fix the fact that Mr. Ruby had stayed too long in the piano room or what had happened at Lily House, but it dawned on her that she and Cassie could salvage Christmas.

She raced from the room, tripping over the dog sprawled across the kitchen threshold. In the darkroom, she flipped on the light and went to her father's worktable. Where was the phone? She pushed aside wrapped presents, the pile of Christmas cards waiting to be mailed, lightbulbs, boxes of film, and two large bags of glazed donuts. When she'd unearthed the phone, she hunted some more and found the message pad where her mother had jotted down Cassie's friend's number.

Her body throbbed. Never before had she stepped onto the tight-rope that stretched between her mother and Cassie, or so boldly asked Cassie to suspend her sense of fairness in order to give something up for her, Ginny. She picked up the phone and dialed.

"It's just one more day," Cassie said when Ginny asked her to come home.

"One more day's too late!" Ginny whispered. "You have to come tomorrow. Mom's really, really sad. And this thing happened today. A big fight at Lily House. Sid was there and . . . something about Bill Holloway. It sounded like he was Sid's father. I think Mom *lied* to us about Sid's father being some guy who ran away." Ginny didn't really care whose son Sid was; she wanted to tell Cassie what had scared her most, which was the sound of her own voice yelling mean things at Sid. But she didn't dare.

Cassie was silent. Then she said, "Ginny . . . every goddamn Christmas, Mom and Fran find something to fight about. They fight about everything. They *always* ruin Christmas! Mom's just making a *scene*, like she always does at Christmas. Try not to let it get to you."

Ginny's anger soared. She pictured Cassie in a room with a crack-ling fire, her cheeks sunburned from a day of skiing, in her parka with the rabbit fur-trimmed hood. Clearly, she had no intention of coming home. Ginny would need to try another tactic. "No, Cassie.

It's your fault. It's *you* this time. She's talking about not even having Christmas because of you! You have to come home! It's not fair!
Come home!"

The sound of her voice commanding Cassie was so alien to
Ginny that she began to cry. When Cassie didn't respond right away,
she panicked and hung up.

Ginny's stomach still hurt when she went to bed. She couldn't
find the sweet spot on her pillow and tossed for a long time.

In the morning, she awoke damp with sweat. The house banged
with commotion and a plaintive wail, "Noooo . . . " pierced the air.
She looked at the time—ten o'clock! She climbed out of bed and
opened her door slowly, just in time to hear her mother sob from
downstairs, "All her life, she's only thought of herself. Never Sid. She
just wanted to hurt him. Sid . . . oh, no one knows how much I loved
him, and now he's lost to me . . . " Her father's low, consolatory tones
wove through her mother's mournful cries.

Ginny struggled to make sense of her mother's words. Could Sid
be dead? she wondered. Did Fran kill him last night after Ginny and
her mother left Lily House? The fighting had certainly felt deadly.

Clutching her nightgown, she stepped to the hall window to look
out at the yard. She didn't see a single ornament or cookie. What had
happened to them? Had her father picked them up after she'd gone to
bed? Had the geese eaten the cookies? She shuddered, thinking about
all the things that could have happened while she was asleep. When
she heard the teakettle whistle from the kitchen, she braced herself
and went downstairs.

At least the piano room had been transformed into the dining
room: signs of Christmas! In the middle of the expanse of Oriental
rug, her father was on his knees, vacuuming up every last muffin
crumb, sucking up the evidence of business that had worn out its

welcome. Everything that was her father's: light stands, typewriter table, camera equipment, now hugged the edges of the room. Files, the desk blotter, scissors, and the ugly green metal tape dispenser were gone; in their places, a red linen runner and a gleaming silver bowl of nuts of all kinds: walnuts, filberts, Brazils. A pair of brass candlesticks with green candles stood on top of the piano, and a small pinecone wreath hung in front of the portrait of Governor Brickman. The folded mahogany dining room table stood in the doorway of the darkroom, awaiting its call like a star in the wings.

Her mother came into the room and said, "Oh, hi, Gin," without a smile. Her eyes were watery, and she didn't remark on how unusually late Ginny had slept. She pointed to the floor under the piano bench.

"Ron, you missed some."

It was the kindest thing she'd said to him in days. She turned to Ginny. "Feel like polishing some silver? Daddy and I have to go over to the hospital in a little while. Fran's *sick*."

Ginny stared hard at her mother, trying to read her. Surely, she wouldn't be thinking about crumbs and silverware if Sid had died, but what was wrong with Fran? She wasn't sick yesterday. She took the jar of polish from her mother. She could think of nothing more comforting, more *normal,* than polishing silver. In the kitchen, she sat at the table filled with silverware and the rarely used silver bowls and poked her rag into the polish, pulling out a pink licorice-smelling glob. She worked the paste into the intricate pattern on the dinner forks. Rubbing away the tarnish was like waking the silverware from a long sleep.

As her parents came in and out of the kitchen, gathering the holiday table settings from the cupboards' deepest recesses, Ginny studied their somber faces for clues. Her mother said something to her father in the piano room, too quietly for Ginny to hear the words.

But as they moved back toward the kitchen her mother mumbled miserably, " . . . everything is always everyone else's fault with her. She just damn well better pull through."

Ginny felt hollow. No one had even asked her if she'd had breakfast, and it was almost noon. When she finished the silver, she took it to the table in the piano room and next to each plate placed a little fork, big fork, knife, and spoon. She gazed at the sparkling, luxuriant table, asserting itself in the little room like a peacock in the barnyard.

So far, her mother hadn't cancelled Christmas, and there was still time to decorate the tree before dinner, when Cassie came home. Ginny pulled on her boots under her nightgown so she could go out to the yard and check on the ornaments. Just as she opened the front door, the phone rang, sounding artificially loud. She stepped outside and shut the door hard behind her. In the trampled snow, she found strands of silver tinsel, an elf's hat, and the glass angel that had always sat at the top of their tree. The angel's wings were still intact, but a piece of her halo had broken off.

The front door banged open. Ginny turned to see her father helping her mother down the steps, even though they weren't icy. At the bottom, they paused and squinted at her as if they were having trouble seeing in the bright snow-light.

"I found the angel," Ginny said, holding it up. "Where're you going?"

Her father was looking at the ground, one arm still around her mother.

"To the hospital," her mother said. "Fran. Well, she's . . . well, Fran died. Unexpectedly."

"*Died?*" Ginny exclaimed. Her teeth chattered; all at once she realized how cold she was, standing in the snow with no coat. "How could she just *die*! She wasn't even *sick* yesterday!"

Her mother hesitated in a way that made Ginny think she was

hiding something and then, looking at the ground she said, "Well, no, she wasn't sick, but . . . well, terrible things happen and . . . "

Ginny gasped. "Did *Sid* kill her?"

Her mother's mouth dropped open. "Ginny," she said, her voice wobbling. "Of course not. What a terrible thing to say. Why would you . . . ?"

Gina's cheeks burned. How could her mother accuse *her* of being terrible after everything *she* had said to Fran yesterday? She could see her mother begin to move toward the car, but she wasn't going to let her get away without some answers. "Then how did she die?"

Her father stared at the ground, but her mother turned to her. "Fran did it to herself, Ginny." She pulled away from Ginny's father and started down the path ahead of him.

Ginny watched their car roll slowly down the driveway as her head filled with all the gruesome ways a person could kill herself. She dropped to the snow, stretched out on her back, and tried to swish out an angel. *Did it to herself.* She cranked her arms up and down but no angel appeared; the snow was too crusty, unyielding.

Back inside, Ginny's legs shook as she stood on the chair to perch the glass angel on top of the bare Christmas tree. When she climbed off the chair and looked up at the tree, she burst into tears. Maybe the angel was still mostly whole, but Ginny felt broken into a million pieces.

She went into the piano room—yesterday the studio, now the dining room again. She stood at the head of the table looking past Great Aunt Louise's candlesticks, the footed silver salt and pepper shakers, the blue and white plates from China, and the crystal goblets she wasn't allowed to carry. She looked past the vase of white chrysanthemums and out of the window. The window, like an eye, was the only thing that stayed the same within these four walls that had so many faces; its view to the driveway's end, where it intersected with the roadways to the rest of the world, would always be the most important feature of the piano room. Her eyes followed the snowbank down the driveway, past the elm tree and her melting fort-ruin, past the playing dogs to where it touched the road. Waiting, hoping with dark fear in her heart, for a car to turn in. For Cassie.

A landscape seen through a window is essentially a backdrop, parallel to the wall, unless we step close to the window and thus leave the room visually to enter the outside space.

Rudolf Arnheim, *The Dynamics of Architectural Form*

Chapter 7

"What's on the agenda today? How about some breakfast?" Lester asked the next morning, when Gina walked into the kitchen. He was dressed in a pale blue plaid shirt and khakis, sitting at the counter cutting a cantaloupe. The room smelled of toast and vibrated with sunniness—yellow walls, yellow cabinets, yellow-and-white curtains. Blue Willow china lined the shelves over the table, and a blue glass vase on the counter was crowded with yellow snapdragons. If the room hadn't reminded her of Monet's Giverny kitchen, Gina would have found the Bridges' paint colors oppressive.

"Oh, no thanks, Lester; too early for me—West Coast time."

Lester eyed her as she slung her purse over her shoulder. "Have I scared you away already?" He reached in his pocket and pulled out his keys. "Why don't you take my car? I'm going to stay put."

Gina thanked him. She was anxious to get out of Lily House before her history with it hijacked her, so had planned to take a walk. But she'd be grateful for the car's air conditioning. On her way to the door, she passed Annie in the dining room with a feather duster.

"This is my job," Annie laughed. "I pick things up, dust under them and put them back. Three or four times a week. Did you know the feather duster was invented in 1870? You'd think that in a hundred and thirty-five years, we'd have moved beyond feather dusters, but no."

Gina laughed. "Have you liked it here, Annie? Being the caretakers and everything?"

"It's glorious!" Annie said. "An honor, really."

Gina found Annie's enthusiasm hard to believe—their confinement to the lesser rooms of the house, the lack of privacy with tourists coming through.

"I love seeing all the curious folks. A group's coming this afternoon," Annie said. "First one in a week and a half. It's been so hot, I think people are mostly going to the beaches."

The day was as warm and humid as the one before, as though night had never divided them. Gina felt calmer in the car but had no idea where she was going; it crossed her mind that she should go to the beach, too. She wound along Pickering Road, an old typewriter on the floor of Lester's Toyota sliding with the curves. When she came to the turnoff for her family's house, there was no one behind her so she stopped and looked up the dirt driveway. She started to turn in, but at the last minute lost her nerve.

She turned onto Halsey Road without a destination. Nothing's changed, she thought, as she surveyed the little houses built too close to the road; she was unsure if this was a comfort or a disappointment. She slowed as she approached the shingled cottage of her childhood friend, Sandy Finch, which, with the exception of the satellite dish, appeared unaltered. Still mint green and the same—well, not the same of course—blue plastic above-ground pool in the yard. Gina was about to move on when Sandy's front door opened and a woman stepped out and glanced at her, holding her gaze just long enough that her features matched an imprint on Gina's memory. *Sandy!* She pumped the gas pedal hard and nearly miscalculated the road's curve.

She could have just as easily slammed on the brakes. But spotting her best friend from junior high whom she hadn't glimpsed since she was fourteen felt like seeing a ghost. She and Sandy had been best friends until a week before Gina left for boarding school, when Sandy's father took the pipe out of his mouth just long enough to say, "Whit's Point schools not good enough foah ya?" Gina had felt cast out, criticized for something she'd barely understood. Things between her and Sandy were never the same.

From the road, Sandy did look great: still voluptuous and crowned by a luxuriant mane of red hair. Gina tilted the mirror briefly to see herself, to check out what Sandy had glimpsed of her and decided with some relief that especially from a distance, she probably hadn't changed much either.

Now, each time Gina passed someone mowing the lawn or stooped over gardening, she morphed them into someone she'd sat next to in the Whit's Point Elementary lunchroom: Robert with the drowned-up-at-the-lake sister; Bonnie in trouble for passing mean notes about their teacher; Natalie crying because MaryAnn told her she smelled. She passed the Baptist church, behind which she'd made out with Teddy Stretch, and then the freshly mown cemetery where she'd smoked her first joint. When she'd gone off to boarding school, it seemed like she might as well have died, as far as her Whit's Point friends were concerned. But that was okay with her. She'd moved on; rivers flowed in one direction—away from their source.

At Route 126, she turned left and drove as far as the lumberyard where her parents had bought two-by-fours just before their accident. When she was in Whit's Point with Cassie, she'd wanted to retrace

---

her parents' drive, but Cassie had been horrified and Gina, too, had finally decided it would be too painful.

Now, she followed the route that anyone in her family could've driven in their sleep. Her parents were excellent drivers and loved their station wagon, but this April they forwent their usual spring drive to Florida in favor of staying home to repair the porch. Lulled by a few days of warm weather, they'd set out for the lumberyard under darkening skies.

Freezing rain, a winding road, a truck—the circumstances of the accident had been thoroughly vetted and couldn't have been more straightforward. But now that Gina's mind was stuck in rewind, it raced backward one-two-three years and paused at her father's heart attack. Her parents had had friends for lunch, and afterward, as the friends drove down the driveway, her father said, "I didn't want to spoil lunch, Ellie, but I've been having chest pains for the past hour." He was admitted to the hospital for a triple bypass.

Later that same day, Gina's mother had said to her on the phone, "It's just terrible. I've never slept in the house alone." Gina had been offended that her mother's biggest concern seemed to be about her own comfort. But she also heard something in her ferociously independent mother's voice that she'd never heard before: helplessness.

Her father had sailed through surgery and recuperation. Always meek, he became more decisive and direct after the bypass, as though repairing his arteries also cleared the avenues for certain ego-boosting fluids. Or, maybe he seized on his close shave with death as an opportunity to live life differently. Her mother, on the other hand, had a hard time recovering; as Ron's outlook became crisper, hers wilted. Worry crept into her joints, and reminders of Ron's and her own mortality refused to go away, collecting like plaque in her mind. She complained of a kind of diffuse weakness and brain-fog that her doctor couldn't diagnose. She became restless and enlisted Ron in running errands with her—errands that often had already been done. The control she'd always enjoyed over her husband and the household wavered; maybe, Gina thought, this had felt like life itself slipping away. She declared to her daughters the imminence of her death.

This was nothing new, her threatening to die. But they'd always taken it seriously, because how could they be sure she didn't mean it? "Now that she has an idea of what it would be like to be alone, it's as though she's determined to die before Dad does," Gina observed to Paul once. She'd felt wicked.

In the year before the accident, despite receiving a clean bill of health from her doctor, Gina's mother began to think even beyond her death into Ron's life as a widower, a territory over which control was impossible. Fear and paranoia surged. "He never tells me where he's going," her mother complained, as if Gina's father were carrying on a secret life. "Who even knows where he is?" she'd say, even as Gina watched her father out the window, loading the wheelbarrow.

On the phone one day, Gina's father told her, "Your mother thinks she's going to die, and I'm going to remarry, and someone will get hold of the damn Washington letters."

And here is where fate might have looked kindly upon her mother. "Let's go get the lumber for the fence," Gina imagined Eleanor saying the day of the accident. Ah, how her mother loved the car—the escape and the sublime security of it! In the car, she could travel with Ron away from the troubling new patterns of home life into a changing land-scape, with a shared destination, everyone present and accounted for. The car had always assured the sameness of their path of travel through life. But with Ron's horizon extending after his bypass and Eleanor's—or at least her perception of it—shrinking, their paths, then, would inevitably diverge. The body had its own destiny, but the car was still in their control, the wheel steering them into the future. Her father would have said, "Now? We haven't even drunk our tea." Her mother:

"C'mon, we'll beat the weather."

There were only the smallest of variables between a car and an accident: a few seconds of misjudgment or distraction, a blind spot in a mirror, blinding light, blinding darkness. Rain, which in tiny increments turned to ice—tiny increments between life and death, increments that ensured Ronald and Eleanor's destination would be, for all eternity, the same.

A deafening screech, the blare of a horn. Gina slammed on her brakes, narrowly avoiding a Honda trying to make a left turn in front of her in the intersection. After she'd presented the best apologetic face she could, the Honda continued its turn. Shaken, she took a deep breath and riveted her attention on the road.

She reached the site of the accident, just past the first sign for the outlet malls, and pulled over. Carefully avoiding the poison ivy, she scrambled down the embankment to the woods of birch and maple and reached to touch the sturdy trunk of the maple closest to the road. Had the car struck this tree, or the one next to it? Gina felt a certain irony, standing in these sun-dappled woods; her mother had been a passionate student of trees, often startling her family during car trips with a command for Ron to pull over so she could get a closer look at a ginkgo or catalpa. Now, the green woods that had always beckoned with their natural innocence took on a sinister glow.

"Everything okay?"

Gina looked up and waved off the concerned passerby hanging out the window of a pickup. She climbed back to the shoulder, legs shaking.

Back in the car, she cranked up the air conditioning, hoping that regulating her microclimate would somehow normalize her thoughts. She slowed as she approached the Old Seeley Farm, noticing that the famously old elm trees that once lined the road had been cut down. A sign at the end of the driveway read "Yankee Properties, LLC." The eighteenth-century farmhouse was crawling with carpenters. But the huge gambrel-roof barn was gone. She pulled over and walked partway up the edge of the property, which had been substantially bulldozed. At the back of the property next to the woods stood a large, new, shingled house crowded with dormers and wrapped with a porch. It was overweight and overwrought for this quiet, country road. A second, nearly identical house was in construction much too close to it, and clearly there would be a few more clones crowding the property before the year was over. "They've just ruined it!" she could imagine her mother declaring.

She turned onto Pickering Road and slowed again as she approached her old driveway, craning to see if there were any cars parked at the house. When she was satisfied there were none, she drove up to the house under the spreading maples she had helped to plant when she was twelve. A huge green debris box—always the first sign of impending construction—sat menacingly in the driveway.

She parked out of sight behind the house and walked to the middle of the front yard, scanning the breadth of the property, dotted with old crab apple, birch, and cherry trees, lilacs and wild rose bushes. The next hill over was crowned with a ridge of houses that faced Pickering Road; when she was growing up, their backs, with their stingy little windows, were turned to the exquisite water view, and owners had let the grass in their yards grow into hay. In the last decade though, French doors and decks had been added to nearly every house, with stairs that spilled onto mowed lawns stretching to the cove's shore. It was as if the enjoyment of natural beauty had finally become fashionable—or perhaps affordable.

For a moment, her attention was snatched by the cove, and she quickly refocused, reminding herself that the house was why she'd come to Maine. Modest but tall, it appeared precariously perched on the hillcrest, with no porch roofs or overhangs, only a few lilac and forsythia bushes to help ground its clapboard walls in the earth that sloped away from it. Cupping her hand against her eye, she framed the structure like a camera, moving her lens over the symmetrically placed windows—one with a shutter missing—and the large, central dormer over the front door. In her lifetime, the house had always been painted white with black shutters.

"The house is worthless," Gina's mother had been fond of saying, as though she were talking about her old potato peeler, not the house she'd presided over for nearly fifty years. The sum of its parts read as an endless list of repairs to her mother and father, merely renters, never owners. They had been grudgingly reimbursed by Mr. Hickle for their improvements, but only for the house's most basic needs—a new roof, a new coat of paint—never for their small repairs and remodels. They had neither the means nor the courage to make big changes to a building that was not their own. "Some day, Hickle's relatives will inherit this heap and make something of it," Gina could remember her father saying about the landlord, as he wrestled with a broken window sash.

But the house had always been *something*, she thought; it was almost iconic with its boxy shape and steeply pitched gables. As she walked the perimeter, it emanated emptiness like a shell on the sand. Its skin was thick and pasty where years of white paint had built up, worn to the wood in others. A trickle of brown stained the clapboards where window trim had rotted and bled. Storm windows had been removed and stacked neatly beside the house. The porch at the back door still looked fresh from the coat of paint her parents had put on a year ago, but the planters there that her mother had lovingly cultivated held only the brown stubs of geraniums. The clothesline that had once run from the shed to the pear tree dangled from its pulley on the wall. In the yard, grass grew thick and high. Lilacs and rhododendrons burst with summer fullness, but it seemed that not even their vitality could nourish the house back to life.

Gina filled with anxious anticipation; she needed to get inside the house before she was discovered there! By now, the house key she'd thrown into the cove in April would be two feet deep in the mud. But on the plane, she'd schemed: she would break in the way she had as a teenager when she'd locked herself out.

She glanced down the driveway to be sure no one was coming, then walked around to the shed off the kitchen. Below the shed's small window, she placed one of the planter boxes from the porch and stood on it, making it barely possible to swing one foot up onto the windowsill, then the other. Once there, she was able to grab just enough of the shed roof to haul herself up onto it. Her forearms burned against the rough asphalt shingles. She scrambled up the shallow sloped roof toward her mother's bedroom window, which she knew had usually been unlocked, and reached to push up the sash. Locked tight! For a moment, she sat on the roof, soaked in sweat, arms raw, staring down at the cove in utter defeat. How rash it had been to throw away that key! But she'd come too far to give up; she couldn't just walk away.

She climbed off the shed roof and once again checked the driveway to be sure she was alone, then dashed to the garage to look for something that would break a window. She found the shovel she'd hoped to use to bury the bottle-headed skunk. In April, she'd forgotten the skunk; from the airport, she'd called to ask their neighbor Jake to dispose of it. Now, she imagined him heaving it into the pile at the dump the way he hefted his lobster traps overboard.

Shovel in hand, Gina circled the house feeling almost delirious from the heat and the headiness of her intention, her heart pounding out its disapproval of the trespassing that would soon become vandalism. She checked the windows to be certain they were all locked and considered which to break. As she came around to the front yard, car tires crunched on the driveway, and she leapt up the front steps to squat out of sight between the bushes flanking the porch. Luckily, the car was only using the driveway to turn around.

Reality smacked her. What was she *doing*! Perhaps she really *had* lost her mind. As her courage dropped away, she reached absentmindedly for the front doorknob and turned it. The door was unlocked. When she pushed it open, the wall of heat hit her first, then the suffocating mustiness.

She stepped inside and gazed up the stair, struck for the first time that there were not just one, but two fundamental rules of feng shui broken by this house: a stair leading directly from the front door, causing good ch'i to flow away, and a bathroom opposite the door—a position that would promote bad health and poverty.

She turned into the living room: a floor and four walls, scarred and dirty, three windows. During the move out when she'd been confined here with Cassie, she'd been unable to see the room through the mess and her fog of emotion. But now, with perfect clarity, her mind's eye furnished the room as it had been when it had *lived*, with a mix of inherited antiques and Miesian-inspired modern pieces: a couch, linen and comfy, an efficient white leatherette swivel chair. A coffee table composed of a clear, acrylic *u* and an old varnished drawing board accommodating precisely two stacks of *Newsweeks* and *Down Easts*. Lamps made from antique glass lanterns, clean-lined ceramics, and paintings of pleasant domestic scenes and waterscapes. Visitors had always said the crowded living room had a year-round warmth; to Gina, its temperature had been as volatile as the seasons.

She pictured her mother now at the round table near the window, watering her potted lilies. A sudden pattering of life filled the house. Not human noises, but those of something small and frantic. She moved cautiously toward the sound, through to the kitchen where a barn swallow was hurtling against the closed window, then diving wildly around the room. Finally, it dropped to the corner of the floor and cocked one eye at her.

She opened the kitchen windows. "Go on out, little bird!" She moved toward the swallow, hoping to shoo it outside. But it rose and fluttered out of the room and disappeared up the stairwell. She followed the bird's soft thumping into Cassie's room. The bird was in the attic now, but the ladder to the opening was gone.

Gina crossed the hall to her old bedroom, where she envisioned her mother, stretching a clean sheet over the bed. She blinked her away and stepped to the window. The cove was half full. Mudflats baked in the hot sun, and she imagined how warm the water would be later, when the tide came back in. She thought of how, as a child, she'd idled on the shore with friends, waiting until the water was high enough to launch into it. Sometimes they'd impatiently wade out to meet it, trudging through the soft mud in their bathing suits, discovering lost swim fins and strange, wormy creatures along the way. In recent years, her own children enjoyed these same timeless pleasures: swimming, boating, beachcombing. Now, she pondered Esther and Ben's city lives and their city windows, with their views of the neighbor's wall. What was a window that didn't give access to even the smallest world beyond the house? she thought. Where were the horizons that her children's daydreams would run out to meet?

Now, something caught Gina's eye, some small bit of red near the shore—a toy or a piece of litter, she thought at first; but when she squinted, she saw there was more than one flash of red. Surveyor's stakes! She felt a sharp stab of possessiveness; for the first time, she let herself think about what Sid might have in mind for the house.

Downstairs, she went out to the shed and peered into a large trash can looking for clues. At the bottom sat a bundle of real estate flyers with photographs that to her critical eye didn't come close to capturing the uniqueness of the house site. She pushed aside foam coffee cups, uncovering the birdhouse she and Cassie had left in the pear tree. Lifting it out, she discovered a folded architectural drawing.

The drawing—so soiled and tattered it looked as if it had been driven over—was labeled "Yankee Properties, LLC" and "245 Pickering Road," but it took a moment for Gina to recognize what she was looking at. On the site plan, the same driveway swooped onto the property from Pickering Road, but now it had a name: "Cove View Pointe." The acreage had been divided into four lots, each with a structure labeled "Cottage," though they were all the full size of a house.

Gina drew a sharp breath and quickly noted the drawing's date: May fifth. Yankee must have decided not to go ahead with the purchase, making it available to Sid. She laid the drawing back in the trash can and set the birdhouse on top of it.

She should've been relieved that at least one design disaster had been averted. But the over-the-top plans, made by someone who didn't *know* the house, seemed to mock her for standing here like a relic on its rotting porch. There'd be more plans soon, of course, and she wondered: when a house was reshaped, were the memories it contained reshaped too? Or simply lost?

The drawings loudly announced that the house was moving on; it had no allegiance to Gina and wouldn't wait for her to be finished with it. She needed to let it go now.

Regard it as just as desirable to build a chicken house as to build a cathedral.

Frank Lloyd Wright

Chapter 8

Gina climbed in the car and drove back to Lily House. Just before turning into the driveway, she pulled over when she spotted Annie with a group of people standing outside the front door. Lily House had been constructed so close to the road that when the stone wall was built to buffer it from traffic, the front door became virtually inaccessible. Now, she could see Annie pointing out the details of the exemplary Georgian colonial—its symmetrical façade with two brick chimneys on each end; five multipaned windows on the upper floor, four on the lower; the central entry with a six-panel door, flanking pilasters and entablature. Lily House, with its esteemed architecture and history, would likely be preserved forever; it would never meet the fate of her family's rental.

Gina pulled into the driveway next to two unfamiliar cars and climbed the porch steps between the orange day lilies that crowded up against the house's lattice base. Once inside the house, she stood for a moment in the hall, eavesdropping on Annie's tour, which had moved upstairs.

"And what is this?" A soft-spoken man asked.

"Oh, that's a radiator. It's for heating the room, but it isn't original."

"How does it work? When did they invent this?" A woman asked.

She was young, Gina could tell. The tour guide laughed, "I don't actually know. But to heat water for their bath, they—"

"Where did they take baths?" a child asked.

"In the basement."

"Where did they go to the bathroom?"

"In chamber pots that they carried to the outhouse."

Silence. "Chamber pots?"

Gina went into the kitchen where there was a note on the counter: *Gina—help yourself to brownies. Paul called. He told me to ask you to please keep your cell phone on. —A*

Gina pulled her cell phone from her purse, feeling bad that she hadn't checked in with Paul since she'd arrived. But she knew calling him would worsen her ambivalence about being away from her family and her confusion about why she'd even come to Whit's Point. She looked at her watch. If she waited until later to return Paul's call, Esther and Ben would be home, too. She turned on her phone to listen to a voicemail from Allison Brink, who was wondering if Gina had had time to work on her great room.

The tour group clumped down the stairs and said their goodbyes to Annie at the back door. Annie whizzed into the kitchen.

"The most darling family from India," she said. "Imagine being from a place like that where things are thousands of years old, being interested in a little old—*young*—house like this. Isn't it wonderful? Yikes! I need lunch." She tied on an apron that said, *I Eat, Therefore I Am.* "How about cheddar and tomato? What have you been up to?" She handed Gina a loaf of bread.

"I went to the house," Gina said, pulling bread slices from the bag. "It was unlocked, so I went in and looked around."

Annie was rinsing a tomato, her back to Gina. There was a small sweat stain at the neckline of her shirt. "How was that?" she asked. "Toasted or not toasted?"

"Pardon?"

"Your bread."

Gina told her not toasted.

"Stick mine in the toaster, would you, dearie?" Annie finished slicing the tomato, opened the refrigerator, and took out a block of cheese.

Gina gathered her courage. "Annie, have you heard anything about Sid's plans?"

"For the house, you mean?" Annie handed Gina the cheese.

The doorbell rang, and Annie dashed to the front door. Gina wondered if she was only imagining that Annie was being evasive. She sliced the cheese and finished making their sandwiches.

When Annie returned, she was waving a package. "My new weeding trowel," she said. "Gee, it's just too damn hot for anything! These look yummy!" She took her sandwich and whisked out the screen door.

Gina ate, though she wasn't hungry. She wished she felt at ease enough with Annie to press her further for information about Sid and the house. On the other hand, whatever Sid had in mind, there was nothing to be done about it because she couldn't imagine being face-to-face with Sid Banton, who in her mind, had become the embodiment of the Banton family's misery.

Ugh! She felt pathetic: afraid to call her family, afraid to face her past. How had she become boxed in by fear and how would she get out?

She decided the only way to escape her anxiety would be to settle down and draw. When she finished eating, she went into the bedroom and laid out the plans she'd made in San Francisco of Allison Brink's project. When Allison gave Gina a tour of her home, Gina was careful, as she was with all her clients, to express interest in only the *bones* of the house, not the *flesh*, and not to let her eyes rest on anything personal: family photographs, medicine vials, messages on the refrigerator door. This was architect protocol. Like a doctor giving a physical, she would no more ask, "Is this your mother in the photograph?" than a doctor would observe, with her patient prone on the table, "Great tan, been on vacation?" Still, later when she'd spent several hours in the house measuring, she'd learned much about Allison; she had a thing for athletic shoes, for instance, as well as French cafe prints, Pepperidge Farm cookies, and mauve.

Standing in her garden, Allison had asked Gina to design a playhouse for her children. "My ex wants to build it himself." She'd snorted when she said this.

Gina gathered her T square and drawing tools to consider Allison's great room. She laid tracing paper over the floor plan and, with her pen, traced the perimeter of the existing kitchen and dining room, leaving out the nest of little spaces people in another century found indispensable: butler's pantry, maid's room, dumbwaiter. By getting rid of them, the kitchen gained eight feet of new window area looking into the garden. She removed the wall separating the narrow kitchen from the dark dining room, making both areas lighter and more spacious, and sketched an island where the wall had been. A hundred times before, she'd made these same moves on someone's plans; each time it had felt like liberating the house so it could breathe.

Hearing voices outside, for the first time Gina took a long look out the window at the garden, an expanse between the house and the garage where Annie was talking quietly to a visitor and fondling the blooms of her tuberoses. The garden was magnificent. Unfussy with its juxtapositions of color, texture, and shape. Annie had planted a sampler of all of Gina's favorite New England flowers: zinnias, tiger lilies and irises, daisies and phlox, lobelia, campanula, hydrangea.

Gina was quite sure that when she was growing up, Fran hadn't kept a garden here.

She went back to work, her tools sticky in her hands, an occasional drop of sweat falling from her forehead onto the drawing. Voices floated in from other rooms. The image of the developer's bloated plan of her family's house occasionally interrupted her concentration. But then she lost herself in the challenge of Allison's great room. The precision and sharp focus of drawing, measuring, drawing, and the clack of the triangle against the T square quieted her like a meditation. There was magic to mechanical drawings; for Gina, they brought a house to life, evoked emotions, and stirred the imagination, the way photographs moved some people. She'd seen her clients become attached to and protective of them, the way they might be of an X-ray of their child's bones. Now, she thought of her father, who'd shared her interest in graphically depicting the world. He'd pored over her architectural drawings with undisguised awe and seemed surprised by the drawings' precision, as if it were not compatible with the grown daughter who appeared sporadically and reticently—sketchlike—against the walls of his house. Those were the moments—leaning over her drawings, walking him through floor plans—when Gina had most connected with him.

For a little while, Annie took a break from gardening and was playing her violin somewhere—upstairs? outside?—the music creating a dreamy ambiance. Annie had taught Gina to play the violin in the fourth-grade coatroom; in the beginning, she'd been wretchedly squeaky on her instrument. But the next year, Annie took her students to the annual children's concert in Portland, and Gina had relished the power of pulling her bow across the strings with a hundred other kids, creating big, beautiful music! Remembering this now, she filled with fresh affection for her parents' old friend.

By two o'clock, she'd finished a scheme she could send to Allison.

As she watched Allison's great room slide through the fax machine, she was surprised by the satisfaction she felt, having solved another house puzzle. It excited her to be able to refresh her clients with a new environment; after all, when a person took a book into nature to read, time would be spent looking for the ideal place to sit, wandering from tree to tree, comparing views from each spot, observing sun angles and wind direction, the relative hospitableness of ground cover. Gina adhered to this same selectivity as she imagined her clients moving about the houses she designed. She created the architectural "weather" they woke up to and came home to every day to feel comforted, loved, and forgiven—and every day that weather had to be *good*. There was *some* nobility in the birthing of Dr. Allison Brink's great room, wasn't there?

She looked again out the window. Annie stooped to pluck strands of a clematis vine from the garden bed. Even in her slouchy, faded gardening clothes, she had an elegance about her; her face, with its sloping forehead, close-set eyes, and prominent nose, brought to mind a regal bird. She worked intently, pulling green twist-ties from her apron pocket, winding them onto the nails in the fence, then around the vine. But the vine was too heavy and pulled the nails out. She stood back to assess the situation, hands on her hips.

Gina went into the kitchen, took the pitcher of iced tea from the refrigerator and two brownies and stepped out into the garden. By this time of the afternoon, her yard in San Francisco would be in wild motion with the fierce summer wind and fog that cruelly stood between her and her little piece of earth. But Annie's garden was silent and still, exuding sensuous aromas of rich, warm earth, and Gina could feel it work its magic on her, making her breathing fuller, softening her layers.

"The garden's amazing, Annie!" she said. "Do you plan it all out before you plant?"

"Oh, heavens, no. I start with the seeds of my favorites and have a loose idea of what I want. Then I see what happens. What grows, what dies—much depends on the weather, of course, and the soil, and how busy I get with other things—and it sort of evolves, and I surrender to it as I tend it. Is designing buildings sort of like that?"

Gina thought about this. "Hmm. Well, I wish it could be more like that. There are so many parameters to pay attention to—program, cost, building codes, neighborhood restrictions, engineering . . . designs evolve when I'm meeting with clients. But, really, we try to plan every little detail before a single nail gets hammered—it's all about control." She laughed.

"Playing my violin for the symphony's a little like that. A hundred years of watching the little black notes on the page, getting them just right so the music will sound the way the composer intended it to. If my mind wanders for a second, I'll make a mistake. But what I love about gardening are the possibilities . . . .." She smiled as she surveyed her garden. "Gorgeous things happen whether I intend them to or not."

Gina heard the wisdom in Annie's words and hoped she would discover such creative balance in her own life.

A hummingbird buzzed by Gina, then hovered with its beak in a gladiolus. "Annie, there's a bird trapped in the house."

Annie turned. "Where?"

"At Mom and Dad's, I mean. I heard it fluttering around in the attic, but the ladder's gone, so I couldn't go up."

"Oh, gosh, poor thing. You can take our ladder over, if you want." Annie held her glass while Gina filled it. "Thanks, hon. The Historical Society replaced this fence, and I've been trying to get the old vine back onto it."

"Why don't I hammer the nails in and get the ties around them while you hold the vines?"

Gina took off her sneakers to let her feet bathe next to Annie's in the cool grass. Annie had on red flip-flops and a Band Aid wrapped her baby toe. Holding the ties between her teeth, Gina reached over a clump of tiger lilies to set the first nail. The scent of damp garden earth and her own sweat mingled; with every nail she hammered, she could feel the tension in her body loosen. The two women worked silently and methodically, swatting mosquitoes with a violence well accepted in these parts, hitching up the vine until most of the fence was covered.

When they got to the corner of the yard Annie stared into the bed of petunias. "I miss your mother and father terribly, you know," she said.

Surprised by Annie's sudden dolefulness, Gina couldn't think of what to say. "You guys spent a lot of years together," she said finally.

"Not just years; we spent a lot of . . . energy together, and I don't mean only in the boats and on the beach with you kids and whatnot. I mean, kids grow up fast. They're with you, what, eighteen years or less? And after that, we parents are still together twenty and thirty years later, grilling hamburger from Tobey's Market or breaking the law by chucking the smelly remains of our lobster feasts into the dumpster at the town dock."

Gina laughed. Annie kneeled to deadhead a petunia. "Lord, how your ma and pa missed you."

A lump rose in Gina's throat; the firm grip of guilt turned the peaceful garden into a trap. She took a breath and stepped back from the flowerbed, all at once feeling her children gone. "It must be a terrible shock when your kids leave home."

Holding the last bit of vine, Annie swiveled and looked at Gina, as if she'd heard the full depth of her fear. "Ayup—it's a toughie," she said, before turning back to the fence. "But you know, it depends on *how* they leave home. If you play your cards right, they come on back and even paint your fences once in a while."

Gina smiled and pounded in the last nail.

Stretched out on the bed that night, Gina closed her eyes and thought about her guardedness with Annie. She'd missed perhaps the only opportunity she'd have to communicate something deeper about her parents. She wondered: *Would* her mother have shared with Annie the kind of intimate things Gina talked about with her closest friends?

She picked up her phone, now nearly desperate to talk to Esther and Ben, hoping to soothe the small injuries of her day. Ben answered, excited to tell her about the giant bubble maker they'd bought at Toys"R"Us. "It was too windy in the yard, so Dad let us do them in the garage so there's, like, soap slime all over the floor! Esther's mad at you, or something."

Gina asked Ben to put Esther on. While she waited, she could hear the hammering scales of *The Rugrats* theme song.

"You *have* to!" she heard Ben yell.

More waiting. Finally, Esther picked up. "Hi," she said weakly. When Gina asked, "What's new?" she said, "Nothing, except Nicky's parents are getting divorced. By the way, I Googled food poisoning, and it doesn't sound anything like how you acted at school that day."

"Oh, Estie . . . I'm sorry about Nicky. And you're right; it wasn't food poisoning, but I'm just fine, and we'll talk all about it when I see you."

Esther was silent for a few moments. "What're you *doing*, anyway?" she finally said. "Can't you just come *home*?" She began to sob.

"Esther? Sweetie, what's the matter?"

Esther struggled to speak. Gina had nearly given up on her when she said, "Other kids see their grandparents on Christmas, not just in the summer! We never spent a single Christmas with Gran and Granddad. It's not fair! Why did we always stay so short in Maine?"

The question left Gina dumbstruck. There was a clattering sound on the phone, as if Esther had dropped the receiver.

"Esther?" Gina waited, close to tears, her stomach twisted in a knot.

Paul picked up the phone. "Hey! How come you didn't call last night?"

"I'm sorry. I was out of it. Boy, Esther's really having a hard time."

"She's tired. And I think she's missing you."

Gina stiffened. "Missing me? I've only been gone two days."

"Yes, but remember, other than when you were east to clean out the house, you've never been away from them for two days in their lives."

The remark pushed all of Gina's buttons. "What are you saying— that I should feel bad about leaving them and bad about *not* leaving them, too?"

Paul was silent. Finally he said, "Gina, I'm not trying to make you feel bad. It's *normal* for Esther to be missing you."

There was that word *normal* again, the surest way to make her feel abnormal. "But she's . . . It's more than that."

"Well, what do *you* think is bothering her?"

"I messed up," Gina said. "We should've spent more time with Mom and Dad. She adored them, and I deprived her."

Gina waited for Paul to refute her claim. But he said, "Don't beat yourself up. If you really want to know, Esther said yesterday that she was afraid you were dying." He laughed.

"*What?*" Gina whispered, afraid Annie and Lester might over-hear. "Why are you laughing?"

"Lighten up, Gina. You know Esther; she's a catastrophizer. She'll be fine. How are you doing?"

"Did you at least reassure her that I'm okay?"

"*Are* you?"

"We're talking about Esther."

"Of course I reassured her. I told her you were on a retreat with the Dalai Lama." Again, he laughed.

Gina fought to contain her vexation. "She needs some attention. Can you just go and make—"

"She was fine before you called, Gina. You know Esther's worrying about what's going on with you—she's trying to understand." Paul spoke calmly, slowly. "She's confused. You melt down at school. You go away alone. Then you don't call. How can I reassure her when I don't know what's going on?"

Paul's list of offenses roiled her. "Paul, I'm . . . I *never* go away. This is very hard for me. I leave for four days—four stupid days! And things there are falling apart. Can you just take care of it, of her?"

Dead silence. Gina looked at her phone; the battery had died. Would Paul think she'd hung up on him? She couldn't remember ever having spoken to him so harshly. Next, she would lose all equilibrium and blame her husband for it, like her mother!

Annie and Lester's bedroom door bumped shut. Alarmed and clammy, Gina went into the bathroom, with a cool soak in mind. She turned on the tub faucet and slumped against the cold, frictionless enamel in just a few inches of water. Closing her eyes, she felt almost human again, but when she opened them, she wasn't prepared for the confrontation with her middle-aged toes, her middle-aged knees and breasts. What did they mean to her anymore? Tonight, they seemed almost to be parts of someone else's body.

She was just stepping out of the tub when again, on the other side of the wall, she heard Annie and Lester thumping around.

Lester's voice: "Why don't you take it off—it's too hot."

Annie: "You're right."

Gina stood dripping on the bath mat, surprised to notice she was holding her breath.

Annie sighed, then Lester. Gina stayed still, listening, evaporating. The bed creaked, and Annie laughed softly. The bed talked more, with rhythm now. A groan, a long silence, another sigh. The low tones of words spoken with affection. Quiet.

A kind of shock took hold of Gina, and she broke out in a new layer of sweat. Looking in the mirror, she stifled a sob rising in her throat. It had been months since she and Paul had made love.

In bed, she churned. Of course, she should've called Paul back on the landline. She should've *tried* to explain to Esther what had happened at school, and she would, soon.

But how would she explain why they'd only gone to Maine once a year? She remembered Esther's last few summers with her grandparents, when she'd spent much of her time combing the blackberry bushes in the field and picking flowers from the garden. "Pick as many as you want, dear; they'll grow right back," Eleanor had told her. Grandmother and granddaughter, exactly the same height that summer, had spent part of every day arranging and tending small bouquets in Eleanor's collection of vases—just one of the many things Gina wished she herself had more time to do with Esther. With bittersweet curiosity, Gina observed her daughter's pure and unfettered enjoyment of her mother, who was careful not to reveal her most troubling side to her grandchildren, only occasionally letting slip a note of bitterness. On what would be the last day they saw Gina's parents alive, as they were leaving down the driveway, Esther had dissolved in tears, as if she knew. Gina had only been able to turn in her seat, reach out, and squeeze Esther's hand.

Gina turned off the light. In the dark, there'd be no chance of escaping her thoughts, of being distracted by the details of the room: the exuberant zinnias, the cheerful flowered sheets, not even the mosquito waiting, bloodthirsty, on the wall.

As she often did when she couldn't sleep, she lured her mind from troublesome territory by returning to the unrealized Marin house, sifting through a kit of parts: morphing volumes, one story and two story, linear and compact; casement windows and sash windows; pitched, arched, and shed roofs; stucco, metal, clapboard, board-and-batten. Piecing together limitless combinations of features, she manipulated her house like a Mr. Potato Head, hoping that eventually the perfect one would reveal itself. Perhaps it was the haphazard sloppiness of the process that sometimes allowed sleep to sneak in and steal her away. But even when sleep did not come, the house she'd hoped to find through her meditation continued to elude her.

Deeper, dreamless sleep darted just ahead of her, leading her through the forest of gnarled anxieties that was insomnia. On her kitchen island, Allison Brink delivered a baby while her children looked on. "Speak to me in English!" she commanded. "Practice the piano while I finish up here." A second later, Allison's kitchen became Gina's parents', filled with dust and plaster. The outside wall of the kitchen had fallen completely away; swallows took turns around the room. "Oh, how gorgeous!" her mother said, putting dinner on the table. "We could leave it open like this and just tell Hickle it fell off." The wall popped up again. Her mother stormed out. A door slammed shut; Gina heard Esther crying but she couldn't turn the knob that would take her to her.

A house is a machine for living in.
          Le Corbusier, *Towards a New Architecture*

KITCHEN
9'-11" X 15'-8"

Lily House had been sold. Ginny hadn't heard a word about why or to whom; her mother had been sulking for three days and sobbing about "all those beautiful family things" and how she'd "never set foot in that house again." Ginny had no inclination to ask her parents about the sale. Questions, she felt intuitively, would only generate more bad humor in the house.

She asked Cassie, who didn't know and didn't seem to care. "Good riddance to Lily House," she'd said.

Ginny, too, was secretly glad Lily House was out of their lives, but she was still shocked; it seemed to her that her mother had worshipped Lily House and had been planning to move into it someday.

She doubted her mother would ever get over this loss. On top of that, it had been wedding season, and her father had been photographing brides nearly every Saturday, "completely ruining the weekends," according to her mother. As excited as Ginny was about finishing seventh grade—all that annoying business of what to wear to school and dancing with short boys was behind her!—she was not at all optimistic about the summer.

But on this first morning of vacation, she was greeted in the kitchen by her parents' cheerful voices drifting in from the shed. The screen door *whacked* behind them as they came into the room.

"Good morning to youooo!" her father warbled, squeezing her shoulders.

Her mother looked fresh and relaxed in her khaki jumper. Gina poured herself a bowl of Rice Krispies and slid onto a chair, feeling the little circles of the caned seat imprinting themselves on her bare thighs. Sun streamed in through the window. Maybe a day for swimming, she thought, turning to check out the cove. The tide was about halfway in and on the outhaul, their dinghy pointed east into a breeze so light it barely wrinkled the water.

Her mother dumped a cup of detergent into the washing machine and then pushed its door shut with her foot. "Well, Gin," she announced, "get ready for a new kitchen! We're going to change this place like you wouldn't believe!"

So that was it—a Project. There were only a few things—sailing, entertaining out-of-town guests, or a Project—that could alter her mother's mood so dramatically. Projects seemed to appear out of nowhere and always involved some aspect of house, boat, or yard maintenance. With this news, a certain equilibrium was achieved between the June day outside and the June day inside, which Ginny experienced as a soaring sense of freedom; the walls of the kitchen seemed almost to evaporate.

Within a few days, the house buzzed with the dismantling of the kitchen. "Take it away!" Ginny's mother exclaimed after breakfast one day.

"Yes, ma'am!" Her father laughed, and Ginny understood that

this really *was* how he wanted to spend his summer vacation.

Ginny watched her parents start at one corner of the kitchen and work counter-clockwise, tearing out the old, preparing for the new. It was reassuring to see them elbow-to-elbow toiling away, dust in their hair. Both of them wore old blue sneakers, her mother's laced only halfway because of her high arches.

"Ron, hold the thing down like this and then pull," her mother instructed as she tore up a square of old linoleum.

"Okay, right-o. Well, that works! Your mother's so clever; isn't she?"

Ron turned and winked at Ginny. What did it mean, that wink? Though it was hard to believe that his flattery was sincere, given the way her mother treated him, Ginny could see in his open expression that it was.

Ginny helped carry out the vertical board cabinets and the black slate sink that she knew had to be ancient because Louisa May Alcott had bought the very same sink for her family's house in Concord. While they were waiting for the new sink to arrive, Ginny and Cassie washed dishes, fruits, and vegetables in the chemical-coated darkroom sink, which to Ginny seemed like a health hazard no matter how careful she was. The new stainless steel sink was built into a new counter that covered the top of the washing machine on one side, the dishwasher on the other. The countertop was plastic laminate trimmed with wood that was finished with the same varnish Ginny had used for the rowboat oars the week before. Above the sink, cabinet faces cut from hollow-core doors were installed. Smooth surfaces! This was the clean, modern look her mother was after.

Every morning, Ginny came downstairs and breathed in the smells of renewal: paint, putty, glue, sawdust. She associated the mostly toxic smells so strongly with her mother's good moods that they always triggered a feeling of well-being.

The Project didn't interfere with the usual goings on of summer; there were drop-in visitors nearly every day, and her mother graciously abandoned her putty knife to play hostess. At the end of the day, she and Ginny's father would clean up the mess, her mother pointing out little piles of dust for him to suck up with the vacuum cleaner. Making dinner, her mother was always a little stooped, looking even smaller than her four feet ten inches, and her sighs reminded everyone of her arthritic back. But during dinner, Ginny could hear in her mother's voice the vigor spawned by the progress of the Project. Chipped beef on toast had never tasted so good.

With Cassie at her summer job at the Navy yard and her parents occupied in the kitchen, Gina's days stretched out before her, breezy and free. On a hot Tuesday, she called to invite Sandy Finch to come over and go swimming. She slipped into Cassie's hand-me-down bathing suit, a luscious orange and purple bikini that made her think of an island paradise. She was thrilled to discover that her breasts finally filled out the skimpy top. In the mirror, she rubbed her hands along the expanse of bare stomach, trying to ignore her hopelessly skinny legs and knees that reminded her of the branches of old apple trees.

Downstairs, her parents were standing in the corner of the kitchen admiring their latest handiwork, small pieces of lumber strewn around their feet. Ginny startled them when she walked in. "Pretty swish," her father said. Her mother just smiled; Ginny knew she'd never liked Cassie's bikini.

Ginny peeked behind the refrigerator, where an old servant's stair had been taken out long ago. It had always seemed odd that there'd been a second staircase in a house that had so little room for a main stair. Even stranger was the idea that there would be maids in such a small house. She'd enjoyed musing about this sneaky staircase and the leftover door-to-nowhere behind Cassie's bed that once had connected her bedroom to the kitchen. Now, her parents had finally claimed this leftover space, and she was impressed by how efficiently they'd made use of it, outfitting it with shelves of varying depths, an area for the vacuum cleaner, and a large masonite pegboard to hold all of the Revere Ware, in order of size.

"Wow!" Ginny turned to see her parents' proud grins. "This gives me an idea." She stepped to the narrow closet where the old water heater stood. "Why don't you clear this out and make it a storage area, too?" she said, opening the closet. "I mean, since there's a new water heater in the cellar, and we don't need this one."

Hands on their hips, her parents stood staring at the water heater closet. Ginny turned and left the kitchen quickly; she'd been enjoying the time to herself and didn't want to be drawn into the Project. Also, Tuesday was her usual day to vacuum, and she hoped they'd forget with all the confusion.

In her room, she grabbed a towel and headed down the hill to the cove with a *National Geographic*. She spread the towel on the grass and stretched out to wait for Sandy, inhaling the smell of fermenting crab apples and grass she'd mowed yesterday. She was transported to the Mayan ruins of the Yucatan until the buzz of lawnmowers and sporadic hammering from the kitchen brought her home again. She sat up to brush an ant off her thigh and spotted Kit, who was messing with a few lobster traps on the shore in front of his house. She wondered if he'd seen her. Just in case he hadn't, she stood and walked out onto the dock where she swished her toe in the water. She lingered, displaying her bikini-clad self for a few drawn-out moments before sitting down. Disappointingly, Kit didn't appear to notice. Until recently, their two-year age difference hadn't gotten in the way of their friendship, but Kit was in high school now, and he'd become mysterious—deep-voiced and tall, his curly blonde hair long and pulled into a ponytail—as if he were someone else altogether. Ginny was very curious about this someone else who'd sprung from her sweet boy companion.

"Where'd you get the bikini?" Sandy broadcasted from the top of the hill. She was wearing a bright pink tank suit, and her thick red hair lay against the ample breasts that were the talk of the boys in their class.

Ginny watched Kit look up from what he was doing and glance over at her. Self-conscious, she plunged off the dock. Sandy ran down the hill and jumped in after her.

"It's freezing!"

"It's not!"

"You lie like a rug!"

They effervesced with wild, breathless giggling brought on by the bracing water, enough silliness to drown them both. Ginny and Sandy had a two-person club and the center of the cove, where they treaded water, was their clubhouse.

"Robert G.!"

"*Hahahaha!* You're crazy! Davey Chick?"

"Rhymes with . . . *Hahaha!*"

Sandy's head pivoted. "Oooh, look!" she said.

"Shhhh . . . I know. But he pretty much ignores me. Watch. He knows it's us out here, but he won't even wave. Stop looking at him! Turn sideways!"

The girls turned to face each other, trying not to giggle. Ginny hoped that Kit would prove her wrong.

The motor on Kit's boat started up, and Ginny turned to look, but Kit didn't wave as he swung the boat around and headed out of the cove. A moment later, they smelled the cigarette he was smoking.

"I told you," Ginny said.

"My sister says he smokes pot."

"Probably everyone does in high school."

Sandy howled. "You *can't* go to boarding school and leave me here alone!"

At that very moment, submerged to her chin, feet pumping, sun hot on her cheeks, at this very place, where the cove and Sandy's million freckles were the center of the universe, Ginny's heart, too, felt torn. "Don't worry! Nothing will change," she promised. But everything *would*, she knew, and on most days, she couldn't wait.

Two days later at lunchtime, Ginny sat on the back porch with her family, devouring a BLT. Cassie dramatically plucked and discarded first the bacon and then the bread from her sandwich as their mother outlined the plan for the afternoon that would include Ginny and Cassie. The conversion of the old water heater closet was nearly finished. The space was a mere eighteen inches wide but Ginny's mother had transformed it into a fine-tuned storage compartment, managing to tweak every square inch to the exact specifications of each furnishing intended for the space. There was a counter-height surface that would hold all of the everyday silverware; below it a liquor cabinet equipped to meet every possible cocktail request and above, a tray cabinet. Ron had painted the shelves that would line the cabinets, and they lay drying on the back porch.

After lunch, Ginny and Cassie worked on their assignment, placing hooks inside the cabinets for cups and cooking implements. Aware of their exacting taskmaster, they carefully measured the location of each screw before putting it in place. By the time they were finished, the shelves were dry, and their father wriggled them into place. "Voilà!" he beamed when the last one was in. The day had grown more humid, and beads of sweat dotted his bald head.

Ginny and Cassie helped move all the dishes from the darkroom onto the kitchen table. Later, after a quick dinner on the porch, they would load them into the refurbished cupboards. Surveying the stacks of plates and bowls, Gina was doubtful that they would fit.

"Great job, girls and boy! We'll go get ice cream cones at The Mrs. And Me to celebrate after dinner!" her mother announced.

Ginny had never seen her mother so happy in the house. Nights since the Project began had been peaceful, not a single middle-of-the-night alarm, no mention of Lily House. When her mother's hands were busy, not with laundry or cooking or cleaning, but with creating something new and useful, the sun seemed to smile more brightly upon their house.

Ginny basked in that light now but then checked herself; a storm could blow in any time with no warning.

Finished with their job in the kitchen, Ginny and Cassie lay in the hammock, Ginny's head at the apple tree end, Cassie's at the birch tree end. Cassie was reading *Anna Karenina*.

"It's really good," she said, when Ginny asked. She ran her thumb over the impressive chunk of pages she'd read. "And the women's names in it are beautiful—not like 'Cassie,' more exotic. Like, instead of 'Ginny,' which sounds like a doll, you could be 'Gina.' Yeah, 'Gina'—it sounds so romantic."

Ginny loved the name immediately. She scrutinized her knees, wondering whether the name "Gina" could sweep her away from ugly scars, closer to the beautiful women in books, and to Cassie, who'd given the name to her.

Tires crackled on the driveway. Ginny rolled over just enough to fix one eye on the Wentworths' woody coming up the hill.

"Mom!" she yelled.

There came a muffled "Oh, God!" from the house.

Like many of her parents' friends, the Wentworths were "summer people" who escaped the cities and suburbs of Massachusetts and points south to their rambling shingled house near the beach in Whit's Point. When summer people came into town to get groceries at Tobey's, they'd stop by the Gilberts' for a glass of iced tea or a cocktail, or both, depending on how long they stayed.

The Wentworths parked behind the house, and Ginny ran inside to put Pepe, who'd spent her days lately perched out of the fray on the living room window molding, back in her cage. Winkie Wentworth was phobic about birds. She was also a gossip, her mother always said, a lover of country clubs, alligator shirts, and all that other summer-people stuff Eleanor called "Joe College," making it a mystery to Ginny why they were friends. Ginny had just closed Pepe's cage when Winkie pressed her nose against the screen door and "Yoo-hooed."

"Come in! Come in!" Ginny's mother crowed, sweeping the Wentworths into the living room as if she'd been hoping all day they'd drop by. There were flecks of putty in her hair, and her denim wrap-around skirt was askew. "Ginny . . . " she tossed over her shoulder. On cue, Ginny slid into the living room as her mother disappeared into the kitchen to rustle up some hors d'oeuvres.

Winkie wore a crisp sleeveless blouse, and when she hugged Ginny with her loose, brown arms, she squeezed out fumes of deodorant and the wine she'd had for lunch, probably at the tennis club. Her hard wicker handbag dug into Ginny's back.

Lyman Wentworth patted Ginny's head, crinkled his bumpy red face into a warm smile and said "Wow! Thirteen!" in a way that made Ginny think of her breasts.

She arranged a smile for the Wentworth kids. She'd known them—Betsy, seventeen, Nate, twelve, and Chris, ten—forever; every summer they'd used up whole cans of *OFF!* playing sardines after dinner. But in recent years, Betsy and Cassie had ditched Ginny and the boys—yup, there Cassie was already, beckoning Betsy upstairs to begin their evening of exclusivity.

But Ginny had news: this year, she was going to park herself in the living room with the adults. The boys saw her sit down on the floor in the corner and headed back outside.

Ron sauntered in from the kitchen. "Well hell-o! Look what the cat dragged in!" He clapped his hands. "What can I wet your whistle with?"

"The usual," Lyman answered, and her father said, "Aye-aye Captain!" All the men in town who sailed were "captains," even though in the Gilbert family, Eleanor had always been the captain. *Casa senza donna, barca senza timone.* A house without a woman, a boat without a rudder.

Lyman and Winkie followed Ron into the kitchen. "Hey, hey— you two have been getting your hands dirty!" Lyman exclaimed. "Wow! Did you get that landlord of yours—Mr. Pickle—to pay for the work?"

"Nope," her father said. "But we finally got a check from the Bucklins for Mary's wedding. Eleanor marched right up their front steps and— "

"Winkie, take a *look!*" her mother broke in. "We even fit the g.d. vaccuum cleaner in. And *this* part was Ginny's brilliant idea!"

When the adults had regrouped in the living room, Winkie said, "What a *sh-hame* the landlord won't pay for French doors in here. I've always thought this room needed French doors and a fireplace. Though the room *is* a little small for a fireplace, I suppose . . . Speaking of which, I dropped in on Annie and Lester yesterday. Honestly, that little place is an unholy mess! Stuff all over the place, dishes in the sink. I think those boys spend too much time alone. I do love Annie, but wouldn't you think she'd take a break from her violin long enough to raise her kids?"

"She better not!" Ginny's mother said. "She's the only one of us doing anything worthwhile! She's my hero!"

Everyone took a sip of their drinks. Winkie said, "I ran into Sid at Tobey's yesterday. He's got one more year at NYU. I asked him if he was staying at Lily House, and he laughed like it was a joke and said he was staying with that awful friend of his—what's his name? Anyway, boy, does Sid look like his father, Bill. Are the Holloways still supporting him?"

Ginny was all ears. So it was true, what Sid had snarled the night Fran died about Bill Holloway being his father and people lying to him. Why *had* everyone lied to him? The subject had appeared to be so explosive that Ginny hadn't dared to ask her mother. Winkie's appetite for gossip, she realized, might be her best shot at learning more. She slumped and looked at the floor, trying to make herself smaller.

"Oh, no, certainly not," her mother said. "The Holloways cut Sid off when he turned twenty-one. That was the deal. But what do I know? I don't have anything to do with the Holloways *or* Sid."

It was the first mean-sounding thing Ginny had heard her mother say in days; it was Winkie's fault, and now her mother threw a startled look at Ginny, as if just realizing she was in the room. "Gin," she said, "how about getting out the Parcheesi for the boys? They loved playing it when they were here last year."

Ginny stood. "They'd love that, dear," Winkie said, giving her the once over. "You're so nice and slim. *Betsy's* really got to lose some weight. She's a slug on the tennis court. So will you be going to

Andrews like Cassie?"

Ginny remembered: her mother didn't disapprove of everything about summer people; Winkie was the reason her mother knew about boarding school. "I hope so," she told Winkie. She slid into the hall and sat down on the stairs so she could keep eavesdropping.

"What a tragedy," Winkie said. "Sid, I mean. And Fran. Why was she so terribly depressed, do you think? Was it losing Bill?"

"Bill?" Eleanor said much too loudly. "Oh, no, Bill and Fran hardly . . ."

She paused. It was curious, Ginny thought, how her mother didn't seem to approve of her much-admired "old friend Bill Hollo-way" when his name was linked with Fran's.

"Fran was depressed before Bill," Eleanor continued. "She just never *did* anything. She had no interests, except bridge. She was always so self-centered—just imagine doing something so terrible like that to your family and friends."

Ginny was scandalized that her mother would be as vicious about Fran when she was dead as she'd been when she was alive. No one had mentioned Fran's suicide in the three years since it had happened, and Ginny was glad. She didn't want to know how Fran had done it because she knew for the rest of her life she'd hold the ghastly image in her mind. But she'd learned something very important since Fran's suicide: her mother had made it clear, despite her recurring howl that she wished she were dead, that someone of her moral character would never kill herself.

"What was the last straw, do you think?" Libby asked. "Does anyone know what happened?"

"Now Winkie, come on," Lyman said.

"No, no," her mother said. "Well, of course Fran was probably in an uproar about what she was going to do once the Holloways stopped giving her and Sid handouts, and she announced to Sid that day that

Bill was his father. Ron, *there*! A mosquito on the wall behind you!"

Ginny heard the smack of a magazine against the wall. That was it then; the topic was dead. Ginny wondered: how could her mother pretend that the things she'd said to Fran that night had had nothing to do with her suicide? The hatefulness that day at Lily House had felt lethal and still sat like a stone in the pit of her stomach.

"Well, your kitchen is going to be just great," Lyman said.

Winkie said, "But all the work you're putting into this house. Aren't you deathly afraid Hickle will kick you out one of these days? Why haven't you moved into Lily House? It's *your* house—you could be living there, instead of here, improving someone *else's* property."

Ginny wished Winkie would just shut up.

"Uh-unh. Nope," her mother said. "I'll never live at Lily House."

"You haven't heard?" Her father chuckled. "Winkie, you mean to tell me you've been in town for twenty-four hours, and you haven't *heard*?"

A short silence. "We sold it," her mother said. "To the New England Historical Society."

Winkie gasped. "You *did*? Why on earth? What about Sid?"

"What *about* Sid?" her mother said. "The house belonged to me. He hasn't spoken to me in years. Why should he get a free vacation house in Maine?"

"You're so right, Ellie," Winkie said. "Everyone says he's a mess anyway—a big drinker. At Tobey's he looked terrible. Have you heard the rumor that he might be a little, you know—"

"Let's not talk about Sid," her mother said. "Fran just ruined him."

"Lily House was costing us an arm and a leg to keep up," her father said. "You should have seen—"

"But why on earth would you sell it to the historical people?" Winkie interrupted. "You couldn't have gotten a very good deal from them. Pickering House went for—"

"Winkie, do you need a refill?" Lyman cut in.

"Stay for dinner!" her mother said, and Ginny's spirits sank even lower. "We'll get some lobbies—it's your first summer weekend here!"

Nate and Chris appeared at the screen door laughing and stepped inside, smelling of grass. "Wanna play Parcheesi?" Ginny asked, leading the boys into the piano room.

Soon, her father was dispatched to fetch lobsters and corn on the cob. "Chickens, Ron, not the one-and-a-quarter pounders," her mother yelled as he went out the door.

Ginny pulled the Parcheesi box from the cabinet and stretched out on her stomach while Nate and Chris set up the game on the floor. After an argument, they finally settled on playing by rules they'd invented. Joni Mitchell's "Blue" poured through the floor of Cassie's room, its mournful tones clashing with the adults' escalating merriment in the living room. Ginny grew crankier by the minute; so often, it seemed, she was merely a witness in this house, on the edge of everyone else's game, trying to understand the rules, trying to understand.

Chris's brown eyes fixed on Ginny. "By the way," he said, "when you lie like that, I can see down your shirt. All . . . the . . . way."

Ginny leapt up, dizzy from the blood leaving her head. Pepe, who had been relocated to the piano room because of the remodel, was making anxious triangles in her cage, hopping from perch to swing to other perch, then back to the first perch, as if in commiseration. Ginny reached out and opened her cage door.

Pepe hopped to the opening and paused before going airborne, beelining for the living room.

"Oh, my God!" Winkie shrieked. "Someone do something about that *bird*!"

Ginny filled with regret as Pepe fluttered back into the piano room, grazing the doorjamb before perching on the window molding. The finch's little black-and-white body throbbed. Ginny shooed her off the molding in the direction of her cage, but she flew straight through the living room. Ginny followed her into the kitchen where she careened recklessly around the room, her radar failing her.

In the living room, everyone was trying to calm down Winkie. Lyman said, "Honey, for Pete's sake, let's go outside if you're going to carry on."

The crowd moved out of the living room to the front yard, letting the screen door bang behind them and sending Pepe into another panic. She circled the kitchen and attempted to land on the cage's hanger, but it was at an awkward angle for her feet. Finally, she settled on the picture molding above the kitchen table. Ginny felt frantic herself now. With one foot on the chair and the other on the table, she was able to move very slowly toward Pepe and gather her in her cupped hands. She felt the relief of a mission accomplished but then, just as suddenly, felt her footing fumble. Her weight came down on the table and a thunderous crash was loosed on the kitchen. A moment after the whole room had seemed to turn sideways, Pepe was still safe within her hands, and Ginny was staring incredulously at the ruin: slices of china in a heap on the floor—red, blue, white, and gold, delicate Chinese scenes—like a heap of fanciful tortilla chips.

She surveyed the table: only half the dishes were still on it. The screen door slammed, her heart pounded, her knees shook. For a moment she wished she could make herself faint like that strange sixth- grader at school. The crash had attracted the kids, and they gathered, gaping, outside the kitchen door. They parted to let Eleanor through. The room filled with steam from boiling pots awaiting lobsters and corn; Pepe's breast pulsed against Ginny's palm as she concentrated hard on the space between her and her mother and the broken dishes.

"Ginny, honey, are you okay?" her mother said. "Better get Pepe back in her cage." She put her hand on Ginny's back, and Ginny felt it reaching through to hold her heart. When she looked at her mother, there was no sign of the mask she wore to be friendly to people like Winkie whom she didn't like or the mask she wore to hide terrible secrets or shout horrible things. Ginny saw a face full of compassion—the one she remembered above her when she lay winded below the tree she'd fallen from, the one after the violin recital at which she'd blanked on her music. *This* was her mother's real face. Wasn't it?

As her mother leaned over and began picking up the pieces, she said, "It happens!"

In those two words, Ginny again felt the power of her mother's unpredictability; her expressions of love could be as blindsiding as her dark fury.

The room became soft again. Ginny slumped into it like a sigh and let go of her tears. She carried Pepe back to her cage, and the kids dispersed. While Winkie and Lyman were still outside, Ginny and her mother worked quickly to clean up the mess.

Soon both families were on the lawn twisting the limbs off lobsters and chomping down on Farmer Burnes's first summer corn. Their chins glistened with butter, and their teeth turned purple from the tiny sweet blueberries they'd waited for all year.

"Girls," Winkie said, holding a muffin aloft and grinning at Ginny and Cassie, "your mother is the *best*."

As they feasted, so did the mosquitoes. When the light grew dim, Ginny, Cassie, Betsy, Chris, and Nate huddled in the lilacs for what would be their last game of sardines.

Ginny slept late the next morning. In the kitchen she found her mother and father on their hands and knees, laying the new black-and- white linoleum in the closet—the last piece of the Project.

She gazed around the room, amazed by its shipshape fullness. With everything tucked away, it was serene and timeless, like a painting: glass lamps and small portraits on the muted tan walls, friendly antique pine furniture, a ceramic bowl of peaches and tomatoes, lilies blooming in pots where geraniums would winter later. But below its pretty surface was a complex machine, replete with cheap hardware that allowed for perfect efficiency. Doors jangled with spatulas, strainers, and bottle openers; there were racks and fasteners jerry-rigged from string and rubber bands to hold boxes, cans, the ironing board, and the vacuum cleaner attachments.

The kitchen was her mother's masterpiece! She had tamed it, squeezed out every ounce of its potential, and most important, regardless of what their lease said, she had made it *hers*.

The new kitchen seemed to refresh the whole house and Ginny's outlook, too. The change, she decided, warranted a new name—*Gina*—that she would begin calling herself this very day and that would propel her more swiftly forward, away.

The structure of life I have described in buildings—the structure which I believe to be objective—is deeply and inextricably connected with the human person, and with the innermost nature of human feeling.

Christopher Alexander, *The Nature of Order*

Chapter 9

On Friday, her second morning in Whit's Point, Gina awoke cranky, hot and sticky, filled with an ingrained imperative to be near the water.

Without stopping to see if Annie and Lester were around, she left Lily House and wandered down the lane behind Tobey's to the town dock, relishing the incremental change in the air coming off the water. She made her way along the wide, splintery dock past men dangling fishing lines and a group of shirtless adolescent boys, their eyes glazed with the boredom of small-town summer. Two boats were secured to the main float at the end of the dock; she was immediately drawn to the one with the square white mast, and, as she came closer, the familiar putty-colored deck and the hull's elegant shape. Could it be her family's old Hinckley, the sloop her parents had sold six years ago?

Intrigued, she took the ramp down to the float for a closer look; when she saw the tell-tale her mother had tied to the starboard stay, she had her answer. A head popped out of the companionway.

"Only a Californian," the man called, "would be wearin' sunglasses at the dock at eight in the morning!"

Gina pulled off her sunglasses and squinted. It was Kit.

"Just teasin' ya, Gina Gilbert!" he laughed. "Good to see you back!"

"Hi!" She stood amazed, looking over the twenty-eight foot sloop she'd sailed for many years with her family.

Kit stood on deck and reached out his hand to her. "Welcome aboard!"

"Do you remember how I lusted after this boat?" he asked when she was settled in the cockpit. "I saw her advertised two years ago and bought her from the Rhode Island guy who bought it from your parents. Such a classic. Your parents took me out on her maybe ten years ago. Your mom really knew how to handle her. How'd your parents manage to have a yacht, anyhow?"

Gina smiled and shrugged, even though she remembered the acquisition of the *yacht* well. It had arrived just after her fourteenth birthday with as much excitement as a new baby.

She walked forward, scanning the boat-filled harbor. It was so unchanged it seemed impossible that twenty-eight years had passed since she and Kit were on the water together. Yet, she also felt how far she'd traveled from here. Did Kit, too, feel this lurch of time and distance? She hadn't read it in his casual manner. Maybe time was different when you lived in one place all your life; like a word seen always in context, you felt unalterable and known.

As Kit coiled a line, Gina stole glances. He'd grown more handsome with age; his face had filled out to a rugged squareness. She admired the sinewy arms that, as a girl, had rescued her on more than one occasion.

She walked back to the cockpit and leaned over the transom to see what name Kit had chosen for the boat. She was surprised to see he'd kept it *Homeward*.

"So what've you been up to in life?" Kit asked, sinking onto the seat beside her. "I heard you went and became an Ivy Leaguer since I saw you last, huh?"

His teasing put her at ease. "I'm still me," she said, "Even so, they granted me a master's degree."

Kit laughed. "I remember your father throwin' his hands in the air. 'Can you believe it? Our daughter at a place like that!'"

Gina smiled. It was true; her parents had been proud. But they often let their daughters know they felt left behind by them. What they never knew was how often Gina herself had felt like an outsider in her different milieus—too hayseed in some, too privileged in others, like here at the town dock.

"What sort of stuff do you design out in California?" Kit asked. When she told him, he laughed. "Houses! They're trouble!" he said.

He shook his head, and Gina sensed he had a story he was eager to tell. "How so?" she asked.

"I tried buildin' a house with the woman I'd been with for a few years, Janice, out on Bailey's Island Road," he said. "She worked with Phelps and Sons—you know that company?" Gina shook her head no. "Well, anyhow, me and Janice liked everything the same—you know: the water, boats, buildin'. We were buildin' the house for ourselves, and like, we thought since we'd built a boat or two together, a house would be the same kinda deal."

"And?"

"Not even close. Houses have those things called foundations, ya know? Once that concrete's poured into the ground, people kinda freak out. But boats . . . "

"Boats are like the anti-house. They're all about impermanence and escape."

Kit bounced his eyebrows up and down at her. "To you, professor, maybe. Not to me—I'm not an escaper type. Anyways, since you're an architect, I think you'll appreciate this story. So, one day Janice and I are layin' floor joists, and out of the blue she says, 'What if this house turns out to be too small?' 'For what?' I asked, and she wouldn't answer. So I said, 'If it's too small, we'll sell it. We don't have to love the house for the rest of our lives just because we built it.' She got all mad. 'How can you say that?' she said. She didn't speak to me for the rest of the day."

Kit stood and went forward to adjust a fender.

When he sat down again, Gina said, "Maybe Janice wasn't talking about the house. Maybe she was talking about having a family?" She assumed she was observing the obvious.

Kit drew in his chin. "Maybe. She was always thinkin' ahead, or about something more. It's my mantra to take one day at a time. Janice knew that. She left before we'd even framed the roof."

Even as a kid, Kit had seemed wise, Gina remembered. Now though, she felt drawn into something more deeply than she wanted to be.

"Janice is already with someone else," Kit said.

"How about you?"

Kit gazed out to sea. "I kind of like being on my own, " he said, turning back to her. "I finished the house—it's awesome."

"You live there?"

"Nope! I live right here, seven months of the year. You're sittin' in my livin' room."

Gina gazed around at the waterlogged boat cushions that lined the varnished cockpit, the paint peeling around the engine gear and fathometer. She thought of the hours spent here with her family, semi-reclined, toes flirting with the cold brass winch, sometimes pleasantly dazed, often half-listening, and other times bored by the protracted exposure to water, sky, sun.

Kit handed her a bottle of Orangina and opened one for himself. As he raised it to his lips, she noticed half his pinky finger was missing.

"Wasn't it hard to give up the house after working so hard on it?" she asked.

"Nah. I wasn't attached. Do you get attached to the houses you design?"

"Not usually. But I'm only with them once a week during construction, not day after day."

"I love buildin', but it's just a job. I sold the house, bought *Homeward,* and nevah looked back."

Gina didn't quite believe him; this boat—Kit's world—seemed tiny. "What's it been like, living in Whit's Point all your life?"

"Hmm. Well . . . it's not like I can compare it to anything else. It's home." He spread his arms as if he meant the whole harbor, the islands, the sea beyond. "Everything I love is here. Why would I live anywhere else?"

It was what her mother and father had always said about Whit's Point. Words she wished *she* could say.

"But I mean . . . a person can feel at home anywhere, right?" Kit said, and Gina thought: he's reassuring me, as always. "Home isn't necessarily just the place you grew up, or the place you live now—it's more like . . . any place that stays alive inside you no matter where you are."

"I guess that's true," Gina said, though right now this notion made her feel all the more conflicted.

"So who ended up with your folks' place, anyway? I know those Yankee people were after it. It would be a crime if someone put up a McMansion there. You checkin' into that? That why you're here?"

"No." Gina felt her defenses rising. "Sid Banton bought the house. There's nothing I can do about whatever he wants to do. It wasn't even our house to begin with." She paused, reaching for things to say. "I'm designing, or trying to design, a house for my family north of San Francisco."

Kit's eyes shifted to the horizon. "Ca-li-fornia," he said, in a way that reminded her of how she—and everyone else in Maine, as far as she could tell—had envisioned the golden state they'd never seen: a playground of endless sun-drenched beaches, plastic people in expensive, spotless cars. "California," Kit said again, as if seeing a mirage. "It *can't* be more beautiful than here!"

Gina smiled. "It's just different," she said, realizing how far from California she felt now. She shifted her gaze to the west, where billowy white and gray clouds were gathering in the hazy sky. Often during a heat wave, they'd sit there all day like that, threatening.

"So how do you feel about Sid owning your place?" Kit asked. "I saw him at the hardware store last week. Haven't seen him in maybe ten years. Barely recognized him. You in touch with him?"

Gina felt her body tighten. "No. Have you seen him in the last couple of days?" she said, trying to sound casual.

"Naw. Boy, he's burned some bridges. Made enough money in New York to buy and sell a few different houses 'round town." He laughed. "I don't know him, but people have always said he's a kinda wheeler-dealer with a drinkin' problem."

This, Gina realized, was why she lived in a big city and not a small town. "So, do people in Whit's Point talk about how messed up the Bantons were?"

Kit smiled. "Relax. First of all, there's nothing special about the Bantons' craziness. Every family's nuts, right? Besides, they don't have to talk to *me* about the Bantons. I was there. Remember?"

Remember was exactly what Gina didn't want to do. But remember she did: Kit *was* there, always. He'd been fun and reliable as a playmate and had grown up to be a kind young man with a crush on her. Gina shrank inwardly, recalling how, when she was seventeen, she'd abruptly ended their friendship.

"Gosh, didn't mean to bum ya out," Kit said, as if reading her thoughts. "All that seems like a long time ago to me. I thought it would to you, too. Hey! Doug! How ya doin'?" Kit smiled and waved to a man in rubber boots coming down the ramp. Turning back to Gina, he said, "Your mom wasn't so bad. I mean, she was always pretty snobby about me and my family when I was a kid. But as soon as she got *Homeward* and started runnin' into me at the dock, we totally bonded. Maybe she shoulda lived on a boat. She was a water person, like me. I think she'd be really happy to know you and I are sittin' here together now."

"Yes," Gina agreed, remembering how her mother had lit up when they were out on the water. "She would be."

Gina was exhausted. She and Kit had been navigating the gaps, calibrating the reach of their conversation—pulling back, casting out, retreating, like yo-yos. She needed to go. She stood to scan the harbor, a wash of blues, grays, and greens, flecked with gulls. It was an uncomplicated, soothing scene, but she was rattled.

Kit took a slug from his drink and stood. "Before you leave, go below and check it out!"

Reluctant but curious, Gina climbed through the companion-way into the cabin, taking in its familiar smell—a mingling of bilge water, wet wood, and canvas. The seat cushions where her family had been rocked to sleep at night were still covered with the blue denim her mother had sewn; two toothbrushes sat in the metal holder her mother had fastened to the galley wall. Gina's fondest memories of family life were from summer cruises down-east on *Homeward*, her mother at the tiller navigating swells with a broad smile, at night, the four of them snug in the cabin.

Kit climbed down behind her just as the wake of a motorboat hit

Homeward. The boat rocked and Gina lurched sideways, nearly losing her balance. She felt Kit's hands take a firm hold on her waist. "Whoa, where're your sea legs?" He laughed and, when the rocking stopped, pulled his hands away.

Gina turned. Her eyes met Kit's, slate-gray with an intensity mitigated by the fine smile lines that fanned from their corners. A familiar sense of him—his gentle touch and salty smell, his protectiveness—flooded her, and she thought of all the small, private spaces, like this one, that she and Kit had shared as kids. Snow caves, rowboats, forts, and beds when they were young enough for sleepovers—they'd huddled to commiserate about the bruises of their complicated childhoods. How could she have known then how rare such resonance and loyal companionship were? Standing with Kit in the cabin, she felt closer than she ever had to the parts of her past that had seemed safe and good.

All this pumped through her mind in the few seconds it took for her to become flustered and say, "It's so cool that you live here." She felt lightheaded, dumb.

Kit smiled, leaned toward her, and reached out his hand. She experienced a visceral memory of pulling away from him, but now she didn't recognize the part of herself that had once needed to and, in fact, was worried about the part that might not want to. But Kit's hand continued to reach beyond her to take hold of something on the shelf.

"One of your father's logbooks," he said, handing it to her. "I guess I've been saving it for you."

Gina looked down at the small black notebook labeled "1977–1979" with her father's perfect printing. "Thank you," she said, hoping he hadn't read the range of emotion that had hijacked her.

Kit turned and she followed him back on deck. "So if you're not lookin' into the house, what're you up to here?" he asked.

A soft breeze touched Gina's cheek. "I'm . . . it's hard to . . . " she fumbled. "I've been feeling out of sorts . . . The thing is, if I can just make this house in California happen, I'll feel better. At the same time, I don't think I can make the house happen until I feel better. And I still can't let go of the old house here."

Kit shook his head and chuckled. "Still tortured! You haven't changed a bit. I mean have you had some untortured years since I saw you last?"

Kit's words jabbed. But he couldn't know just how tortured she'd been feeling recently, and she saw in his eyes that his remark had more to do with the hurt she'd inflicted on him years ago.

Was there a point in addressing her regrets now? She thought of her missed opportunity with Annie yesterday. "I was really confused back then," she said. "I had a lot going on and . . . You were always so kind." She felt her cheeks flush. Her words hardly seemed adequate, but they were something, at least.

When Kit smiled, a shyness softening his lined face, she felt rewarded. "Well, we were both lonely, huh?" he said, as if addressing her implied apology. "Our parents believed us kids were immune to their crap. Eleanor really got to you, and when my dad left my mom, it was just the beginning of trouble for me." He stood. "Anyway, about the house—you'll figure it out, right? That's why you've come out here. And then you'll feel better!"

An outboard motor started up at the float, enveloping them in a cloud of gasoline fumes. Gina looked at her watch. "Yes. I just need to get down to it!"

She put out her hand, but Kit surprised her with a hug. "Hey— come look for me next time you're at the dock," he said. "Oof! You're stiff as a two-by-four. I can tell you're needin' a good row!"

The feeling of Kit's arms around her awakened a slumbering sadness that threatened to draw her too deeply into her younger self. She pulled back from their embrace. "Yes. I think I do need a row!"

Kit pointed behind her at a float crowded with skiffs and inflatable rubber dinghys. "You can take out my boat, even if I'm not around," he said. "It's the shell secured with a red line over there. The oars are in the clubhouse with my name on them."

"Thanks a lot," she said, smiling. "That would be really great."

But in a quick couple of days, she thought with some relief, she'd be gone.

The Plan is the generator. Without the plan, you have lack of order, and willfulness. The Plan holds in itself the essence of sensation.
                          Le Corbusier, *Towards a New Architecture*

Chapter 10

As she walked up the ramp and down the dock, Gina pulsed with all that Kit had stirred up. Crossing the street in front of Tobey's, she forgot to look and had to make a dash for the sidewalk to avoid a car.

By the time she reached Lily House, she understood that Kit was right: she hadn't yet found what she'd come to Whit's Point for and had to return to the old house. She marched down Pickering Road and stood again in the front yard.

Nothing had changed since yesterday, not the stifling heat that by now had burned the blue out of the sky, nor the white husk of a house, nothing except the cove, which held an hour's less water than it had at the same time yesterday. From the yard, she sized up the house, trying to imagine what she would do to it if it were her architectural project. But no matter how she pushed and pulled its walls in her mind, appending the old house with new rooms or windows, a coherent vision of an improved house didn't come to her. It was what it was—unmalleable, complete. And yet it left her feeling incomplete.

The house looked back at her, as confounding and impenetrable as her mother. But it was a *house*—wood, glass, lines and angles—

and she was an architect; she had the tools to get inside and *know* this entity.

All at once it struck her: she would make drawings of the house. Usually, drawings marked a beginning of something new. She'd ask her client, "What do you want?" and turn the answer into a plan, the plan into a house. Now, she would work backward—more like an archaeologist than an architect—and with her drawings deconstruct the house wall by wall in hopes of discovering what she wanted from it.

Propelled by this mission, she mostly ran the quarter-mile to and from Annie and Lester's to fetch paper, clipboard, her tape measure and camera. When she got back to the house, she had to sit under the birch tree to catch her breath and cool off.

On the pad of paper, she sketched the footprint of the house on which she would put her exterior measurements. She stood and walked the house's perimeter, hooking the measuring tape on each corner and dragging it along the wall. She placed each ground-floor window on the plan, noting its distance from the ends of the wall. Then she added the front and back doors, the porches and steps leading from them, and the shed off the kitchen.

As she measured, she felt drawn to the house in a new way, not unlike what she'd felt with Kit in *Homeward*'s cabin: an appreciation that came from not only a shared history but also a more focused and seasoned perspective.

She finished the plan of the exterior walls and collapsed under the tree again to gaze at what she'd drawn. For every wiggly line that represented a wall of the house, there were four more parallel to it that merely served the purpose of noting dimensions. There was no hierarchy in this kind of sketch, just a mess of lines and numbers that were legible mostly only to the measurer. Yet there was strict, underlying precision in the apparent disarray, which later would translate into a plan that documented the house to within a quarter of an inch. This preliminary work had always suited Gina: the part of her that liked to scrawl with pen and paper, the part of her that wanted to create order by revealing a house's factual image. A house's history could be uncovered in these lines, and its future would rest on their foundation. Now, she experienced something different as she recorded this house: the lines and numbers were alive on the paper, a breathing reality that revived her family's past.

The front door was still unlocked. She glanced down the driveway before pushing it open. Willing herself through the house's stuffy rooms, she quickly sketched the floor plan: living room, kitchen, piano room, and darkroom, grouped around the steep stair. Then she went upstairs, where the walls of the four bedrooms aligned with those below. "We're all on top of each other!" her mother often complained, and indeed they were; the "foursquare" house, popular everywhere in America at the turn of the century, defined family life with its compact, centralized plan. It was the floor plan of choice for Gina's clients who strove for togetherness; her wealthier clients, however, chose houses with wings where they could flee from their children and their caregivers, their housekeepers, and cooks.

Now, Gina set out to assign dimensions to her lines, at times on her hands and knees reaching inside closets with her measuring tape, once feeling a splinter pierce her palm. It was an intimate exercise, and although she went about it with a mechanical efficiency, emotion welled up in her; she was as close as she could be to the wood bones and plaster skin of the organism that had been her family. She became acutely aware of how her mother saturated every inch of the house, imagining her poking the nose of the vacuum cleaner under beds and into closets, mopping the kitchen floor, brushing paint on the old radiators. Gina would never again touch her mother, and the darker corners of her mother's mind would remain a mystery. But with her tools, as Gina probed and recorded every bump and recess that her mother had inhabited, she felt somehow closer to her.

Finished measuring, she walked through the rooms of the house one last time, letting her eyes rest idly on their barren landscape. There were footprints left by objects that had defined each room: the faded rectangle where a tiny Dutch painting of a fishing boat had hung, the hook for her father's hat, the dent left by the living room doorknob where it had repeatedly punched the wall, the ghosts of rugs where the floor had been painted around them. In the kitchen, two holes marked where the birdcage had hung next to the window; cup and utensil hooks still remained in the kitchen cabinets. There were no architectural details in these rooms, only the simplest flat baseboards, window and door trim. Probably only one other person had drawn this house—its builder. Who had he been? she wondered. Perhaps it was the fate of a rental to never be fully known.

As she closed the front door, she heard the stirrings of the trapped bird from the attic and scolded herself for not remembering to bring Annie and Lester's ladder.

She returned to Lily House wilted, blisters from her flip-flops burning between her toes. Dirt clung to her damp skin, and her palm throbbed from the splinter, long and lodged deep. A note sat on the island in the kitchen.

Gina, I'm heading to a symphony conference in Portland and won't be home till after dinner. Lester's helping a friend set up his computer, then going to a book sale at the church. He said he'd be back before one so if he's not, call the Coast Guard! Leftover lasagna in the fridge for you 2 tonight. A.

Gina looked at the clock: twelve forty-five. Why would Annie worry about Lester? He seemed very capable.

She changed out of her filthy clothes, washed her hands and face, and removed the splinter. On her phone, she saw that Paul had called without leaving a message. She left him a perfunctory voicemail saying all was well, then went into the sunroom. The drawing she'd faxed to Allison Brink was waiting for her in the fax machine with Allison's notes of approval, questions about details, and a shy-looking arrow pointing to the space between the kitchen island and dining room. Here, Allison had drawn a dashed line in the exact place where Gina had taken out the wall.

She'd added a note:

I love having this wall gone, but could we design a really neat move-able screen here, so that when I entertain, I can have privacy from the housekeeper and kids in the kitchen? Also, the kids' father says he really wants to build the playhouse before summer's over—any progress on that?

Cranky, Gina tapped out an email to Allison on her phone:

Allison, You named this your "great room" not your "sometimes a great room." You're lonely and longing for your children's company—why predict that you'll want to shut them out once you've let them in?

She quickly deleted it and wrote:

Allison, trust your instincts about taking the wall down. I think you're going to love the openness. Of course, once you've lived in it a while, if you find yourself wanting a screen, you can always have one made.

The measurements of her parents' house stared up at her from the table. She sat down, pulled out a sheet of fresh vellum, taped it to the desk, and sharpened her lead. Sticky from the heat, her fingers left prints on the paper as she set down her scale to measure the first line. She sharpened her lead. Studied the numbers on her drawing.

Stood and pulled down the shade halfway to shut out the sun, then went into the bathroom and splashed water on her face. Realizing she was thirsty, she fetched a glass of water from the kitchen and took it to the desk. She sat down, picked up her leadholder and sharpened it for a third time. She glanced at the clock: one forty-five. She'd been procrastinating for an hour! Finally, Annie's joke about calling the Coast Guard got the best of her. She decided to walk to the church in hopes of intercepting Lester at the book sale.

The sidewalk along Pickering Road had given Gina her very first taste of freedom as a child, but now as she scuffed along the worn concrete squares, she considered the constraints of marriage and aging. Lester had been the one to whom people had gone for advice and comfort; now he created concern when he was a little late getting home—in the middle of a hot but otherwise fine day! But then, she herself had fantasized that Ben had been kidnapped at school with a kind of terror she couldn't have imagined before she had children. And Paul—his close monitoring of her lately had made her feel claustrophobic. (And now she realized she'd again left her phone at the house.) She thought of Kit's apparent contentedness, pictured him in the morning, emerging from *Homeward*'s cabin to assess water and sky before rowing ashore to spend the day building boats. No one was worrying about him, and he seemed to be doing very well. Was it not possible to maintain at least a *feeling* of independence when you were married and raising a family?

She crossed the lawn in front of Whit's Point Congregational Church—a typical eighteenth-century New England structure with white clapboards and two tall windows flanking the forest green front door. The church had no adornment except a steeple stump that lacked a culminating spire. Several tables scantily lined with books were set up on the grass, and people were milling and chatting. Gina scanned the crowd but didn't see Lester or recognize anyone else.

The church doors were open, and she stepped inside to cool off. Funerals and weddings—since she'd stopped attending Sunday school at age eleven, they were the only occasions that had brought her to the church. She remembered seeing Cassie walk into the foyer before her parents' service, flanked by Wes and their three teenagers. The sun pouring in through the doors was so bright that Gina had trouble seeing their faces. Backlit figures bent to hug Cassie, and she flapped and nodded in her usual, demonstrative way. Unlike Gina, she'd continued to be in touch with old family friends and had always thrived on ceremony. On her wedding day, Cassie'd come down the aisle of this very church—could it have been the same red carpet?—on their father's arm, looking bridal-radiant in ivory and flower-child vintage, even though their mother had quipped that she might have considered a red dress "under the circumstances."

Back outside, Gina scanned the book tables once more for Lester and this time spotted Lowell Strong, the church's minister, stooping to listen to the woman standing with him. Lowell had conducted the wedding ceremonies for both Gilbert sisters, presided over Fran's funeral, and come out of retirement to perform Gina's parents' service. Gina remembered him the day of the funeral, ascending slowly and gracefully to the pulpit, announcing gravely, "This day has come much too soon."

Looking up now, Lowell spotted Gina and waved as she crossed the lawn.

"How wonderful to see you here," he said when she walked up. "I was hoping you Gilbert girls weren't gone for good!"

Gina felt touched by his warmth but saddened, too, by the notion of being *gone for good*. She asked about Lester, and Lowell said he'd seen him at the book sale about an hour ago. As Gina said goodbye, he clasped her hand, and she was struck by the tears in his eyes that seemed to say that whether or not it had mattered to her, she'd always be a part of this community.

Gina walked back to Lily House, opened the front door and yelled, "Lester?"

No answer. It was two-thirty. She paced in the kitchen, wolfing down some yogurt that barely put a dent in her hunger, and sat on the back steps staring into the garden. Why didn't these older people carry cell phones! Suddenly realizing her own carelessness, she went into the house and turned on her phone. It rang immediately, displaying Paul's number.

When she answered, Paul asked sharply, "What's going on there? How come you don't answer your phone?"

"I forgot to take it with me. Everything okay?"

"Could you try to remember to have your phone with you? We need to be able to be in touch. I want to know how you're doing."

Gina felt awful—harassed and at the same time guilty for not sharing with Paul everything she was experiencing. "I'm fine, Paul; please stop worrying. I just need this time to . . . " Time to *what?* "I'm going to make drawings of the house."

A long pause. Then, Paul said, "That's a great idea. For a keep-sake, you mean?"

She was grateful for this simplistic interpretation: everyone understood a *souvenir*. "Yeah," she said. "What's going on there?"

"I went to Marin to check on things. Today's one of those perfect summer days up there."

Marin, Gina thought. Dry brown grass, empty blue skies. Did she even remember how it smelled?

"Seventy-nine degrees," Paul said. "People wearing shorts, eating ice cream cones—the whole nine yards. Being on the site reminded me how ready I am to move. But, then I had this thought." He paused. Finally he said, "We need to talk seriously about this project."

Gina panicked. "Can I call you back later?" she interrupted. "I need to find Lester—he's kind of disappeared, and Annie's worried. I'll call you back. "

Paul sighed. "Okay, well please try to. I hope he's all right."

When they'd hung up, Gina slapped a mosquito on her cheek so hard that her eyes watered and her hand tingled for a long time afterward. Of all times for Paul to want "serious talk" about the Marin house! Just the thought of it yanked at the delicate threads that were keeping her grounded here.

And, she realized now, he hadn't told her how Esther and Ben were doing.

Her San Francisco life bearing down on her, she was determined to get the as-builts of her family's house done. She convinced herself that Lester must have stopped in to see a friend. As soon as the drawings were done, she'd call back Paul.

She shut everything out except the paper in front of her. Hunched over the table, she broke a sweat and two leads as she began the ground floor plan. The first three lines she drew were wrong, and she nearly wore a hole in the vellum erasing them. But then, they began to fall into place almost on their own.

When she'd added the interior doors to the plan, she stood back from her work. For a contractor, most lines on a drawing represented something to be bought at the lumber store; to Gina the lines represented every surface she had touched, listened to, or looked through. But the bold curves of the doors described nothing tangible; they were about the kinetic quality of the house, and they posed questions—"Who's there? What's going on in

there? Can I come in? When will you come home?"—that filled
its rooms as they swung back and forth, tracing their invisible arcs over and over again, unifying or dividing spaces
and people. Now they seemed irrelevant, and she scrubbed them
from the paper.

With the first floor plan complete, she printed the name of each
room on the drawing. She hesitated when she came to the room that
had been her father's darkroom until he retired and it became the
dining room. After some consideration she printed "DR," pleased by
the coincidence.

Long before she'd been drawn to architecture, her father had
helped lay the groundwork for her career by inviting her into his
private domain—the darkroom—to teach her the magic of his own
art. With a smile this memory brought, she erased "DR" and in its
place wrote, "Darkroom."

At a certain age, most children have the desire to build some sort of shelter. It may be a real cave dug into a bank, or a primitive hut of rough boards . . . The child's play is continued in the grown-up's creation . . . he progresses from the cave game to more and more refined methods of enclosing space.

Steen Eiler Rasmussen, *Experiencing Architecture*

DARKROOM
10'- 7" X 17'-6"

"Can I come in, Dad?" Gina leaned into the darkroom door and pressed her ear against it.

"Hold on a minute, honey."

She stayed slumped against the closed door, waiting. She had tremendous respect for this door. Unofficially, the darkroom doors were the only ones in the house that were allowed to be closed during waking hours, besides the bathroom's and her mother's, when she was sulking. No one ever told Gina and Cassie directly that they shouldn't retreat behind doors; this was her mother's unspoken rule. A closed door would lend itself to all kinds of interpretations—a desire for privacy, for instance, which might be viewed as rejection or rebellion. When the darkroom doors were closed, though, it was a straightforward, technical matter of having to make the room dark. They even had locks.

Her mother was coming downstairs. "Virginia?"

Eleanor had taken to calling Gina "Virginia," her full name, ever since Cassie had come up with the idea of "Gina." It was her mother's way of protesting. "Gina? Italian, isn't it?" was all she'd said when Gina had announced the change three years ago.

Gina was relieved when the bolt on the darkroom door scraped in the lock, the door gave way, and she fell into the dim glow of the yellow safety lights. She locked the door behind her.

"What's cookin', chum?" her father asked.

"Sick of researching my art history paper. Would this be a good time to print my stuff?"

Ron plucked a photo from the stop bath and dropped it into the water tray. "Sure. I developed your roll this morning. It'll just take a minute for me to finish these up."

Gina went to the other end of the room and hoisted herself up on her father's worktable to wait. She loved the darkroom; it was her favorite room in the house. Its furniture—mostly machines—had a purposefulness and objectivity to them, unlike the fought-over Banton antiques elsewhere. The darkroom teemed with an industry that had nothing whatsoever to do with the household, but rather was dedicated to life in the outside world. Hanging above the table was a photo calendar showing March with one of her father's typical boat and lighthouse scenes, and next to it a large-format picture of Whit's Point Harbor and outlying islands, framed on the left side by a huge elm tree. Foreground, middle ground, background—Gina had begun to see this as her father's compositional trademark. On the adjacent wall was a photo of Vice President Nixon enjoying a lobster dinner at a picnic table with Pat, Tricia, and Julie; Nixon wore a boldly striped polo shirt and Pat a puffy skirt and a kerchief tied too tightly around her neck (you could tell it was bright red and matched her lipstick, even though the photo was black and white). Julie and Tricia, in matching sunsuits, scrunched their faces at the lobster-eating ordeal.

Gina remembered how proud her father had been to be asked to take the portraits.

The lights snapped on; Gina felt her sleepy reverie shrink away.

"Let's get these babies into the washer!" Ron upended the tray of limp photos into the print washer and flipped a switch, starting the big cylindrical cage turning in the tub of water. The room filled with a pleasant sloshing. Beyond it, Gina could hear the clanging of pots in the kitchen. She glanced at the clock—five-thirty—still early.

Ron held up Gina's negatives, pictures she'd taken of a few friends and of her artwork, for her college portfolio. "Want to take a look?"

She hopped off the table and stood next to her father while he brought her first frame into focus with the enlarger. The darkness created an intimacy she hadn't felt with him since he used to wake her for school with his tender caress of her cheek. At times like this, she could believe that underneath the submissive man she witnessed with her mother, there was a strong father who could help teach Gina to recognize and make the best use of her power in the world. She watched his confident hand adjust the aperture, his muscular arm below his rolled-up sleeve; they'd always seemed incongruous, but reassuring, on his wiry frame. A grainy face appeared and disappeared on the back of his hand as it passed over the easel.

"See what you want to do," Ron offered, backing away.

Gina moved the head of the enlarger up and down, watching her boyfriend Mark's face shrink and grow until the image filled the paper just right.

"That's a great one—of Mark?" her father ventured, and she told him yes.

He'd met Mark once and had commented to Gina that he didn't "quite know what to make of him." Gina was not at all surprised; her father and Mark couldn't have been more different. Mark was one of the courageous boys who drifted down to the all-girls Andrews from the more prestigious boys prep school up the street. These boys parked themselves on the couches in the girls' dorm common rooms, offering cigarettes while taking inventory of the girls. In pasty Whit's Point, Gina had never met a boy like Mark, with such dark hair and eyes, so witty and self-assured. At prep school, it was *cool* to be smart. When Gina had remarked on this to Cassie, she'd said, "They're smarter and more interesting because they're all rich." Since starting at Andrews, Cassie had felt insecure about her upbringing "in the sticks," but by the time Gina got there, Andrews students had long since traded in status symbols for a studied attempt at care-free sloppiness.

Of course, there were still some signifiers of wealth at Andrews: expensive stereo equipment, braces, nose jobs, ski vacations in Vail, and the river of cash flowing into the procurement of alcohol and drugs. What a laugh that her mother had believed her daughters' morality would be better protected at boarding school than in Whit's Point! Most of the supervising adults at Andrews were caring but quite a few spent their free time in much the same way as their students. (Mr. Grand, the history teacher, was known to be sleeping with a senior but at least she was eighteen.) At times Gina found the freedom at school overwhelming; it was a lot to manage work, fun, sleep, and the 24-7 demand for emergency peer counseling that substituted for parenting.

But Gina had never spent a homesick day at Andrews. To be surrounded by so many interesting girls! Like having more sisters— slightly wounded sisters. Daughters of divorce, alcoholism, illness, and death: escapees, all. She loved how the place engaged her every molecule, how revelations seemed to come in the breakfast biscuits, how there was room for her to feel, to express, to create. She loved the three art studios—the ceramics room especially, where she worked until midnight some nights, building her clay ruins.

She loved being out of earshot of her mother.

So when her parents told her in September that she might not be able to return to Andrews for her senior year because of money problems, she secretly cried nearly every night for three months. It was never brought up again until they were driving her back to school after Christmas vacation and she asked from the backseat, "So, am I going to graduate from Andrews or not, do you think?"

"Yes, of course," her mother said. "You're going to graduate from Andrews."

That was the end of it—subject closed, as usual on the topic of money. Gina held in her explosive relief until they'd left her at the dorm, and then she and her roommates gyrated to the Rolling Stones in a four-person bear hug.

Now, she slipped the photograph of Mark into the tray of chemicals. It would always be magic to her the way a blank surface would slowly fill in with life. Peering at Mark's portrait, she thought of the letter she'd just received from him, covered with painstakingly drawn caricatures of his teachers. She plucked the print from the last tray and clothespinned it to the line hanging over the sink. She hoped he'd call.

She sat on the stool poking the tongs at the prints in the tray, tasting the pungent chemicals they soaked in. As her sculptures took shape on the paper, she felt pleased that in two dimensions the pieces—a series of "rooms," made from raku-fired porcelain slabs— had lost little of their mystery and power. This was the first body of work she felt was truly hers.

For an instant, she was pulled away by the sound of dinner preparations beyond the darkroom door. But her father switched on the print dryer, and its hum brought her back inside. She left the finished prints in the rinse tray and pulled the stool over to the dryer. When she and Cassie were little, they'd peel the prints from the hot silver drum quickly to avoid burning their fingers, then make a pile of them, dry and slightly curled like autumn leaves. Now, she picked off a photograph of a group of mostly smiling people posing against a layer of orange day lilies in front of Lily House: her mother, her grandparents, Fran, and a toddler—probably Sid—grinning and straddling a large, spotted dog. The women's skirts were skewed by the wind.

"Oh, take a look at this!" Her father plucked from the belt a photograph of her mother, dressed in an antique gown, standing on the stair at Lily House. "I took this the day I met her. The Historical people hired me, and Mom was the only one tiny enough to fit into Mary Banton's dress. It was raining that day, and muddy in the driveway, so I picked Mom up and carried her across Lily House's threshold. Isn't she a beauty? She was the classiest girl around."

"Yeah," Gina said. Her mother looked both regal and sultry, like a very short movie star. She imagined her father, falling in love through his viewfinder. But as always, she felt both mystified and irritated by the adoration in his eyes that she'd come to understand was what stood between him and the imperative to protect his daughters from their mother.

More pictures of Lily House rolled out on the dryer belt: Lily House in all seasons, in the snow and spring, windows lit up at night; it was a photo-worthy house. From looking at the merry faces of the people gathered around it, you could almost believe it had once been the magical place her mother always said it was. Next came a series of recent photographs, clinical portraits of each room from every angle. Rooms of four-posted beds, curvy Victorian couches, caned chairs, clashing oriental rugs and stern portraits everywhere.

When Gina asked about the photos, her father said, "Mom wanted them, to keep track of furniture and paintings and whatnot. She doesn't trust the Historical Society."

"Why did she sell the house to them, then? I thought she wanted to live in Lily House someday—she always worshipped it. Did she sell it because of . . . what happened with Fran?"

"Fran?" Her father cocked his head. "No, I don't think so. I don't think Mom ever wanted to live at Lily House. She likes it here, being on the water."

Not for the first time lately, Gina had the thought that her father might not just be long-suffering but also oblivious.

Just once, Gina had asked her mother why she'd sold Lily House to the Historical Society, but her mother had changed the subject. Gina figured it was because the sale had to do with the taboo subject of money. "But why'd she'd sell to *them*?" she pressed her father now.

"She wanted to be able to sell it to someone for a better price—a lot more than what we ended up getting from the Historical people. If she had, we would've gotten our hands on all these *things* in the house." He pointed at the photograph of Lily House's dining room sideboard. "But we couldn't because the Washington letters never showed up."

"I don't get it. What do the Washington letters have to do with anything?"

"Your grandpa wrote in his will that if the letters weren't found, Lily House and everything in it had to be sold to the Historical Society so they could protect the hidden letters. *If* they're even there. Isn't that silly? But remember: don't say anything to anyone about the letters; it's a Banton family secret, like all the others." His chuckle came out more like a cough.

Gina felt an irrepressible urge to pour all of her questions into the dark room. This must have been what a confessional felt like! "How come Mom never talks about the fact that Bill Holloway was Sid's father?" she blurted.

Her father sighed and shifted his weight. "It's a long story. Mom will tell you about it sometime." He shook his head. "Those Bantons. They're quite a bunch."

It was the only indictment about family Gina had ever heard her father make, and it seemed to include her mother, since she and Sid were the only Bantons left. The safety of the darkroom must have emboldened him, too.

She took another chance. "Don't you think there's something *wrong* with the Bantons?"

"Oh, well, I'm not sure how you mean that . . . Sid's a little light in his loafers; is that what you mean?"

"What? No, I don't mean . . . " Gina felt embarrassed for Sid and angry at the same time. "Who cares about that?"

"Well, maybe you kids don't, but it's a little tough to swallow. For adults. Parents."

"Like who? He doesn't have parents. Why do you care? He doesn't even talk to us."

"Oh, I'm not saying I care, particularly. They have a right to the way they want to live, as far as that goes. But it was pretty hard on Mom and Fran."

Gina thought of all the pain Fran and her mother had caused the family and even though she had no reason to feel protective of her estranged cousin, she couldn't help feeling indignant that he was being implicated in their misery. She felt herself shut down.

The hum of the dryer filled the room as they continued to pick prints off the belt.

After several minutes, her father said, "I didn't mean to sound like I don't approve of how Sid is. It's just that with Sid, it's not so simple. Remember, he's *Sidney Banton*. The last in the famous line of Sidney Bantons. There was a certain expectation. Your mother thinks that was the last straw for Fran. That night she did herself in. Sid told her about . . . " here, her father dropped his voice, "being a homosexual."

Gina's jaw was clenched tight. Taking a breath, she aimed to take a good shot at her father. "I was there that day," she said. "It wasn't because of Sid. Fran and Mom were totally out of control. *Both* of them." To twist the knife, she added, "Cassie thinks Mom's sick and needs a psychiatrist."

"Oh?" Her father laughed, infuriating her. "She does, huh? Well, Mom and Fran did always have their problems with each other. And Mom has had her ups and downs, but it's not all *that* bad; is it?"

The intimacy Gina had felt earlier shrunk into the room's yellowed darkness. She was struck with an urge to grab her father and shake him out of his . . . amnesia, or stupor, or whatever it was.

Ron held up a photograph. "Look at this great Chippendale desk. Sidney Banton's very own."

Gina didn't look.

"Virginia, are you in there?" her mother's voice shot through the darkroom door.

Gina ignored her.

"Virginia?" Eleanor yelled again. "Phone's for you. It's Mark. We're going to eat!"

Gina picked up the phone on her father's worktable. "Hi, Gina Lo-La," Mark said.

Gina turned her back to the room and moved her lips closer to the receiver to ask him how he was. She'd hoped he'd call, but not now, with her father standing right there.

"Four days into vacation, and I'm already going nuts," Mark complained. "Rachel has three other pre-pubes here all the time, Martin is king, and Trudy thinks she's my best friend, only hipper."

Gina remembered being scandalized the first time she'd heard Mark call his parents by their first names. During parents' weekend,

Trudy's skin-tight jeans and silk halter top had made her a standout among the other khakis-and-wool-skirted parents. She'd never met a parent she'd call *sexy*. Her own mother snorted in disgust at the Closeup toothpaste ads and ruined every TV make-out scene with her loud negative commentary about *swapping spit*. In their house, Gina's sexuality slinked off like a guilty dog.

Mark was focused 100 percent on losing his virginity, and Gina was the girl he intended to lose it with. She was flattered; he was handsome and smooth, never fumbling a kiss. She loved lying next to him in the field near school, skin against skin. Peeling off clothes, breaking the rules sneaking into his dorm room—minutes charged with the exciting danger of getting caught. She thought now of the night last month he'd thrown pebbles at her window, and she'd sneaked out of her dorm to find him huddled against the maple tree. He'd just returned from the funeral of a best friend back home who'd crashed his car. When he laid his head in Gina's lap and cried, she felt more alive and purposeful than she ever had, more connected to everything—to Mark, to the trees just beginning to push out tiny buds—and grounded by the profoundness of this act of comforting that transcended her middle-of-the-night fatigue, the rules they were breaking, the exam she had the next day.

These feelings, Gina realized, had little to do with wanting to have sex. She had no intention of losing her virginity to Mark. She'd told him so. First of all, she wasn't ready (the reason she gave him), and she wasn't in love with him (the reason she didn't give him), if she even knew what love was. Furthermore, the horniness that peppered his every joke and gesture was a turnoff.

There were plenty of other girls who might have been *ready*, but Mark soldiered on with determination and loyalty—not her father's hangdog kind of loyalty but the frisky kind. She was *worth* waiting for! What she was willing to give, she figured, must have been worth what she was not willing to give up.

Though sometimes—like now as he pleaded, "Can't you pul-eeze get your bod down here for a couple of days?"—he made her seriously doubt that he was interested in anything more than her body.

"I'm still not feeling good." She coughed a juicy cough. "Plus," she whispered, "we can't afford the bus fare right now."

This was sort of true. Her father had been short of work for the past three months, and while she was home they'd been eating waffles and canned tuna for dinner.

"That sucks. D'you miss me?"

"Yeah, I do," she said, though she realized she'd missed him more before he'd called.

"I want you, Lo. I can't stand having to wait until school on Monday. Please come visit—I'll pay for the ticket."

Gina turned again and glanced at Mark's confident face hanging on the line, dripping into the sink. She hated his begging. "I can't—really—I mean, I want to, but I'm sick, and I've got my art history paper to write."

"Ron?" her mother's bark, through the door. "What are you waiting for, a personal invitation?"

"Oh—dinnertime already? Be right there!" her father chirped. So innocent, as if he hadn't heard the reproach. "Gina . . . " Looking deflated, he gestured toward the door.

"Mark, I've gotta go eat—I'll call you back later, okay?"

"Maybe we can do some more after dinner," her father said, when Gina had hung up. "We'll see what Mom wants to do." His sorry tone meant there would be no more darkroom revelations tonight.

Silently, they finished loading the washer.

Gina took hold of the doorknob just as her father placed a firm hand on her shoulder.

"You know, honey, if Mark really cares about you, he won't pressure you like that."

He'd startled her. From what remote region of him had this protectiveness suddenly emerged? She wanted to linger, to make sense of this fatherly concern. But it had come too late; the minute they left the darkroom, she knew, it would evaporate.

"Don't worry," she said, unlocking the door and stepping into the angry, bright light of the kitchen.

Valid ambiguity promotes useful flexibility . . . The calculated ambiguity of expression is based on the confusion of experience as reflected in the architectural program. This promotes richness of meaning over clarity of meaning.
Robert Venturi, *Complexity and Contradiction in Architecture*

Chapter 11

Gina was eager to finish drawing the plans, but her concern about Lester grew. Could he be quietly working somewhere in the house? She went outside, lifted the old wood doors on the cellar bulkhead and stepped down into the dark, dirt-floor space. The light caught the metal of a hanging chain, and she pulled it, illuminating a workbench with all kinds of tools, a stack of logs, an old lawnmower, and some beach chairs. No sign of Lester.

Perhaps he was asleep upstairs. She went inside and stepped gingerly up to the second floor where she couldn't remember ever having been. There were three bedrooms opposite the stair. She quickly peeked into them, then turned down the hall where the two main bedrooms occupied the front of the house, facing Pickering Road. One of them had been the original Sidney Banton's; she recognized his writing desk from her father's photographs. The room appeared untouched, its bookshelves lined with old leather volumes. She turned and faced the closed door across the hall and a chill ran through her as she realized it probably led to the room where Fran had died. Heart thrumming, she put her ear to the door, all at once thinking of the trapped bird at her parents' house.

"Lester?" she said quietly. She knocked and, hearing nothing, she reached for the doorknob. A loud *pop! pop! pop!* made her lunge for the stair but then she realized a car on Pickering Road had backfired. She took a breath and opened the bedroom door.

To her great relief, the room had been divested of all signs of habitation and was being used for storage. Boxes and furniture filled the furnace-like space; she recognized a couch slipcovered in peony chintz from Annie and Lester's old house. She wondered if it was an accident or because of Fran's untimely death that this room had been relegated to storage. Would its disuse honor Fran or merely preserve the tragedy by remaining a metaphor for a life not fully lived?

Gina stepped around the boxes to look out the window facing east. From this high perspective, she could see that despite Annie's description of letting the plants, time, and weather inform her gardening, there was nevertheless a pleasing structure to her garden. And something else caught her eye: on the old barn, a skylight running the length of its roof. A skylight! In Whit's Point, this was such an unexpectedly modern sight it might as well have been a spaceship perched on the shingled ridge. She ran downstairs and outside to investigate.

The barn was large relative to the house and had the saggy look of a forgotten outbuilding, though its clapboards were freshly painted. The padlock that hung from the door latch was unlocked.

She pulled open the door and what came to life before her was so unexpected she nearly gasped: a soaring, bright, open space enclosed by whitewashed walls, a refinished wide board floor and an exposed beam ceiling strung with light cables. A huge wooden fan was suspended from the center truss, whirring loudly. On the walls hung several richly colored rugs: Navajo, Oaxacan, and Turkish, perhaps souvenirs from Annie and Lester's travels. At the end of the room where Gina stood was an upright piano; next to it, Annie's violin and a music stand that held the music for a Bach concerto. A pile of music books, notebooks, envelopes of photographs and a half-full coffee cup emblazoned with a treble signature were scattered across a large unfinished pine table. In the corner nearest the door stood the ladder Gina needed and Annie's garden tools: rake and spade, a watering can, and a bucket that held a dibble, trowel, and pruning shears.

Gina froze. She felt she'd stumbled upon something intensely private—sacred, like the forts she'd built as a child. The place was the personification of Annie and Lester—tall and powerful, warm and engaging. Slowly, she moved to the center of the room where she could fully absorb the life emanating from its walls. Under the skylight the space was so luxuriously unfettered—defined only by a large worn oriental rug and a single overstuffed chair—she wanted to spread her arms and dance!

At the opposite end of the room stood metal shelving that held journals, books, stacks of letters. A laptop sat on a heavy antique desk with ornate metal drawer pulls—Lester's desk, Gina guessed. She slipped behind the Japanese screen that obscured the remainder of the room, and jumped when she spotted Lester's crutch, then Lester himself, lying flat on his back on the floor, his eyes closed. She rushed to him.

"Lester, are you hurt?"

Lester squinted up at her. His face was drained of color, his shirt soaked with perspiration. "Oh, Gina, thank goodness you're here, dear. I must have dozed off, and I'm awfully thirsty. I–I– slipped and fell. Annie hasn't come home yet?"

"No, she hasn't. How long have you been here?"

"I don't know; too long. I called for Annie but . . . oh, gosh, I just stepped on a damn piece of paper and *fwitt!* My legs flew out from under me, and I couldn't reach my crutch. I think you'd better not move me—it's my leg or my hip."

Gina called 911 and grabbed a cushion to put under Lester's head. She tilted a glass of water to his lips, and he drank.

"Annie?" he said into the glass.

"She'll be back later, Lester. I've called for help."

"Where's Annie?" Lester asked as the ambulance wound its way along Pickering Road.

When Gina reminded him she was at the symphony, he said, "That's right. She'll be home after dinner." He turned away as if to contemplate this possibility, and Gina would always remember how changed he seemed at that moment, how his confidence had seemed to wither as confusion and pain filled his face.

"What time is it then, Ginny?"

"It's three." She turned her watch to him, and he squinted at the numbers.

"Oh, well, I meant to tell her to fill the gas tank before she left," he said and closed his eyes.

The ambulance flew over the Whit's Point Bridge. As Gina watched Lester's chest rise and fall with his heavy breathing, her own chest tightened against her racing heart. What if Lester had had a stroke or a heart attack? Perhaps if she hadn't been so all-consumed with this house business, she would have found him sooner!

The paramedic finished examining him and sat down, looking relieved. "No major breaks at least—we'll see what the X-rays tell us."

Lester said, "I just need some Advil and a good stiff drink."

Gina couldn't remember ever having been at the Riversport hospital, a fact that seemed strange to her now. She'd been in board-ing school when her mother had had a hysterectomy, in California when her father had had his bypass. She'd always imagined her local hospital would be a sorry, outdated version of the cold and sterile medical centers in San Francisco. But Riversport looked more like a Marriott Hotel, with carpeting instead of linoleum, potted plants everywhere, landscapes by local artists on the walls, even a plate of oatmeal cookies on the admittance desk. There were only four others in the waiting room, one a mother holding a young child. Nurses and doctors passing through the ER lobby actually smiled and said hello.

Gina sat next to Lester's gurney furiously filling out forms with the information Lester gave her.

"Ginny, you're a dear," Lester said when she'd finished with the forms.

Gina felt undeserving of his appreciation, but there was such sweetness in his voice she impulsively took his hand. It was large and sticky in hers. "Let's hope they can see you quickly. Can I get you anything?"

Lester asked for more water, and when he finished drinking, he took a deep breath. "Oh dear . . . you know, I'm a little rattled. I can't remember where, exactly, you said Annie was going. The symphony was it? Goodness. I think I need a little nap. Ayuh—that's what I need."

While Lester slept, Gina turned on her cell phone and a text from Allison leapt onto the screen: *Any thoughts re: playhouse?* Gina thought of Annie and Lester's studio overflowing with character, and all the other secret places in her life, real and imagined. *I think you should let the kids design it and help build it,* she texted back. *They'll be so much happier with the results!*

She called the Maine Symphony office in Portland and asked them to try to track down Annie. Then she left a message for Paul, telling him about Lester's fall.

A nurse came over to take Lester's pulse. "I'm afraid we're unusually busy with a couple of critical cases," she said, turning to Gina. Her face was kind and so wide that her ears seemed to disappear. "You might want to get a cup of coffee in the cafeteria. Your father may have a wait."

Gina let the mistake go. Thinking Lester might be hungry since he'd gone without lunch, she bought him a sandwich and some iced tea. He was still asleep when she returned, and she picked up a copy of *Dream House* magazine from the table next to her. *Make your home your dream-come-true*, the cover said. *House, home*—real-estate agents and journalists used the two words interchangeably even though one was concrete, or wood or brick as the case may be, and the other abstract, subjective. The magazine was repellent; the houses sprawled almost pornographically across its pages. A gaudy sunset shot from across a lighted infinity pool; a room jammed with African artifacts and hide-covered furniture; a garage full of vintage cars; and a media room stacked floor to ceiling with equipment. The rooms had been composed by a stylist, then composed again through the lens of the photographer—they were compositions of compositions that provided no sense of the houses' spaces, of architecture. *Dream houses?* No room here for dreams.

Gina dropped the magazine on the table. The truth was, the professional magazines stacked in her office didn't do much better. They published *art* houses—not for the approval of consumers but for that of architects—commissioned by people whose primary motivation was to own an award-winning house. Sometimes the carte blanche they gave their architects resulted in a building that was architecturally extraordinary *and* an efficient and comfortable dwelling. But often, awards were given to projects that were low-functioning and proud of it; while their inhabitants publicly pronounced their architects *brilliant*, in private, they cursed the flat roof that didn't drain, the clanging metal stair, the skylight over the bed that cut short their sleep.

It was challenging to strike the right balance, and Gina had made her share of mistakes; with time, she'd learned to recognize which projects would inevitably compromise her aesthetic—occasionally resulting in her not taking one on—and when her vision would seriously impede utility. The Stones had given her tremendous freedom with their house, and she hoped it would showcase her artistry while also realizing their visions and needs.

As if summoned, her phone vibrated in her pocket; she pulled it out to find Jeffrey Stone's number striped across her screensaver photo of Esther and Ben.

Jeff left a vexed-sounding message:

"Gina, having trouble reaching you—we've got an emergency here with the neighborhood outreach meeting—pretty stiff opposition. Expect an email from our neighbor Henchew—something about aquifers and wild parrots. Anyway, Mitzi's very upset and would appreciate a call from you. Thanks."

"An emergency," Gina thought, frowning at the irony. She checked her email and sure enough, there was a message from H. H. Henchew, the owner of both a major airline and the nation's top pet food chain who'd built a seventeen-thousand square foot mansion in the style Gina dubbed "Chateaucoco." He'd typed his email in uppercase as if lower case wouldn't have made his points loudly enough.

RE: NEIGHBORHOOD OUTREACH MEETING FOR STONE RESIDENCE. MULTIPLE NEIGHBORS OPPOSE THIS PROJECT BASED ON

1) THE DISTURBANCE OF EXISTING AQUIFER CAUSING

FLOODING DOWNHILL OF THE HOUSE
2) DISTURBANCE OF SUBTERRANEAN HABITAT
3) POSSIBLE DISTURBANCE OF EXISITING UNKNOWN
FAULTS THAT COULD CAUSE EARTHQUAKE
4) OVERSIZED WINDOWS ON UPPER LEVELS POSE
DIRECT THREAT TO THE WILD PARROTS OF TELEGRAPH
HILL WHO WILL FLY INTO GLASS DURING MIGRATIONS
AND FALL TO THEIR DEATH.
WE LOOK FORWARD TO DISCUSSING THESE CONCERNS
AT THE MEETING.

It would be a long fight but not an unfamiliar one. Gina's stomach complained; anxiety tugged at her. She turned off her phone and ate half the sandwich she'd bought while people swam about, speaking with urgency. The child slumped in his mother's arms, staring at Gina through glazed eyes: a fever—a high one she could tell. She closed her eyes and leaned her head back against the wall.

"Gina? Are you all right?"

When she opened her eyes, Lester was peering at her.

Before she could answer, the nurse was over them, standing so close to Lester that her pillowy stomach touched his hand. "I'm going to take you two into the exam room. But I can't guarantee you'll be seen right away," she said.

"That catnap did me good," Lester said when they were settled and alone.

The room was tiny and windowless, but the air conditioning felt heavenly. Gina gave Lester the sandwich half, and he nibbled at it.

"I think I was a bit heat-stricken. The painkillers are helping, too; I feel downright zippy. Just can't for the life of me figure out how I could've landed on my rear end so fast! What an old man. Annie's gonna let me have it!" He laughed, and Gina laughed too, amazed and relieved by his good humor. "How did it go today?" he asked.

"Oh, I just went to the house." She considered telling him about measuring but was afraid he'd ask her why and what would she say?

"You did, eh? Bring back old times?"

"Oh, yes . . . you know . . . the best of times, the worst of times . . ." Gina laughed but without warning, her eyes flooded.

Lester noticed and reached over and gave her a pat. "You know, things were very different, back a generation," he said. "All those rules. What you talked about, what you didn't."

The silence that filled the room was so dense it was hard for Gina to breathe. In her experience, nobody in Maine ever talked about *anything*, and here Lester was, plunging right into something deep. She felt disoriented, as if she'd stumbled into the middle of someone else's conversation.

"People," Lester said. "I even got into trouble talking about my high school kids with their folks. People didn't air their laundry the way you all do. You just rolled with it."

Airing laundry? Gina tingled with anticipation, remaining silent so she wouldn't interrupt Lester's stream of consciousness. It had to be the painkillers that had made him so forthcoming.

"Your mother—she was expert at putting on a good face in public. Not so good at it at home, I suspect." Finally Lester turned and looked at her with such kindness she had to look away. "Listen to me; I'm a lunatic!" he exclaimed. "Have I said too much?"

Gina did her best to feign unconcern but noticed she'd slid to the edge of her chair. "No, no," she said. "You're right, Lester. Please keep going."

"Your mother was a chipper gal around all us pals. But one night . . . I remember . . . you and Cassie were little tykes, and your father called looking for Eleanor. She'd stormed out and hadn't said where to. It didn't sound so serious; what housewife didn't get worked up every now and then? But your dad, he was one distraught man. I could tell there was more to it. I told him, 'Talk to her doctor,' but Ron and I both knew she wasn't the kind of person who took orders. In all those years, he and I never spoke about such a thing again."

Was that all, Gina wondered, after all that build up?

"Things seemed to settle down, anyhow," Lester said. "Ron and Eleanor, they were good . . . good *together*. Remember how your father used to say, 'Can you imagine me without Eleanor? A boat without a rudder!'"

Casa senza donna, barca senza timone. Gina inwardly cringed; her father's adage had made him sound proud of his inadequacy.

And Lester: she chafed at his loyalty, his apparent determination to tie up her parents' marriage with a bow. She swallowed a lump in her throat. "There were two children in that boat," she managed to say, "and the rudder was broken."

Gina hesitated, worried about speaking so openly. But the unscripted way in which they'd been thrown together seemed to forecast that rules were going to be abandoned. "Lester, Mom was always wailing that she wanted to die," she blurted. "My whole childhood, I was gauging the level of danger I was in of losing my mother." Her eyes filled with emotion, but she pushed onward. "She terrified us. And she accused Dad, insulted him, and he never stood up to her. About anything." She wanted to keep going, wanted to say, "He never stood up for us," but didn't dare; her cheeks burned from the shock of her own allegations.

Lester appeared unphased by her outburst. "Now you're not talking about your mother. You're talking about some demon in her that took over and waged war."

Gina realized now that he knew much more about what went on in their house than he'd first let on. "Yes," she said matter-of-factly. "A doctor I once talked to called that demon 'agitated depression with borderline personality disorder.'"

Lester grinned at Gina's big, hairy words, and she felt as if she were shrinking in her chair. It *was* pathetic, wasn't it, to be rehashing your deceased parents' parenting to one of their best friends lying in the emergency room? But this was the conversation she'd been waiting all her life to have with her mother.

"Your mother should've seen a doctor, yup, but she wouldn't," Lester said. "And should your father have fought with her to? Be glad, my dear, that he did not. He wouldn't have done anything that might've caused him to lose his family. If Eleanor had gone to a doctor, she'd have denied everything, refused help. You *know* that's true. What good would a diagnosis have been?"

"It might have helped us—Cassie and me."

"How so?"

"My doctor's diagnosis of Mom was an explanation—the only one ever offered me—for why she raged and seemed to have no empathy about how it affected her kids. A diagnosis made it possible for me to tell myself she wasn't a bad mother, just *sick*."

Sick, Gina thought. Such an ugly word.

Lester was silent. Finally he said, "Did *sick* make it more possible for you to love her?"

Gina's chest tightened in the chilled air. "I don't know. No. Maybe. I don't know." It was the truth, and she felt ashamed.

Lester's warm smile reassured her. "'Sick' doesn't explain everything." He thumped his chest and cleared his throat but remained quiet for a few moments. Finally he said, "Your mother . . . you know, she had dreams. There was . . . well, for starters, she'd wanted a career. She'd wanted to go to art school. She worked in that publishing house in Boston so she could make enough money to go. Then she met your dad up here, and . . . " He stopped. Then he said, "But you know all that. Maybe what you *don't* realize is that your mother certainly loved your father. You'll have to believe me about that. But then things . . . things happened fast for them."

Lester stopped abruptly. Gina opened her mouth to say something that would urge him on, but already their conversation had been so rousing that she felt suddenly shy, like when you were on a date and good things were happening too quickly.

"Ginny," Lester said, "get out of this refrigerator and go stretch your legs."

Gina left the room disappointed; Lester had seemed on the verge of spilling something important. As nervous as she was about all she'd said, she felt somehow powerful, too.

Her mind shifted to matters beyond: Annie, Paul, Mitzi. As she got to the end of the corridor, her phone chimed; she realized there'd been no service in the exam room. Paul had tried to reach her twice. She checked with the receptionist to see if Annie had called the hospital—she had—then ducked into a small lounge area to phone Mitzi.

"Gina, thank God!" Mitzi's pitch rose an octave. "The neighbors are like a *mob* . . . They don't speak to us on the street! Except one older woman who said to me, 'Why do you *need* all this? You don't even have children.' " Gina couldn't stifle a gasp. Mitzi began to cry. "I don't judge them; why do they judge me? I mean, they have no idea. Me and my mom, when I was a kid . . . we lived in studio apartments—*eight* of them in eighteen years! Jeffrey and I are going to make this house so beautiful. Why do they hate us so much? How can we ever live there after this?"

The rawness of Mitzi's pain touched off a sudden protectiveness in Gina, and she wished she were there in person to put her mind at rest. "Mitzi," she said calmly, "it's a tough neighborhood you live in. A lot of powerful people without enough to do. Try not to take it personally. This happens all the time on projects. They don't hate you; think of them as bored dogs patrolling the fences around their castles, barking at whatever comes near. You've excited them. They like excitement."

"They seemed determined to shut down the project. Should we sell the house?" Mitzi sniffed.

"No," Gina said, "of course not! Everything we've planned is legal, and we've done all our homework with respect to engineering and soils reports. After we meet with the neighbors, we'll thoroughly address each of their complaints in a way you and Jeff are okay with. Then we'll meet with them again. I'm completely confident that the mob will disperse. I know this seems unbelievable, but my experience has been that once you finish the project, your neighbors happily welcome you because then you're one of *them*."

"Really?" Mitzi said weakly. "It's so hard to imagine."

"I know, but I see it every time."

Mitzi was quiet. Then she took a deep breath and said, "*Ohmygod.* Okay, so I just have to not let them get to me. Okay. Okay. Now for the good news: I'm pregnant!"

Gina filled with a joy that seemed to silence all the nerve-wracking noise around her. "Aw, Mitzi, that's wonderful! I'm thrilled for you!"

When they hung up, Gina felt lighter. She tried to reach Paul, and when his voicemail picked up, she left a message telling him about Lester.

She made her way back down the corridors to Lester's room, marveling at how Lester, who'd been only an old family friend just two days ago, suddenly had become a confidant, and a challenging one at that. Would he reveal more or be regretful of having shared so much already? When was the right time to tell certain truths to the next generation and how much should one tell them? Too soon or not enough could frighten them; too much could burden.

"Why did we always stay so short?" She remembered Esther's penetrating question.

How and when would Gina explain to Esther why they hadn't spent more time in Maine? In guiding her children, what would she choose to reveal about her history, her mistakes and regrets?

For the first time since she'd left her family in San Francisco, she dared to feel how much she missed them. She'd traveled even further from them than she'd intended—across a continent and then, unexpectedly, deeply into the past.

It is not in the designer's power determinately to vary degrees and places of darkness, but it is altogether in his power to vary in determined directions his degrees of light.

John Ruskin, *The Seven Lamps of Architecture*

Chapter 12

Lester was out of the room when Gina returned, but soon he arrived on his gurney, pushed by a young attendant.

"Good news!" Lester announced. "The X-ray says no breaks, no surgery. But I'll have to stay and see the orthopedic guy in the morning." When the attendant had left the room, Lester pointed at her phone. "Taking care of some business on your little miracle machine there?"

"Yeah." She laughed. "Believe it or not, it does make things easier to manage."

Lester was quiet for a few moments. Finally he asked again, "Have I said too much?"

"No, no. I really appreciate being able to talk about Mom and Dad. When we were growing up, Mom was very unhappy. They were so different . . . It was hard to figure out how they got together in the first place. And why they stayed together."

"I think Ron had never met someone like your mother, and he

loved that about her. They came from different worlds, but Ron seemed just fine with her friends, even though they were partiers—quick-witted college kids—and Ron was . . . more modest. His aspirations were focused on Whit's Point. You know, in a way, he was the perfect cure for . . . well . . . your mother had had her share of heartbreak, and Ron probably made her feel in control of her life again."

Gina was about to say, "Tell me about the heartbreak!" when the nurse stuck her head in to check Lester's vitals. She adjusted his pillow and, as she was leaving, wagged a finger at Lester. "Don't wear yourself out, Mr. Bridges."

"We're on a mission," Lester said, winking at Gina.

She understood then that it wasn't just the medication making him candid. Suddenly, it felt like a gift, not an accident that had brought her together with Lester in the cold, confining room. Her parents had never needed caring for in this way; their accident had cheated her of an essential chapter in a family's life cycle—the one in which she could have held her mother's or father's hand and perhaps for once, been able to comfort them.

Lester batted at a fly. "Remember your ma's spider phobia? She didn't let herself think about certain things because it would have been like picking up a rock and finding a bunch of hairy spiders under it."

"But what *were* those spiders?" Gina pressed. When he didn't respond right away, she said, "I mean, aside from the fact that she was bitter about being a creative person stuck as a housewife."

"Oh, you bet—never underestimate *that*," Lester said. "I think as much as she loved her home and her family, she felt trapped."

All at once, Gina's mind flashed with the images she'd had at the house during the past two days, of her mother industrious and always caretaking, bending her small frame into that endless list of chores. "Let me out," she'd seemed to be saying.

"Annie says I didn't know how good I had it, having a wife who worked and did everything else, too." Lester looked pensively at the ceiling for a few moments, then turned to her. "What about you? You a happy working mother?"

Gina smiled and pushed back the emotion welling up in her. "Something happens when you become a mother . . . your ideas about fulfillment change. For starters, giving birth is a peak experience, like . . . like scaling a peak. Even better, I bet." She was speaking in generalities; how could she know they were true for anyone but her? If she'd dared, she'd tell him that for her, motherhood was the anchor she'd never had. The chance to love as a mother in a way she'd failed to as a daughter, to whisper *I love you* in Esther and Ben's ears—words her parents had never said to her—and understand by the way her children pulled her closer, that they knew she meant it. But how could it be that the very thing that had made her most content in life had also made her feel the most vulnerable?

"Motherhood . . . " she went on. "Every mother I know is searching for balance. We're chronically conflicted and often judged. And we're our own harshest critics." Her eyes filled as she pictured Esther's solemn face at the airport, and she could see in Lester's expression that he noticed. "I've been very afraid for my kids at times . . . too much so. It's like . . . like I'm walking around with my organs on the outside of my body."

"It makes sense, doesn't it? You felt unprotected as a kid; why wouldn't you be afraid with your own kids?"

Gina smiled warmly and nodded, rendered mute by the power of Lester's words. How was it possible that one sentence could clarify years of struggle?

Lester dramatically raised one eyebrow. "So . . . is that a *yes*? Is there hope that happiness can spring from this motherhood maelstrom?"

Gina laughed. "Yes, yes. Happiness springs . . . in the most surprising ways."

They were silent for a few minutes. The fluorescent tube overhead flickered, then steadied.

"Ron must've felt Eleanor knew best with you girls," Lester said. "It's probably different for you; probably you and Paul take turns at the helm. I know Annie and I do. Sometimes I want her to take care of things. Other times I'm annoyed when she does. Now with this—" he pointed to his hip—"she's going to be waiting on me for weeks. I hate the thought!"

"Yes," Gina agreed, "I know *exactly* what you mean." For months, she'd been trying to stifle her grief and feelings of weakness because they made her feel like her mother, whose unhappiness had been unfathomable. And, Paul's worrying and insistent caring for her had reminded her of her father's constant and ineffective placating. Gina had been pushing Paul away when she'd needed him most. He couldn't win and now, she felt ashamed. "Damned if you do and damned if you don't," she thought aloud. It was one of her father's many sayings.

Lester laughed. "'If it ain't one thing, it's another!'"

Remembering her father's bottomless pocket of clichés, the jolly spin they put on life, Gina began to laugh, too. Her body was loosening, coming alive.

"At a certain point, you've *got* to laugh," Lester said. "Do you know what your mother had done? That night your dad came looking for her at our house? She'd taken all the dinner she'd cooked . . . still in its pots and pans . . . She . . . *ha ha*! Oh my Lord! She took them down to the dock and pitched them into the cove. Then she drove herself to the Howard Johnson's for fried clams. The next day, your dad waited for low tide, put on his rubbah boots and fished the pots out of the mud."

Gina had no memory of this and Lester's account struck her as hilarious. They both rocked with a fresh round of laughter.

When they stopped, she felt like staying quiet, like pausing along a trail to enjoy a view. The room became porous again to the voices that came and went over the intercom. For what seemed a long time, Lester stared at the ceiling, then closed his eyes. Watching his hand rise and fall where it lay on his chest, Gina filled with a deep affection.

When something loudly bumped the door, Lester's eyes popped open, and he turned to her.

"Do you think you can forgive her?"

Gina was unprepared. This was a question to ask on a beach where it could be carried off by a gust, not in a windowless box where it bounced off the walls, looking for a way out. She wondered: if her mother had ever once said she was sorry for anything, if she'd asked for forgiveness, wouldn't that in itself have made her forgivable?

She couldn't yet find an answer for Lester.

"People talk a lot about forgiveness," he said. "Real forgiveness is not possible sometimes. And anything less than the real thing demeans."

Gina smiled. He must have been one hell of a guidance counselor.

Lester was being moved from the ER exam room to a hospital bed when Annie arrived at eight o'clock. Her face was strained with worry, and she moved uncomfortably in her beige linen suit and pumps.

"Lester! What on earth?" She rushed past Gina to his bed and pressed his arm.

"Now don't scold me. I wasn't getting into trouble; I just got up to grab a book from the shelf. Did you have enough gas?"

"Stop about the gas! I was fine. You tripped? You slipped?" Her annoyance couldn't disguise her fear.

"Oh, Lord, I don't remember. It's my damn hip though. I'll see the orthopedic guy in the morning."

Annie fanned her face with a pamphlet that said *Heartstrong*!

"Geesh! Do you know it's still eighty-two degrees out there? Gina, you must be exhausted. Go home now, dearie. Take a cool shower and have something to eat."

Gina wasn't eager to go. But it was time to leave the two of them alone. She gave Lester's hand a squeeze, and when he smiled, she felt a shift inside her, something moving over to make room for something else.

Lily House spooked her when she walked in, heavy with the day. Without Annie and Lester's renewing presence, it seemed to return to the sad Lily House of her memory. When the phone rang and she startled, she realized how tense she was. She let it ring and pulled vegetables for a salad from the refrigerator. The answering machine beeped. Worried that Annie might be trying to reach her, she listened to the message.

"Mom, it's Mike. I got your message. Wondering how Dad's doing . . . hoping he's okay. Give me a call and let me know. Karen and I are happy to fly home if you need us. Okay. Give a call. Love you."

Gina tried to picture Mike, whom she hadn't seen since a Whit's Point Sunday night picnic when she was twelve or thirteen, and wondered if she'd be able find his phone number to call him back. She went into Annie and Lester's bedroom where Annie's little antique desk was covered with bills, newspaper clippings, and receipts. Above the desk hung a group of family photographs, some of which Gina knew had been taken by her father. Tall and athletically built, Mike and his brother Randy both had their mother's close-set eyes. In one picture, the boys, in their twenties, stood with Annie between them, their arms firmly around her shoulders. There was a comfortableness about their posture, as if they'd found themselves together this way often. Gina couldn't remember an equivalent photograph in her parents' collection.

"I've always preferred the company of men. I always thought I'd have sons," Gina remembered her mother saying. The betrayal within had hurt Cassie the most, but Gina had felt it, too. Sometimes Gina imagined that her mother lumped her grown daughters in with those "unpreferred" women who were jealous and cagey, prone to stealing anything you cared about. She'd even managed to make her daughters' growing up seem like a spiteful act of stealing from her.

Eleanor had been careful to amend: "Having girls turned out perfectly." But it hadn't really. Girls were pricklier than boys and unwittingly tuned to their mothers' variability. This was true of Esther, too, but Gina welcomed the challenge to get it right with Esther, which is why their current misunderstanding plagued her so.

Gina spotted a typed list of phone numbers and was about to call back Mike when the phone rang again.

"Who's this?" a man asked when Gina answered.

When she told him, he said "Oh, hi, Gina. It's Mike. Mom mentioned you'd be visiting. I hope all's well with you . . . Mom called an hour or more ago when we were out on the boat. I'm wondering about Dad—do you know if he's okay?"

Gina told Mike all that she knew. Mike worried that he and Karen should fly back from Alaska, but Gina reassured him that Lester was being well taken care of.

"Okay, well, tell Mom to call me when she gets home. And can you let me know if something changes? Thanks for everything. I'm so grateful you're there. Mom was thrilled that you were going to stay with them. You can probably tell she loves having *girls* around!"

When they hung up, Gina felt something settle inside her, as if she was in just the right place for the first time since she'd boarded the plane in San Francisco. But she was exhausted to the bone. She made her salad, ate it quickly, and went straight to bed. When she'd stretched out, she called home.

Ben answered. "I have a birthday present for you!"

"You do? I can't wait to get home and see it!"

"It's a really, really super special present! Here's Dad."

"What are you doing for your birthday tomorrow?" Paul asked.

"I haven't had a chance to think about it. Hopefully, Lester will come home tomorrow. I'll call you at some point so I can talk to the kids and tell them we'll have cake when I get back on Sunday."

"Okay . . . I'm thinking of taking them up to Point Reyes tomorrow. I'm not sure. If I do, there might not be phone service. But in any case, we'll be home by seven or so."

Gina's heart sank at the thought that she would miss a fun family outing on her birthday. "Okay," she said.

"Oh, so get this," Paul said. "Esther insisted I take her to Mervyn's to buy a bra. Apparently, she's been wanting one for months. Of course, I haven't seen it on her and have no idea if it fits, so you'll have to see."

Paul's pleasure that Esther would trust him with this errand was so evident that Gina withheld her surprise; Esther didn't even have buds! "It sounds like things are going well there," she said.

"It's been really nice to be with the kids alone. You all right?"

"I'm glad I came." She'd begun to feel that this was true.

After they'd hung up, Gina pictured Paul in the house with the kids and thought of Lester's comment about parents "taking turns at the helm." This had not been easy for her with Paul. As sure as she'd been about him when they married, she'd plunged into motherhood with eyes wide open, high beams on, unable to trust that they'd avoid making her parents' mistakes. She tried to *be there* for Esther and Ben, in six places at the same time if needed. To be, it occurred to her now, both the mother and father she hadn't had, even though the very qualities that made Paul an extraordinary partner—his warmth and sensitivity, patience, and quick sense of humor—made him an exceptional father, too.

She had work to do! Loving not only meant *being there*, but also taking turns, trusting, knowing when to leave and let go.

Memories of Lester's close call and their conversation replayed in her mind. She wondered whether she should stay an extra day to help Annie and worried about finishing the drawings of the house. She wouldn't even pretend to be able to fall asleep. She switched on the light and took *Homeward*'s logbook from the table. The pages rippled in the fan's breeze as she turned the log's first entry, in her father's hand.

August 24, 1977

Ellie, Ron, and Gina and one happy pup aboard. Made it to the Isles of Maine last night in an hour forty with Cap'n Eleanor at the helm. Woke up to fog. Some roll but not uncomfortable. E made pancakes for all, complete with blueberries and maple syrup. Went ashore on Little Neck Is. Explored abandoned house and grounds. Yellow seaweed, light rocks, patches of grass, dark rich green spruce. Like a primeval forest blended by the misty soft light. Rain caught us on the rocky beach, and we took shelter under the spruces that march down to the shore. Finally braced the elements and putted back to Homeward. Spent time housekeeping, reading. Wonderful lazy day.

Closing the logbook, she wondered: how had she come, so suddenly it seemed, to be forty-five? That day her father wrote about—cold rain, the shallow cave they'd explored, filled with fluorescent green mosses—was still vivid, though she had been only seventeen. She remembered how contented her mother and father had seemed, immersed in nature's elements and later, tucked in *Homeward*'s cabin, out of the pouring rain. Usually, these occasional peaceful interludes with her family would buoy her with reassurance. But that August, she couldn't be comforted. She'd never felt more alone.

Outside and inside are both intimate—they are always ready to be reversed, to exchange their hostility. If there exists a border-line surface between such an inside and outside, this surface is painful on both sides.

Gaston Bachelard, The Poetics of Space

CASSIE'S ROOM
12'-11" X 9'-3"

Eleanor's unfinished paintings filled Gina's room, so Gina was staying in Cassie's for the summer, which was painted lavender and faced the driveway.

It was a curse to be stuck for three months in Whit's Point where she'd lost touch with even her closest friends. During her first year at Andrews, Gina always called Sandy when she was home, but Sandy was never around. After a while, she'd given up.

"You'll need some buffers there," Cassie had advised Gina. "Invite some people up." Since her girlfriends at Andrews lived too far away, she invited Mark, who would come at the end of July. In the meantime, all she was equipped with were her worries about college applications and a weighty reading list of Hermann Hesse.

There was her four-days-a-week job at a sandwich shop, but it too felt alien. When she'd heard about the job, she'd pictured a Formica-filled room teeming with flirty, tan teenagers making ice cream cones and flipping burgers. But this sandwich shop, set in a colonial house buried deep within the four-acre Riversport Historic Preservation Project, was a small triangle of space behind the wood counter that formed its hypotenuse. The walls of the room were painted Williamsburg blue. She and her mother had selected two dresses for her that would complement the genteel setting; both were covered with small flowers, and one was trimmed with a little lace on the collar.

She worked alone. Her customers were the employees of the Preservation Project: the blacksmith, the gift shop cashiers, the costumed docents who took tourists through the twelve historic houses; and the tourists themselves, bringing their fascination with all things old.

One day she looked up from the cucumber and tomato sandwich she was making to see Kit, like an apparition from the modern world, his long hair, beard, and denim shirt powdered with dust. She hadn't seen him in three years and felt a confusing surge of excitement she knew she'd have to suppress or she'd scare him off.

"Well, hey," he said, his smile shy. "How long have you been workin' here?"

Suddenly self-conscious in her girly dress, Gina folded her arms across her stomach. When she told him just a week he said, "Cool. Can you make me a ham and Swiss on rye, please? That would be great."

Gina moved from the refrigerator to the bread to the cutting board, feeling Kit's eyes on her. "So what do you do here?" she asked when he'd paid her for the sandwich.

"I'm the boat builder—in the shop by the Governor Goodwin house. Come check it out sometime."

During the next week, Kit came in for his ham and Swiss at lunchtime and sometimes a cookie in the late afternoon, ordering trancelike, watching her get his order together in a way that made her reluctant to say anything that might break the spell he seemed to be under. She fantasized that he'd become captivated by the lilac-scented innocence of the scene in which she played, so harmoniously enhanced by every detail: the smaller-than-life scale of the doors, the divided pane windows, the delicate stencils along the top of the wall, the vase of wildflowers on the counter, and the bit of lace that brushed her cheek when she leaned over the cutting board. What was he seeing when he looked at her? A child he once knew? A seductress? She couldn't guess; there were many days when she felt every bit as innocent, as *colonial,* as the cream, pink, and blue dress she wore. Still, on other days, she felt she was somehow tricking him; that Kit, like herself, was seeing not Gina, but something he could no longer have.

Cassie was in love. "Shacking up!" Eleanor shrieked at Ron when they returned from their surprise visit to Cassie. They'd driven three hours to her apartment and knocked on her door at ten in the morning. Dropping in was Eleanor's habit with friends and family; she wouldn't consider calling ahead—for fear, Gina suspected, of being turned down. She'd ambushed Cassie a few other times, but this time, Wes, Cassie's boyfriend of two years, had answered the door in his boxers.

Gina walked to Tobey's Market to call Cassie on the pay phone. "The morality police!" Cassie grumbled. "You should've seen her face—it was like I'd stabbed her through the heart!"

Gina decided not to share that her mother had been crying on and off ever since, and cracked, "Why buy the cow, when you can get the milk free!"

"I've never felt this way about someone before," Cassie said. "Wes is so wonderful." *Won-der-ful* unfurled like a lazy wave; it was the first time in her life Gina had heard the sound of real, swooning love, and for some reason, it made her want to cry.

There was a pause she would always remember: the smell of the Juicy Fruit gum stuck to the telephone infusing her sense of loss. It reminded her of when her family had gone swimming at Lake Winnepesaukee, and for the first time Cassie was allowed to swim beyond the necklace of buoys that separated safe from dangerous. After that day, she never again swam inside the buoys with Gina. Gina had worried; would she be safe without her big sister?

Cassie was in love now, and even though she'd left home a long time ago, she'd formed a new kind of bond that could take her even further away. In her mind, Gina too had traveled far from Whit's Point, but her body still got driven to Maine and parked high and dry every year about the same time that the boats in town got released from their cradles back into the water.

"That's so neat, Cass." She wanted badly to sound happy for her, since no one else at home was.

Gina said goodbye to Cassie and walked home along Pickering Road's narrow sidewalk feeling tall and out of scale next to the small houses that sat practically on the street Their blank windows seemed to stare as she slipped by. I'll get used to it, she told herself; it was always like this at the beginning of summer: the dissociation, the self-consciousness that came from being recognized, but not really known. After a few more weeks, she'd feel the warm moist air, the cool grass, and salty water welcoming her back into the landscape, and she would belong.

Three weeks after she'd started her job, lonely and heady with Kit's daily dose of admiration, Gina surprised herself one day after work by walking right up to him while he was sanding a boat bottom. "Hi," she said.

Kit looked up, startled. She smiled. She'd taken out her barrettes so her hair could drift around her face, and she was carrying her shoes. Kit scanned her as if she might not be the same girl he'd only seen behind a counter. "Hi," he said.

"Are you almost done for the day? I'm going to walk over to the wharf to look at the schooner, and I was wondering if you'd like to . . . "

"Oh," Kit said.

He surveyed the shop. There were tools and sawdust everywhere; clearly, he wasn't ready to close up. But she could feel his wanting to go, could feel he wouldn't say no.

"Sure," he said. "I can just come back after to clean up."

She smiled and brushed her hand down her dress, smoothing it against her body.

Kit locked the barn door, and as they traversed the grounds of the Preservation Project, Gina realized that she'd premeditated only the invitation and had no idea what should come next. She was glad that without the counter between them, Kit seemed more relaxed and chatty. He'd recently run into her parents at the town dock and admired their new boat, *Homeward*. "Did you see them movin' those houses?" he asked.

"It was kind of strange," Gina said, remembering the three historic houses that had been relocated to the Preservation Project from another part of town. "They looked so undignified stacked on those truck beds. I mean, the idea of just up and moving a house from the place it's been standing for a few hundred years. Like moving an old tree. Or a famous ruin. It almost seems sacrilegious."

Kit said, "Hmm. I hadn't thought of it that way. I guess because I'm a builder, I just think of the buildings in terms of their construction, not as something with roots in a place."

A builder. "So, where do you go to college?" she asked.

Kit laughed and Gina, realizing her error, flushed with embarrassment. "I don't," he said. "I'm a full-time boatwright." He told her about the rowing shells he and his father made that were sleek and fast—nothing like the traditional wood dories he built at the Preservation Project.

They crossed the street, and halfway down the old wood wharf where the historic schooner was docked, a sharp pain pierced the ball of Gina's foot. Kit took her hand and led her to a bench along the wharf's railing where she hitched up her dress and crossed her foot over her knee so they could examine it. "Piece of glass in there," Kit said. He was leaning so close she could smell the sweetness of the sawdust in his hair. He stood and searched his pockets. "Rats. Tell you what—if you can sort of hop back to the shop with me, I've got some tweezers there." He wrapped his arm firmly around her waist—a necessary and natural gesture, but one that made her feel cared for in a way she'd never been before. "Go ahead and lean on me," he said.

Back at the shop, he pulled a chair close to hers and held her foot in his lap. The old barn—filled with the fragrance of wood and varnish and decorated with antique tools—transported Gina back to all the special places she'd spent time with Kit when they were younger. Now, it felt romantic to be entrusting her foot to him. In seconds, he'd removed the piece of glass. He dabbed first aid cream on the wound and put on a Band-Aid.

"Ah . . . what a relief! Thank you!" Gina laughed and kicked her repaired foot in the air. When she looked at Kit again, his eyes were sparkling.

"You're lovely," he said. His eyes held hers long enough that she had to look away. "Well. I guess I better get this place cleaned up, and we should both get home."

The encounter with Kit took on magic in the following days; every time he walked out of the sandwich shop, Gina remembered the very lovely way he'd said *lovely* and the way it had made her feel ... well, *lovely*. Certainly, *lovely* was not the kind of word favored by Mark, who described her breasts as "boobalicious." So she said *yes* when Kit asked if she'd like to go out rowing with him the next Saturday, and the following one, too.

Their outings on the water provided vital respite from her parents. The third time Gina was leaving the house to go rowing with Kit, her mother said, "What's all this about?"

"What?" Gina said.

"Why are you spending so much time with Kit?"

Gina read her mother's disapproval and seized the opportunity to provoke her. "He's really great," she said.

"I'm sure. Has he gone to college yet?"

"Nope. Didn't need to, to build boats."

"Well, don't take his interest in you too seriously."

Furious, Gina decided that from here on out, she'd make sure to torture her mother by announcing her "dates" with Kit.

Kit was an attentive listener, and she took full advantage, freely complaining to him about her home life. He was *kind*, never forgetting to stow cookies and an extra sweater for her, just in case. She felt a natural ease with him—a familiarity deep in her bones. But she had to admit to herself that although his obvious crush on her felt exciting, she wasn't attracted to Kit. It was possible that he was "too nice," the words she and her friends used to describe boys who weren't sexy to them. While masquerading for her mother, she'd have to be careful not to stoke his romantic interest. Besides, she had a boyfriend.

Sitting cross-legged on the end of the bed wrapped in a blanket, Gina read Mark's letter for the second time. *It is not really horniness at all,* he'd written, in response to a letter she'd sent to him about not wanting to feel pressured into having sex all the time.

Mark as you see him now, is the product of a great deal of hurt,
abused trust, and self-hatred. Mark's social life, especially the
last few years since he left his nerd scene in Manhattan and
tried to make it in WASP-ville, Connecticut, was nightmarish . . .

Gina was riveted by these worldly revelations. What was "WASP"? After describing several cycles of self-loathing and cockiness, Mark came to his conclusion, which was that he felt most loved

. . . when my head is buried in your neck and my hands in your
jeans; yes, behind the tree, in the car, under the table. P.S. As for
loving you for your body, have you looked in the mirror lately?
You gotta know, honey, there's some hungry men out there, and
some of us still wear retainers at night.

A snorting bull illustrated the P.S.

Ugh! He was infuriating! He could talk circles around her, seducing her with his vulnerability, scaring her with his effrontery.

She missed him.

She folded the letter, stuffed it into the envelope, and hid it with her journal in the bottom drawer, under Cassie's Miss Andrews Academy Award, which she had dubbed "the good girl award."

On the day that Mark was to arrive, Gina felt gorgeous. She'd acquired a deep tan and her long hair was sun-streaked from her days at the beach. She put on her light blue halter top and looked in the mirror—yep, she was looking good and felt strong, more than ready to take on Mark.

At five o'clock she put down the top on their recently purchased secondhand Mustang and climbed into the driver's seat. The car smelled warm and leathery. She'd only had her learner's permit for a week and already loved to drive. She cocked the rearview mirror to check her face as her father sat down next to her—oh, if she could just save forever this perfect moment of anticipation, this feeling of omnipotence and today's zitless face that looked at her from the mirror! She drove slowly and carefully to the Trailways station, savoring her excitement. When they pulled in, Mark bounced down the bus steps wearing jeans, a denim jacket, and carrying a backpack, looking even sexier than she'd remembered him. He fingered his dark shoulder-length hair behind his ear as he surveyed the parking lot.

"Mark!" Gina called.

"How goes it?" Her father said when Mark shook his hand. Ron climbed into the backseat, and Mark sat down next to Gina. His clothes smelled deliciously of detergent and cigarette smoke. As he leaned over to give her a little kiss near her ear, he put his hand on her knee and quickly slid it up to the top of her thigh, nestling it between her legs. Unnerved, with one eye on her father in the rearview mirror, Gina pushed his hand away.

On the way home, twice she nearly turned left into oncoming traffic.

"God, you're lookin' good, Gina Lo-La." After Gina's mother had greeted Mark and gone inside, Mark slipped his hands around Gina's waist. "Have you missed me?"

"Yeah."

A little breeze brushed her bare back and made her shiver. Mark rubbed her breasts with both hands. "Ooh, I've missed my friends," he cooed.

Gina pulled away from him as her mother popped out of the screen door holding a Coke for Mark. "Virginia, why don't you get the stuff to set the table out here. It's such a gorgeous evening. *Paper* plates."

Gina went inside to get silverware, napkins, and the flimsy paper plates that always soaked through before you were halfway done with a lobster. When she returned, Mark and her parents were standing with their toes against the garden, their focus cast over the hill, out to sea.

"With a southwesterly wind like this, we can get to the Isles of Maine in less than two hours," her mother was saying.

"No kidding," Mark said. "So Eleanor, have you always been a sailor?"

"Oh, yes. We'd take the train up from Long Island for the summer at Lily House—my family's house. I was the only girl around here who sailed in those days, and my old friend Bill Holloway and I . . . we usually won all the Sunday races."

"A good sailor, this Bill?" Mark said. He shifted to glance at Gina, and she smiled. She loved his sly command of her mother. She set four places at the table, then stretched out in the hammock, just within earshot.

"Oh, *yehhhhhs!*" Her mother said in that breathy Hollywood way. "Bill was my best friend. He went to Yale and then was a lieutenant in the Air Force—his plane was shot down in the Korean War. But anyway, on my twenty-first birthday, Bill rowed me blindfolded out to Miller's Island—that's the one there, with the lighthouse. It was the most beautiful day. We had a fire on the rocks and baked lobster and potatoes . . . isn't it funny, I remember he'd forgotten a flashlight. But we didn't care . . . "

Bill Holloway's name always came up when Eleanor was talking about sailing, but the older Gina got, the more starry-eyed her mother's references to him became. Gina had tried to ignore this disturbing lapse, but now she heard something clear as a bell in her mother's story: unrequited love. It was disgusting! Bill Holloway had been her sister Fran's fiancé and Sid's father! Gina checked Mark's expression; he appeared to be amused by it all.

"Anyway," Eleanor went on, "the tide went out, and we had to haul the boat halfway across the island to get it back in the water. It was very late . . . my sister Fran was *furious* when I got home . . . "

Gina watched a mountainous white cloud float in front of the sun, making the world dimmer for a minute.

"You have to watch the tide here," Eleanor said. "The current in the river will suck you all the way up to the naval prison. Our girls figured that out the hard way." She paused and flapped her arms. "What a day! It would have been nice to get out on the water, but Ron just wants to putter, I guess." Her mother laughed as if it were just a little joke, but Gina bristled at her deteriorating tone. "I've been trying to get him to take the storm windows off for two months, so what's he doing on the most beautiful day in July?" Eleanor gestured to the two windows propped up against the house. "Oh, this house is a dump! But isn't it marvelous? It's the best piece of property on the cove, the one with the *real* view straight out the harbor. I wanted to live in this house the very first time I laid eyes on it."

Right now, in fact, Gina thought her mother looked as if she were stoned on the view.

"I hope at least Ron's putting the lobsters in. I still can't stand doing that, you know, even after all these years!"

When Eleanor had gone into the house, Mark flung himself on top of Gina in the hammock and buried his face in her hair. "She's all right," he said. "Not so bad. Who's this Bill guy? She clearly had the hots for *that* dude."

"The guy she wishes she'd married, I'm pretty sure," she said.

"So, Mark, have you given any thought to where you might apply to college in the fall?" Eleanor asked when they'd sat down for dinner.

The little patch of flat grass at the edge of the hill facing the cove was their makeshift patio where they put their table. A *real* patio was on her mother's "if this house were mine" list. There were only three plastic chairs with the table, so Ron had brought out a wood one for Mark. Gina shifted her seat a little so she could have a better view of the cove. It was a gentle evening; a layer of stratus clouds took the sharpness out of the blue sky and even though the breeze had died down, the mosquitoes hadn't yet found them. With the question about college, Gina became hopeful that the conversation might advance beyond her mother's past.

"Well, so far, I'm thinking maybe Harvard, Stanford, and possibly Berkeley."

"Really? California? Good for you—an adventurer, like me! Of course, I didn't get to go to college because . . . well, anyway . . . "

Her mother rolled her eyes and laughed. What a hypocrite she was to make Mark sound like some kind of pioneer! She would never let Gina apply to a college that far away.

"I hope you're going to put some thought into their art programs," her mother went on. "You've got such talent."

The way she tilted her head! Gina thought. Was she *flirting* with him?

"I hear you've been doing some painting yourself. You must've inherited Gina's talent." Mark winked at Eleanor.

"Oh, there's talent in the Banton family all right. That's my family, I mean. In fact my nephew, Sid, is a marvelous painter. He *was*, anyway. He's thrown all that talent away to work in the antiques business." She tsked, casting her glance into the distance, then caught herself and looked back at Mark. "Well of course, Virginia's the *real* artist in the family," she said, smiling. She turned to Gina. "How about those . . . clay sculptures you did for your . . . semantics project?"

"Semiotics," Mark corrected.

Her mother snapped a leg off her lobster. "Oh right. *Semiotics.*"

Gina tried to ignore the conversation, turning to the cove where two kids were swimming off their rowboat. She waited for the delayed rattle of oarlocks and the *thwack!* as they hit the water.

"The pieces are very evocative, though, aren't they?" Mark said. "Romantic. Like Stonehenge in *Tess of the D'Urbervilles.*"

He was masterful!

"I think you have something there," her mother said, even though Gina was quite sure her mother had never read Hardy. "Virginia, sweetie, could you go in and get another Coke for Mark?"

"That's okay—I'll get one," Mark said. He rose from his chair, producing an awful crack. "Uh-oh," he groaned, looking down at the stretcher he'd snapped off.

"Don't even think about it!" Eleanor said. "That chair's so old, it's probably been repaired a hundred times. Cassandra Westwick's chair," she added.

"Cassandra West . . . " Mark took a second look at the chair.

"Cassandra was a relative of ours—a Salem witch," Eleanor said. "Since Cassie was supposed to be born on Halloween, we thought it would be fun to give her a witch name."

In her head, Gina did the math. She noted Cassie's birthday: September eighteenth, nineteen fifty-five. Her parents were married in nineteen fifty-five, too, in February. Seven months. How premature could a baby be? "What? Cassie was premature?" she said.

"Certainly," her mother said.

"I'm sure Gina's told you about her other famous American ancestors?" her father said.

"Dad," Gina protested. "I'm sure Mark has his own famous American ancestors and doesn't— "

"No, no. I don't. I'm Jewish, remember?" Mark said.

"Oh, well, that's all right then," her father said. Under the table, Gina felt the wind of her mother's leg kicking her father.

Before Mark was up the next morning, Gina rode her old bike to the phone booth at Tobey's. She had to call Cassie; she couldn't get the mystery about Cassie's birth out of her head. She'd never heard that Cassie was almost six weeks premature and had been a small baby.

"Oh yeah," Cassie sleepily confirmed on the phone. "Did it just occur to you? Why else do you think they'd get married in the winter— in *Maine*?"

Now, her mother's ranting about Cassie's immorality filled Gina with fury. She wanted Cassie to share her outrage or at least to wonder with her how the pregnancy might have happened. But she realized that Cassie probably had no answers and worse, was not even interested in speculating. She was *gone*; that was all. Gina let their conversation wind down with chitchat and rode home.

Back at the house, she examined a photograph of her mother and father on the hall desk, taken when her mother was probably not yet thirty. Gina had walked past this picture thousands of times, but hadn't seen the two people she saw now, perched on the deck of a sailboat, their strong, tan limbs touching. Her mother had made love to this man! Impossible! Though her father often embraced her mother, she never reached out for him, except to push him away. Yet once, she'd wanted him enough to let herself go too far.

"Hi, Lo." Mark's voice drifted down the stairwell; she looked up to see him pointing a sword at her.

"Handle with care. It's from the War of 1812."

Mark put the sword away, came downstairs, and rested his chin on Gina's shoulder. "Your mom? Sexy lady," he observed about the photograph of her mother, toned and confident posing in her shorts. "And her daughter, too."

Gina and Mark drove the Mustang to the beach the next two days and stayed all afternoon. It was cozy, lying next to Mark in a sweet cloud of Coppertone. Through the triangle of space between her arm and the towel, she watched teenagers strutting self-consciously along the sand and thought of all the days she'd come here alone. Now, she basked in the supernal comfort of being a girl with her boyfriend at the beach. Her eyes followed the sexy curves of Mark's sun-bronzed back to where they formed a little valley at the top of his swimsuit. In this idyllic landscape, crowded with mothers and small children, she could run her hand across his warm skin without the risk of initiating something more. If only this delicious attraction she felt from a short distance didn't evaporate as soon as Mark put his moves on her!

"Why don't you take the dinghy out for a sail?" Gina's father suggested as he was stepping out the front door the next day. He and her mother were driving to Boston to pick up a new tripod and wouldn't be home until three. At the bottom of the steps he turned and said, "Watch the current in the river, though, if you're out when the tide turns."

"Do Ron and Eleanor ever go anywhere without each other?" Mark asked Gina when they were rigging the sail. He held the bag and pulled out bunches of sail while Gina slid the clips onto the mast.

"No," she said. "You make them sound devoted."

"Your father is. He's like, dorky-in-love. It would drive my parents nuts to be around each other all the time."

Her father *was* dorky-in-love, Gina thought; lately, this had been making her kind of sick. "They don't have sex," she said, remembering the porn videos Mark had found in his father's drawer. "At least your parents have sex."

"Yup. Of *that* we can be sure."

Gina tugged the halyard, and the sail slid up the mast, flapping in the breeze. The tide was still more than an hour from being high, so they had to push the boat over the mud with the oars to get it afloat. Gina took the tiller, and when they reached the mouth of the cove, she put the centerboard down. The boat heeled nicely on a steady forward course. It was a perfect sailing day; with the wind from the southwest, she could stay on this tack all the way to the lighthouse. She took a deep breath, pulling in the fresh salty air, and leaned back against a cushion. Strands of hair caressed her face, and the sun warmed the top of her thighs. Everything felt right. She was already sad about Mark's leaving tomorrow.

Mark took off his shirt, stretched out on the center seat and was soon asleep. When they reached Miller's Island, Gina pushed the tiller hard to come about. The sail flapped wildly then caught the breeze, turning the boat on its ear. Mark jerked awake. "Whoa!" he howled, sitting up and squinting in the bright light. He reached over and took his sunglasses out of his shirt pocket.

"Do you wanna sail?" Gina asked.

"Sure." Mark's sweatshirt was in the hold, and he reached under it and pulled out a beer.

"Did you just take that from the fridge?"

"Don't worry; they won't notice."

They changed places, and he took the tiller. Gina peeled down to her bathing suit and stretched out on the seat. She closed her eyes and listened to the water swooshing against the hull.

Mark touched her shoulder. "Come on down here and sit by me," he said.

He finished his beer and sank it overboard, then propped up a cushion for her. Gina slid over to sit cross-legged next to him on the damp floorboards. When he put his arm around her shoulder and slid his hand into her bathing suit top, she concentrated on not letting her urge to pull away spoil the sublime afternoon. But conversation died instantly upon Mark's hand making contact with her palest flesh; in the brilliant daylight while motorboats whizzed by, she felt awkward. Mark seemed to feel only her breast. As soon as she managed to, she put his hand out of her mind. Mark reached over, took hers and plunged it into his bathing suit. It was always like this: his telling her hands what to do. "Just hold it there, okay?" he said. He tilted his head back and pushed his hardness into her hand.

"Mark, c'mon." Gina pulled her hand away. "You aren't even paying attention to the wind. We're luffing—head off a little."

She reached for her shirt and Mark made his sad dog-face. Now she felt like a meanie and a prude. What was *wrong* with her?

By the time they'd sailed around the island, the breeze had died to a mere breath. Mark let the sheet run free until the sail was all the way out on a reach.

"The tide's high," Gina said when they reached the cove. She pulled up the centerboard and dangled her fingers in the water. "It's soupy! Feel it!"

Mark dragged his hand overboard and smiled. Gina stood up and let the sail drop with the halyard. After they'd furled the sail and secured the boat on the outhaul, they dove into the water. Mark bee-lined for the shore, but Gina swam to the middle of the cove where she stopped and treaded water. She looked around her at the green fields and barns, the apple trees and rickety docks that rimmed the water. The cove was sacred to her, the center of a small, safe universe. A place where she could be buffered, weightless and free. She thought of Sandy—how she missed their swims together.

"Come out!" she yelled to Mark.

"I'm tired and hungry," he called back. "Come back in, okay?"

Gina was disappointed, but hungry, too. She sidestroked in to the dock, and they climbed the hill. She pulled out the garden hose so they could rinse off the salt water and tinsel-shaped strands of seaweed.

Her parents hadn't remembered to open the windows before going out, and the house's heavy, mildewy air blanketed the light heartedness she'd felt outside. As she and Mark went upstairs to get dressed, a hornet bombed across the hall, just missing her head. She checked the clock: one-thirty; still an hour or so before her parents would be home. They parted ways in the hall, Mark going to the guest room, she to Cassie's to change. She started to shut the door but decided it would be unfriendly and left it ajar. Within moments, Mark came in with his suit off, drying his hair with a towel. She reached for her clothes on the bed, and he looped the towel around her stomach from behind, pulling her body against his. He purred into her ear, smelling of beer. "Let me dress you," he said, and she thought, *He won't try anything new here.* He unclipped her bathing suit top and pushed her bottoms down to her knees with his thumbs, then pressed them to the floor with his foot. A wave of queasiness— or was it just hunger?—rolled over her. She pulled away. Mark turned and kicked the bedroom door shut with his foot.

"Mark—" his name caught in her throat.

"Shhh, don't worry."

His face was flushed, unyielding as his eyes moved up and down her body. "Mark!" More emphatic this time, but he pressed his lips against hers, and his tongue moved frantically around in her mouth. Heat and fear, his hands on her breasts again. The wooden monkey that had once been hers looked down at her from the new shelves her parents had just built where the old door to the maid's stair had once been. Hands slid around her damp body. On the bureau, a photograph of Cassie and Gina under the apple tree. In the picture, Cassie was just the age Gina was now; she wasn't smiling because moments before, Eleanor had told her she couldn't go out that night with Billy Cutler in his Chevy. Mark's mouth was on her nipple, and he nudged her backward toward the bed. Their skin touched everywhere; everywhere was wet, slippery. Determination seemed to harden Mark's whole body as he arched her back and eased her down, letting her head fall into the nubby cotton of the bedspread. Below him now, she felt small, limp. She gripped the rug with her toes. "Mark, what are you doing?" As if she didn't know. "We can't . . . " Was he seeing her? No. His eyes roamed, never meeting hers. He was all hands and then he was leaning into her, and she tightened her thighs against his weight, but they trembled. Where was her strength? *No, Mark.*

"No, Mark!" Had she said it out loud? Yes, she must have because his hand slid over her mouth, his eyes were closed, and he was saying, "Shhh, it's okay. You're so beautiful." And then footsteps—was it?—on the stair. Had her parents come home early? "Shhh," Mark said again, because he had heard it, too, and she froze, taking herself outside the room now, listening beyond their breathing, beyond what pinched and pulled, listening to the walls, barely feeling him slip inside her; yes, she was certain now, steps and the closing of the bathroom door. Must not make a sound. Not a sound. Slipping in and out, hurting her, stuffing her resistance farther and farther up inside her, his breath stealing hers.

The awful ache in her back stopped. Her whole body pounded. She listened. Goose bumps broke out on her skin, as if every inch of her was extending itself to hear. Mark stood over her and offered his hands to pull her up off the bed. A hideous calm spread over his face.

"Did you—" she breathed, her hand over her mouth.

"Uh-huh," he nodded with a look of blissful apology.

"Virginia?" Her mother's voice, from the bathroom.

"Not anymore," Mark snickered.

Shock sucked the noisiness from Gina's head, sharpened her

senses. The critical seconds that would hold an expected response began to pass. In another era, she realized, she would've been able to escape from here, open that door and slip down the maid's stair into the kitchen. She heard her own voice: strange, cheerful, almost singing out, "What, Mom?"

"Could you come here for a minute?"

Gina threw on her jeans and tee shirt and carried her sore and shaky body down the hall toward the long mirror, concentrating on her face, wanting to cry out at the girl she saw there but working on a smile—no, not a smile, just a look of insouciance—as she reached for the bathroom doorknob. She opened the door. Her mother sat on the closed toilet holding a nail clipper. "Yeah?" Gina chirped, searching her body for an innocent gesture, then flicking her hair behind her shoulder.

Her mother hunched, apparently examining her fingernails. She spread her hand on her thigh and with the other, began to clip. *Clip!* The nail hit the linoleum floor with an impossibly loud *tick*. Only under extreme duress would her sanitary-minded mother litter the floor with her nails.

"Where's Mark? What're you doing?" Her mother asked, not looking up. *Clip, tick.*

Clip, tick.

Gina shivered from a chill that seemed to emanate from her mother. She realized that coming on the heels of Cassie's misdeed, her own might be the one to put her mother over the edge. Gina could do this; she could lie. "We went swimming and Mark's changing. In the guest room."

Her mother's head shook like a bobble-head doll's. She'd clipped all the nails on her hand but she started in on them again, thumb first. *Clip, tick, clip, tick.* "Nobody knows . . . " she said miserably. "Why do I even bother? I might as well drop dead."

Her nails were cut to the quick. When she squeezed the clipper down on her nonexistent baby fingernail, she flinched and thrust the finger in her mouth. Gina half expected her to slump off the toilet onto the linoleum.

Eleanor looked up at her with a penetrating gaze. "I was just changing," Gina said.

So easy to say what should have been, what they both wanted to believe. Gina and Eleanor, looking across that tiny room at each other, constructing a truth from a lie.

When her mother had gone downstairs, Gina climbed into the bathtub and lay with her ears submerged. Her heart raced and for once, she welcomed the rush of adrenaline that would keep her from sinking and betraying her lie.

The water in the tub tilted when she moved, spilling into the overflow drain with a gurgle. She surveyed the room, pulling each detail into her like breaths of air: a claw-foot tub standing on a black-and-white linoleum floor, an old porcelain sink with brass faucets; above the sink, a glass shelf with her mother's make-up collection: two lipsticks, two bottles of Max Factor foundation, a bottle of Chanel #9. Faded peach bath towels and delicate objects lined the room: a silver bowl full of shells, a white porcelain baby's hand for holding rings. The ashtray, *casa senza donna, barca senza timone*. It was a cozy, feminine room, a place to linger.

She pulled her face underwater, and when she came up, her eyes strayed to the ugly rings of rust where the sink pipes connected with the wall. Mildew speckled the wall above her head, the linoleum behind the toilet was peeling up. The house was beginning to fall apart. The skin around her thumbs and toes was wrinkling. It was a different body now, stretched out before her; she would need to watch it carefully. She ducked once more, opening her mouth, flushing him from every orifice.

In Cassie's room, her insides churned. She dressed quickly, then read three chapters of *Rosshalde* without a single word of it lodging in her head. She stood and left the room. When she crept past the guest room, Mark was stretched out on the bed reading, his shirt off, ankles crossed and one hand cradling his head. He turned and smiled at her. He was *victorious!*

She hated him.

She drifted down the stairs and out the door, across the front yard to the crest of the hill, where she sat down behind the rose bush. The tide was on its way out, and the mudflats stretched out brown and life-less, as if the cove's soul were being taken with the tide. But it would be reborn an infinite number of times each time the water returned: blue, green, still and reflective, rippled and dancing, frozen white.

She drew her knees up under her chin. There was no rebirth for her, only moving forward from this day, forward in this body—the same, yet irreversibly changed.

"Gina." Mark had come out of the house, and he sat down beside her without touching. "Are you sad?" he asked sheepishly.

Sad? Not sad; sadness was heavy and still, when feelings finally came to rest. Hers still whirled furiously around her like birds afraid to light. "Nope," she said, her eyes fixed on the dinghy, stranded on the mud.

It was the closest thing to the truth she would ever again bother to tell him.

"Come on now, kiddo. Get up and get going. Don't take yourself so seriously." Gina's mother snapped up the shade and whisked out of the room.

Gina put down her book and looked at the clock. It was eleven. Tuesday. Mark had left ten days ago; her period was three days late.

As soon as Gina felt reasonably assured that an exchange with her mother about the incident was never going to take place, her rage toward Mark began to consume her. Then, the long summer days grew hotter, the light more golden, the zinnias in the garden reached their glorious peak, and her anger boomeranged. How could I have been so careless? Why wasn't I stronger? She let her feelings loose in her journal, writing around the event, careful not to name it.

Cassie's room was a mess. In three days, Gina hadn't even bothered to open the window. The stuffier the room became, the less inclined she felt to leave it, as though she were being slowly absorbed into its walls. She rolled over and flipped to the end of her book. Ten more pages of summer reading, six more weeks of summer. Downstairs, her mother was giving her father his daily dose of hell; no doubt he was paying for the sins of his daughters. It suddenly occurred to her: it was not only her mother who made her crazy, but the *house*, too. If she lived in a long, modern ranch house like Mark's, in a room like his at the end of a wing, she could do whatever she wanted and have total privacy. *Wings*: she needed them.

She kicked off the covers and flew out of bed.

When she rode into Tobey's parking lot, a pickup filled with lobster traps and stinking of bait was parked next to the phone booth and a man in filthy khakis was using the phone. This she hadn't counted on. She had to spill her guts to someone *now* while she still had the nerve. "Cassie," she would say, "I did a terrible thing." No. "Cassie, a terrible thing happened. Cassie, Mark . . . " What? Mark what? "Cassie, Mark and I made love in your room." *Ha!* Made love.

Had sex. So many ways to say it, but none of them fit. "Gina," Cassie would cry out. "Do you use birth control?"

"Cassie, Mark just attacked me," she could say, just to make it simple. "What an asshole!" Cassie might say, and she might be right, but she might not be, either.

Gina rode in circles in the parking lot, stirring up clouds of dust around her. The man in the phone booth had turned around, and she frowned at him for looking at her, the letch. When he left the booth, she picked up the phone and dialed Cassie's number; it rang, and she hung up. Because the only thing more humiliating than the truth would be the telling of it.

"Gina!"

Gina turned toward the voice to see Kit strolling across the street. He'd shaved his beard.

She brushed her hair out of her face and forced a smile.

"You okay?" he asked.

"Yeah, I'm fine. I was just going to call Cassie. I like to use the pay phone because . . . " Flustered, she rolled her eyes and fought back tears.

Kit turned toward the harbor, giving her a moment. "I just went down to the dock and put my shell in the water. I've been repairin' it all week. Are you sure you're okay?" he asked again, turning back to her and putting his hand on her bike to steady it.

"I'm fine," she said. "Just having a bad day."

"But it's still early! How bad could it be?"

Gina looked up at his open smile, the blue sky framing his head. She hadn't noticed how clear a day it was. Or anything about the weather lately. The traffic was picking up on the road and shirtless boys—"wharf rats"—were heading down to the town dock to hang out.

"Wanna go rowin'?"

"Now?" Gina realized she'd do anything not to go home.

"It's so great to have a friend who can *row*!" Kit said.

Gina followed the rhythm of his strokes as they sliced through the harbor and out past the islands. She breathed in the reviving air rising from the blue. For a long time, she didn't look up from her hands as they pulled back, forward, back, forward. A song came into her head, its notes aligning with her strokes, and she watched the muscles in her thighs flex, her arms tighten and extend, until they were not just legs and arms, but *her* legs and arms again. "Friend," he'd said. Exactly what she needed to hear; exactly what she needed.

They reached Miller's Island where the lighthouse stood. "Let's pull the boat up on the beach for a bit!" Kit called.

"Okay," she said, though she'd been enjoying the rowing and the quiet distance it allowed.

They climbed out of the shell, and she followed him to the abandoned house where the lighthouse keeper had lived before the light became electronically operated. When they stepped onto the broken floorboards of the porch, Kit looked out to sea and spread his arms. "Wouldn't this be an amazin' place to live? Surrounded by water, no cars . . . no noise except the foghorn and the birds."

Gina smiled and nodded, wishing she could hear that music now, over the crescendo of her worries. She left the porch and wandered slowly across the scruffy grass and tangle of sweet peas, then scrambled over the rocks until she found a large flat one to sit on. She was hoping Kit would follow her.

He didn't. He inspected the house inside and out, then walked to the southernmost edge of the small island. Gina watched him meandering along the shore, every now and then stooping to pick up something. Slowly, he made his way back to her and held his fist out. She opened her hand and on it, he deposited several pieces of sea glass, all of them blue, the color most treasured by beachcombers.

He sat on the rock with his back to hers, nearly touching. "It's great out here. All that talk with the tourists at the Project can get to me. By the time the weekend rolls around, I need some time to be alone."

Alone. Only during the past week did Gina understand what alone really meant. She swallowed and pushed back tears, relieved that Kit couldn't see her face.

When she didn't answer, Kit asked, "So how was the visit with your boyfriend?"

Emotion overwhelmed her; embarrassed, she covered her face with her hands. Kit stood and found a rock where he could sit facing her.

"We broke up," she managed.

"Aw. I'm sorry. Could ya use a hug?"

She nodded. When he put his arms around her, she felt ten years old, thirteen, seventeen. It was a hug she had needed for a very long time.

Kit pulled back, his hand gently holding her wrist, and kissed her lightly on the lips. When he pulled away, she did her best to smile, stood, and walked toward the boat.

"Should we get rowing now?" she called over her shoulder, knowing this would be the last time they would cross the harbor together, the last time she would be, for Kit, *a friend who can row*.

Architecture is to be regarded by us with the most serious thought. We may
live without her, and worship without her, but we cannot remember without her.
                              John Ruskin, *The Seven Lamps of Architecture*

Chapter 13

"He's a tough old guy," Annie pronounced to Gina in the morning as she hauled her hose around the garden. Green shears leaned from the pocket of her khaki shorts. "I sure wish Mike and Karen weren't off in Alaska. But we'll be all right."

"I know you will," Gina said, thinking, you have to be. You have a barn full of life waiting to be created. "But since Lester can't come home today, I'm going to stay an extra day."

Annie insisted she and Lester would be fine, but her eyes were owlish from fatigue, and she was wearing her shirt inside out. Gina sat down on the stoop. Her drawings would have to wait while she kept Annie company. The air smelled different this morning, she noticed—sweeter, maybe. The heat was still overbearing, but now and then a tiny breeze touched the grass.

"Thank goodness you saw the skylight and found the studio!" Annie said, shaking her head. "I'd been meaning to show it to you. We only put in the skylight and new lighting two years ago, but we've had the studio, mmm . . . almost five years. Your dad helped Lester with the floor, and your ma and I painted. I think at the time they'd temporarily run out of projects at their house, so they were *thrilled* when we recruited them. Especially since your mother could hardly bear to go inside the house. When we finished the studio . . . oh, they loved it! We'd have our gin and tonics right there on the big rug."

If her parents had mentioned it, Gina had forgotten. The brightness of the studio shone through in Annie's words, and Gina felt a corner of herself light up, too, as she pictured the four old friends together. Her father would have loved the idea of the studio since he'd given up his darkroom when he'd retired. Her mother would have admired the modern lighting and the wide-open space.

"They were the only ones who knew about it," Annie went on. "Everyone needs a little hideaway; don't they? But, oh my, what a job!" she said. "First, there was the termite problem, then the family of raccoons nesting in the wall. Let's see . . . half the foundation needed replacing. What else? We put in a new beam . . . "

Gina listened with fascination. She could see how, when her mother was at her creative and energetic best, she and Annie would have hit it off. They had their shared interests—nature, the arts, *projects*. But also, the two women seemed unflappable in the face of construction, despite, or maybe because of, their relative lack of resources. Was this Yankee stoicism or just the way they were? Each time Annie said "Ellie" with affection in her voice, the idea of her mother as companionable became more real. It seemed her growing fondness for Annie was opening up her heart to her mother, too.

Annie stooped to turn off the hose, picked up something small from the flowerbed and threw it over the fence. "You know," she said, "the day we christened the studio, your mother said, 'Now's your chance. Tell Lester if he doesn't quit smoking, you'll lock him out of here.' It worked! Well, I mean, it took two years, and I did have to actually lock him out once or twice." Annie laughed. "Your mother was really the first—well, maybe the second—feminist in town, you know. She was one of the few people who understood I needed my career with the symphony."

"Mom really admired you, Annie."

Annie turned and looked at the studio, her eyes moist. When her lip quivered, and she began to cry, Gina stood up to hug her. The back of Annie's shirt was damp, and she smelled of rosemary. "They hadn't even drunk their tea!" she said, wagging a limp lily. Gina thought of Annie going into her parents' house the day of the accident, and all at once the dam she'd been shoring up for months burst. She cried into Annie's collar with such abandon that for a few moments, she forgot where she was. When she finally stopped, she felt Annie's arms tight around her and filled with the deepest comfort she'd felt since her parents' accident.

They remained in their embrace for several minutes. Finally, Annie stepped back and smiled warmly through her tears. She turned on the garden hose, and Gina returned to the stoop.

"Sometimes I think your mother and I were born a generation too early." Annie said. "Ellie wanted her children to have the things she didn't—the important things, not material things—and by golly, she made it happen. She made you girls independent. She certainly got that part right."

Annie looked over her shoulder at Gina with a smile and hint of mischief. "Of course, you and I both know that most days, she regretted the *independent* part."

Gina laughed. The siren at the firehouse sang out, triggering a chorus of dog barking.

"I hope you've had time to do what you came here for," Annie said. "I confess I snooped a little and noticed you're making some drawings of the old house. What a wonderful idea." She turned again and cocked her head worriedly. "I've been afraid to ask, but I hope you aren't upset about Sid's buying it. You know, he's really okay. He's settled down . . . been with the same man for years now. We're just relieved developers didn't get their hands on that property. Imagine how they could've ruined it." She shook her head. "Sid must've paid a bundle. But he did well in the antiquities business, I guess, and his different real-estate deals. Who knows? Maybe he inherited some Holloway money."

Gina felt at ease with Annie now and knew she wouldn't hold back her questions. "Annie, why do you think Mom never talked about Bill Holloway being Sid's father? And how did Bill end up with Fran, anyway? Cassie and I were sure it was Mom who was in love with Bill."

The admission seemed to suck up what little air was in the garden. Annie turned abruptly, apparently forgetting she was holding the hose. It soaked the front of her skirt, but she seemed not to notice. "Well, yes. She was in love. With Bill. Bill and Ellie were great pals and sailed together every weekend. But . . . Bill was with your Aunt Fran, and when she got pregnant . . . Oh golly. I feel like the town crier." Gina smiled to let her know it was okay to go on. Annie shifted around the garden, keeping her back to Gina. "When your grandpa found out Fran was pregnant, he told her he'd give her Lily House if she and Bill got engaged. Then, when she was five months along and Bill's plane was shot down, the stuffy Holloways, who never approved of Fran, asked that the whole affair—meaning Sid—be kept unattached to their family name. So, Fran had to invent a runaway father for her own baby. Your mother must have been devastated by Bill's death, too, but what could she do? She'd been in love with her sister's man. She just stowed her sadness away somewhere, I suppose."

Gina pictured Bill Holloway, who'd shown up so often in her

mother's photograph collection. Even until recently, her mother's feelings for Bill had surfaced with a discomforting freshness, as though her love for him had been flash-frozen, preserved at its peak by Bill's untimely death.

"So do you think Dad was just sort of a port in the storm for Mom, after Bill died?"

"Oh, no. Well, let's see. Honestly? I can't say. But . . . it wasn't like your parents had a shotgun wedding." The words themselves popped like gunfire. "Cassie wasn't planned, but I'm quite sure your mother and father were headed for the altar anyway."

Gina was so taken aback by Annie's candor that she almost laughed. Her parents had never discussed Cassie's unplanned birth; it'd been only a murmur between Cassie and Gina—The Legend of Cassandra the Witch, To Be Born on Halloween! Annie must not have realized Gina's mother had never told her and Cassie the truth.

Annie said, "Ellie had a thing for Bill, it's true, but Bill was . . . well, for lack of a better word, a *playboy*. I like to think there came a time when your mother understood that he wouldn't have made the best family man. But you know, when someone dies young, tragically like that, it's easy to romanticize. Your mother moved on with her life for the most part. But Fran . . . " Annie shook her head. "She was *stuck* and no one seemed to be able to help her."

Silently, Gina tried to piece together the parts of the family story she *hadn't* heard through the walls of houses.

"Annie, how did Fran die? How'd she do it?"

Annie had put down the hose and began fastidiously snipping the blades of grass that leaned into her flowerbed. "Pills," she said. "Quick and painless, not messy." She smacked a mosquito on her leg. "That poor kid. What a life. You know that Sid lived with your parents for a little while when he was a boy?"

Gina nodded. "Cassie told me. But Mom never mentioned it."

Annie shook her head. "So much shame back then. Fran took too many pills that time, too. Sid found her on the kitchen floor after school." She sat back on her heels and wiped her brow. "Anyway, your parents loved having Sid living with them. He was very upset about having to leave your place when Fran came out of the hospital, which of course made things between Ellie and Fran just terrible. You'd think Fran would have been grateful, but she was very jealous of Sid's affection for Ellie. Sid was a born sailor, like his father Bill, and Ellie took him out every chance she got."

She stood to turn off the hose and brushed by Gina, giving her a pat on the head. "Be right back," she said, going inside.

Gina felt glued to the stoop, weighted by all she'd learned. She pondered how shared feelings could pull people closer, or, left unaddressed, like a misplaced or forgotten line in a drawing, could change the course of lives. There were no blueprints for a human life, no architect to pore over details that would ensure a sound and enduring structure. When a house was designed, it was imperative that every line tell the truth: the thickness of plywood, the width of a beam, the spacing of rebar. Since each dimension affected every part of the structure, one wrong line in a drawing would send a ripple of error through the entire project, resulting in a cacophony of complaints from contractors, clients, building inspectors. Everything would have to be adjusted to accommodate the untruth; otherwise, a costly correction would later have to be made.

When it came to human lives, corrections were only occasionally made; life grew around a secret like skin around a splinter.

How might everything have been different for her mother had Fran not become pregnant with Bill Holloway's child? Sid's birth and secret paternity had torn up the landscape of her mother's, Fran's, and Sid's lives. Her mother's own unplanned pregnancy had spawned a marriage, a child, then another child, followed by a lifetime of wondering how things might have been different.

Gina had been her mother once, both blessed by and chained to her body's potential to conceive. That August, every day she didn't bleed felt like her future burning down like a matchstick. Like her mother and Fran, she'd hidden the injury of a mistake to avoid shame, never telling Cassie or anyone else about Mark's pressing her into Cassie's bed. The day before she left for school, she awoke with her period. She sobbed and put on a sunny yellow halter top, as if to reclaim her imperiled girlhood. She imagined she was lucky—that her fear and pain had been carried away in her blood, and she never stopped to think what she'd have done if she'd been unlucky.

After Mark, there were more Marks—cocky, mysterious, unreliable men, never *nice* enough to remind her of her father's passivity and weakness. Eventually, in Paul, she found the qualities her more mature self craved in a partner, and the passion, too. Perhaps she'd finally learned, or had just been lucky again.

But what if she'd been *unlucky* that summer and like her mother and Fran, hadn't had the choice of ending her pregnancy? She couldn't have lived in disgrace under her parents' roof and couldn't have stayed with Mark. Perhaps under the circumstances, she would've reconsidered the spark she didn't feel with Kit, would've decided his passionate feelings for her and kindness were enough. Would they have built a family together only later to find out that Kit preferred "being on my own?" Or, would they both have discovered that family life was fulfilling, even without mutual passion?

Perhaps this was what Annie and Lester had been saying to Gina: that love had many faces and formulas and could be built even on an uncertain foundation; that although Cassie was unplanned, there was nothing accidental about the way Eleanor and Ron had raised their girls. Through hardship and mental illness, they'd nurtured their family—imperfectly, but with determination and pride. And love, albeit a love that was wrapped in thorns and stewed in tears.

When her parents dropped her off for her last year at Andrews, Gina got out of the car and her mother stared at her wistfully, as if taking her in for the first time, or the last, or as if presaging that Gina would never live at home again. Gina shut the car door gently so it wouldn't feel like a slam. Still, as they drove off, she saw her mother hang her head.

How would it feel to have one door after another slammed in your face? Perhaps, after a while, if one were a fighter—and her mother surely was—one would punch at anything that looked potentially harmful. Even or maybe especially, the love of a good man or the voices of independent daughters.

Now, it was Gina who rested her head in her hands. Perhaps compassion, even when it came too late, was close enough to forgiveness.

Annie pushed through the screen door with two glasses of iced tea. She handed one to Gina and sat on the step next to her. "I wonder what Sid will do to the house," she said. "All the things your mother always wanted to do, probably."

This prospect was painful for Gina. "It should be a basic human right to change your living space as your life and family change. Mom and Dad never had that chance."

"Yes," Annie said. "They changed it in little ways. But your mother had such dreams for the house. 'Our little piece of heaven,' she called it. She would never have survived not living on the water. She and your dad wanted to buy it, you know."

Surprised by how happy Annie's words had made her, Gina asked, "Why didn't they?"

Annie sighed. "Money. Your mother never gave up hope that they'd find the Washington letters here and then they'd be able to sell the house and everything in it. When she finally sold it to the Historical Society, there wasn't enough money to buy your house and pay your school tuition, too. Ellie and Ron knew what their priorities were! Well, and they were able to buy that beautiful boat, *Homeward*."

Annie stood and turned on the hose, directing it at her bare feet. "Ahh, this is just what I needed," she said. She turned it off again, and the plumbing whined. Taking the shears from her pocket, she leaned to cut a bouquet of zinnias and handed them to Gina. "Happy birthday!"

"Annie!" Delighted, Gina stood and gave her a big hug. "How did you know?"

"A little birdie told me. Zinnias are your favorite, right? You used to come and pick them at our old house when you were very little— before you were even in school, I think."

A gust of wind, like a stranger, entered the garden. Annie craned her neck to look at the sky. "I don't know why I even bothered to water," she said. "It smells like rain."

Annie left for the hospital at noon. Gina ate lunch and called Paul to tell him she was delaying her return by a day, but she couldn't get through; she supposed he was already on his way to Point Reyes with the kids, and out of range. She stripped all the beds and put the sheets in the washing machine. Moving slowly in the heat, she did a thorough cleaning of the kitchen. Then, she drove Lester's car to the big supermarket in Riversport to stock up on groceries.

When she returned to Lily House, Annie wasn't yet home. She tried Paul again, but still no luck.

At last, she seemed to have a window of time to finish the drawings of her family's house. She had a snack and went to the desk, where she laid out a sheet for the second-floor plan. From her measurements, she drew the four bedrooms and bathroom, then stood back to evaluate. Something looked not quite right. Usually when she made as-built drawings, there were a few conflicting measurements that required some head scratching or a second visit to a house, but she hadn't expected this with a house she knew so well. She untaped the plan from the table, spread out the drawing of the first floor and aligned the second-floor plan over it. There was a knot of disagreeing lines in the area where the maid's stair connecting Cassie's room to the kitchen had been removed and the pantry added. She tried to recreate in her mind the inches of space that weren't accounted for in her lines. Once, she remembered there had been a door to nowhere in Cassie's room that she'd opened as a child to discover a slot of leftover space in front of the wall studs framing the bathroom. Now, she recalled the feeling of her hand stretching into that cavity, a question forming in that dark, hidden place.

She sprang from her chair. She would need a hammer! She searched the drawers in Annie and Lester's kitchen, finding no tools. Remembering Annie's gardening equipment, she ran out to the garage only to realize she'd locked the padlock on the door before going to the hospital with Lester. She wandered through the rooms of Lily House, finally spotting a brass fireplace poker—it would be awkward, but would no doubt do the trick. She stuffed her measuring tape and pad of paper into her bag and was headed out with the poker when a car door slammed outside.

*It was once thought that the physical environment determined the charac-
ter of life. When that view collapsed, the natural reaction was to insist that
environment had no consequence whatever. But each view rests on the fallacy
of the other. Organism and environment interact; environment is both social
and physical. One cannot predict the nature of a man from the landscape he
lives in, but neither can one foretell what he will do or feel without knowing
the landscape.*

Kevin Lynch, *Site Planning*

Chapter 14

Gina froze. She looked at her watch: six-thirty. Would the car be
Annie, coming home for dinner? How would she slip unseen out of
the house? She darted into the dining room to replace the poker, then
peeked out the window at the driveway. There, wrinkled and sleepy,
stumbling toward the porch from a rental car, was Ben. Gina dropped
her bag, dashed outside and intercepted him on the porch.

"Happy birthday, Mom," he croaked, throwing his arms around
her waist. "We're here! That's your present!"

"You guys! I can't believe it!" Gina cried, struggling to shift gears.

Esther trailed behind Ben, waiting for Gina to greet her. Gina
gently extricated herself from Ben's hug and wrapped her arms
around her, taking in her bubble-gummy smell. How she'd missed
her family's touch, their voices! So much had happened; three days
had felt like three weeks.

"Happy birthday, Mom," Esther said. "It's so hot. Ouch! Be careful; you're squeezing my bruise I got at Aikido."

Gina's eyes met Paul's as he got out of the car grinning and holding a bouquet of white roses. He leaned over Esther and kissed Gina lightly on the lips. "Sorry you couldn't get us on the phone," he said, laughing. "Happy birthday."

Gina's mind buzzed with the mystery she'd just uncovered in the plans. But she didn't want it to detract from this lovely surprise. She released Esther and hugged Paul tightly. "I'm so happy you guys came!"

Esther and Ben had never visited Lily House and once inside, they wandered from room to room. Gina pointed out a few important artifacts, identified family members in portraits, and told them that while a lot of places made the claim, George Washington had really slept in this house. They appeared spellbound by a genuine fascination that Gina had never felt as a child.

"And the president sat right here," Gina told them, stroking the mahogany arm of the lolling chair.

Ben was dying to sit in the chair; Gina told him she was sorry he couldn't because it was a national treasure.

"Look!" Esther said, pointing to a collection of framed photographs of Bantons who'd lived in Lily House for generations. "I think I've seen this picture of Gran before. She was standing right over there on the stairs, right?"

"Right," Gina said. She'd overlooked the photograph her father had taken of her mother on the day they met, and now she filled with pleasure knowing her mother would always have a presence here, in her beloved Lily House.

So," Gina said, turning to Paul, "Annie must've known you were coming?"

Paul nodded. "It's not our style to spring major surprises. But, I was pretty sure you would've told us not to come if I'd asked, and we all really wanted to. I hope it's okay?"

The truth was, Gina was so distracted thinking about how she would get back to the house with the fireplace poker, she wasn't sure. "Yes!" she said. "I just have to . . . Maybe we should get a room at the Marriot. I'm concerned about the extra confusion here."

"I know. I thought about that on the way out. So Esther had this idea. We brought the camping gear—I've reserved a campsite for us starting tomorrow night at Hermit Island. I figured since you and I had originally planned to be away for the week . . . " he looked at Gina hopefully.

Gina had only been half listening, "Oh! Oh yes! That works, camping's a great idea," she finally said. "But I don't think I should leave Whit's Point until Lester comes home."

"That's fine; we'll go to the campground and you can take the bus up the next day or whatever. But tonight, Esther was hoping we could camp at the old house. What do you think?"

For a moment, Gina had serious doubts. "We'd be trespassing," she said. Then she realized that one way or the other, she was going to the house and the sooner the better. "But it's not a problem if no one knows."

Paul smiled. "You don't think Sid would be okay with your spending one night there—for old times' sake?"

"I'd have to ask him, which I'm not going to do. I've managed to get this far without having to deal with him."

Paul shrugged. "Okay. I just thought you might sleep better if you did." He smiled slyly, and she narrowed her eyes at him.

Gina made quesadillas and drummed her fingers on the table as Ben and Esther dawdled over the food. They were too hot, they complained, so she bribed them with the promise for a swim in the cove.

"Night swimming!" Ben exclaimed, hopping on one foot.

While Paul washed the dishes, she went to get the poker from the dining room and shut it in the trunk of the rental car.

By the time they left Lily House the light was nearly gone from the sky. They pulled the car around the back of the old house, out of sight from the road. When Paul opened the trunk to get the camping gear, Gina reached in for the poker.

"What's that for?" Paul asked. "Expecting the bogeyman?"

"You'll see."

Inside, they dumped their bags in the hall and the four of them shuffled through the rooms, brightening patches of wall with their flashlights. Gina moved from window to window, flinging them open. Breathe! she thought. Let all remaining ch'i flow away—it's too late now.

Upstairs, Gina and Paul spread two tarps out on the floors of her parents' and her old bedrooms.

"It's even dirtier than a campsite," Esther grumbled.

"Hey, nature girl, where's your sense of adventure?" Paul teased. "You're the one who wanted to camp out here."

Gina could see that Esther was in no mood for Paul's teasing; she looked inconsolably sad. It was too much to be here, feeling her grandparents gone, and Gina had the impulse to whisk her away.

But when they got to Cassie's room, her heart thrummed. She couldn't wait. She ran downstairs and returned with the fireplace poker, careful not to check her family's expressions. "I think there's something here. Something I need to get to," she said. "Stand out in the hall, okay?"

"Gina?" Paul said. "What in the world are you doing? I thought you were afraid of trespassing."

"You'll see. I have to do this, okay? Just step out there with the kids," she said, giving him a gentle push. "You can see from there."

Obediently, Paul shifted out of the room and stood in the doorway with Esther and Ben. Gina's mission caught fire inside her. She positioned the flashlight on the floor and planted herself in front of the shallow shelves her parents had built into the wall when they'd removed the old door. Bending low, she drew back the poker and thrust it at the wall below the shelves.

"Mom!" Esther shrieked. "What're you doing!"

"Esther, Don't yell!" Ben cried. "You guys are scaring me!"

Gina noted Paul's silence and was grateful he didn't try to stop her. The sheet rock had punctured easily, requiring disappointingly little force. But the narrow poker made too neat a hole—it would take an hour to open the wall! She flipped the poker around, held it like a bat and, aiming its fat, heavy handle, took a swing. This time, the handle struck the wall hard, breaking through with a satisfying crunch. She lost her grip on the narrow poker and dropped it.

"Gina, are you looking for something?" Paul said with an unnatural calm, as if he were trying to talk a person off a ledge. "Because there are less destructive ways to . . . "

She felt crazed, but she knew exactly what she was doing. "I have to! Wait, you'll see!" She turned to Paul, her eyes pleading with him to show Esther and Ben that he trusted her. He nodded. She wiped her sweaty, plaster-coated hands on her shorts and raised the poker again, tightening her grasp.

"Daddy," she heard Esther murmur. "What's *wrong* with her? She's scaring me again."

"Shh, its okay. Let's wait and see."

Gina held her breath and hit the wall again and again. She could hear Ben whimper, but she kept going. Dust filled the air. Her hands throbbed. But her energy rose with every arc she swung, each blow settling a score with the walls of this house. *For trapping. For not sheltering. For nights of trembling. For harboring demons and secrets. For fostering blame and guilt. For remaining standing, impassively, after her parents had died.*

When her shoulder began to burn, she stopped. She kneeled in front of the hole she'd made and snaking her hand through the gash, touched the wood studs. There were about six inches of dead space between them and the inside of Cassie's wall; the slot extended the length of the bathroom and accounted for the missing inches on her plan. As a first and second grader, she'd been intrigued with this secret place and had hidden her Halloween candy just inside. Now, her heart quickened as she stretched as far as she could to reach along the floor behind the wall. She felt the paper first, then the shape. She folded her hand around her prize and drew it out.

In the beam of her flashlight was a gift, still wrapped in green and red holly paper and bearing a tag that said "For Eleanor." An innocent little package, hidden by Gina herself when she was ten in a rush of confusing emotion, on a day she'd tried without success to forget. She rippled with anticipation of what she held. At last, she turned the flashlight on her family. Ben and Esther were glued to Paul's sides, Ben with his thumb in his mouth.

"I found it!" she said. She jumped up and the three of them silently followed her into her parents' bedroom. "Sit down here, and I'll show you. But first, I need to wash my hands." After she'd scrubbed off the dirt with some shampoo Paul had fished from his bag, Gina kneeled on the tarp.

Paul and the children huddled around her, and she handed the flashlight to Esther. "Be my light," she said. She blew the dust from the package and pulled the end of a ribbon whose thirty-five-year-old knot easily released. Peeling the paper away, the lines of sepia ink took shape before her: "G. Washington."

Instantly, memories scrambled to arrange themselves. Gina recalled Fran's furtive look and shaking hand as she slipped the package into her game bag. Glancing up at Sid's flushed face. Her disappointment when she got home to discover the gift was for her mother, not her. Now, the significance of her aunt's attempt to give the Washington letters to her mother struck her: Fran had told Sid who his father was, had made sure the letters were put in the right hands. She'd been putting her affairs in order before her suicide.

It was not the flying knives at Lily House that day that had killed Fran; she had planned it all.

Like Annie and Lester's revelations, the discovery of the letters had exposed the foundation of secrets, lies, and misunderstandings on which Gina's family had built up their fortress walls. She'd built her own wall-of-forgetting to keep out things she didn't understand; now, she felt that wall coming down. In its place she would construct a new understanding that could be built on truth.

Esther and Ben huddled closer as Gina unwrapped the bundle and laid out six letters on the floor. Esther was the first to register what they were looking at. "Mom!" she gasped, her fingers dancing above the pages. "It says 'Thomas Jefferson' on this one! And this one . . . 'G. Washington'!"

Ben pushed his face closer to the pages. "It's hard to read."

"Don't touch it!" Esther scolded, yanking his hand off one of the letters.

"It's okay, Estie, you can touch. We'll be some of the last people who have the chance to. But don't pick them up because they're very fragile."

Gina looked up at Paul, beaming. "Wow!" he said. "I'm speechless."

For several minutes, the four of them squatted silently over the letters, taking them in.

"But Mom, who put them in the wall?" Esther asked.

"I did. When I was your age." Gina explained why she'd hidden the gift, how she'd forgotten about it, and how her parents had closed it in when they remodeled the house. "People in our family have been trying to find them for a long time."

"Is someone going to get mad at you?" Ben asked.

Gina laughed. "No, I don't think so," she said. But there *was* Sid, whom she wouldn't let herself think about yet.

"Then can we go swimming now? It's so hot."

Gina stood and looked out the window where heavy clouds covered the moon and the cove was a large dark void in the landscape. Crickets rioted; mosquitoes whined at the screen. She was covered with dirt and dust and craving the cove water more than she had all week. "Yes, let's go swimming!" she sang.

Ben, Gina, and Paul quickly slipped into their suits.

"I don't really want to swim," Esther said.

Usually, Gina was the one to coax the kids into a plan, but Paul beat her to it this time.

"Aw, Estie, the cool water will feel good. And Mom really wants us to swim with her. It's her special place, and it's her birthday. Besides, remember how much you liked swimming all the way across the cove last summer?"

Gina noted Esther's hesitation. Finally, perhaps remembering last summer or considering the alternative of sitting by herself in the dark house, Esther put on her suit. Paul grabbed the flashlight, and the four of them ran outside and down the hill to the rickety dock. The tide was so high the water skimmed the dock boards.

"It's warm! It's warm!" Ben squealed, hopping from foot to foot.

They stood for a few moments watching shadows shift as the moon ducked in and out of the clouds. Soon, mosquitoes found them, and they had to wriggle to keep them from landing. Gina stepped to the edge of the dock, leaned forward, and sliced through the water with a shallow dive.

She came to the surface just as Paul said, "C'mon, guys!" and dove from the dock.

Esther jumped, and Ben splashed in next to her. Wild giggling erupted.

"Don't touch the bottom, Esther," Ben warned. "There's crabs!"

"They're more afraid of you than you are of them!" Esther said with authority.

Gina laughed—it was a line her mother had always used to make her young daughters feel safe in the ocean. Here—where the waters were dark and your body dangled into a crude world of crustaceans and barnacle-covered rocks, beer bottle shards and strands of seaweed that would wind spookily around your limbs—swimming required a special trust.

Paul sidled up to Gina and put his hand around her waist. "I missed you," he said, "and I've missed this."

"Me too. I'm so glad you came. Thank you. It was just the right thing." She kissed his salty lips.

When Ben and Esther were tired, Paul swam with them back to shore. The three of them hauled themselves out on the dock and stood in the dark waiting for Gina.

"Go on in—I'll be up in a minute," she called.

She swam away from the dock without looking back. When she reached the middle of the cove, she stopped to gaze at the soft house lights that dotted the hill. Each bright window illuminated the life within; a TV in one revealed a life within a life. Her parents' house was a fading shroud—its interior made irrelevant, as though Christo himself had thrown a huge white sheet over it. For a moment, the clouds parted; the full moon floated like a porcelain plate on the high tide. She waited. Finally, when the darting glow of her family's light brought the house alive again, she dove.

Underwater again, she felt the thrill of unaccountability, of disappearing from the earth. Underwater—where the daily insistence of concerns and negotiations was short-circuited by the happy propulsion of arms and legs defending her buoyancy, where only a single question, the one that pressed against her chest, mattered: how much air remained? *Swimming*—like making love.

It was late by the time Ben and Esther fell asleep on top of their sleeping bags. Gina and Paul couldn't wait until morning to look more closely at the letters. They sat side by side taking turns holding the flashlight, reading, becoming more used to the graceful but difficult script the more they read. The letters were brief and surprisingly to the point—no Watergate Tapes, but Jefferson and Washington sparred like the politicians they were.

When they'd finished reading, they folded up the letters and lay on their backs, silently enjoying the occasional breeze sweeping their damp skin. The sky rumbled.

"I can't believe those two great presidents," Paul said. "How lovely their handwriting was, and how scathing their language. I can see where it would've been bad news for Jefferson, had the letters been published—I mean, he called Washington's administration 'aristocratic and monarchical.' And I loved, 'Your military prefers the calm of despotism to the boisterous sea of liberty!' Them's fightin' words!"

Gina looked at Paul, admiring his handsome profile in the dark. She remembered the feeling of freedom she'd had in the cove. "I prefer the 'boisterous sea of liberty' myself; don't you?" she said.

When Paul turned to her, his expression filled with warmth and knowing, she rolled over and pressed her body against his, sticky with salt. He stroked the hollow between her hipbones, and she shivered. Her every cell had been awakened by her discovery, the cove water, the sounds of a summer night outside the window. They made love slowly and silently, attending carefully to each familiar touch.

When they were finished, they put space between them to let their skin cool. Gina reached for Paul's hand. "I've made it so hard for all of you lately," she said.

"Shhh . . . it's okay."

"It's not entirely okay," she said firmly but gently. "We need to talk about what's been happening with me—not tonight, but soon."

"Good. I've been wanting to talk about it, too."

They lay quiet for a while. Gina had begun to drift off when Paul said, "Gina, about Marin."

"Tomorrow," she said sleepily.

"I need to get this off my chest."

She was fully alert now, eyes wide open.

"While you were gone," Paul went on, "I really thought about why it's taking us so long to build a house there. I mean, don't you think it's because it's not really right for us?"

She hadn't seen this coming. Paul had always been so enthusiastic about the property; did he honestly have second thoughts or was this merely a tactic to draw out her feelings?

Paul pulled back to look at her. "Gina? Am I all wrong about this?"

"No," she said. "I thought it was just me."

"If you had doubts, why didn't you say something?"

"I wasn't sure. I thought I had a . . . a design block, or a flaw because I couldn't fall in love with the property. I mean, everyone keeps telling us how beautiful it is. And it *is* beautiful . . . "

"Yes. Yet, somehow, after two years, it hasn't won your heart. If I'd been paying attention, I'd have realized sooner that this was also true for me. I've been so focused on the idea of . . . honestly? . . . of getting out of my family's house and having a place that's really *ours*, that I overlooked the most important thing: it's not what we really want."

A tear slid down Gina's cheek, the dissolution of the dream she and Paul had believed they shared. "It's missing something."

"Yes," Paul said.

More thunder, closer now. Gina got up and went to the window, as she had thousands of times in this house. Tonight, she registered this movement to be as profound as it was familiar and ordinary. It was this power they'd been missing at the Marin property, the inducement that can draw one away—even from the person to whom you've just made love—to the window, again and again.

If I were asked to name the chief benefit of the house, I should say: the house shelters daydreaming, the house protects the dreamer, the house allows one to dream in peace.

Gaston Bachelard, *The Poetics of Space*

Chapter 15

Gina shot up in her sleeping bag, struggling to sort out the signals that had aroused her from her barely-sleep.

She turned to find Esther kneeling next to her. "There's a tapping noise," she whispered. "I can't sleep."

The trapped bird, Gina thought. But she wouldn't say, because Esther, the nature lover, would worry, and it was too late to do anything about it. "Let's snuggle."

Esther stretched out next to her for the first time in a year, since she'd stopped appearing at her parents' bedroom door every morning. Now, Gina appreciated the soft skin of her daughter's arms, the sweet-salty smell of her hair, her pepperminty breath.

All at once, rain came down in torrents outside; thunder roared.

"Thunderstorms are exciting," Esther said. "I wish we had them more in San Francisco. Were you afraid of them when you were little?"

"Just once," Gina said. "When I was about your age. Cassie and I were on a sailing trip with Gran and Grandpa. We were headed down east on a borrowed boat for a week, and one very foggy day, we were trying to enter a harbor, and Gran couldn't see the buoys that marked the channel. Out of nowhere the wind came up, and it started to rain and thunder. We were flying into the harbor, and suddenly we could hear waves crashing, way too close. Then we saw the huge rocks of the shore right in front of us. We were soaring toward them!"

"Were you scared?"

"Gran gave us all orders, and we were scurrying around trimming lines and slipping all over the deck. Gran kept yelling, 'We've got it— don't worry! Hang on!' As soon as she'd come about and we were out of danger, I remember she said, 'That was quite an adventure!'"

"She wasn't scared?"

"If she was, she wasn't showing it. And you know what? Because she seemed so sure of herself, we never believed we weren't safe." Again, Gina thought: *casa senza donna, barca senza timone.*

The storm still raged, but the intervals between the lightning and thunder were lengthening. Gina and Esther were silent for a few moments.

"Estie?" Gina finally said.

"Hmm?"

"I just want you to know that I'm fine and my coming here had nothing to do with you or Ben or Dad. At school that day I—"

"I know," Esther interrupted. "Daddy told me. He said you were so sad about Gran and Grandpa that it made you scared when we couldn't find Ben. Do you think we could paint my room a different color when we get home?" Gina smiled to herself, realizing that in the wide gap between Esther's two thoughts lay her trust, assurance, and forgiveness. Gina had some explaining to do still, but for now, as far as Esther was concerned, the case was closed.

"Yes, a new color!" Gina agreed. "It's time for something new!"

They awoke to sunshine, though thunderclouds still mush-roomed on the horizon.

"So what will you do with the letters?" They were Paul's first words when he opened his eyes. Gina had hardly slept, wondering the same thing. "Will you call Cassie? How about Sid?"

She groaned, thinking about the mess she'd made in Cassie's room and the inevitable conversation she'd have to have with Sid. It was like having a hangover after an especially adventurous night. But, she had the letters! "I'm thinking about it," she said.

In daylight, the dirty, dilapidated house lost any alluring mystery it had had the night before. Paul wanted to help Gina clean up Cassie's room, but Gina wished to spare Esther and Ben another scene should someone discover them there. They packed up the camping gear and tumbled outside, glad to be in the fresh air. There were now three debris boxes sitting in the driveway, Gina noted.

"Goodbye, house," Ben said almost cheerfully.

Esther, if not Ben, seemed to feel the gravity of his words. She turned tentatively to glance at the house, then committed to a brisk jaunt to the car. After discussing the logistics of their rendezvous in Portland, Paul and Gina shared a long embrace and reluctantly said goodbye.

In the garage, Gina grabbed the shovel and an empty cardboard box and carried them into the house. Remembering she still needed the dimensions of the wall cavity for her drawings, she grabbed her bag that held the measuring tape and the Washington letters and headed upstairs to Cassie's room. Reaching inside the hole she'd made, she measured in all directions and recorded her findings.

Hands on her hips, she contemplated the chunks of sheet rock and dust littering the floor. What was the point of cleaning it up? she thought; there'd still be a huge hole in the wall! She shoveled the rubble into the box and used her hands to sweep up the smaller bits of debris. Her knees stung from kneeling in the plaster, and she could feel the grit of it in her teeth.

Downstairs, the front door banged open.

"Hello?" A man's wary voice.

Her heart galloped. Who could it be? She hadn't heard a car come in the driveway. Fear gripped her, shutting down all reason. She picked up the poker and silently slipped it inside the opening in the wall. As if hiding it would disguise what had happened here!

Once again she was trapped in Cassie's room, listening beyond her body's anxious grinding, needing to leave or be caught at the scene of her crime. *Was* it a crime? Covered in dust and sweat, she stood motionless in the airless room.

"Anyone here?" Heavy footsteps. Whoever it was seemed to be moving into the living room. She wondered if she could sneak down the stairs and escape out the door.

From the kitchen, a cell phone's boisterous ring. Gina put the Washington letters in her bag, slung it over her shoulder and crept to the top of the stairs, legs shaking.

"Hello? Yes. I'm at the house now," a voice said. "Yes, have you got the ladder? Okay. Pick me up then."

She was halfway downstairs when she heard the cell phone snap shut. Feet clunked through the living room. Her heart banged.

"Who the hell are you?" An older, bloated version of Sid stood at the bottom of the stair peering up at her, sweat trickling down his cheek. "Oh," he said, "you're a Gilbert, aren't you. So maybe you know how to get a bird out of the attic. It's two-hundred degrees up there!"

"I'm Gina . . . Ginny," she said. "Sorry if I startled you. I hope it's okay . . . yeah, I heard the bird, but the ladder's gone and . . . " She was babbling. He was a total stranger—no, more like a character she would know from TV.

Sid's laugh, sharp like glass. "What brings you here? You look like you crawled through a war zone." His hands settled on his hips, making him even wider.

It's my house! she wanted to shout. "I just came to . . . I'm leaving, actually."

"Whoa," Sid said. "I don't mean to sound like the Inquisition. Let's see. Are you looking for something? There's not a thing here but a very confused bird. I'm waiting for a ladder to get it out."

With some effort, Sid bent to pick up a nail on the floor. Gina wiped her brow and steadied herself. "I'm making some drawings," she said. "Of the house."

"Really! That's great—a drawing to remember it by?"

"Yes, a *souvenir*. I've finished measuring. I was just leaving." She was clammy and lightheaded, and the constriction in her chest made it hard to breathe. She held the railing and concentrated on her feet slowly moving down the steep stairs toward the front door. Sid's eyes were on her.

"You okay?" he asked.

"Sure. Hot . . . "

When she reached the bottom step, Sid sighed. "Well. So we end up seeing each other after all."

Did she only imagine a sardonic curl of his lip? She reached into her bag and pressed the letters deeper. There were three feet between the bottom of the stairs and the front door; Sid's pink button-down shirt seemed to fill all of them. Gina waited for him to move and when he didn't, she could no longer contain her panic. She was out of air.

"I can't . . . I need to . . . "

"Hey. Get a grip now; it's okay."

Why doesn't he move? She lunged to get around him, but he put his hand on her shoulder.

"Ginny," he said.

She jerked away. "Please move! I can't breathe!"

Sid shifted and through her haze, she saw the slice of lawn beyond the front door widen, and then his hand was on her elbow,

and she vaguely understood he was helping her outside. She kneeled
on the lawn, gasping for air, horrified when Sid crouched next to her.
"C'mon; let me help you up."

"Please go! I can't breathe!"

"You can. Just take it slow."

"I can't! Dammit, leave me alone! I just . . . need to . . . " The apple
tree was slanting menacingly toward her, the ground slipping from
underneath her. She clutched the grass in her hands to keep herself
from floating off.

"Ginny, stay with me now. We're here, at the old house. You're fine.
Now I'm going to pull you up . . . " He stood, reaching for her hands.
"And we're just going to . . . Come over here with me."

Gina closed her eyes and felt her resistance drop away. She
reached out her hands and let Sid tow her.

"Open your eyes, Ginny; you'll like what you see. One of the
most beautiful places on earth. Hear that? That's the new launch
horn over at the yacht club."

She heard nothing. Her body seemed to be collapsing in on itself.
When she opened her eyes, she and Sid were standing at the edge of
the hill overlooking the cove. Sid's hand was firm on her shoulder but
not holding her there.

"What could be more peaceful than this? It makes you believe
everything's right in the world; doesn't it?"

She heard him; notes of sincerity, like a gentle chime, had
slipped through.

"Take it easy now. Just listen to your breath—in, out. That's it—
in and out. Slower, now, and a bigger exhale. Can you slow it down?
That's it. You're doing great."

In and out. Gina let her eyes drift from one landmark to another.
In and out. She was vaguely aware of Sid's voice, guiding her breathing as her awareness, like a rising sun, left its dark otherworld and

stretched out its rays, illuminating the scene in front of her. She fixed her eyes on the light playing on the water's surface and breathed. She felt the skin on the back of her neck drying, heard the chatter of terns, and looked up to see their arc in the sky. The ambient sounds of her childhood gradually drowned out her breathing. Her heart began to quiet.

Sid's hand slid off her shoulder. For several minutes they stood, silently surveying the cove.

Finally Sid said, "How long have you been having panic attacks?"

*Panic attack*s. For the past few months, those two words had popped in and out of her mind like gophers in a field, and she'd been plugging the holes as fast as she could.

"I had my first one when I was twenty-two," Sid said. "Right after I graduated from college. Came on right out of the blue. My last one was about two years ago. I'm an expert at them. Grannie had them, you know. Of course, back then they just called Grannie *neurotic*. You feeling okay now?"

"Okay," she said, though she still trembled.

She kept her eyes on the cove. She imagined the refreshment of the cool water and if she'd thought her legs could run, she might have bolted down the hill and jumped in.

"Sure is beautiful today. I must say I was pretty surprised neither of you Gilbert girls wanted this place. Not that I would've wished fighting with those idiot developers on you. I won't even tell you what they had in mind. It was criminal."

The image of the developers' subdivision punched Gina so hard she had to close her eyes again.

"I'd hoped to tell you in person, but . . . Life's full of surprises, isn't it? No one ever thought they'd see Sid sober, but I have been, one year and counting."

Sid was silent for a few moments. Finally he said, "That was the best damn year and a half of my life, living here." Gina looked at him; his eyes locked with hers. "Ever wonder how it would have all turned out if Eleanor hadn't handed me back to Mother? I dreamed of coming back to this spot all my life."

Gina had to look away to buy time, to think of what to say. Remembering the letters in her bag, she broke out in a fresh layer of sweat.

"Well, I don't suppose you wanna be rehashing stuff that happened years ago. What's past is past."

Gina turned to Sid again, realizing suddenly that he'd moved past a place where she'd been stuck. His eyes filled and for a moment, she was afraid he was going to cry. If he did, she knew she would, too. But as he scanned the cove, an expression of pure joy smoothed away his wrinkles of melancholy.

"This place . . . " he said. "This place was paradise. It *is* paradise. Not like . . . *Lily House*. I forgave your mother, you know. I forgave her for everything. I probably would have drowned at Lily House. I forgave her and never had the chance to tell her. I forgave her because . . . "

He leaned over and picked up a crab apple. Straining, he hurled it down the hill. It hit the dock with a short *pop!* before bouncing into the water. "Because before you even existed, Ginny Gilbert, your mother was like a mother to me." He shifted on his feet, then turned, his eyes searching hers. "Do you understand? I couldn't even bring myself to go to the funeral. Isn't that pathetic? I couldn't . . . it was just too much . . . loss." His face crumpled, then composed itself again.

In her depleted, defenseless state, Gina experienced Sid's every word and gesture as acutely as she had as a child. But now, she understood that his words were sincere and the pain he expressed had been theirs to share. "Sid . . . " she started.

A Lexus SUV pulled into the driveway and honked. The driver, a slim man wearing white shorts and a red baseball cap, got out and pulled a ladder out of the car. As he approached them he said, "We can't stop, Sid. We're already gonna be late."

Sid took the ladder from him and said, "Say hi to my cuz, Gina. Gina, this is my partner, Bart."

Bart took off his hat and did a playful bow. "Hi, Sid's cuz," he said.

His smile was warm, but Gina was still too rattled to muster anything but a handshake and a hello. She froze as Sid carried the ladder into the house, terrified that he'd take it up to Cassie's room and see the mess. But he left it inside the front door.

"Well," he said when he came outside again. "We're going to Ogunquit for the day. How long are you in town?"

"I leave tomorrow."

"When tomorrow?"

"Early."

She wondered if Sid was trying to figure out whether they could still meet. But he said, "Okay," and for a moment his gaze slipped sideways, as if there was something more he wanted to say. "Well, have fun making the house drawings—you'll be glad to have them."

He and Bart climbed into the SUV, and Sid waved as it pulled out of the driveway.

Gina dashed inside and ran upstairs to Cassie's room to grab the shovel and box. But Sid would know it was she who'd made the hole! "I was looking for my old diary in the wall," she imagined telling him. Lying would be absurd; he'd see right through it. And wrong—the letters belonged to him, too. What should she do? She'd talk to Cassie. Would Cassie want to tell Sid?

She was hopelessly scattered, couldn't think, and now the poor bird was banging around the attic.

Gina went downstairs to get the ladder and carried it to Cassie's room, careful not to bang anything, realizing the silliness of worrying about minor scratches after she'd practically destroyed a whole wall. She leaned the ladder below the attic door and took the flashlight from her bag. Then she climbed the ladder and pulled herself through the tiny opening into the musty, roasting-hot space.

From the corner, a sudden fluttering of wings. She moved toward the sound, crouching low along the splintery floor, careful not to let the flashlight beam touch the already terrified bird. She pointed the light at a triangular hole in the gable end that was once a vent but was now open to the air. She hoped to steer the bird toward it.

All at once the swallow was airborne, crashing into the rough, sloped roof boards. Gina stood and moved closer to the end of the attic space, gradually confining it, and before long it was trapped in a tiny area, its only escape being the vent opening. She shined the light on the hole, still careful not to illuminate the bird. Slowly, she raised her arms. For a moment, the bird appeared frantic in the spotlight and then seemed to slip almost accidentally through the opening.

She climbed down the ladder, at first thinking she'd put it back downstairs where Sid had left it. But then she decided to leave it under the attic door to let him know that she, too, had cared about the captive bird.

In an inclusive rather than an exclusive kind of architecture, there is room for the fragment, for contradiction, for improvement, and for the tensions these produce . . . An architecture of complexity and contradiction has a special obligation toward the whole: its truth must be in its totality . . . It must embody the difficult unity of inclusion rather than the easy unity of exclusion. More is not less.

Robert Venturi, Complexity and Contradiction in Architecture

Chapter 16

Annie wasn't home when Gina got back to Lily House. She looked for a note that would update her about Lester, but there was none.

She took a cold shower to try to calm herself. After a bowl of yogurt, she picked up the phone to call Cassie. She put it down. She started to dial Paul's cell, then hung up. She brewed some coffee and gulped down half a cup while staring at the Washington letters, try-ing to figure out when to tell Cassie and what to tell Sid. She realized she couldn't tell Cassie until she'd decided whether to tell Sid. She didn't want to be swayed by Cassie's opinion—and Cassie would have a strong one. At least Sid would be in Ogunquit for the day, so she had a little time to think before he discovered the hole. She paced around the kitchen, wiping the clean counters with a sponge.

Drawing! It would help her think. She went into the study and, with her new measurement, easily resolved the lines of the second-floor plan. She constructed the north, south, east, and west elevations of the

house, her hands translating her measurements into lines, lines forming house-portraits on the page.

The elevations represented the building as it had been conceived,
before time had wrinkled its clapboards and tugged at its eaves. When
she finished drawing, the house stared up at her, taking her aback
in its poker-faced simplicity. It was considered a Victorian, like her
house in San Francisco, but its austerity made it seem wholly unre-
lated to its fanciful West Coast cousin.

In the dimming, muggy stillness, she looked at the house and
knew that her time with it was finished and that Sid's had begun.
Until today, the notion of her cousin ending up with the house had
seemed abstract, almost farcical. But seeing him in the flesh and
hearing the emotion in his voice made it real. Now, she noticed with
surprise that the feelings gripping her didn't include resentment or
regret. And, she knew what she needed to do about the letters. She
steeled herself and dialed Cassie's number.

"What's the asshole going to do to the house?" Cassie sputtered
when Gina told her about running into Sid.

Gina spoke slowly to compensate for her sister's agitation. "I
didn't ask—I was too freaked out. But Cassie, he fought off developers to buy it. He assumed we knew; I'm sure he was trying to get in
touch with us because he wanted to tell us. He'd thought we'd want
the house. But we *didn't*."

"Are you defending Sid now? That's not the point, that we didn't
want the house! The point is . . . the point is he just had to have it.
Because he didn't get Lily House! Mom must be rolling over in her
grave!"

"No, Cass, he's really attached to the place. The landscape . . .
the cove. The way Mom was, and we are." Gina hurriedly related Sid's
revelations, ignoring Cassie's gasps of disbelief. "He's not the nasty

train wreck we remember from our childhood," Gina said. "He seems to have made peace with the world."

Cassie wouldn't hear her. "It feels like he stole our house! He's a psycho!" She wailed. "Like the rest of the Bantons! If my kids have their genes . . . "

Her anxiety still reverberating, Gina felt the sting of Cassie's lumping her in with the "psycho" Bantons, and it reminded her too much of their mother's dismissal of Fran's misery. "Cassie, at the house, I had a panic attack."

"Who wouldn't have, running into Sid? Why'd you go to Whit's Point alone, anyway? Why didn't you tell me?"

Gina ignored her questions, determined to make her listen. "I mean a full-blown I'm-gonna-die panic attack, Cassie. I had one earlier this summer, too, but never told anyone. Except my doctor."

"Gina, you're stressed out and—"

"I want you to listen!" Gina said. She described everything she'd felt and all that Sid had done to help her, sparing no detail.

Cassie was silent for a few moments. Finally, when she said sadly, "Oh, Gina," Gina knew she'd gotten through to her big-hearted sister.

Then, she told her about finding the Washington letters.

Cassie gasped. When Gina finished telling about hiding the letters, they both fell silent. Gina imagined that Cassie, too, was trying to make sense of the events leading up to the canceled Christmas.

Finally, Cassie said, "If Mom and Fran hadn't always been at war with each other, you wouldn't have felt you had to hide the package. And if Mom had gotten the letters . . . ugh! So many *ifs*! Do you realize how close we came to losing them? I can't believe it, Gina. Imagine what they must be worth! I'm dying to see them!"

"Is there any chance you could come up here tomorrow?"

"*Tomorrow*?" Cassie sighed. "Oh, Gina. I wish you'd told me you were coming; we could've had a birthday party! Let's see. Umm . . .

So I have to be at a job in Brockton in the afternoon, but if I came up really early, yeah. I could, I guess—I could get there between eight-thirty and nine. Where should we meet?"

"At our house."

"You think that's a good idea?"

"Yes, I do."

When she and Cassie had hung up, Gina searched for Sid's phone number in Cassie's old email, took a deep breath, and called him. Sid didn't answer, so she left a message that she had something important to discuss and asked him to meet her at the house at nine-thirty the next morning.

In the morning, Gina sat on the front steps of the old house wait-ing for Cassie. Lester had been kept at the hospital overnight; he'd had a slight fever in the afternoon. But this morning it was gone, and Lester's doctor felt confident that he'd be able to come home at the end of the day. Gina decided to delay her trip to meet Paul and the kids until tomorrow so she could help Annie bring Lester back to Lily House and get him settled.

Now, she was restless with anticipation. Sid had left her a mes-sage after dinner agreeing to meet her at the house, and she was hoping that Cassie would get there before him so she'd have time to warn her Sid was coming.

But Cassie didn't pull in until nine-thirty. "The traffic on 128 was horrible!" she complained when she opened the car door. As she was getting out, Sid's van turned into the driveway.

Gina gave her a big hug. "Sid's meeting us," she said quickly, still in their embrace. "I asked him to come so we could talk about what to do with the letters."

Cassie pulled back and turned to see the car coming up the hill, her mouth gaping in disbelief. "Oh Gina, I just *can't*. It's just too much. You should've warned me."

"I was afraid you wouldn't come," Gina said. "I promise it'll be okay. It will be. You'll see." She smiled and waved at Sid. "I haven't told him I found the letters yet. But he's had a whole career of selling this kind of stuff, and he'll know exactly what we should do with them."

"Why do you think you can trust him?"

"Cassie! Why should he trust *us*? We're the ones who made the letters disappear."

Cassie shuddered. "God. Okay," she said, gritting her teeth as Sid's car door slammed. "But I'm not going to talk to him about our house."

"Okay. You're allowed."

Sid came around the corner wearing black shorts and a sky-blue polo shirt. "Well. It's both Gilbert girls. What's the occasion—are we going to have a passing-of-property ceremony?"

Cassie wagged her fingers hello at Sid, and when he wagged his back in imitation, Gina wondered how she was going to get through the next hour with them. She led them into the living room where the letters, rewrapped in the original Christmas paper, were sitting in the middle of the floor. "Sit here," she ordered, pointing to the floor.

"Christmas in August!" Sid chuckled, and Gina suddenly realized the full burden of Christmas associations that she might be loading on him. Might he even remember the wrapping paper? "Is it for me or Cassie?" he asked.

"Both." Gina told Sid to open the package. He started peeling off the Christmas paper, and when he realized what was inside, he let out a big laugh.

"What the hell . . . where have you been keeping these all this time?" He handed a few of the envelopes to Cassie, who carefully extracted the letters and opened them on the floor in front of her. For the first time in a long time, she seemed speechless; Gina hoped it was because she was engrossed and not that she was furious with her.

"Before you look at them," Gina said, "come with me, and I'll show you where they were."

Cassie and Sid followed her upstairs, and when Cassie saw the hole in the wall of her old room, she gasped, "Gina!" and cast a worried look at Sid.

"I'll pay to get it fixed," Gina said quickly.

Sid laughed. "No need. It's not a problem," he said. "Really. And anyway, are you *kidding*? Look what you found in there!"

Relieved, Gina recounted the story of how the letters traveled from Lily House in her bag to the hiding place in Cassie's wall.

"Mother told me she'd given them to Ellie," Sid said. "I didn't even know Mother had them. She must've found them somewhere in Lily House and never told anyone. I couldn't figure out why they never surfaced and figured Ellie was hiding them."

Back downstairs, the three of them sat silently on the floor while reading the letters.

"Wow," Sid finally said. "They're really something, aren't they? Do you know the story?"

Gina shook her head. "Only the gist."

"They were never supposed to have seen the light of day because they would've been such bad PR for Jefferson. The way it got started was, Jefferson had written to this libertarian friend in Italy, calling Washington 'Anglican' and 'monarchical' and a bunch of other unflattering stuff. The letter was published overseas and then re-translated and published in the States by Noah Webster—the dictionary guy. So then Washington got pissed off, and he and Jefferson shared a few nasty rounds of correspondence, which of course our very own Sidney Banton was the messenger for. Apparently, a couple of people at Mount Vernon read the letters, and after a few drinks Banton gossiped about their content. Jefferson's political enemies would've had a field day if they'd been made public—dissing the first president was totally uncool—and then suddenly the letters were nowhere to be found. Banton denied their existence. Banton's biographer said publicly that he believed Jefferson had asked Banton to destroy them. But privately he thought Washington had brought the letters to Lily House when he visited Banton here in 1789 and that Banton had hidden them. Jefferson rewarded Banton for the rest of his life for keeping the letters private—writing recommendations for him and eventually hiring him as a consul general."

The living room was silent except for peeping crickets and the occasional swish of a car on Pickering Road. Cassie pinned her stare on the letters as if they might float away.

"Whaddya think, girls, should we hide them away for another two hundred years?"

Cassie's head jerked up, her eyes flashing with panic.

"Kidding!" Sid laughed and patted Cassie on the back; she smiled wanly.

Gina was counting on Sid to be the authority on what should be done with the letters and hoped she wasn't wrong to trust him. Especially because Cassie was now giving her a *look*.

"I suppose I should be jumping up and down about these," Sid said. "But all I can think about is all the anger and betrayal they represent—the secrecy around two fighting presidents . . . then the secrecy between two fighting sisters. These damn letters held our family and Lily House hostage."

Sid sighed and rested his face in his hands for a moment. The barren little room that moments before had tingled with excitement turned desolate. Gina stood and walked to the window. Black clouds towered over the cove; behind her, she could hear Cassie sniffling.

"I believe in new beginnings, though," Sid said. "I've had a few already. The booze didn't manage to kill me and neither did *the plague*, which is nothing short of a miracle. You kind of look at life differently when you've been given the chance even to just keep going. It turns out no matter how damaged you are it's possible to find love that's not treacherous. That's what matters, right?"

Gina turned just as Cassie let out a sloppy sob. She watched Sid stroke her sister's back and thought, this is what a miracle is: a sea change happening here, in this family, in this house.

By the time Cassie had to leave for Brockton, they had a plan for the letters. Sid knew whom to contact to ensure they would be bought by a private collector who'd be obligated to donate them to the Library of Congress within a few years' time.

"I'm driving these to the bank vault this morning," he said.

Gina had brought the lock of Martha Washington's hair and the piece of Washington's cloak, and she and Cassie agreed to add them to the collection of letters. "No more disappearing acts for these things," she said.

In the driveway, the cousins did the unimaginable and hugged goodbye; Gina felt the possibility of family where there had been none. The new one, free of the possessions and history that had joined and then divided them, would be brought together by an appreciation for what they'd lost and could find again on their own terms.

Cassie and Gina climbed into Cassie's car. Sid cast a stormy look at Gina through the window. "You're headed back to San Fran this morning, right?" he said.

"No, no. I decided to stay till tomorrow to help out Annie and Lester."

"Oh." Sid looked at his feet. "I thought you'd be leaving today.

Well. I'm really sorry." He turned and gestured at the house. "About all this. I hope you'll understand."

"Of course I do," Gina said, wondering why, after today's reconciliation, he'd still be worried. "I *do* understand."

Sid looked thoroughly unconvinced. "Well, I don't know." He looked from Cassie to Gina. "But you're all the family I've got. So let's not be strangers, okay?"

At the bottom of the driveway, just as Cassie turned onto Pickering Road and burst into tears, Gina glanced back up at the house. Sid was standing on the slope of the front yard, hands on his hips, gazing up at the house. Or perhaps it was the house who stared down at him, asking *him* now, "What will become of me?"

Things are either devolving toward, or evolving from, nothingness . . .
While the universe destructs it also constructs. New things emerge out of
nothingness . . . And nothingness itself—instead of being empty space . . .
is alive with possibility.
                        Leonard Koren, *Wabi-Sabi for Artists, Designers, Poets and Philosophers*

Chapter 17

Cassie pulled in at Lily House to drop off Gina. "We have to celebrate," she said. "Paul told me on the sly he was coming out here and invited me and Wes to meet you guys at the end of the week at Hermit Island. Is that okay? I'll bring fabulous food. I have some amazing new summer salad recipes I'm doing with tomatoes and corn."

"Great! But we'll accept you without food, too, you know. We'll celebrate, yes!"

"I don't mean celebrate just the letters, though. It's something else. I've always felt . . . like there was this part of me that stayed hard— like in some avocados, or those peaches that never ripen right. And right now, I feel all soft, like a juicy, sweet honeydew. You know what I mean?"

Gina laughed. "I know exactly what you mean." She leaned to hug Cassie. "I love you, Cass; thanks for being such an awesome big . . . honeydew."

When Cassie had gone, Gina walked into the house, and Annie gave her the good news that Lester would be ready to come home at six o'clock. By two, she and Gina were finished with the house chores and grocery shopping. Annie needed a nap.

Gina badly needed a nap, too, but what she *craved*, she realized, was a row. She left Lily House and walked to the town dock to look for Kit. *Homeward* was not on her mooring. She sat at the top of the ramp to wait for him, leaning against the dock railing with two teenaged girls in bikini tops and tiny shorts who were sharing a cigarette. Three boys in swim trunks were horsing around, pushing each other off the float into the water. Half an hour passed. Boats came and went from the float, picking up or dropping off passengers who talked of more thunderstorms.

After a few more minutes, Gina decided to take Kit up on his offer that she could use his boat anytime and fetched the oars from the clubhouse.

In the two-person shell, she felt in charge of the oars, as though no time had passed since her last row with Kit, the summer she was seventeen. The boat glided with neat precision as she threaded her way through the yachts in the harbor. She read their names to herself as she passed: *Take Flight, Tinkerbell, Southerly*—names that, unlike *Homeward*, seemed to promise escape.

Her eyes swept the scenery, and she silently named the points of land and the islands, the two rivers and small coves that sneaked inland. Unlike San Francisco, where the earth came to a sudden, plunging end, here the horizontal landscape made its slow reach toward the ocean, low hills rolling into fields that stretched out to marshes and rocks, and more rocks, smaller and smaller until, in some places, pebbles yielded a crescent of sand—a gift to the people who celebrated this union of sea and earth. The intimate landscape fostered a relationship with the water that was more like poetry than sport.

She reached the outer edge of the harbor, where, on the afternoon of the funeral, she and Cassie had taken a friend's boat out to scatter

Eleanor and Ron's ashes. The April air had been bitter; Gina remembered wondering what could possibly prepare a person to toss the flaky remains of another person into the sea. But, as she watched them dance and dissipate on the rippling sea, she knew for certain it was exactly the right thing.

The Isles of Maine appeared, dark humps on the horizon. She passed Miller's Island, shrouded with dozens of black cormorants, and thought of the day she and Kit had pulled his shell up on the island's shore, how he'd said he savored his time alone and how alone it had made her feel. For her, too, solitude had had its rich reward, making her more aware of the exquisite comfort of nature. But feeling isolated even in the presence of those who loved her, as she had that summer and again in recent months, had made *alone* unbearably lonely.

In just a few days, with each new and old door she'd opened—to Annie and Lester, to Sid and Kit—that loneliness had backed away another step. Even now, separated from her family and slipping into the blank, gray expanse of ocean while a storm was brewing, she felt sheltered.

She understood how Kit could make a boat his home. When summers rolled around and the breeze came up, he would move *Homeward*, finding other ports to explore before returning to his mooring. His home was always with him though the ocean was bigger than anything; his world was not so small, after all. By drawing the house, she, too, had taken this home inside her and would carry it everywhere.

Gina looked up at the darkening sky: it was time to turn inland. As the boat skimmed the gray surface, the resistance against her oars seemed to nearly vanish. Thunder rolled through the sky, and the blackest clouds were nearly over her. Sweat trickled down her cheek as she picked up her pace.

When she reached the inner harbor, the sky roared with startling fury. Gina scanned the shoreline for her parents' house, picking
her way along the hills until she recognized the neighboring houses.
But something looked different; she couldn't find the house. Had
the trees grown up in front of it? Again, she identified each house
until she came to the spot where the house should have been, but it
wasn't visible. It must have been behind the grove of birch trees on
the island.

It was nearly high tide—the cove would be full. She decided to
row into it one last time. She maneuvered through the harbor, surrounded by a flotilla of pleasure boats beelining for their moorings.
Despite the imminent rain, the offshore air blew hot again, and she
was soaked from the exercise.

Slipping now between the inner islands, she realized she'd passed
the last opportunity to spot the house before she rounded the point
into the cove. A gust of wind curved the tops of tall pine trees and
sent halyards clanging against masts. A flock of terns rose abruptly
from the rocks. Lightning cracked the dome of the foamy, black sky,
and rain poured down as she entered the cove. She turned, wiped
her eyes, and scanned the surrounding hills. What was she seeing?
It wasn't right. When thunder exploded, she thought it could be the
sound of her heart bursting. She pumped the oars without turning
again. Was she dreaming? Would she awaken and find herself tangled
in a mess of sheets?

When she reached her parents' dock, she barely found the
strength to pull herself out of the boat. Head down in the rain, she
made the slippery climb up the hill, her fingers touching the grass
to keep from falling. Before she'd even reached the top, she could
smell what was coming. There was a certain odor that rose from the
new ruins of a house; it was released when the bowels of the house

were exposed: earth and rotting wood, microbes and fungi fed by dampness, fuel. Now, she also recognized the distinctive scent of her parents' cellar—a fusion of kerosene, paint, and turpentine.

She stood in the rain, legs shaking. The debris boxes hunkered in the driveway, overflowing with the bones and tissue of the house. Piles of doors and windows lay neatly beside the stack of storm windows. She fixed her eyes on the only part of the house that still projected from the ground—the ragged bricks rimming the hole that had been the cellar. The deep, mud-filled rectangle appeared small and too crude to have been the foundation for any house. But she was grateful for it now, as it was the only room that could not be carried off.

She waited for the shock; strangely, it didn't come. Perhaps the strenuous row had left her too enervated to respond with anything but a languid sadness. She hadn't allowed herself to predict this outcome, though she herself had recommended the demolition of several houses too dilapidated or unworthy of their sites to save. When a house design required vast remodeling, it was almost always more economical to start over, building from the ground up. To the client, demolition had been nothing more than the necessary first phase of construction. A house that had taken months to build and had been lived in for generations could be taken down in a few hours. She was humbled now to think that although she'd felt remorse for sentencing a house to such an abrupt end, she'd never stood in the shoes of the people who might drive by one day to see the house they'd made their home replaced by another.

This was what Sid had meant this morning when he said he was sorry about the house; had she not delayed her departure, she would've been spared. News of this death, too, would've come in a phone call. She was glad to be here to witness the physicality of dying that she'd been robbed of when her parents had died suddenly, leaving her with only death's finality. In her head, where houses marched through like soldiers for inspection, she'd known the house's time had come; now in her heart she felt it, too. Stripped of the physical evidence of her family and relieved of its responsibility to shelter, it had ceased being a home. On its long journey it ended as it had begun: as simply a *house*. The truth was, she'd never envisioned a new life for this house, just as Sid hadn't for his new family. Its life had belonged to her family—the Gilberts—even though its wood and plaster had belonged to someone else.

A four-foot circle of purple irises stood on the edge of the yard, its geometry now oddly conspicuous on the deconstructed site. She picked the irises—all of them—and threw them one by one into the cellar, assigning a family name to each, starting with her parents and ending with Ben, the youngest grandchild. Some of the flowers disappeared into puddles, but she was captivated by the way the others transformed the house-ruin with their delicate color.

The house was gone, and with it its power, both wondrous and terrible. There were no more questions to be asked of it; memories and secrets trapped within its walls had been freed.

She stood and looked out over the hill at the cove. The house existed only on paper now, but this place her mother had chosen—its exquisite composition of landforms and water, sensuous contours of hills and shoreline, play of shadow and light—had provided the unfailing comfort to her children that she could not, and it would go on living, unaltered by the changes in the lives it touched.

Now it was Sid's turn to build a life here, and it was right. He would nurture this place with his deepest appreciation and spirit of renewal. Perhaps in this world there were no owners or renters, only borrowers choosing a bit of ground to call home during their short stay on earth. We must choose carefully, Gina thought; when we set our walls down to enclose something ordinary or extraordinary, we must be passionate about what we capture, inside and out.

The rain moved away, taking with it the white noise and watery lens that had blurred her senses. The bright world looked new, full of color and contrast. Gina studied what she could see now that this place had no structure. From the front yard, she could see the apple trees in the backyard; from the backyard, she saw past the birch tree, across the hills all the way to Kit's old house. She'd grown accustomed to looking at the world from the perspectives dictated by the house: separated and obscured by walls, framed by windows. Now, the cove and harbor were visible from the entire hilltop, and the landscape ran together—north, south, east and west.

Into this opening came an answer to her uncertainty about *home*. Not to her mind's eye, in lines or planes or in a misty-edged snapshot of a house, but as an essence.

She welcomed the dry breeze that aroused a tingle of anticipation. Tonight, Lester would come home to resume his life with Annie. Tomorrow, Gina would join her family in their tent. Before Ben and Esther went to sleep, she would kiss them and feel her time with them not dwindling but instead, stretching out like an uncharted ocean. When she returned to San Francisco, she would roll the Banton doorknocker over in her hands, excited to imagine its next home. In the coolness of their tall Victorian bedroom, when the windows had gone black with night, she would look between them at the photograph of the cove—the window that was always open, always light.

Thank You

To all the writers who have moved and inspired me. Novels have always seemed like miracles to me, and if I'd really understood how hard it is to write one, I never would have tried.

I am enormously grateful to Jay Schaefer, who edited with equal parts patience and passion, for his deep understanding of this work, his gentle and respectful nudging to make it better, and brilliant literary contributions.

To Lisa McGuinness, Rose Wright, Andy Carpenter and Andy Ross for everything they've done to bring this book to light.

To the amazing women and dear friends who read and provided their wise insights and decade-long encouragement: Anita Amirrezvani, Isabelle Beekman, Carolyn Cooke, Sylvia Dworkin, Jeanne Felton, Katherine Forrest, Laurie Fox, Peggy Greenough and her book group, Nancy Hardin, Anne Hogeland, Tess Uriza Holthe, Marion Irwin, Cary Nowell, Jamie Raab, Suzanne Schutte, Jessica Straus, Elise Trumbull, Lorna Walker, Janet Warren and Molly Wheelwright.

To Rennie McQuilkin, who showed me that writing was not only a useful way to work out teen angst, but also something that could be meaningful to others—or not...but in any case, it doesn't matter; we write because we can't not write.

To Kris Picklesimer, whose deep compassion coaxed words out of hiding when nothing else seemed possible.

To my parents, Alice and Douglas, who taught me to regard the world each day with curiosity and astonishment, and my sisters, Beverley Daniel and Gay Armsden, for sharing with me that wonder and the shelter of their enduring love.

Deepest thanks to my husband, Lewis Butler, whose love, friendship, support, and unfaltering *joie de vivre* have made my writing life possible, and to our children, Elena and Tobias Butler, who brought me home when they were born.